# MARTYRLAND

# MARTYRLAND

## THE PERILS OF THE PERSECUTION

## A TALE OF THE DAYS OF THE SCOTTISH COVENANTERS

### ROBERT SIMPSON

SOLID GROUND CHRISTIAN BOOKS

BIRMINGHAM, ALABAMA USA

Solid Ground Christian Books
PO Box 660132
Birmingham, AL 35266
205-443-0311
sgcb@charter.net
http://solid-ground-books.com

**MARTYRLAND**
**The Perils of the Persecution**
*A Tale of the Days of the Scottish Covenanters*
Robert Simpson (1792-1867)

*Solid Ground Classic Reprints*

First edition May 2006

Cover work by Borgo Design, Tuscaloosa, AL
Contact them at nelbrown@comcast.net

*Cover image is taken from the painting by*
*William H. Weatherhead, "The Covenanters"*

Special Thanks to Pastor Robert Elliott of the Reformed
Baptist Church of Riverside, CA who told us about this book
and who wrote the excellent Introduction to our new edition.

1-59925-074-8

# CONTENTS

# INTRODUCTION AND APPRECIATION

The success of John Knox in reforming Scotland was so significant that in 1560 Scotland 'officially' became a Reformed Nation. However, one hundred years later as Charles II ascended the throne it became obvious that his appearance of friendship with the Scottish Presbyterians was a sham and a show, intended to deceive in order that Scotland would support his claim upon the throne.

Supporting Charles II was one of the most foolish things the people of Scotland have ever done. He manifested an unquenchable desire for attention and entertainment and tragically the church was, to him, just another forum over which he would exercise his petty will!

All that had been accomplished at the Reformation was under serious threat. The cruel monarch imposed a law (1661) that made it illegal for a local congregation to choose its own Pastor based upon biblical qualifications. Prelacy, as it was called, placed this responsibility in the hands of Bishops, who ultimately were answerable, not to Christ the true Head of the Church, but to Charles II. The next step, which was quickly taken, was to throw Pastors out of their churches and replace them with mere 'puppets of the King.'

Needless to say the godly people who had been well trained and schooled in the Scriptures would not, could not, settle for such intrusion into their worship.

They hungered for the Word of God to be preached, and were disgusted at the strange doctrine being foisted upon them as they gathered with God's people on the Lord's Day. They recognized no Head of the Church save Jesus Christ and wanted no preachers save those their head called to Himself and then sent to feed His sheep.

The cruelty of Charles II caused many who had covenanted to follow Christ also to take up arms to defend their homes and families from Charles' marauding men. Military characters such as Richard Cameron came to the fore whose actions were heroic and brave as he sought to take on the might of the English King.

However, the men that held together the cause of the Covenanters were not those who fought heroically at Drumclog or Bothwell Bridge. It was, rather, the faithful preachers, having been ousted from their churches who would meet their congregations secretly in the middle of the damp moorlands of the Scottish Southwest. Preachers, like Alexander (Sandy) Peden were forced to live as fugitives, often in caves or in the homes of those who loved them and their message. They would stay in such homes for no more than a night or two before having to move on, lest their presence should bring the whole household into serious danger or even death at the end of an English soldier's musket.

The safest meeting places were well beyond the villages and towns, over hills and bogs (marshes) and often under cover of darkness. Many who escaped death by Charles' soldiers found that the inclement conditions of their gatherings (called Conventicles) took their toll and often carried them to the grave. Typically, young and old would venture out on days or nights that ordinarily would have been spent around the hearth. But for the sake of their true Monarch (Jesus Christ) they would leave the safety of home and walk to out-of-the-way locations, they would then congregate in absolute silence, sometimes waiting for hours for the preacher to be safely conducted to them. Their patience rewarded and discomfort forgotten they would spend hours gladly singing praise to God and being fed upon gospel truth. The cold, the dampness, the terrain took many a dear old saint home to meet their Lord earlier than would otherwise have been the case.

To be caught having any involvement in a Conventicle would at times result in a trial for treason and then death, but often the trial was by-passed and the red-coats would hasten the Covenanters departure by murdering them in cold blood, without any judicial hearing.

Over 18,000 saints of God had been martyred before the ascension of William III to the throne of England and the subsequent "Glorious Revolution" which brought an end to the terrible persecutions. There was now no need to escape to 'The Land of the Free' on the other side of the Atlantic. Instead once again the gospel was freely preached by men appointed by the true Head of the Church.

There are many historical records and accounts of the exploits of the Covenanters, but *Martyrland* stands in a league all of its own. If you would like to be transported in your imagination back to the 17th Century and enabled to vividly hear, and see, and smell, and feel all that went on, then this book is going to capture your mind in a way that you will not easily forget!

Living and preaching in Sanquhar, a little town at the center of the Covenanting cause, gave its author tremendous insight into the lives and personalities of the Covenanters. Some of his characters are fictional, created in order to help us get close to those who lived in the days of persecution. One cannot help but wonder how many couples like Gilbert and Grizzy are vividly represented by Gilbert and his wife Grizzy. Like the vast majority of Covenanters they are simple farming people, with a deep love for one another and for God. You will also meet the greatly used Sandy Peden whose life and service for Christ is worthy of your further research. Simpson weaves many actual incidents and characters into this story in a way that brings it all to life.

While ministering in the little Scottish village of New Cumnock, I became aware that all around me there were memorials to martyrs who had died because they would allow no other King but Jesus to rule in His church. It became a favorite pastime of mine to walk up a hill or over a moor to reach those sites, and when there read the account of the death of Charles' victims. I also read a great deal trying to understand their theology, philosophies and priorities, but when one of the dear men from the church I was pastoring (Tom McGinn, thank you!) placed *Martyrland* in my hand, a richer dimension of who these people were, and what it was like to live as one of them dawned on me. I was not only surrounded by the hills and glens that my Protestant forefathers walked, I almost thought I could hear their voices and see their worn out but happy faces!

One piece of friendly advice: Don't let your Spouse know of this book until AFTER you have read it. I made that mistake, and for a few weeks my wife and I were racing to be first in bed so as to get first dabs on what still remains our favorite historical narrative!

Pastor Robert Elliott
Reformed Baptist Church
Riverside, California USA

# Chronological Summary

1560 Reformed Faith established as national religion of Scotland.

1580 Protestant leaders pledge themselves to support the Reformed doctrine and discipline in The National Covenant.

1603 Union of the Crowns [James VI of Scotland becomes James I of England].

1610 Bishops established in Scotland by royal authority.

1618 The Five Articles of Perth. The King seeks to conform Scottish worship to the pattern of the Anglican Church

1625 Accession of Charles I who pursues his father's policy.

1637 Rejection of Archbishop Laud's Liturgy. Jenny Geddes throws stool in St. Giles.

1638 Signing of the National Covenant. Presbyterianism re-established and the independence of the Church re-asserted.

1639-40 First and Second Bishops' Wars.

1642-48 First and Second Civil Wars.

1643 Signing of the Solemn League and Covenant. English Puritans and Scottish Presbyterians pledge their nations to uniformity in religion according to the Word of God.

1643-49 Westminster Assembly of Divines.

1651 The Scots crown Charles II at Scone but Oliver Cromwell subdues their country.

1660 The Restoration of the monarchy. Charles II throws off his former allegiance to the Scottish Presbyterians.

1661 Prelacy re-established by law.

1662 Over three hundred ministers turned out of their parishes. Field-preaching and Conventicles introduced.

1663 Government attempts to limit Conventicles. Persecution commences.

1666 Covenanter rising ends with defeat at Rullion Green.

1669 A Declaration of Indulgence which results in division of Covenanters into the 'indulged' and the 'non-indulged'.

1670 'Field-meetings' made treasonable and preaching at such meetings becomes a capital offence.

1679 Murder of Archbishop Sharp [3 May]. Covenanters defeat Government forces at Drumclog [I June] Covenanters defeated at Bothwell Bridge [22 June]

1680 Covenanters defeated at Ayrsmoss. Richard Cameron killed.

1684-85 'The Killing Times' - the period of hottest persecution.

1685 Accession of James II.

1688 Capture and execution of James Renwick, the last of the Covenanting martyrs. The Glorious Revolution. The Church of Scotland is restored to her spiritual freedom

# Glossary of Some Names from *Martyrland*

These are but a few of the numerous names found within the pages of this historical novel. The reader is urged to make a list of names in the story and seek information on those not listed below.

**John Brown** (referred to as Priesthill) - A peasant farmer from Priesthill, (3 miles North of Muirkirk) who was known for his honesty and ability to teach young men the Word of God. Three of his students who studied Scripture with him at the table of his one roomed farmhouse were martyred for the faith. John's martyrdom took place at the hands of the wicked Claverhouse and is one of the most moving stories of the Covenanting period.

**Richard Cameron** - Cameron was schoolmaster of his native village until he became chaplain and tutor to Sir William Scott of Harden. In 1673 he began to preach in the open air, under the influence of the Covenanter John Welch. Strongly opposing the measures aimed at reestablishing the Episcopal Church in Scotland, and objecting to any state control of the church, he led a small company who, in the Sanquhar Declaration (1680), disowned the royal authority of Charles II. A price was set on Cameron's head and within a short time he and a little band of supporters were overtaken by royal troops. Cameron and many of his group were killed in 1680.

**Alexander Peden** - One of the greatest of all Covenanting preachers. He has been called "The Prophet of the Covenant" because of the poignancy and amazing relevancy of his utterances. Often young men accompanying him to field meetings would wear masks similar to the one he wore and only when the coast was clear would they all remove them thus revealing which one was Peden. This was done to prevent assassins having their way.

**John Graham/ Bonnie Dundee/ Claverhouse** - He was descended from King Robert III and had inherited the estate of Claverhouse near Dundee. He was as loyal to the King as he was vain and vicious. He spent many years hunting out Covenanters and killing them in cold blood. He was called Bonnie Dundee because he gave as much attention to his looks as a vain woman. (Bonnie= pretty)

**Battle of Drumclog** - On 1 June 1679 the Covenanters routed Claverhouse's army causing him to flee to Glasgow.

**Battle of Bothwell Bridge** - Shortly after the success of Drumclog the Covenanters lost this battle. Not many lives were lost during the battle; however upon retreating the Covenanters found they became easy pickings. Hundreds were imprisoned and sent on ships to America (Virginia), however 200 drowned when their ship sank.

**James Renwick** - (1662-1688) He spent the last five years of his short life traveling around Scotland preaching powerful sermons. The success of the Word of God under his ministry made him one of the chief targets of Charles II cronies. He was martyred in Edinburgh on Feb.17th 1688. His head and hands were severed and placed on display at a few of Edinburgh's city gates.

**James Sharp** - (1613-1679) A Presbyterian minister, and later Archbishop of St Andrews (1661-1679). Having been at one time involved with the Covenanters he represented all that 'treachery' represented. As Archbishop of St. Andrews he embarked on a severe policy of repression against the Covenanters. He was killed by Covenanters in 1679.

# MARTYRLAND

## The Perils of the Persecution

*A Tale of the Days of the Scottish Covenanters*

"The Church shall never perish!
Her dear Lord to defend,
To guide, sustain, and cherish,
Is with her to the end:
Though there be those who hate her,
And false sons in her pale,
Against or foe or traitor
She ever shall prevail."
- **Samuel Stone**

*"They wandered about in sheepskins and goatskins;
being destitute, afflicted, tormented; (Of whom the world
was not worthy) they wandered in deserts, and in
mountains, and in dens and caves of the earth...
Wherefore seeing we also are compassed about with so
great a cloud of witnesses, let us lay aside every weight,
and the sin which doth so easily beset us, and let us run
with patience the race that is set before us, Looking
unto Jesus the author and finisher of our faith; who for
the joy that was set before him endured the cross,
despising the shame, and is set down at the right hand
of the throne of God. "* - **Hebrews 11:37,38; 12:1,2**

"Jesus, Thou Friend divine,
Our Savior and our King,
Thy hand from every snare and foe
Shall great deliverance bring.

Sure as Thy truth shall last,
To Zion shall be given
The brightest glories earth can yield
And brighter bliss of Heaven."
-**Timothy Dwight**

# MARTYRLAND;

OR

# THE PERILS OF THE PERSECUTION.

## CHAPTER I.

PATRICK WALKER tells us that "In the year 1683 was such a long and great frost, that from November to the middle of March, there was no labouring of the ground; yet even before the *snow* fell, when the earth was as iron, how many graves were in the West of Scotland, in desert places, in ones, twos, threes, fours, fives together, which was no imaginary thing—many are yet alive who measured them with their staves, exactly the deepness, breadth, and length of other graves, and the lump of earth lying whole together at their sides, which they set their feet upon, and handled them with their hands, which many concluded afterwards, did presage the two bloody slaughter-years that followed, 1684 and 1685, wherein eighty-two of the Lord's suffering people were suddenly and cruelly murdered in desert places."

This storm, which began in the eighty-two, was more especially felt in the wild parts of the country, and along the upland wastes. The desert of Kyle was severely visited, and its solitudes rendered still more solitary. In this district there lived an honest farmer and his wife who were warmly attached to the Covenanting cause. Gilbert Fleming's family consisted only of three persons—himself, his wife, Grizzy Grey, and a herd-boy, named Sandy. The

frost of this dreary winter hardened the moors and mosses
like a board, a suitable platform on which to spread the
mantling of deep snow which was speedily to succeed, and
to cause such devestation among the flocks of sheep in the
wilds as had scarcely ever been known.

On the evening of the day on which the snow began to
fall, two Covenanting brethren, in full flight before a company of troopers, from Muirkirk, took refuge in the upland
parts of the wilderness of Kyle, and there hid themselves
from their pursuers.   This was the more easily done, as the
dusk of the evening was now setting in.   The troopers finding it in vain to pursue, especially as the snow was thick-
ening, retreated with all speed to their quarters.   The two
worthies, exhausted with their flight, and shivering in the
cold, cowered down in the shelter of a deep moss hag, which
threatened, in a brief space, to become their grave, as the
twirling snow-flakes were beginning to form a wreath at
their feet.

"What shall we do ?" said one, "for if we remain here all
night we shall not see the morning."   "No," said the other,
"we must make our retreat ; it is not yet dark, and besides
it is full moon, and we will hold on our way to some place
of refuge in this weary waste."   "John," said Willie, "I see
it all now ; Gilbert Fleming has often invited me to his
house, and I have not hitherto availed myself of the invitation ; this is our time of need, and I am sure we shall
meet with a cordial welcome."   "Ay," said John, "but
where shall we find the hut, even if it be hereabouts ?
What hand to turn to we know not—every object is now
white, and we shall not be able to distinguish a house of any
kind."   "Let us try, however," said Willie ; "we may not,
perchance, be so far from our object, and the Lord, who
leads the blind by a way that they know not, has not permitted us to be chased into this moor for nothing."   "You
are right, my friend, yonder it is ; see you not that twink-

ling light on the moor! it shines brighter because of the snow. It may not be the house we are seeking, but it will at least be a shelter." In a brief space they reached a cottage—it was the house they sought—the house of Gilbert Fleming of the Miny. They entered, and the greeting was most cordial. "You are welcome for our Master's sake," cried honest Gilbert; "but how found you the way on such a night as this?" "A light guided us," they replied, "flickering from the window of your cottage." "O, how wonderful is that!" said Grizzy; "we never put a light in the window for fear of leading the enemy to us; but this evening I felt an unusual prompting to put the candle there, and you see what has come of it. The snaw might have been your winding-sheet, had you not found our house. This is the Lord's doing, and to Him be our acknowledgment."

This was a happy meeting. The wanderers were glad to find a shelter, and the inmates were as glad to receive them. For in those days the worthy inhabitants of the moorlands deemed it a privilege to have the opportunity of exercising hospitality to Christ's people for His sake. They knew who had said, "A cup of cold water given to a disciple in the name of a disciple shall not lose its reward," and they were soon to find the truth of this, as will appear in the subseparts of our sketch. The evening was spent in conversing on Zion's troubles, and the support which the Lord affords His people in persecuting times.

The wanderers slept soundly after the previous day's harassing toil; and worthy Gilbert, saluting them in the morning, congratulated them on the fact that the snow being drifted to a great depth over all the face of the moorland, there was no fear of being assailed by the troopers, who must now be besieged in their own garrison by the storm. It was in such circumstances chiefly that the moorlanders deemed themselves impregnable, and could sleep securely on their beds, free from all fear of the enemy.

"But," said Willie, "who can tell how long this storm may last ? and, if we be shut up here for a whole winter, we will eat you up, for, being often straitened for provisions, our appetites are keen, and, it may be, we shall not be easily satisfied." "Eat us up !" exclaimed Gilbert, "no fear of that, and even though you should, you shall be welcome to share the last morsel wi' us. But na, na, lads, there's nae fear o' being eaten up here—last week I brocht o'er the hard surface o' the muirs a whole melder fresh frae the mill ; besides nae lack o' barley flour for scones. The big beef boat is fu' to the brim ; we hae plenty o' buirdly kebboeks o' our ain making ; and we hae rowth o' maut for a brewst, to serve us when the cows in the byre are yell. And I canna but look on this as a very particular providence ; for two things were before us which we didna forsee—your coming to the house, and the visitation o' this storm. If either had come before the inlaying of our winter's provision, what could we have done ? But the Great and Kind One who foresees all, has now supplied us beforehand, and I consider myself honoured that He has sent you to board with us for a season. I have my own forebodings that the storm is not to continue for a day or two only, but it may be for weeks, and we are prepared for it."

It was indeed a terrible morning—the commencement of a storm that lasted for about four months. When the two men looked from the door—for the windows were literally blocked up—they were astonished at the appearance of the waste. Not an object or single feature of the former landscape was now to be seen ; the drift was pouring in streams along the surface of the snow, and so dense was the smoking trail that it was both blinding and suffocating. It was obviously a storm in earnest, one of those terrific visitations with which the uplands were occasionally assailed in those days. The fitful blasts of these hurricanes sometimes continued for a whole week without intermission, night and day, the snow either falling incessantly from the sky, or its light particles driven continuously before the wind. The desolation caused in this way was incalculable—houses, and flocks and men being buried indiscriminately below the drifted mass. We who live in these times, when no such storms are known, can scarcely have any correct idea of such a visitation. Many of the upland farmers were utterly ruined ; everything they possessed in the form of sheep and cattle was destroyed, and themselves, in many cases, thrown as beggars on the world's wide waste. Hunger and sickness were the accompaniments ; and a sort of pestilence invaded the households of the rural districts, working fearful havock, sometimes carrying off whole families, whose bodies could not be conveyed to a churchyard, and were, consequently, buried in the wilds. This accounts for the circumstances which appeared to Patrick Walker as being something akin to the miraculous, namely, open graves discovered in the moors by the casual passenger, as he wended his lonely way through the wastes. They were veritable graves, intended as the receptacles of those who died of the prevalent diseases.

Honest Gilbert's farm-stocking consisted of three score of sheep on the moor, four cows in the byre, and two horses in the stable. On this he was enabled to support himself, and to pay his small rent on the term-day. On seeing the storm raving without, he exclaimed in grateful exaltation, "How happy am I to think that the cows and horses are so snugly housed ! We have abundance of fodder gathered in the warm days of summer, and as for the hay, I think we never had the like of it in quality; Providence foresaw what we were to need." "But maister, maister," cried the herd-boy, "what o' the sheep; hae ye forgotten them ?" "The sheep, callan', the sheep, it never entered my mind we had sheep, alas ! my saxty puir sheep, they are a' buried deep aneath the snaw, and what to do I wot na." The two

friends smiled at the perplexity of their host, for they were
shepherds themselves, stout and stalwart men both, who
had exhumed many a sheep from the lairy moss hag, and
dug many a score from beneath the drifted snow ; and they
deemed it no insuperable task to rescue their host's sheep
from their perilous position. "Ye are smiling, I see, my
friends, and I think I can guess your meaning. But ken
ye, I can scarcely walk to the door, as I am so crippled wi'
pains in this shivering weather ; and if a' the cattle on my
bit farm should perish, I couldna help to rescue ane o' them.
Ye thought that ye were our debtors for gi'en ye lodgin',
and lang lodgin' too ; but I forsee that in the lang-run we
will be your debtors, rather than you ours. What could
that silly bit callan' do, if left to him ? and my puir wife
there couldna do muckle mair. If the Maister, whom ye
serve, and whose cause we are willing to suffer for, has sent
you here for the preservation of your lives, He has sent you
here also for the preservation of my little property. Go
and manage the sheep as you please."

The men made instant preparation for the work ; but
where were the sheep to be found ! "I gathered them,"
said Sandy, "into the hollow between the twa knowes to
the east there, and they cannot be far aff." The hollow
alluded to was filled with drifted snow, and it was obvious
that it would require no small exertion to excavate the
flock. The men, with little Sandy, however, succeeded in
making an opening on one side, where the snow was several
feet deep, and having extricated one, another followed, and
another, till, after long and exhausting toil, they succeeded
in setting free the whole sixty, whose destruction would
have been inevitable if such assistance had not been rendered. Thus honest Gilbert's little stock was recovered to
his unspeakable satisfaction, and the men were beyond
measure gratified at having it in their power to render him
this service.

On the forenoon of next day a circumstance occurred which perplexed the whole party not a little. The drift was still streaming along the waste, and the snow had gathered to the depth of between two and three feet, for in the higher parts of the country the storms rage with double fury, and pile the snow to twice or thrice the quantity that falls in the same time in the lower parts. Sandy reported that, as he and his collie were tumbling among the snow, as boys sometimes delight to do, he observed the marks of human feet, and that at a considerable distance from the dwelling-house. The holes, he said, were deep, and partly blown up by the drift, but that they were foot-prints he was certain, and they appeared to be those of two persons. The footsteps now became a matter of grave consideration. Could they be wanderers? Could they be soldiers? Could they be robbers? Which? This last supposition was suggested by a not uncommon fact; for many took occasion, from the disorders of the times, to engage in plundering raids throughout the country, especially in the upland parts. They visited farm-houses carrying off butter, and cheese, and poultry, and whatever suited them. It became necessary, therefore, for the peasantry to be as much on their guard against such parties as against the troopers themselves. The conclusion, however, to which the friends came was, that whatever might be the character and occupation of these lost ones, they were at least human beings, whom it was their duty to seek out, and endeavour to save. But the question came to be, Where were they to be found? The waste was now covered with snow several feet deep, and the foot-marks, it was concluded, must, ere this, have been drifted over. Gilbert thought that the most likely spot for the men to resort to would be the old vault at the ruin called the *Auchty*, which was originally a baronial residence in the moor: and he proposed that it should be visited. The Auchty was at a short distance from the dwelling-

house, so that, under the guidance of Sandy and his dog,
the two friends, he supposed, would be able to find it.
Accordingly, the party set out, and after deep wading and
tumbling in the soft wreaths, they reached the entrance of
the vault, the mouth of which was partly concealed by some
hazel bushes growing near it.   The dog led the way, and
began to bark whenever he reached the entrance.   "Is
there anybody here ?" cried Willie.   "There are two men
here," exclaimed a voice, tremulous with cold.   "On the
night of the storm we lost our way in the moor, when we
accidentally came against the hazel bush, and found the entrance into this vault, which has screened us from the tempest, and which the Master whom we serve, and in whose
cause we suffer hardship, has made a Bethel to us."   "We
hail you, then, as suffering brethren ; come with us, and, if
you have strength to plod through the snow and drift, you
shall soon find yourselves in a comfortable habitation."
The men then issued from the dark receptacle, and the
whole party, in a brief space, stood before a rousing fire of
peats in the kitchen of the Miny.   Gilbert received them
exultingly, when he learned who they were, and deemed
himself twice blessed in being honoured to entertain another
party of Christ's suffering people.

"We come," said the strangers, "from the wilds of Carsphairn, which we left the other day, as we learned that the
soldiers were in search of us.   As we were obliged to flee,
we thought we would like to visit the Upper Ward of Lanarkshire, where, we understand, many experienced Christians live, and where the blood of many of the Lord's people had been shed.   We traversed the base of the lofty
Cairnsmuir, and up towards the head of the Ken, and struck
across the mountains by the lonely Monthraw, and then
down into the defile of the Afton, and, crossing the upper
part of Nithsdale, we came into the moors of Kyle, and
wandered till we reached this neighbourhood, with the snow

blowing strongly in our faces. In passing along the frozen mosses, we were in no fear of sinking, but we were in fear of perishing in the snow ; we plodded on, however, lifting up our prayers for guidance to the God who knew our way, and who could lead us to a place of shelter. In a brief space, our progress was arrested by a tuft of hazel bushes lying in our path, and, as they seemed to afford us a screen from the blast, we crept down close beside them. This afforded us a breathing time and a grateful relief from the choking drift. While we sat here, as thankfully as ever Jonah did under his gourd at Nineveh, a hare or fox sprang out between us—apparently from some recess behind ; on searching for which, we found an opening, which we entered, and found within a spacious apartment, as dry as dust on the floor, and not a puff of wind. To understand the true state of matters, we struck a light (for you see we carry with us small fire-arms for self-defence), and kindling a piece of paper, held it up as a torch, and found that we were under the strongly-built arch of some old tower, where we might remain with safety, at least for one night. Finding on the floor a considerable quantity of withered brush-wood and tufts of dried heath, we proceeded to collect materials for a fire, which we soon kindled, and warmed ourselves. We next discovered several stone seats placed close by the wall, here and there, around the vault ; on these we rested, and, drawing our fire nearer the side where we sat, felt ourselves very comfortable, for we were now in a receptacle unspeakably preferable to the cold, dripping caves in the sides of the hills, where, as we supposed, not a few of our fellow-sufferers might, at the moment, be imprisoned. The smoke did not annoy us, for it went straight out by the hole at which we entered. Our hearts rose in thanksgiving to the great Preserver of our lives, who had so wondrously guided our steps to such a retreat. Having prayed together, we wrapped ourselves in our plaids and fell fast asleep, and

scarcely awoke till the morning began to peep in at the entrance to the vault.

"We roused ourselves, and proceeded to collect materials
for a fire, and soon the whole interior was lighted up with
the cheerful blaze. But now a new difficulty presented
itself, the smoke did not seem to escape, but collected in a
dense, suffocating cloud above our head—we ran to the entrance for breath, and found that it was all filled with snow,
excepting a small space near the upper part, which could
scarcely admit a man's arm. We began to clear the aperture, and forced our way with difficulty to the outside,
when we could scarcely keep our feet for the fury of the
tempest, which, coming from the east, did not blow into
the mouth of our recess. No sooner did we open the outlet, which we did with our bare hands, than the smoke
rushed out, and we resolved to remain contentedly another
day in our stronghold."

"But," exclaimed honest Gilbert, who listened with deep
interest to the men's story, "where did your breakfast come
from ? What was your condition on the score of food ?"
"Here," said they, "we were not altogether at a loss.
When we travel to any distance from home, in these times,
we always carry with us a suitable supply of provisions, so
we had a pretty good stock of bread and cheese at least ;
and, as we passed through the moors there, a friendly woman
whose hut we entered for the purpose of resting for a few
minutes, presented each of us with a goodly bottle of milk,
fresh from the cow. This we found to be a boon far more
valuable than we at first conceived ; for I know not what we
would have done in the vault without some liquid. We
spent the day in no little comfort ; but the thought began
to haunt us that probably wo might be storm-stayed here,
and if this should be the case, the vault must become our
sepulchre. It was this which, on the second morning of our
residence here, prompted us to issue from our retreat, to

look abroad over the face of the moorland, if possible to descry a human habitation. We set out in the face of the blast, and found that the snow could not be less than three feet deep, and in many places twice that depth, and the drift still streaming along without any abatement. Having wandered about for a while without discovering any habitation, we began to fear lest our footsteps should be effaced, and we would not be able to trace our way back again. When we re-entered the vault, we began to be oppressed with forebodings somewhat dismal; and to fortify our confidence in God, we agreed to fall on our knees and pray. We committed our way to Him who had hitherto guided us, and asked deliverance, and we arose from our knees full of confidence in God, leaving the result entirely to His disposal. Scarcely had we seated ourselves in our stony chairs, when we observed a dark shadow at the mouth of the entrance, and heard a voice asking, ' Is there anybody here ?' It was a human voice, and that was welcome ; and so the matter has issued in our appearing here under your hospitable roof, and our satisfaction is the greater to find that we are in the midst of friends and of brethren in the same common cause."

"Weel," exclaimed Grizzy, "I hae gotten my dream read. I dreamed that twa o' our sheep had wandered frae the lave, and that some o' the dragoons passing through the moor, huntit their cruel dogs at the twa puir things, till, bleetin' and forfochen, they escaped into the auld vowt, and the dogs foregetherin' wi' a hare, ran after it ; and sae ye're welcome here for our Master's sake, in whose cause ye suffer."

Gilbert, who was transported at finding himself in the company of such men, to whom it was in his power, and in his heart, to do a service, exclaimed, " It's just ae wonder after another ; ye were heard in being directed to the vault, and ye were heard when praying in the vault. What a

Master we serve! O! if we had only a minister wi' us,
what a happy time we might spend!" "Hoot awa', Gibby,
my man," said Grizzy, "we mauna fa' that; I think ye hae
here men wi' ye that may weel serve in the stead o' ony
minister, even o' Saunders himsel', although there is naebody I like better to see dit our door than Saunders Peden,
for he aye brings his Master wi' him. Ye hae a' the company that ye'll get as long as this storm lasts, and let us be
thankfu' for what we have."

While good Grizzy was talking she was preparing a
hearty breakfast of warm, rich brose—the common food of
those times—and the two cold and hungry strangers partook of a plentiful meal, and were refreshed. "But," said
they, "how came you to the mouth of the vault to seek for
persons there?" Gilbert then rehearsed the story of the
herd-boy and his dog when tumbling among the snow.
"This," said he, "led, in answer to your prayers, to your
deliverance at the very nick of time, for, you see, the storm
is as constant as ever, and another day might have sealed
your doom; but the Lord is wonderful in working in reply
to the supplications of His people in the hour of their distress. We are a witnessing remnant, and we may look for
some special interposition in our behalf."

The men from Carsphairn were quite delighted with their
reception, and with the comfortable abode into which they
were introduced—they recognised the Divine hand in the
whole case, and a sentence of one of the conventicle
preachers came vividly before them, "Let no one fear a
suffering lot for Christ."

But the affairs of honest Gilbert were to be attended to,
as well as the entertaining of strangers. The sheep had
been excavated from the snow, but were still in a perilous
condition on a knoll in the vicinity of the house, and it was
necessary that their safety should be looked to. The storm
did not seem to abate, and the face of the moorland bore

the most dismal aspect imaginable. Not an object was to be seen, for the driving of the snow was like a dense mist all around. It was now plain that, unless the storm should abate, the poor flock would not be able to keep their ground. A plan was adopted which entirely answered the end. A large out-house, frail indeed, both in its walls and its roof, but which, with a little trouble, could be repaired, was selected as a shelter for the poor animals. Into this place the sheep were collected and furnished with abundance of hay; and now the minds of all were greatly at ease. Gilbert's property was secured, and in this the men rejoiced; the men's lives were spared, and this gave Gilbert unspeakable delight. The work of digging out the sheep from the snow, and of preparing them a shelter in the outhouse was no Herculean task for a few strong men; but a work was before them which they could not foresee, nor guess at, and which was to tax their energy and skill to the utmost. An event was about to occur, which we may well believe to have been the main reason for which Providence had brought these four men together, at this juncture in the house of the Miny. This event does not immediately follow the incidents which we have just now narrated, but will turn up in its order.

---

## CHAPTER II.

JUST before the fugitives had reached the Miny, to which the persecution and the snow-storm together had driven them, Gilbert Fleming had got his little crop safely gathered into the barn-yard, and part of it turned into rich, sweet oatmeal, now snugly pressed into the meal-ark. But the bulk of the produce yet stood in the stack-yard. To thresh it himself, sore pained as he was at every joint by the severity of the weather, was more than Gilbert could have accomplished; but it was no heavy task for the

strangers, so that he had soon what was needed for fodder
to the cattle, and for corn to the horses, to keep them in
good condition against the spring labour.   The men could
not be idle, and they belaboured the lusty sheaves on the
barn-floor, with swinging flails, by turns every day.   In a
few weeks they had large heaps of yellow grain laid on the
floor ; and as Gilbert had intended to thatch his house
before the storm began, they prepared the straw with a
view to thatch it themselves if an opportunity should offer.
In this way a large quantity of straw was piled up to the
roof of the barn to be in readiness.   Our reason for
mentioning these things will afterwards be seen.

As a specimen of the Covenanters' Sabbath, when public
ordinances were beyond reach, the first Sabbath after the
arrival at the Miny may here be noticed.   The friends had
anticipated a day of much spiritual enjoyment, and they
were not disappointed.   A Sabbath among the religious
moorland peasantry was a Sabbath indeed.   It was with
them a strictly sanctified day, and not a day of religious
pretension.   It was a season on which they sought to worship God, and to worship Him in spirit and in truth.
Gilbert and his friends rose at the first peep of dawn, and
after secret prayer, family devotion was observed.   This
done, breakfast was set on the table, which in the rural
parts, consisted of rich oatmeal brose, in which was hid a
goodly lump of fragrant butter, which, to the hungry
appetite, afforded a rare repast.   " Now, friends," said Gilbert, " I suppose all of you will be equally inclined with me
to keep the Sabbath-day as it ought to be kept.   I am in
the habit of collecting my little family around me, when I
endeavour to imitate the order of the services of the Kirk
as near as may be.   I do not preach ; but if I had the gift
I do not see what should hinder me from speaking to my
neighbours of a Saviour, even though it should resemble
preaching ; but I read a sermon from a godly book which

I have here on the shelf. Now, I have been thinking that, as there are five men of us here, one of us should begin with praise, the next read a chapter and pray, the third read the sermon, the fourth pray, and the last conclude with a psalm. This, I think, would be a profitable way of spending the forenoon of the Sabbath, and we can either repeat the same in the afternoon, or spend it in religious conversation, as may be found suitable." Gilbert's proposal was cordially agreed to, and the Sabbath was spent accordingly.

The conversation in the evening, however, seemed to be the most lively and impressive part of that day's exercise. Every one appeared to be deeply affected with the various spiritual topics that came incidentally before them. The tears were seen frequently to start into the eyes of the little herd-boy, and steal silently down his cheeks. God was in the midst of them. They were a portion of His church enduring tribulation for His sake. A large portion of spiritual influence manifestly rested on them, and their hearts were comforted. Cold and inclement as it was without, the vitality of a spiritual warmth was felt within. Not a few meetings had been held in Gilbert's house, but none were to be compared with this. A spiritual joyousness seemed to pervade the company, and every one felt happier than he even chose to express. There was the communion of the saints, and there was communion with God, and what more was needed? Such heavenly repasts were required to fortify the Lord's people in those trying times, for they had much to endure, and, like Elijah in the desert when journeying to Horeb, they needed food in the strength of which to prosecute their pilgrimage. This Sabbath was one of a long series which they were to spend under Gilbert's roof, in the heart of this lonely desert, and every succeeding one was equal to it, for the manna became sweeter and more plentiful every day they gathered it. "Noo, Gibby," said Grizzy, with a heart full of heavenly exultation, "ye thocht our little company wad be perfect, if we had only a minister amang us, and ye looked out at the window as wistfully as if ye had expected auld Saunders would come stottin' o'er the muirs as he used to do in the fine days o' simmer ; but hae we not been as weel entertained, seeing the great Master of assemblies has been wi' us Himsel' ?"

The storm continued to rave, and the snow was driven in wild eddies. Gilbert's farm steading was now completely covered over, behind and before, and no light peered into the interior save what descended by the chimney. All this was dreary enough, but still the snugness and comfort within doors cheered the hearts of the little group gathered round the hearth. Yet the possibility of being shut up here for weeks to come was not pleasant to so many active-minded persons. When the desire was expressed on the part of the strangers to be serviceable to the household in any way they could, Gilbert replied, "Indeed ye hae served me weel enough already, I think ; ye hae saved my puir sheep, ye hae thrashed a gude part o' my corn, and what service ye may yet be able to render us before ye leave this house, only He who foresees a' things can tell ; so, therefore, dinna put yoursel's about—things may turn up that ye may get to do." Grizzy, who was busy about the house and heard the conversation, said, "There is plenty o' yarn hingin' frae the baulks ; if ony o' ye can work a stockin', ye may get that to do." Here was work at once for the two shepherds. The men from Carsphairn were one a tailor and the other a shoemaker ; and as the house plenishing included two webs of home-made cloth, ready for the flying tailor from the head of Douglas Water, whenever the necessities of Gilbert's wardrobe should require him to be sent for, as well as plenty of leather and other materials to make shoes for the household, whenever the jaunting cobbler from Muirkirk should come round, each commenced his appropriate work, while work within doors only could be accomplished ; and thus all things went comfortably on.

In a few days the storm partially abated; the clouds began to disperse, and the bright sun shone out once more in the clear sky. The scene was now visible, and what a scene! not a black spot was to be seen on hill or dale—all was one uniform sheet of whiteness, exhibiting that velvet appearance peculaliar to deep snow. The frost now began above the snow as it had done beneath it, and the bright glancing of the frozen surface on the sides of the hills, which had been partially softened by the mid-day warmth, reflected the flashing rays of the sun as if from a mass of polished silver. It was a thing both beautiful and melancholy to behold. All communication between neighbours was cut off. No one could assist another; and who could tell what misery was experienced within the lowly huts buried deep in the drifted snow throughout the waste? There might be sickness where no medical aid could be obtained; there might be want of food where no supplies could be had; there might be loneliness without a single being to speak with, and perplexities of many kinds that could not be remedied. Even the dead might be lying in their shrouds, with no possibility of obtaining burial. The friends in Gilbert's comfortable home ruminated on all these things, and became the more thankful when they thought on the distress of others.

As the clear weather continued, it occured to the Carsphairn brethren that they would like once more to visit the Auchty, and survey the vault in which they had at first taken refuge. "The Auchty," exclaimed Gilbert, "a cauld, gloomy vowt wi' naething in't but foxes, and fumarts, and wulcats, and queer-looking craters frae the muirs." A visit, however, was determined on; but it was clear that it must be by the cutting of a passage through the snow, and this would require some exertion from the four stout men. There was no want of implements for the undertaking, and as it afforded something like active exercise, it was prosecuted in high spirits. At length they reached the mouth of the vault, which was closed up with snow ; but this was soon cleared away, and they stood beneath the arch. A huge pile of peats was kindled in the midst of the floor, and the smoke, as formerly, curled out at the opening, but none of the "eldrich craters," which Gilbert enumerated, were to be found in the apartment. After having satisfied their curiosity, they returned along the avenue which they had formed.

The intercourse which Gilbert Fleming held with his friends was of the most agreeable and edifying nature—no idle discourse, no gossiping, no merely careless or worldly conversation. Their position as Covenanting brethren, obnoxious to the rulers of the period, and liable at any time to be captured or shot on the spot, superinduced a serious-ness and a spirituality which were observable in their entire demeanour. No subjects of conversation, therefore, suited their taste and their circumstances, but topics of a religious caste. One cold and inclement day, as they were gathered round the pile of peats that blazed on the hearth, every one at his own proper occupation, the shepherds at their stock-ings, the tailor and the shoemaker plying the awl and the needle, the guidewife spinning in the corner, the boy teaz-ing the wool, and Gilbert stretched at his length on the "lang settle" behind the hallen, bearing his pains as best he could, the conversation took a turn on conventicle preaching. "Were ye at Hyndbottom," said he, "ony o' ye, that day that Cameron preached so shortly before his death, from the text 'Ye will not come unto me that ye might have life ?'" "We were there," replied the shepherds from Lesmahagow, "and a great crowd there was from all the surrounding parishes." "I remember," said Gilbert, "how urgently he pressed the acceptance of Christ that day on his hearers ; we offer Him, he cried, unto you in the parish of Auchenleck, Douglas, Crawfordjohn, and all ye that live

thereabout, and what say ye? will ye take Him? tell us
what ye say, for we take instruments before these hills and
mountains around us that we have offered Him to you this
day." "Ay, Gibby," said Grizzy, "and I mind how he
cried and pointed wi' his hand, 'look over to the Shawhead
and these hills, and take a look at them; for they are a'
witnesses now, and when ye are dying, they shall come before your face. We take every one of you witness against
another; and will not that aggravate your sorrow when
they come into your mind and conscience, saying, we heard
you invited and obtested to come to Christ, and yet ye
would not; now we are witnesses against you?' It was
then, I remember, that the whole congregation began to
weep, and when he observed it, he cried out, 'I see some
tenderness among you, and that is favourable to look upon,
but yet that is not all. The angels will go up to report before the throne what every one's choice has been this day, and
thus they will say—There were some in the parishes of Auchenleck, Douglas, and Crawfordjohn, that have received the
Lord Jesus Christ, and He is become their Lord, and this will
be welcome news there.' These were his very words." "O but
that was an unco day!" said Gilbert. "I thought I was at
the very gates of heaven itself, when sitting on the wild
muir in Hyndbottom. There was scarcely a dry eye in the
whole company. He was so affected that he could not
speak, and leaned his brow on the Bible, and the tears wet-
ted a' the leaves like a shower of rain." "Ay," said Grizzy,
"the strong man bowed himself, for his great heart was
pained and full of yearning for souls. I remember a puir
young lassie sittin' beside me on the bent, and her bit napkin, which she held to her een, was a' drenched through and
through wi' greeting. It was naething to see the women
greet, but it was extraordinar' to see strong men, and
auld men, a' meltit into tears, and standing wi' faces as if
they had been washed wi' a shower." "I was sitting close

beside my father," said John from Lesmahagow, "and he
shook as if he had had an ague : and on his right hand
there was a tall, swarthy man, with a firm and manly
aspect, who seemed for a while to resist the general emotion;
but by degrees his countenance relaxed, and the tears
streamed down his cheeks.   He had his bonnet in his hand,
with which he sometimes wiped his eyes, and sometimes he
dashed the tears away with the big sleeve of his coat, and
at other times with his rough bare hand."   "Yes," said
Gilbert, " the very rocks seemed to melt, and the heart of
stone within was softened.   They talk of the Kirk o' Shotts ;
but I question if the Kirk o' Shotts can be compared to
Hyndbottom.   The fruits o' Hyndbottom dinna soon vanish :
the martyrdom of the minister so quickly after served as a
standing application of the sermon, and enforces its truth
till the present hour."   "We never had the opportunity of
hearing Cameron," said one of the men from Carsphairn ;
"but we have had many a meeting in our wilds kept by
men who, no doubt, have visited your uplands."   "Ay,"
said Grizzy, "gude Mr Peden tells us that there are nae
Christians like the Christians o' Carsphairn, nane that hae
mair moyen at the throne of grace than they."   "Yes,"
said Gilbert, "and ye hae had an eminently godly minister,
John Semple, who watered the deserts around you.   I hae
heard him at the Sanquhar sacrament, and the sweet
impression has scarcely left me to this day."   "It was under
his ministry," said the men, "that we were brought to the
Saviour, and never can we forget the name of that saintly
man."   "Continue," added Grizzy, "to live as a credit to
that good man's name.   You are but men in your prime
yet, and ye may hae muckle to try you ere a' be done ; for,
tak' my word for it, the persecution is not yet at an end,
and we hae need o' patience, for a suffering lot is before us.
We cannot tell how soon we may be wrapped in a bluidy
winding-sheet, and hidden in a mossy graff."

In this general way did the friends converse when seated round the fire, each at his work, and in this little group none seemed more attentive to what was said than little Sandy. A new field of vision was opening on his youthful mind, and the great matters of salvation were beginning to be of all things the most important to him. Thus, as the elderly were more exposed to the fierce blasts of persecution that swept them away from the earth, a young generation came up among them to supply the void, that there might be no lack when a sacrifice was required.

The weather still continued clear, calm, and frosty, and the earth groaned under its superincumbent mass of deep snow—every cottage and farm-steading in the uplands was like Jericho straitly shut up—none went out and none came in. The snow was generally as highly piled up as the tops of the houses. This was strictly the case with good Gilbert Fleming's farm-steading. It was drifted up round and round, and to a person at a little distance nothing would have indicated its existence but a sturdy column of smoke that issued apparently from the interior of a hillock of solid snow. The two shepherds conceived the design of clearing a pretty wide space along the entire length of the front of the building, that ample room might be made for entering the out-houses where the sheep and cattle were confined, instead of getting to them from the interior by means of the doors leading off to the right and left from the kitchen. The four powerful men, each with a broad mouthed shovel in his hand, cleared the space with nearly as much expedition as they made the road to the Auchty. By this means a great relief was afforded both for additional fuel and for water. The fine well, which formed a natural basin at the bottom of a knoll at the end of the buildings, could now be reached, and saved the prisoners from having recourse to the melting of the snow in pots and kettles over the fire, to obtain water for culinary purposes, and for drink

to the beasts in the stalls.  This was considered a great
achievement, and there was now a walk, in a straight line,
from the further end of the steading down to the vault—a
walk which was frequently used for exercise.

This being accomplished, they next thought of repairing
the roof of the houses.  It was no difficult thing to clear
the snow from the thatch, and a space was soon laid bare
from the vent of the dwelling house for a number of yards
on the side of the cow-house, as this was the place where
they wished to make the experiment.  The farm-steading
of the Miny consisted of a row of low buildings, the
dwelling-house occupying the centre, the byre and stable
stretching to the west, and the barn and the outhouse, in
which the sheep were sheltered, stretching eastward.  We
now approach an event for which all this work was a suitable preparation.  The men had finished what they intended,
in removing part of the heavy mass of snow from the roof
next the dwelling house, and were just about to descend, as
the evening was stealing on, when the herd-boy exclaimed,
"Maister,'maister, here's auld Eddie !"  "Auld Eddie wha?"
said Gilbert.  "Auld Eddie Cringan and his cuddie, standing on the top o' the snaw wreath at the end o' the house."
"The callan's gaen gyte ; it's a vision, it's a vision."  "May
be, but Eddie's there at ony rate, and he's crying to help
him doon."  "Eddie, is that you?"  "Indeed is it, Gibby ;
it's a' that ye'll get for auld Eddie."  "O dear man, that's
miraculous ; it's like walkin' on the water without sinkin'."
"But ye could walk on the water if it was frozen, Gibby,
couldna ye?  Now the snaw is frozen as hard as a board,
so that a gude skater could flighter his way from Glenbuck
to this in an hour."  "Where hae ye come frae, Eddie?"
exclaimed Grizzy in great astonishment, "Where hae ye
come frae in this deep snaw?"  "I hae come frae the head
o' Douglas Water, and I hae come here just wi' the article
ye ken ; but come and help me down, and I will tell ye a'

about it." The strangers were both astonished and amused
at the apparition of Eddie, a personage of whom they had
never heard, and with their spades soon made a way for
his descent. But the arrival of Eddie revealed a circumstance which now gave them some uneasiness, and of which
they had never dreamed, namely, that the snow could be
traversed, and that now there was no security against a
visit from the soldiers, who were lying at Muirkirk, waiting
an opportunity of invading the moorlands. They naturally
looked out on the surface of the waste with some anxiety.

Eddie Cringan was a noted character in the district, and
a warm friend to the Covenanters. Though he never himself took any decided part, he traversed the moors with his
donkey, having a *creel* attached to each side of the animal,
while he himself occupied the seat between them. His
cuddie was a strong creature, and well fitted for the moorlands ; and wherever Eddie came, both he and his companion
were treated with much hospitality. His journeys were
short, and in general he was in no hurry in shifting his
quarters. His company was always entertaining, as he
brought all the news of the country, which he gathered on
his way, and had the faculty of retailing ; besides, he was
a pious person, and a thoroughly honest man, who could
keep a secret, and would sooner have lost his life than be-
trayed any of the covenanting friends. Eddie carried keel
for the shepherds in the upland parts, and professed to
gather eggs from the farmers' wives ; and in these two things
he drove a considerable trade. But there was another article, or rather other two articles, which lay more concealed
in the bottom of his creels—these were gunpowder and
shot. The keel covered the one and the eggs the other,
and nobody knew that his donkey carried such materials
but the Covenanting friends, for whose benefit especially he
dealt in them. Self-preservation required the persecuted
people to keep weapons of defence, and there was no way

of getting the material for their fire-arms but through such
a medium as Eddie.    Hence, his visits were always acceptable.

Eddie had long traversed the district; but it was observed
that he seldom lodged a night in the house of a Prelatist,
for there he never found himself at home.    Eddie was an
original after his sort, and was, withal, a privileged person.
He could rally with the dragoons, and make himself amusing
with their commanders, whom he frequently met in their
raids, but always passed without suspicion.

Eddie, finding that the snow was so hardened by the keen
frost that he might safely venture on its surface, resolved
to visit his friends in the moors.    He set out to the Miny
to see how it fared with its inmates ; and a little before
dark he presented himself there as we have seen.    He was
received with all cordiality, and placed in the warmest corner, after the creel which contained the gunpowder was suit-
ably disposed of.    Few visitors were more welcome here
than Eddie, as he was one whom all could trust, and who
sometimes brought important intelligence respecting the
movements of the enemy.    Eddie having been comfortably
seated by the fire, with a *bicker* of rich, steaming brose resting on his knee, and an enormous ram-horn spoon in his
hand, observed :—" I never travelled these moors so lightly
along as I have done this day, and the animal, even in the
softest parts, never sank above the hoof.    I came round by
the edge of Cairntable, and called at no house till I reached
this, and I saw the face of no living creature, and I am sure
none saw me."

" Think ye, Eddie," said Gilbert, " that there is no likelihood of the troopers coming out if the snow keeps hard ?'
" Na, na, there's nae fear o' that ; the cuddie and me came
lightly o'er the snaw, but their heavy horses would sink to
the belly at the very first step.    They are fond enough o'
mischief, but they hae little notion o' sinking themselves,

man and horse, in a bottomless snaw wreath—na, na, they are no the chaps for that, and so ye needna fear a visit frae them, tak' my word for't."

"O, Eddie," cried Grizzy, "how glad I am to see ye! I was just thinking about ye the other day, and said to mysel', We'll no see Eddie the year, nor hear what is doing ayont the muirs; but ye are here after a', and ye are welcome to our biggin." "Thank ye, gudewife, I kent I was welcome, else I wadna hae been here; and if I can help you in onything I'll be glad to do it." Such was Eddie's reception at the Miny.

---

## CHAPTER III.

THE day after Eddie Cringan's arrival at the Miny was ushered in with a dense, white mist, which covered all the moorlands, and which Eddie called "the wraith of snaw." Before the day broke, the boy had gone to do his work in the stable, having in his hand a lighted candle, which he placed in a slit, made in the end of a stick inserted into the wall. While he was busy in the stalls, the stick and candle fell into the heart of a loose heap of dry straw, and in an instant all was in a blaze. The boy alarmed the household with a sudden scream, when all rushed in, and found the stable full of flame and smoke. The horses were prancing, the cows lowing, and all in confusion. It was expected that the whole steading would be reduced to ashes in a brief space. The shepherds instantly released the terrified animals, and commanded the boy to drive them to the Auchty, and place them in the vault. Poor Gilbert was in sore distress. Stiff and pained at every joint, he could not help himself, so that he had nothing in prospect but the entire destruction of his property. The flames were making progress—they had caught on the roof;

but the superincumbent weight of snow began to melt by
the heat, and prevented their more rapid diffusion. It occurred to the shepherds that the place in the roof, which
had been cleared of the snow, should be instantly broken
down to prevent a communication with the dwelling-house.
This was done without delay, and the flames were arrested
in their progress toward that quarter. This was so far sat-
isfactory ; but a puff of wind would have mocked all their
precautions.

The roof above where the horses stood now fell in with a
crash, and snow, and fire, and smoke, were all mingled together—the air getting freely in forced the flame toward
the thatch of the byre, and in a short time it also fell in.
The whole west end of the steading was thus a ruin. The
great anxiety was now to preserve the other buildings in the
line ; and the dwelling-house became, of course, the object
of solicitude. The thatch below the snow was dry, and the
fear was lest the embers should get in among the combus-
tible matter immediately above the kitchen. Buckets of
water were brought from the well, and dashed in on the
edge among the straw, and all around the bottom of the
vent. At this work of extinction all the hands about the
house laboured assidiously, hour after hour, till the fire was
fairly brought under, and nothing but smouldering ashes
lay on the floor, with a load of snow pressing heavily upon
them. The dwelling-house was now considered secure, and
they began to breathe more freely. It was agreed that no
attempt should be made to remove the smoking rubbish
from the interior till the next day, when it was expected
that the melting of the snow would extinguish the last par-
ticle of the burning.

The next care was the cattle in the vault. Abundance of
hay was conveyed to them, and the horses were tied in a
corner by themselves. When all things were properly
arranged, and the day drawing near its close, the household

were gathered round the hearth, honest Gilbert could not
suppress his emotions. "I see," said the good man, "I
plainly see why the path to the Auchty was cut through
the deep snow, and why the space in the front of the house
had been cleared, and why the well was opened up, and why
part of the roof of the office-houses nearest the kitchen had been
so far prepared to cut the connection between the two, and
I see how God has sent you all here about me, a poor helpless man, and the more helpless, that I am labouring under
this pain, and I could do nothing though the whole had been
burned to a cinder.    I praise and thank Him who takes care
of me and mine, and who works deliverance so wonderful."
"Ay," exclaimed Eddie, "and what a favour is it that this
was a misty day! for if the weather had been as clear as we
have seen it, the flames and the smoke issuing from your
burning house, like a ship on fire in the midst of the blue
ocean, would have attracted more eyes than you would care
for, and, it may be, some would have come, foes as well as
friends, to see what was the matter, and the hiding-place of
your true friends around here might have been discovered
—I ken what I say." "I see now," said Grizzy, "the meaning of the apostle's words—'Be not forgetful to entertain
strangers, for thereby some have entertained angels una-
wares.'   It was for Christ's sake we admitted these wandering friends into our house, and we have been richly repaid,
for, as Mr Peden says, 'we never can get aforehand wi' Him;
gi'e as we like, He gi'es far ayont us.'   In what condition
would my puir husband and mysel' hae been this night, had
it not been for your hands?   But He sent you, and to Him
be the praise."   "I was aye fear'd," said the kind-hearted
Gilbert, "I was aye fear'd that ye wad think yourselves
unco indebted to us for the bit hospitality ye had received,
and this vexed me; but now the tables are turned, and it is
we that are your debtors, and we can never repay ye, but
He will do it by whom ye stand."

After a hearty meal, which repaired the exhaustion of the
preceding day, it is needless to say with what grateful
hearts the little group surrounded the domestic altar to give
praise and thanks to the Preserver of their lives. It was
agreed that they should keep watch by turns during the
night, lest any untoward incident should befall.

The next day's work was to clear out the interior of the
burnt house, with a view to repair as speedily as possible
the entire damage ; and here the four men, with Eddie and
the boy, set vigorously to work, and before the day was
half spent, a thorough clearance was made. The roof was
repaired, for there was plenty of *cabers*, as Gilbert called
them, or spars of wood, lying at the end of the house, which
were easily made available for roofing; and the turfs, though
some of them were wasted, were generally fit for the purpose of clothing the framework ; and then there was an
abundance of straw in the barn, and all prepared for the
purpose of thatching—and so by the end of the week all
was restored, but in a much more substantial fashion than
before. The horses and the cows were brought up from the
vault, and placed in their stalls as formerly—and now the
evil passed away as if it never had been—like some of
those hasty storms that sweep over the moorlands and leave
a perfect calm behind.

The mist now cleared away, and the bleak and shivering
aspect of the desert again appeared. The surface of the
snow was now very much hardened, so that travelling was
no difficulty. This circumstance rendered the inmates of
the Miny somewhat uneasy, especially after the following
statements made by Eddie. Throughout the district Eddie
was regarded as a sort of privileged person, and went under
the familiar appelation of Eddie the Keelman, or Keel
Eddie. But Eddie was a shrewd man, kind, and truly
pious, and a man of a very self-denying disposition, calcul-
ating more the interest of others than his own. We have

said that Eddie was not understood as strictly belonging to
the Covenanting party, at least in any ostensible way,
though his leanings were mainly on their side, so that he
held intercourse with dragoons as well as with those whom
they persecuted.

"As I was coming along," said Eddie, "by the head o'
Douglas Water on the day that the snow began to fa', I met
a company o' troopers. I kent the captain weel, and he
began to rally me on my puir equipage, compared wi' his
gallant war-steed. 'Weel a weel,' says I, 'yer honour, if
yer horses be brawly harnessed, ye're no o'er weel clad
yourselves; there's a batch o' chaps that's come enow to
Douglas that dings you outright—they are a' clad brent
new frae tap to tae, in bonny bright red, but your coats are
turned sae blae in the hue that they need a bit o' my keel
to bring back the colour.' 'Never mind, Eddie,' said he,
'orders are given to cleed us all anew before the winter sets
fully in—but who is the commander of the Douglas party?"
'O,' said I, 'its that scape-grace, Peter Inglis.' 'Peter
Inglis! I thought he had been garrisoned in Hell's Byke in
Lesmahagow.' 'So he was, but he has come buzzin' out o'
that byke, and a' his bees at his back, and noo they are
skeppit in the Red Ha' in Douglas.' 'So ho,' he cried, and
rode off. But the thing that I am ga'en to tell is this;
there's a blade, a dragoon in this party, they ca' Geordy
Ga', a fine chiel; I kent his father weel, he was a douce
man, auld Saunders Ga'—he was one o' the cottars o' Carmacoup. It was a waefu' day that o' their flittin', when so
many godly families were driven frae the skirts o' Cairntable; and when thirty chimnies ceased to smoke on the
fair lands o' Carmacoup, and a' for keeping a gude conscience. But Geordy means nae ill; he just wantit to be a
sodger, and a sodger he is. Geordy tells me he never puts
lead in his pistol, and when he fires, it does nae harm, but
makes as loud a noise as ony o' them. Weel, as I was sayin',

Geordy was in the troop, and when he saw me and the captain haverin' thegether, he fell into the rear, and so, when the party scampered off, Geordy cries, ' Eddie, hae ye ony tobacco ?' ' I dinna ken but I hae,' I says, and so he fell back, for a' this was a pretence, for he just wanted to speak wi' me, for aye when we forgethered we taigled a blink, for ye see I sometimes get news frae Geordy : so as I was taking out the tobacco, I says, ' Geordy, what's in the wind enow ?' ' O,' says he, ' we are on the chase the day ; twa herd lads frae Lesmahagow side were seen hereabouts, and we are after them ; and last night we got notice of other two men frae Carsphairn hand—the one a tailor, and the other a shoemaker—that have been seen coming down the Afton, and then directing their course to the upper parts of Kyle ; at least so say the spies from New Cumnock.   But I hope we'll make nothing of it—now ye hae my secret, and good day."

" I now began to think what I should do, and so, praying earnestly for Divine direction, I rode to Glenbuck, for the snow was beginning to fa', and there I was stormstayed till the day ye saw me on the cuddie on the tap o' the snaw."

This concerned the party not a little, and Eddie was not at all aware of the persons who were before him.   The news, however, fell like a blight on the hearts of the four men.   They now perceived that they were marked men, and that the pursuit of them was not merely incidental. They were near the troopers, and the snow was hard, and who could guess what might happen?   " Eddie," said Gilbert, " ye see before ye the four men ye hae been speaking o', and they hae been wi' me since the beginning o' the storm, and they are welcome to stay to the end of it, and shall stay ;—but do ye think, Eddie, that the troopers will venture out?"   " Not with their horses at any rate, and I dinna think they will be inclined to travel so far on foot, and so, I think, ye may rest at ease."

The next morning, however, put an end to their fears, the storm had commenced anew, and with all its former violence; "the wraith o' snaw" had boded the reality. The road to the Auchty was drifted up *queem*, as Eddie called it, that is, filled from side to side, and all the spaces about in like manner. The inmates were now quite at their ease—no visit from the soldiers was contemplated, nor even from unfriendly neighbours. It became obvious that the residence of the friends at the Miny was not to be of short duration, and every one was thankful for the comfortable quarters in which Providence had placed them. Never, perhaps, was there a happier group met around the genial hearth. " I think," said Eddie, looking up to the roof of the kitchen, where the product of Grizzy's spinning-wheel was suspended, "I reckon, gudewife, that ye will hae a gude sale for yer yairn the year; wha do ye deal wi'?" "Wi' Priesthill, Eddie, the Christian carrier; we get frae him the price that's ga'en, and he sells it at Lourie's fair in Hamilton." "He's a rare man, John Brown," said Gilbert, "he is the flower of the desert. Mr Peden says he'll be shot some day, for his Master's image is too deeply imprinted on his forehead to escape the notice of the enemy." "But I am sure," said Grizzy, "he never was out; he was not at Drumclog, nor at Bothwell, nor at Ayr's Moss; and what for should they shoot him who is so blameless a character?" "But," replied Eddie, "he does not attend the curate, and that wi' the enemy is reason enough ; and as for his blamelessness, they hate him jist the mair for that. Hech, sirs, but these are waefu' times in which we live !" "I never heard a man pray like Priesthill," said Willie from Lesmahagow, "and though he has a stammer in his speech at other times, yet when he is on his knees, the words come from him like a stream. It is a treat beyond compare to spend a day with him in company with my cousin David Steel, and others in our neighbourhood. It is like heaven upon earth

to be with these men ; they converse as if they were on the
very borders of the other world, and expected every
hour to step into it." "That's the communion o' the
saints," said Grizzy, "and if that is sweet on earth what
must it be in heaven !"

"Have ye heard onything o' young Renwick in your
travels, Eddie? he commenced his ministry sometime ago
in Darmead Moss; but I hae heard nothing o' him since."
"I have not seen him ; but Priesthill tells me that he has
been at Priesthill, and that he was greatly taken with him."
"Ay, the famous days of field conventicles are over now,"
said Grizzy ; "Welsh is away, and Cameron, and Cargill,
and Kid, and King, and many a famous preacher whose
voice shouted on our hill sides, and in our glens and mosses ;
yes, they are a' away now, and my heart is wae to think
on't ; but the Lord can revive His work in the midst of the
years."

It was on a dark stormy night in the end of December,
as the cheerful household in the kitchen of the Miny were
conversing together, when a loud and furious knocking was
heard at the door. The party was astonished, and gazed
on one another. "What can this be ?" exclaimed Gilbert ;
"who can be abroad on such a night as this?" The knocking was repeated—the shepherds cast a hasty glance to the
place where their fire-arms had been laid—the men from
Carsphairn instinctively placed their hands on their
weapons of defence, and all were prepared for a vigorous
resistance in case of an onslaughter—"Let be," said Eddie,
"let be ; I'll gang to the door and see ;" and, to his astonishment there stood the cuddy, his head and ears all dusted
with the snow, and looking as earnestly as if he sought a
special interview with his master. "How came ye here,
donkey," said Eddie, "and what want ye?" The wind had
blown open the door of the outhouse in which the sheep
and the donkey were confined, and the poor animal, impatient

with thirst, had broken his halter, and was ranging about for water, as was obvious from his thrusting his mouth with violence into the pail that stood in the entry where the door was opened. He was then conducted to his stall, and the fear of the party gave place to the out-bursts of merriment at the incident. "Eddie," said the men, whom the uncere-monious visit of the donkey had at first somewhat discon-certed, "where do you think might be the safest place in these parts for concealment, in case the troopers should direct their raids against us? We have had a good chase from them already on the day the snow began to fall, and it was our flight before them that drove us to this place —the very party you met was that which pursued us. Now, what is your opinion with regard to a place of con-cealment?" "A place o' concealment!" said Eddie, "where could ye find a better place than this, and where will ye find a landlord that will make ye more welcome? There's no a retreat in a' the muirs like this ; and I can tell ye a secret about this place that, may be, nane o' ye kens o'. We a' hae come through changes in our lifetime, and I hae come through some. I was ance what I am not now. I was at one time in the smuggling trade, and, along with others, carried brandy on pack-horses frae the Galloway coast, and traded secretly as we travelled the wild parts of the country, and we had our customers baith among gentle and semple. But I gave up that occupation lang, lang syne, for I saw the evil o't. But what I was ga'en to say is this : the Auchty was one o' our lodging places—the very Auchty down the brae there—and that was the way it got the word o' being hauntit, and we took care to keep up the report, for it served our purpose, and served it weel. Now, in the Auchty, there is the big vault you see on entering, but there is mair than that ; there are other chambers, and one in particular, on the right hand at the far end, that is entered by a neat door wi' a little arch. Within this apart-

ment I hae sleepit mony a canny night wi' the brandy
piled up in little kegs in the dark corner.   There is here a
fine fire-place, and room for two or three beds, and the
floor beneath is as dry as that hearthstane.   Here a dozen
of persons could lodge wi' a' comfort and safety in spite o' a'
the dragoons in the district; but I need say nae mair at
present; we'll visit the vowt in company, and ye shall see
what ye think of it."   "I see now," said Gilbert, "how
the Auchty has got sic a bad name, and let it keep it ; it
may be of use to us another day."

Next day the storm still continued, and the drift blowing
straight in the front of the house—the wind, rebounding
from the wall, formed a narrow trench between the bottom
of the wall and the mass of snow beyond, which revealed
the way in which the donkey had found his path to the
door.   Happiness and thankfulness reigned in the household
of the Miny, and none enjoyed them more than Eddie.
Plenty to eat and drink, abundance of fuel, warm beds to
rest on, and a rampart of deep snow round and round the
lowly habitation, which was every day becoming more and
more impregnable; who cared for spies or troopers now?
they could lie down and rise up, and none to make them
afraid ; they were fully sensible of their great privileges,
and wished to demean themselves accordingly ; for many of
their suffering brethren were in a very different position,
who bore all meekly and in perfect resignation to their
Master's will.   "I hae been thinkin'," said Grizzy, as she
was plying at the wheel, and preparing the yarn for Priesthill's next visit, "I hae just been thinkin', that we should
express our gratitude to God in a more particular way than
we have yet done; and what think ye, sirs, o' keepin' a day
o' thanksgiving for a' His mercies?"   This was instantly
agreed to, and the morrow was appointed for that end, to
be kept as religiously as even a Sabbath-day.   The morrow
came, and all addressed themselves to the exercise, and such

a day was scarcely ever spent at the Miny. The Lord was
in the midst of His people ; and though they were but a
little flock, they were carefully tended by the Great Shepherd, who dealt kindly with them, and blessed them
with His peace. These sacred meetings were little
Bethels for God's presence ; and some of those who survived
what Patrick Walker calls "the gude, ill time of persecution,"
declared that they would gladly suffer all over again to
enjoy those seasons of high communion which they then
experienced. On this day was the household at the Miny
blessed, and fortified in their faith and constancy for whatever might betide in the sad years that were yet to come.

"It strikes me," said Grizzy, "that the worst o' these ill
times is not come to yet with the suffering remnant in this
bluidy land. It may be there will be sadder days still. I
had a heavy dream the other night ; I thought I saw the
sodgers running through muir and moss, and shooting the
fleeing folk, and hackin at them wi' their swords ; and I
heard loud screams, and waefu' moanings, and saw the red
bluid gushing, and a black, black cloud hovering over the
house o' the lone Priesthill, and I awoke wi' a weary heart ;
I fear there is dark, dark work to follow. Claverhouse has
been raging fearfully since Bothwell, and muckle precious
bluid has been shed in the muirs since then, and greatly do
I dread that a' that has yet happened is but little to what
is near to come." "Hoot awa', Grizzy," said Gilbert, "ye
pay o'er muckle attention to dreams ; we mauna heed a'
that runs through the mind in sleep ; ye are aye ready to
look at the dark side o' the cloud." "And how can I help
it Gibby, my man, when I see nae ither side to look to? but
the Lord will be our helper, and we must e'en put our trust
in Him." "I was lately," said Eddie, "in the house of
James Brown of Paddock Holm' in Douglas Water, and he
was saying that Mr Peden had the same dark inklins, that
there were waefu' things abiding us." "I never see that

godly man Priesthill but my heart fills," said Grizzy ; "I
mind weel what Mr Peden said to Isabel Weir on the day
o' their wedding, to keep a winding-sheet beside her, for it
might be hastily needed some misty morning.   What a loss
wouldna John Brown be ! what an example he is to a' the
country round ; and then there is Isabel and the puir
bairns.   But the Lord will do what is best, and let the
warst come ; I think my heart clings just the closer to His
cause, and to His people for His sake.   It comforts me
muckle to think that the Lord is wi' His people in the
furnace.   We are aye safe when we are near Him, and it is
sweet, sweet to hear His voice, 'It is I ; be not afraid.'
How muckle should it confirm our faith in Him, when we
see that not one of our friends that have been ta'en away,
were without His presence in their last trial, and that they
a' died in the full assurance of their salvation, and I hae
little doubt, when our trying hour comes, but we'll find it
the same."

"These are indeed sad times," said John of Lesmahagow ;
"we know not what hand to turn to ; we are safe neither
at home nor abroad, neither in the desert wilds nor in the
crowded city ; all alike is danger.   The enemy is everywhere, and the spies, and the curates, and the lairds, are
equally set against us ; and what is as bad, many of our
neighbours have cooled to us, and some of them are now
ready to do us an unkindly turn as even our avowed
enemies.   How few, in many of the parishes, are the real
friends of our cause !   We cannot get up conventicles now
as we once did ; and where a meeting does take place, how
scanty is the attendance !   It is true, our leading preachers
are now mostly off the field, and the attractions are not
quite the same.   What the young Renwick may do we cannot say ; he is yet to be tried, and the Lord may honour
him to do something among us.   I trust a revival shall yet
take place, and that 'the desert shall rejoice and blossom as

the rose.' The Lord's work will not stand still, and He will carry it through in the face of all opposition. As to the dangers and privations of the times, it concerns me but little for my own part, for I can beg a morsel of bread at a friendly door for Christ's sake ; I can lodge at night in the cave or in the thicket, safe under the guardianship of Him in whose cause we suffer, and I am as willing to part with my life, when He calls for it, as to keep it. As to all this my mind is made up, and I have counted the cost ; I am as contented to suffer as to be exempted from suffering, just as He shall decide, though suffering is just as painful to me as it is to others, and for its own sake equally undesirable. But I have a father and mother, both in their old age, and helpless, and it is for their sake that I could wish to live and be serviceable. My friend here and I are cousins ; we are both of the Thomsons of Lesmahagow, and we are not ashamed of the connection. As soon as our Covenanting leanings, and our frequenting of conventicles became known to the enemy, we were regarded as disaffected persons, and the soldiers were frequently sent in quest of us. We were successful in evading them, till one Sabbath evening, in coming over a lonely moor, we encountered, all at once, a party of troopers, who emerged from a hollow place in the waste, and suspecting that we might be conventiclers, they pursued. We fled, but in vain ; for as the moor was hard and benty, they easily gained upon us, and threatened instant death unless we surrendered. We were now in their power, and they conducted us across the moorland, till we reached the high road. We came to a small inn on the wayside ; this they entered, and locked us in the stable beside the horses. They sat long, and drank deep, and at last were completely overpowered with the liquor. On learning the state of matters, we resolved on our escape. We got up among the joists, and finding that the roofing was very slender, we tore aside the turf, and the dusk of

the evening favouring us, we stole easily out, and ran across
the fields till we reached a ravine, where we concealed ourselves among the bushes.   How the troopers managed the
affair, we know not; but in the dark we reached our
homes.   My father and mother were much concerned, for
they now saw that I was really in danger, and that there
was nothing for it but instant flight.   To this I was greatly
averse, for I was their only support in their old age, and I
could have laid down my life for theirs at any time.   But
necessity compelled me; for one night, all on a sudden, our
house was surrounded by the soldiers.   Happily I was from
home at a prayer meeting, and on my return, as I came
near the house, which contained all that was dearest to me
on earth, I heard confused voices ; and not knowing what
might be the matter, I slipt behind a peat-stack, a short way
from the house, and saw at once how matters stood.   The
troopers were mounting their horses, and as their road lay
opposite to where I was standing, I waited till they withdrew.   When I entered, I found my dear parents greatly
distressed about me.   I remained till the morning, when it
was agreed that I should depart; and my cousin here
being exactly in the same predicament, we resolved to set
out in company.   Before our departure, however, I made
arrangements with some kindly neighbours to look after
my parents, and having given them what money I had, we
left our homes, and have been wandering here and there
ever since, till the day the snow began to fall.   We were
again in full flight before the enemy, when the Lord guided
us to your friendly abode."   "Yes," said Gilbert, "the Lord
*has* sent ye here, and abide ye here, for He may have more
work for ye before ye leave this place."

## CHAPTER IV.

DAYS passed on, and though the snow ceased to fall, yet there was a strong "yerd drift" which filled all the hollows far and near. The inmates of the Miny were all busy, each in his own way; and as the boy was teasing the wool, Eddie was carding for the gudewife, and amply supplied the rowans for "the muckle wheel."

"Eddie," said Gilbert, "do ye ken that the laird has made me his gamekeeper, at least on the farm here? He has given me a' in charge, and for my trouble he discounts five pounds off the rent, so that I pay just fifteen pounds now instead of twenty, and he also allows me to take a hare when I please, only no to abuse discretion, like." "And what has put a' that in the laird's head?" "The poachers, the poachers, to be sure. They come frae Cumnock and Muirkirk, and the places round, and work sad havoc among the muirs; and the laird thought if I would take the thing in hand it might keep them in awe; and so I am to take my pistols and scatter a wheen lead draps about their heels."

"Gilbert," said one of the shepherds, "would there be any offence in catching a hare among the snow?" "Nane, nane whatever; but where are the hares to be found now? They are a' smoored in their wee saft dens aneath the heavy snaw-wreaths." "There are hares yet," said the boy, "I saw ane ga'en hirplin' down by the Auchty." "I'll warrant there are hares in the vowt, and that's ane o' them that has been out seekin' a kail blade or an auld stock to nibble at; so let us to the Auchty the morn," cried Eddie.

The morrow came, and the four men, with Eddie and the boy, succeeded in opening up the way by mid-day. When they came to the mouth of the vault, and had cleared away the snow, and were about to enter, something was heard within. "Hist," said Eddie; "heard ye ever the like o'

that ?  What an unearthly sound !"  They listened, and
soft voices took up the strain of the sweet singer of Israel,
and sang with a melancholy cadence the following lines :—

> "Oh, let the prisoner's sigh ascend
> Before Thy Throne on high,
> Preserve those in Thy mighty power
> That are designed to die."

The sound died away, and the arch of the cavern re-echoed
for a few seconds the heavenly melody.  "There are worshippers here," said Willie of Lesmahagow, "let us search
them out, for they must be sore bested."  "Is there any
person here ?" he exclaimed ; but no voice responded.  "If
there be any here, let them not be afraid to speak, for we
are the friends of the sufferers."  "There are two persons
here," said a feeble voice from the extremity of the vault.
"Let us strike up a light," said Willie, "and see what is the
matter."  This done, they searched the vault, but found
nothing.  "Turn to the right," cried Eddie, "to the chamber I spake of."  They did so ; and there lay on a quantity
of straw which had been gathered from the litter of the cows
where they stood in the vault, two emaciated individuals
in almost the last stage of exhaustion.  "Who are you, and
whence come you ?"  "We are two wanderers for conscience
ʳ˄ke.  We left the upper parts of Nithsdale on the day the
ı ʾond snow began to fall.  We found our way to this place
iı. he evening and we have been here ever since."  "Let
us arry them instantly to the Miny," cried Eddie, "and
run, boy, for a hand-barrow."  Sandy came in breathless
haste to the kitchen.  "What's the matter wi' the callan ?"
said Grizzy.  "I want the hand-barrow ; there are twa men
dying in the 'bogle hole.'"  He flew off like an arrow, and
entered the vault with the barrow.  One of the men was
placed on it, and in a few minutes was laid on a warm bed
in the kitchen, and in a few minutes more the other was laid
beside him.  The men were so feeble that they could scarcely

speak; but, restoratives being applied, they gradually came round, and in a few days were fairly in a convalescent state. Eddie had now a full opportunity of investigating the vault, and of pointing out to his friends some of its secrecies, which, all agreed, were most suitable as a retreat from the face of the persecutor.

The story of the new-comers was brief. They were travelling towards the Water of Douglas, and intended, on the night they reached the vault to go to Friarminion—a place well known in the persecuting times, and in the vicinity of Hyndbottom. They continued in the vault for some days and nights, having only a little provision which they carried with them, on which to subsist, and their thirst was quenched by mouthfuls of snow. The cold, the fatigue, and the destitution brought on sickness, under which they laboured for a considerable time, but, by the fostering care of Grizzy, and the blessing of Him in whose cause they suffered, they were restored to perfect health. It is impossible to express the thankfulness of the poor men for the seasonable assistance afforded them in the vault, from which they never expected to come out alive. But low as their condition was, and near the end of their pilgrimage as they appeared to be, their hearts were full of heavenly comfort, and they were ready to depart when the Master called them. They were in the habit, like Paul and Silas, of singing praises to God in their prison-house: and it was when uttering a song of praise that their feeble voices caught the ears of the men as they were entering the vault, and which led them to their retreat.

This long winter was scarcely half over when the sick men were brought from the vault, so that the party had much intercourse, and that of the most profitable kind.

"What sort of a person," said Gilbert one day to the men from Carsphairn, "is your curate?" "Peter Pearson," said they, "is a very violent man; he can by no means endure the Noncomformists; he is constantly spying out their

haunts, and lodging information against them, and in consequence of this we were obliged to flee from our homes.
Our old minister, John Semple, reared a great many godly
persons in the district around ; so that when the curate
came, he found a large proportion of the parish in the covenanting interest." "But was he not an indulged minister ?"
"Yes, he accepted of the indulgence in the sixty-nine, and
he lived to the seventy-seven, an earnest, a devoted servant
of Christ." "I dinna apprave o' the indulgence," said Gilbert. "What for no ?" said Eddie ; "I am sure there are
many gude gospel preachers among them." "Ah, Eddie,"
said Grizzy, "ye dinna see the thing in the true light yet."
"Maybe no, gudewife ; Priesthill sometimes tells me that."
"Weel, Eddie, I hope ye'll come to take a mair consistent
view o' matters, and wha kens but ye may yet bear yer testimony in the Grassmarket !" "Weel, gudewife, if it should
be sae, I'll have nae objections if my end be as happy a ane
as I saw Cargill's to be."

"Have ye visited the Crawick, Eddie, in yer journeyings
of late ?" said Gilbert. "Yes, I was down there amang the
herds wi' keel some months syne, and I saw yer auld neighbour, William Tait, at Whitecleuch. He is still the same
zealous man, contending for the right way. There's a race
o' grand folks in the bonny valley o' the Crawick—there's
many a praying family there, and many a religious meeting
kept among them unknown to the enemy ; and the thick
woods on the breast of the hills and in the deep glens are
favourable to concealment. There's a batch o' houses on
the brae on the upper side o' the wood, they ca' Spoath,
where lives a man no' a whit inferior to our ain Priesthill
over the height there. He collects the families around him
on the Sabbath evenings, and prays wi' them, and exhorts
them just like ony minister. I hae heard him mysel' mair
than ance." "That will be auld Bryce Cairns. I have
met with him frequently at the conventicles in our moors

here. Mr Peden has a home there, and often holds a conventicle in the Crawick when the troopers are not in the neighbourhood." "Ay," said Eddie, "the woods o' Crawick are close and dark, and the sodgers cannot easily thread their way through them. There's the haunted linn, a fine retreat, which no dragoon dare enter for fear of meeting wi' something that's no canny." "But, Eddie, it appears wonderfu' to me how such meetings can be permitted so frequently in a place so near the toun of Sanquhar, where there is a curate, and where the soldiers are so often quartered in the castle." "It's no wonderfu' at a', when ye consider that the curate is James Kirkwood, a man who is secretly mair a friend to the Covenanters than to his own party. He takes every opportunity of screening them, and it is weel kent among themsel's that he allows them the key o' the kirk to meet there in the night season in the cauld winter weather. And though dowf and eerie sounds are heard in the kirkyard at the dead o' night, the folk never imagine that they proceed frae a company o' puir, prayin' people, but think that ghosts and bogles are haunting the dreary place o' the dead in the mirk night, and this prevents discovery. Kirkwood is a muckle respeckit man by our friends in the upper parts o' Nithsdale. He differs widely frae his brethren, though I do not take him to be a religious man for a' that. He is often wi' the family in the castle, and is never absent when Airly and his troopers come ; for he is a great wag, and Queensberry, the lord of the manor, is mightily entertained by him. But none of us need be afraid of the curate of Sanquhar, for it would be the last thing he would do to injure us."

"They are a douce and orderly set o' folk down by yonder. I was there that day that Michael Cameron published his brother's declaration at the Cross o' Sanquhar. I happened to be down wi' a cargo o' keel to the provost : for ye see he has a number of farms in the neighbourhood, and he

needs something in my line. And so, as I was saying, I
happened to be there, when about twenty stalwart, grave-
looking men entered the town, and walked deliberately
down the street. I happened to get my eye on our friend,
Laing of Blagannoch ; and I thought there was something
in the wind, though I could not guess preceesely what it
was. The men, with a great crowd o' women and bairns
after them, walked up to the Cross, and Michael, getting to
the foot of it, read aloud the declaration, and fastened it to
the pillar, and, without saying a word, quietly walked up
the street, and the men at his back. By this time the
whole town was turned out. The street was lined on baith
sides, and not a tongue was lifted against them ; and they
moved on wi' as muckle solemnity as if they had been following a coffin to the kirkyard. The crowd closed in behind
them, and seemed deeply to sympathise wi' them. It was
fortunate there were no sodgers in the castle at the time ;
and so they retired without molestation till they turned aff
into the valley of the Crawick, where, in the thick woods,
they could bid defiance to pursuit. When they were gone,
the provost whispered in my ear, ' Eddie, these are worthy
men, and I am glad, for their sake, that there were none of
the military about the place ; and, as for the magistrates,
we could do nothing. But it is a bold step wi' a witness,
and they must just look to themselves." " Ay," said Gilbert, " the Sanquhar Declaration has cost us much, and it
may cost us more yet ; but we are a' prepared to maintain
its principles, cost us what it may."

One gloomy day in February, when the storm was raging
without, every one intent on his own occupation, and none
inclined to speak much :—" A plack for yer thought, gudeman," said Grizzy to Gilbert, as he lay stretched on the
langsettle, and was staring wistfully into the fire. " I was
just thinking," he replied, " on the many sweet days we
have had at these conventicles, and how the hand of the

Lord has been seen, many a time, in warding off danger.
I remember the meeting at Friarminion, when Mr Peden
preached. It was in the high days of summer, and a large
company had collected on the bonny green by the burn-
side. The lark was singing high in the air, and the cheery
sun shone without a cloud. We were a happy company,
met afar in the wilderness to worship God—the God of our
salvation, whatever might betide. But though no dragoons
had been near, danger seemed to arise from another quarter. The early morning had been clear and somewhat cold,
and by mid-day a dark thunder-cloud began to gather on
the lofty top of Mount Stewart, near the wilds of Hyndbottom, and in a short time it became terrible to look on.
Being on the hill straight above us, it began to move in our
direction. The thunder was beginning to mutter in its
bosom, and some of the heavy raindrops were falling. The
people crept close together, and gathered their plaids over
their heads, and tried to listen to what the man of God
was saying. Mr Peden observed the confusion ; and seeing
the fearful cloud gradually descending, and growing darker
and darker, he paused in his discourse, and said :—'I see,
sirs, that ye are put about, and there is cause for it. I
never saw a heavier cloud hang over our heads in these
deserts before, and I have preached in many a storm, both
in summer and in winter ; but the Lord is the Hearer of
prayer, and let us cry to Him who is able to screen us in
the day of His fierce tempest.' He then poured out a prayer,
the like of which, for fervour of spirit, and confidence in
God, I scarcely ever listened to. When he ended, the
people were greatly composed, and sat quietly down to wait
the result, and Mr Peden went on with his discourse. In a
short time the cloud began to move, and crept from one
hilltop to another, till, gathering in great bulk, it rested
over the heights of Penbreck and Cairntable, when it poured
out its waters in such gushing torrents that all the hills

ʋith foam, and all the streams flooded from bank ꞓnmuir water became unfordable, and the Douger seen so high. The thunder was fearful, and resou⸺ from height to height like the loud cannon on the battle-field. The lightning tore up the bent, and splintered the rocks on the hills. We regarded our deliverance as an answer to prayer; for had the cloud burst upon us, as it appeared to do elsewhere, in what a distressful condition must our meeting have been placed ! Mr Peden improved the occasion in an address that went to the hearts of all. And a shower of another kind than the rain we dreaded from the bosom of that dark cloud, under which we cowered, came upon us; for the Great Master of Assemblies shed down His Holy Spirit to revive our hearts, and quicken us in our religious exercises, so that in spirit we were wafted away heavenwards, to be fed with heavenly manna, and draw water out of the wells of salvation. John Weir, that old experienced Christian, used to say that he never enjoyed the gracious presence of God so manifestly as on that occasion."

"The sky cleared, and the sun shone brightly, reminding us of the countenance of Him who is the Sun of Righteousness. After the services, a circumstance occurred which gave the company some uneasiness. Laing of Blagannoch got his eye on an object in the midst of a thick bush of brakens on the hill, a short distance from the meeting-place, and, suspecting that all was not right, determined, when the congregation broke up, to ascertain what it was. With two other stout men, to whom he had given the hint, he set out to the braken bush, and, to their surprise, a man started up and fled. They pursued and caught him just as he was drawing his pistol to shoot. They quickly secured him, and found that he was Sandilands, the spy from Crawfordjohn. They carried him to Blagannoch, and kept him there a prisoner for some time, and then dismissed him under certain obligations, and with suitable advices."

"Mr Peden went to Shawhead ; and Priesthill, who was at the meeting, came to our house and spent the night with us, for the waters were high. And what a night was that! The conventicle to us was much, but this was more. The saintly man seemed as an angel dropped down from heaven in the midst of us. How spiritual his conversation, and what a prayer when he addressed the throne of grace ! I will never forget that night."

"We feared the storm," continued Gilbert, "but the storm saved us. It drove back the troopers to Muirkirk, who, having received information, were on their way to disperse us. The roaring of the thunder terrified them ; the startling glare of the lightning scared the horses ; and the deluge from the firmament hindered their passage through the waters, and thus they were forced to retreat to their quarters. We thought the cloud looked on us with an angry scowl ; but it came as a friend, and was like the pillar of cloud between the Israelites and the Egyptians at the Red Sea. I think that nothing but the immediate presence of God, comforting the hearts of His people in so extra-ordinary a manner, could stimulate so many to go out to these dangerous conventicles. And so, gudewife, ye hae my thought for yer plack."

---

## CHAPTER V.

WE now advance into that dismal period commonly called "the killing time," or the slaughter years, namely, the 1684 and 1685, "wherein," as Patrick Walker remarks, "no fewer than eighty-two of the Lord's people were shot in cold blood in the moorlands and desert places," in consequence of that military license which, by the "bluidly council" that sat in Edinburgh, and direct-ed all the movements of the persecution, was indiscriminately

conferred upon the soldiers. The distress caused by this
means in the upland parts is indescribable. An adequate
account of the barbarities, and cruelties, and brutalities
exercised by the soldiery in those woeful years has never
yet been given, and probably, at this distance of time, cannot now be given, at least in that fulness of detail necessary to bring out the real facts of the case in the entire
depths and darkness of their atrocity. The wailing throughout the bleeding land, where the fierceness of the tempest
was more especially felt, namely, in the five western counties,
was almost universal. There was scarcely a family, perhaps,
of those at least who professed Covenanting principles, that
had not sustained an injury directly or indirectly, not
merely in the loss of their property and liberty, but in the
loss of life among their kindred, if not in their own domestic circle. The wilder places in the south and west were
literally made a hunting-field, within whose spacious limits
the soldiers roamed at large, and, without restraint, killed,
or mained, or captured at their will. It is over a part of
this field, then, that we mean to roam in our subsequent
sketches, as it regards the period more especially to which
we have alluded.

The cautious keelman had always affirmed that there was
not a place of more perfect security in all the moorlands
than the Miny ; and he was right. From the time that
honest Gilbert was invested with the office of gamekeeper,
the commander of the troopers, who lay at Muirkirk, entertained a good opinion of him ; and more especially from
the day that he was seen by the troopers firing his pistol
after the poachers, as they conceived, who fled across the
moor, and left the heather burning at their heels from the
flaming colfin that fell on the dry bent. This circumstance
became a safeguard to the household of the Miny, and prevented many a discovery that would otherwise have been
made. It now became Gilbert's uniform practice that, when

any of the friends in hiding with him left his house, he ran
after them bawling and firing his piece with vehemence ; so
that when any of the troopers or other suspicious persons
happened to be in sight, the conclusion drawn by them was
that the worthy man was chasing disaffected persons from
his laird's lands.  This, in a great degree, shielded him from
the suspicions of the soldiers ; while another circumstance
shielded him from the suspicions of the curate.  The Miny
lay at the farthest point eastward from the Parish Church
of Auchenleck.  It might be twelve long miles into the
very heart of the moors, owing to the well-known irregular
outline of the parochial boundary.  In those days travelling
in the moorlands was no easy matter, nor is it yet ; and the
curate of Auchenleck, not knowing, perhaps, that such a
place as the Miny existed, never visited the spot ; and as
to the curate of Muirkirk, it was beyond his jurisdiction.
However it was, it so happened that honest Gilbert Fleming
was not troubled by the curates.

This state of things was highly favourable to the wanderers that frequented those parts ; and it was right that
there should be cities of refuge here and there in the wilds,
not only hiding-places in ravines, in thickets, and in caves,
but in dwelling-houses, where food and comfortable accommodation might be had with some degree of security.  Bad
as things were, they would have been much worse had there
not been such places of occasional shelter.  The Great
Master had provided hospices in different localities in the
wide wilderness, and even in situations where one would
think it impossible, owing to the supervision of the spies
and the military ; but such is the fact that these places did
exist—rarely, it is true, but still they existed : and Gilbert
Fleming's house was a specimen.

But then incidents befel which rendered even these places
of resort of little avail, unless in peculiar circumstances.
No one of these places could be absolutely exempted from

a visit from the soldiers, because they were tracing the
moors and glens in every direction ; sometimes for mere
sport, sometimes in quest of fugitives, and sometimes in
marching from one part to another. The Miny, owing to
its situation in the moss (for the Celtic word *mini* literally
signifies moss), was difficult of approach to the horsemen,
and this, for one reason, might render their visits more
sparing, still absolute exemption could not be counted on,
for the troopers were often in sight, and therefore a descent
on the Miny might at any time be made, and made, too,
when it would be very inconvenient. Besides, though the
worthy farmer, and gamekeeper to the laird, stood in the
good graces of the commander of the soldiers at Muirkirk,
who could tell how soon he might be removed to another
station, and a fresh one come in his stead, who might be of
a very different disposition ? This idea began to impress
the mind of honest Gilbert somewhat painfully, and he expressed his suspicions to his worthy spouse, who was always
ready to sympathise with him. " Indeed, gudeman," quoth
Grizzy, " I hae had the same misgivings for a gude while
past, though I did not wish to trouble you wi' what ye
might consider my groundless fears ; but naebody can look
at the black cloud that is lowering o'er our heads, a cloud
blacker far, and mair exceedin' fearfu', than the cloud
that hung o'er the conventicle that day at Friarminion
when Mr Peden preached ; and God grant that this cloud
may pass away as it did ! But, Gibby, my man, though
our trust is to be entirely in the Lord, yet it is our duty to
be looking about us. We hae been lang here, and mony a
happy day we hae had even in those troublous times. The
Lord has honoured us to feed many of His hungry people
for His sake, and to afford them a place o' shelter, and we
hae never had cause to rue that. Ye mind the time o' the
great snaw-storm, and how the Lord blessed us baith afore
and after, and how He made our house a Bethel. I wonder

if a' our friends are alive who consorted wi' us at that time ;
but, Gibby, we maun look to oursel's ; I mean we must
provide for the warst." "And what can we do, my dear
Grizzy ? I had amaist ca'd ye Grace, only I didna wish to
abuse that sacred word, by making it a sinfu' craiter's
name. I say, what can we do, we are twa helpless folk ?
I wish we had Eddie here, for there's mair wit about that
body than his ain, and his advice has often helped us in a
pinch. Eddie is an honest body, and I hae great depen-
dence to place on his opinion. I wish I heard the clatter
o' the cuddie's feet at the door." "And I think ye hae yer
wish," said Grizzy, "for I hear a tramplin' in the close."
And there was a trampling in the close, but it was not the
feet of Eddie's cuddie, it was that of far different customers ;
it was a company of troopers. "Keep us a'," exclaimed
Grizzy, "what's this ?" "It's e'en the sodgers, my woman ;
it's the sodgers themsel's ; but let us be kind to them—it
may be they mean nae harm." The men dismounted, and
entered. "Good morning, honest Gilbert," said the commander, "we have just come to bid you farewell. We are
going to shift our quarters ; and as we were coursing along
the hillside yonder, and descending on the moor, and being
pretty near your house, I thought I would just call for a
moment, and say that we are going to leave the neighbourhood." "We are glad to receive your friendly call," said
Gilbert, much relieved from his anxieties. "I am sorry yer
ga'en to leave us, for it may be the next who comes will not
be so neighbourly." "Why, as to that, I cannot say ; but
Captain Crichton and his troopers are to supply our place ;
only we leave three of our men to instruct him with regard
to the localities, and to impart to him our own experience
with regard to matters in these parts ; and this, you know,
is a considerable help to a new company. George Ga' here,
and these other two fellows are to be left." Gilbert was
inwardly pleased to learn that Geordy Ga' was to be one of

the party ; for he had often heard Eddie speak favourably
of him as one that sympathised with the sufferers, and who
was in the habit of conveying much useful information to
them by means of persons whom he could trust, and especially the keelman, in whom he had the most perfect
confidence ; for Eddie had often dandled him on his knee,
when a child, in his father's house, among the cottars of
Carmacoup, so that Geordy had contracted a strong affection
for Eddie, and ever regarded him as a second father.   When
the troopers were gone, Gilbert expressed his satisfaction
to Grizzy that Geordy was still to be in their neighbourhood, and that, through Eddie's means, some good might be
done.   "But wha," said she, "is this Crichton that is coming to be the evil spirit in our wilderness? If I mistake
not, his hands are stained wi' bluid, wi' the red bluid o' the
Lord's people, and if sae, we needna expect muckle gude at
his hand."

It was indeed as Grizzy opined.   Crichton was truly the
evil genius of his party.   He was a fierce, indomitable person, who cared as little for the shedding of human blood, as
for the spilling of water on the ground.   He was in every
respect a fit instrument in the hand of the faction that employed him.   He fought under Claverhouse at Bothwell
Bridge, and earned the approbation of his master.   He was
fired with a keen spirit of revenge against the Covenanters,
and used the full military license that was granted in the
*eighty-four*, with the utmost latitude, and without the least
scruple of conscience.   His dragoons were like himself, an
outrageous, riotous, murdering band.   Crichton's troop was
reckoned one of the very worst that infested the uplands.
They stole and plundered at their pleasure ; and from mere
wantonness in wickedness they scrupled not to set
fire to dwelling-houses, to burn the stacks of corn in
the barn-yards ; to kill the sheep and roast them on the
spot ; to drive away the cows, and sell them to the first

purchaser; and to appropriate the horses on the farm-
steadings to their own immediate use—all this was perpetrated with the approbation, and even by the express command of their Captain. The men were licentious : they
abused women in their own houses, and threatened instant
death to any who dared to remonstrate. They were scarcely
ever sober, for drunkenness was characteristic of the whole
of the persecuting party, from the men who sat in the council down to the lowest of the soldiery—the curates, the
lairds, the informers, and the mass of the irreligious populace were more or less addicted to this vice. It is not to be
wondered at, then, that Crichton, a drunken, swaggering,
blustering, cruel-hearted cavalier, should have his imitators
in his own troop, and men who, though they could not
easily excel their master, would yet strive to resemble him,
and, if possible, to become his equals. Crichton's name was
a terror to the poor peasantry—whether they belonged to
the Covenanting party or not—for he was alike indiscriminate in his ravages whenever it suited his purpose; and
complaint was of no avail, it was even worse, for it often
brought the severest chastisement on the head of those who
dared to vent a single murmur. The names of Lagg and
Claverhouse were not more feared by the poor people than
that of Crichton, especially in the districts in which he was
located. Crichton's name was not so well known in the new
district to which he was appointed, but this ignorance was
not of long continuance ; he soon made himself infamously
known, and his deeds of outrage soon spread consternation
throughout the uplands of Kyle, and Lanarkshire, and
Nithsdale. Such was the man, with his troopers, who came
to be quartered about Muirkirk, and of whom the household
of the Miny was ere long taught to stand in awe.

The furnace of the persecution was now heated seven
times; and it was the determination of the Prelatists utterly
to exterminate the Noncomformists. No half measures

were to be resorted to any longer—it was either instant
submission or instant death—the ground must be cleared,
and every encumbrance removed, for the election of prelacy
in all its perfection. The vigorous measures now adopted,
and the indiscriminate murders which now took place in the
retreats of the mountains and in the dreary wilderness, compelled the suffering party to resort to certain means for
their own defence. They accordingly published what is
called their "Apologetic Declaration," wherein they broadly
stated that they would defend themselves when attacked
by their enemies, and that they might expect something of
the same measure to be dealt to them as they dealt to
others—in shooting the helpless Covenanters in the wastes.
This declaration, though never intended to be acted on, had
the effect desired, for it retarded the impetuosity of the
soldiery—who, in the main, were cowards—especially in
certain circumstances, for they now dreaded an assault from
the thickets by the waysides, or from the covert of the moss-
hag, or from behind the screen of the mist which came trail-
ing along the mountain's brow, or came sailing down the
gorges of the narrow glens. The Apologetic Declaration,
then, which in appearance seemed to be founded on the
principle of retaliation, prevented much mischief, and was a
powerful bridle to rein in the reckless and head-strong
troopers. Both officers and men felt awed by this bold and
defiant manifesto ; and not a few lives were spared, that
otherwise might have been sacrificed to the wantonness of
a brutal soldiery.

Crichton, from his quarters in Muirkirk, sallied out in
every direction over the surrounding district, keen and intent on his mission of evil. It was a rough district over
which he presided—rough in aspect—bristling with heathy
hills, intersected with powerful mountain currents, and
overspread here and there with extensive plains of moss,
and which none but those well acquainted with the topo-

graphy of the desert might venture with safety to enter on. This rendered this particular locality a tolerably secure retreat to the wanderers who sought in its wilds a hiding-place. Cairntable, and Wardlaw, and the hills above Glenbuck, the wilds of Ayr's Moss, and Wellwood, and Glenmuir, and all the surrounding scene—now full of Covenanting interest, but terribly wild in its features, as it borders on Douglas, and Sanquhar, and Crawfordjohn—were just the places to traverse which suited the taste of the troopers, who scoured hill and dale with as much hilarity as if they were bounding after the timid hare or the wild fowls of the desert. It was there the birds had perched, and it was there that the net was to be spread to catch them.

As Crichton was true to the work which his masters had assigned him, he frequently sent out detached parties in various directions, on raids of mischief among the peaceable peasantry. One day a small company of his troopers, under the command of one Cochrane, was ravaging the parts about Cairntable, and seizing on any stray person they could find. They were all highly inflamed with liqour, for they sometimes carried whisky or brandy with them, in small tin flasks, of which they partook without restraint, and frequently were so intoxicated that they could not sit on their horses. They were descending the hill, at the bottom of which they proceeded along at full gallop, and not being aware of the spongy nature of the ground that lay before them, some of the horses sank to the belly, and when, after much tugging and swearing, they extricated the poor animals, they proceeded at the same rate over the more solid parts of the moor, scarcely knowing whether they were on horseback or on foot. At length one of the heavy steeds stumbled and precipitated his rider, with all his accoutrements, in full dash to the ground. This formed an episode of no little merriment to his fellows, who rode on, screaming and swearing, without offering him a helping hand. " Let

him lie there," said one, "no matter though his brains be
scattered on the bent." "It will teach him better manners,"
said another, "than to attempt to ride before his betters."
"Ay," exclaimed a third, "let him seek the good graces of
Crichton now, by showing who is the best moss-trooper ; I
trow this will stop his vaunting." In this manner—for
there is no real friendship among wicked men—they coursed
along, jeering and gibing, and left their companion to his
fate in the moss. All this was witnessed by three of the
Covenanting brethren who lay concealed in a hollow on the
face of the hill. They pitied the poor man who lay prostrate
and motionless on the moor, and they determined to render
him, if alive, what assistance they could, and, if dead, to
bury him in the moss. Accordingly, they rose from their
lair, and began to descend the hill. By this time the
troopers began to consider themselves, and to think what
account they should render for the loss of their companion,
and that, if they could not bring him home alive, they
would at least secure the horse—an article that could be
less spared than his rider. Accordingly, they retraced their
steps in a body, and soon came in sight of the animal grazing quietly on the moor, and this guided them to the precise
spot. The three men, who had by this time approached
the fallen trooper—who appeared to be more stunned than
injured, and who, through the effects of the liquor, was
sound asleep on the brink of a deep moss hag—the three
men now observed the approach of the dragoons, riding
more warily along the precarious surface, and, judging it
high time to make their retreat, betook themselves to the
hill.

On seeing this, the troopers spurred their steeds to their
utmost speed, and seizing the hard ground on the base of
the height, rode furiously after the fugitives. Their companion lying in the moss was not for a moment regarded ;
but the horse without his rider galloped hilariously after the

cavalcade, and neighed, and sprang from side to side, feeling himself, no doubt, much lightened without the heavy dragoon who usually bestrode him.   One idea, and only one, possessed the troopers; and Cochrane thought that he would put a new feather in his cap if he could either kill or capture the rebels who were in full flight before him.   The pursuit was hot; it was a day in autumn, and the sky was clear, and objects could be discerned at a great distance. The poor men rounded the hill, and for a few minutes were out of the sight of the horsemen, but in a brief space they observed their pursuers, who seemed to follow with undeviating instinct their very footsteps.   In the hollow below there lay a pretty extensive moss, into the heart of which it was their intention to run.   In this they succeeded, and plunged sometimes to the waist in the deep hags; and, struggling onwards, reached a green spot on which they flung themselves prostrate—more dead than alive.   The troopers stood to consider.   It was obvious their horses could not enter the morass ; but their fire-arms were in instant requisition, and ball after ball went whizzing over the surface of the moor ; but the shot was innocuous—it could not reach the object ; and so the poor fugitives lay panting on the mossy platform, but perfectly secure, at least as far as the firing was concerned.

Cochrane, however, was not to be baffled in this way.   If one plan did not succeed, another might, and therefore he determined that the moss should be entered on foot.   The troopers were six in all; three were commanded to dismount, while Cochrane himself kept the horses, and three were directed to ride round the moss, and to attack the fugitives on the other side, or, at least, to prevent their escape while the men on foot were gradually approaching within gunshot.   The three brethren seeing the predicament in which they were now placed, rose from their resting-place and cleared the morass before the horsemen came

round. They fled to the height on the other side, and the
men in the moss being recalled, the whole party, with Cochrane at their head, rode furiously to join the three in advance. This was quickly done, and the entire party were
again in full pursuit of the poor exhausted fugitives. It
soon became evident that escape was impossible, for their
strength failed them every yard they trode, and the powerful
horses of the troopers were rapidly gaining ground. One of
the brethren fell through sheer exhaustion, but speedily
recovering himself, rose and fled with the rest. By this
time they were nearing the edge of a ravine, precipitous in
its sides, and filled with dense hazel-wood and birches. To
gain this was their only hope, but the troopers were at
hand, and discharging a volley after them, the balls went
booming past their ears, and, at the very first, one of the
party fell. Another volley ; and the remaining two were
on the very brink of the gully, and tumbled over among
the thickets, while the shot went rustling among the leaves.
The soldiers had now done their work ; one lay weltering
in his blood on the turf, and the other two, as they conceived, had received the fatal shot, and had tumbled lifeless
into the ravine. Cochrane now retreated, leaving his victims to be buried out of sight by any that choose to take
upon them the task. This was the custom ; the bodies of
the Covenanters that were shot in the wilds were left
where they fell to rot in the sun, or to be devoured by beasts
of prey. The troopers that day thought they had performed
a meritorious deed, and no compunctious visiting touched
their conscience.

The men in the ravine, who had sustained only some
slight bruises in falling among the bushes, perceiving that
the hubbub had ceased, and not knowing the fate of their
companion, ventured to scramble up to the edge of the plain
ground to ascertain how matters stood ; saw the horsemen
departing in the distance, and the body of their friend lying

in his blood on the bent. As they approached, they found that life was not extinct, though the body was literally bathed in a pool of blood. The dying man raised his eyes when his friends addressed him, for he knew their familiar voices. "I am dying," he feebly articulated; "I am dying, but I am happy, happy, yes happy; and if I had a thousand lives, I would willingly lay them all down, deliberately, one after another, for Christ's sake. O! it is sweet to suffer for Christ. Many a pleasant hour have I spent in religious ordinances, but I never spent a happier season than since these balls went through my body. I shall soon see Him whom my soul loveth, and 'who loved me and gave Himself for me.' I shall soon get the martyr's crown; but think not, dear friends, that I am trusting on *my* sufferings for Christ for my salvation—no, no; all my trust is on *His* suffering for me. I renounce all my own merits, and all my confidence is in that precious blood which was shed as an atonement for human sin. I know God has received me for Christ's sake—I feel it; I feel it in my heart He has sealed me unto the day of redemption. I now die as a witness for Christ, and what a privilege is that! Continue, my beloved friends, continue steadfast in the good cause; and let no one fear a suffering lot for Christ. O! He is near me; I think I see Him. I am just coming Lord Jesus." After a pause he added : "Bear my love to my dear mother, my brothers and sisters; my father has already borne his testimony for Christ, and maybe his spirit will come along with angels and conduct my soul to glory. I leave my love to all my suffering brethren. I forgive my enemies. Kiss me, my dear friends, and then I will die, and——" He could say no more, for the purple tide of life had now welled itself away, and he sweetly fell asleep in the Lord.

The great question now was what was to be done with the body of the slaughtered man; buried it must be of

course, but how buried? They had no implements where-
with to dig a grave in that lonely spot. They therefore
resolved to seek 'the nearest house in the waste, and procure
assistance if possible. In the meantime, they covered the
body with the leafy branches which they tore from the
bushes in the linn, to prevent it from being attacked by
prowling animals or otherwise insulted. This act of theirs
reminds us of the story of little robin red-breasts hiding
the babes in the woods with leaves. They left the spot in
quest of friendly aid—for they were strangers, and knew
not where to direct their steps. The sun was setting in
lurid majesty in the western sky, for his rays were bedim-
med by a thick and dubious haze. A house was visible in
the distance by means of a column of blue smoke that
issued tardily from the vent in the stillness of the evening.
By this they were guided in their movements, and, not
knowing what reception they might find, they proceeded
with some degree of hesitancy. That house, however, was
the Miny. Gilbert and his wife, with Sandy the boy, were
its only occupants at the time, and, with downcast spirits,
were conversing on the troubles of the times. "I dinna
like," said Grizzy, "the look o' that sun at his setting the
night ; it seems as if his face was covered wi' a cloth dipped
in blood : it's fearfu' to look at." "Hoot awa, woman, ye
are aye thinkin' o' bluid." "And can I miss," she replied,
"when there has been sae muckle bluid shed in these moorlands, and when we canna tell how soon our ain may dye
the heather bloom? I had an unco dream yesternight. I
thought I was reading these verses in the Hebrews, 'They
were stoned, they were sawn asunder ; were tempted, were
slain with the sword ; they wandered about in sheep-skins
and goat-skins, being destitute, afflicted, tormented, of
whom the world was not worthy ; they wandered in deserts,
and in mountains, and in dens, and caves of the earth.'
And just as I was reading, there fell two draps o' bright

red bluid on the very words, and I closed the book, for I could read nae mair. And then I thought I went to the end o' the house, and saw, in the dark muir, a deep, deep grave, wi' the black moss lying at the side, and I awoke in a fright." At this moment a gentle rapping was heard at the door, and the two men stood before it. Gilbert kindly asked them to enter, not knowing exactly whether to consider them friends or foes. In a brief space, however, suspicion vanished on both sides, and the men were found to be brethren in affliction, and the house was found to be a shelter to wanderers. The men told their story, and requested help to bury their friend on the hill. "There noo," exclaimed Grizzy, "I hae my dream read. Gibby, my man, ye see there is mair in dreams than some folk weel wot o'."

Arrangements were instantly made for proceeding to the height, but Gilbert thought it would be better to wait till the night set in, to prevent discovery. In the meantime Grizzy covered the hospitable board with her usual consideration, rightly judging that the poor men must be faint with hunger. "What is the name of this place," said one of the strangers, as they were partaking of the repast, "what is the name of this place?" It is called the Miny," replied Gilbert. "And are you Gilbert Fleming?" asked he. "I am," replied the honest landlord. "Then," said he, "we know you well, though we never saw your face before. Our friends who have enjoyed your hospitality have often told us of you, and little did we think that we were near so friendly an abode." The darkness had now set in, and Gilbert, with the men, proceeded along the dreary moss—the footing of which was somewhat dangerous in the dark; but Sandy followed with a lantern, which, when they were about half-a-mile from the house, was lighted, and no sooner—a precaution which was necessary. On reaching the place, the body was uncovered, and gently removed from its lair, and then the grave was dug in the precise

spot where the martyr fell.  The moss was easily cut, and
the face having been bound with a napkin, the corpse was
gently lowered into its narrow bed.  Before the moss was
thrown in, the body was strewed over with leaves stripped
from the branches, and then all was covered up, and two
stones were placed—the one at the head and the other at
the foot of the grave—to mark the resting-place of the
martyr.  The body-clothes of those who were shot in lonely
places generally formed their winding-sheet, so that when
some of these graves were recently opened, the apparel,
dyed in the moss, seemed quite fresh.  The little company,
with faces bathed in tears, knelt down around the grave,
and prayed, and the Comforter was with them and filled
their hearts with peace.  They then returned from the spot,
and left their martyred brother to sleep in his gory shroud
till the blessed resurrection.

## CHAPTER VI.

THE next morning, as the party were seated round
the breakfast-table, the men, in answer to Gilbert's
inquiry, informed him that they came from the
Glenkens in Galloway, and that the one was a weaver and
the other a shepherd.  "It was," said they, "from the two
men from Carsphairn whom you so kindly entertained during the great snow-storm—the tailor and the shoemaker—
that we got our information concerning you; but little did
we reck that we ourselves would come under your roof to
be witness of the truth of what they told us, and to partake
of your hospitality."  "And how fares it," asked Gilbert, "with the honest men ?"  "Both are in their
graves; the tailor died first."  "And how died he?" asked
Gilbert.  "The death of a martyr," replied the elder of the
two, with the tear in his eye; "he died an honoured wit-

ness for the truth by the hand of the infamous Lagg. You are to understand that, since the military license was granted, two garrisons have been established in the wilds of Carsphairn, to suppress the Covenanting spirit that was so largely manifested in the upper parts of Galloway. After the death of the godly Mr Semple, there was found to exist in those parts a greater number of Nonconformists than was anticipated by the ruling party, and these increased rather than diminished; because, the locality being wild and mountainous, many fled thither from the low country for security, among the almost inaccessible hills and deep glens. The curate was a man of a very fierce temper, and very cruel to the Covenanting brethren; and, indeed so very mischievous was he—like another Bishop Sharp—that his conduct could be borne with no longer, and he was shot by the Black MacMichael, brother to the saintly Daniel, who lives at Lurgfoot, in the parish of Morton. The killing of the curate was condemned by all of us, and though the perpetrator attempted to show cause, and meant it in self-defence, yet we found it necessary to expel him from our society, and to hold him responsible for the deed. The curate was indeed a bad man, but he ought to have been left in the hands of Him who hath said, 'Vengeance is mine, and I will repay.'

"The curate was in the habit of lodging information against our brethren, and of instigating the soldiers to deeds of cruelty. The garrisons were well manned, abundance of soldiers were always at command, and Lagg possessed the full means of gratifying his savage temper. There were four of us in all, who used to keep together in our wanderings and hidings: we two here, with the tailor and the shoemaker. One day we had retired to a hollow place on the slope of a rugged height that overlooked the village of Carsphairn, and not seeing any of the soldiers moving about Lagg's quarters—of which we had a full view—we began

to think ourselves pretty secure, and resolved to send one
of our party to the village in quest of provisions. As we
were deliberating on this, a powerful dog bounded past us
in pursuit of some object. Still suspecting nothing, we
rose instinctively to our feet, to look abroad over the heath,
and, to our surprise, a company of burly troopers was just
at hand. It was obvious that they were not so much in
pursuit of wanderers as of game ; but, however it was, we
were discovered, and the whole party rushed furiously forward, with the terrible Lagg at their head. I shall never
forget the look of that man—his ferocious aspect—his
blood-shot eyes—his bluff countenance, unusually reddened
with wine—with his lips wide apart, and teeth exposed--as
if he would have torn us in pieces like a tiger. 'Whence
are you?' he sternly asked ; 'you are a company of rebels,
and you are our prisoners.' 'No,' replied the tailor, who
was our spokesman, 'no, we are not rebels ; we are loyal
subjects of the King of kings ; they only are rebels who
disregard His authority ; we are not.' 'So ho, you are
true blue I see ; you are fowls of the right feather ; we have
been pursuing the wild birds all day, and have caught only
a brace or two, but now we have caught, all at once, a whole
covey. What say you? Do you own the Sanquhar
Declaration?—was Bothwell Bridge rebellion?—was the
Bishop's death murder?—do you own the Apologetic
Declaration?' On he went in this strain, without waiting
for an answer to the particular questions, and ordered us
instantly to prepare for death. The troopers were commanded to stand in a row, and to be ready to fire. We
were arranged in a line, that the shot might hit us with
more precision. We all bent on our knees and uttered a
short prayer to the God of our life ; and, I believe, we
never felt more composed all our days, than when we
expected the murderous shot to be poured into our bodies.
The soldiers were drawn up in rank immediately before us,

and I could see from their faces that it was a matter of sport to them to be employed as our executioners. The most perfect indifference seemed to rest on every countenance ; for such work was now become to them a matter of ordinary occurrence. At this critical moment, a person who seemed to be a commander of one of the garrisons, and who had that day joined Lagg for their sport on the hill, took him aside and whispered something in his ear. Lagg then turned and said he would carry us to the garrison as his prisoners, but that he would first make an example of one of us on the spot. The tailor was the individual fixed on, and we were commanded to withdraw to the one side. We wished to stand by our dear companion in life and in death, but the soldiers forcibly separated us. The tailor then stood forth alone, as the selected victim for the present. He was an uncommonly devout man, and a fine-looking person, as you may remember, and about twenty-five years of age. As he stood ready to be offered, he assumed an unwonton dignity of aspect. His countenance was lit from heaven, as if a preternatural beam of light streamed down on it. We were all struck with wonder. I could easily see that Lagg's own face changed colour, and the other commander retreated and turned his back. The soldiers alone maintained the same unmoved posture. Our dear friend, then—with his eyes fixed on heaven, and his hands lifted up—exclaimed, 'Into thy hands I commit my spirit, for thou hast redeemed me, O Lord God of truth ;' and scarcely had the words escaped his lips when the shots passed through his body, and he fell on the heath, and died without a groan. His departure was instantaneous. The soldiers left the scene of slaughter without uttering a word, while they carried us with them ; and I could see that Lagg and his associate were silent till they reached the bottom of the hill ; 'surely,' thought I, 'this will spoil one evening's festivity at least, in Lagg's quarters.' "

"But what became of you?" inquired Gilbert, who hung
with burning anxiety on the man's narrative, "what became
of you?" "We were conveyed to Garryhorn, Lagg's residence in Carsphairn, and were put in an empty out-house,
where was abundance of straw on which we could lie all
night; for rest we expected none, not so much from outward fear, as from thinking on the sad scene we had
witnessed on the hill. The person who conducted us
to our lodging, locked the door firmly behind him; and we
lay down, expecting to meet the fate of our companion in
the morning, for we had no doubt that Lagg had reserved
us for a tragic end, although, perhaps, he meant to gather
something from us by a rigid examination. No mercy was
to be expected from him, after the way in which he used
that worthy gentleman, Mr Bell of Whiteside, in Galloway,
whom he shot without mercy, and for which cruel deed
Kenmuir threatened to run him through the body with his
naked sword, and would have done it, had not Claverhouse,
who was present, interfered. I say no mercy was to be
expected from Lagg, unless 'hot water could be found
beneath cold ice.' And so we lay among the straw like
sheep awaiting the slaughter knife. On looking round our
apartment, however—before the darkness came on—one of
us observed a back door which was barred in the inside, and
without a lock.' This was an unexpected discovery; and
fearing lest the soldiers should be sent to guard us through
the night, we resolved to make our escape whenever the
murkiness of the evening should favour our attempt.
Accordingly, no person disturbed us, none came with food,
and none came to guard, and so, quietly drawing the
bolt, we issued from our prison-house, and fairly made our
escape." "I feel," said Gilbert, "I can now more easily
draw my breath. But what of the martyred body on the
hill?" "We instantly repaired to the house of a friend who
lived at some distance from the village, and who accom-

panied us in the darkness, as you did last night, and we
buried our slaughtered companion in silence." "And was
he who was shot yesterday one of the three?" "He was."
"And did you not recognise him?" "He was the shoemaker, but his face was so disfigured——" Here poor
Grizzy burst into an uncontrollable flood of tears; her warm
and womanly heart was all dissolved, and had they been
her sons, her own dear children, she could not have felt a
deeper anguish. The two godly men she had entertained
during the storm, and whose conversation was so heavenly,
and so edifying to all the household, were now in their
graves. But it was "the Killing Time," and God's saints
were slaughtered wherever they were found. No wonder
that Mr Renwick exclaimed, "The moors and the mosses
of the West of Scotland are flowered with martyrs."
Honest Gilbert sat as one stupified, and his utterance was
choked with grief. At length he exclaimed, "Alas! my
brothers;" but he had occasion to utter more exclamations
of this kind ere all was done.

It was in the autumn when these things occurred in the
neighbourhood of the Miny; and as the harvest was drawing near a close, Gilbert had finished the cutting of his
corn, and it only remained to gather it into the barn-yard.
The two men from the Glenkens, to whom he had shown
kindness, were desirous to assist in getting the corn stacked;
and they so addressed themselves to the work, that in a
short time all was secured in good condition; and it was
well, for in a few days there fell such a torrent of rain,
which continued for so long time as would have rotted the
sheaves in the fields, and "made the harvest a heap in the
day of grief and of desperate sorrow." Some days before
the rain fell, and as all were busy in the barn-yard, Sandy
announced the coming of Eddie and his cuddie along the
moor. "I am most happy to hear it," said Gllbert, "for
he may bring news that will be of some consequence to us;

I hae been lang wearying for his coming." The men had heard of Eddie from their companions, so that though they had forgotten his name, it did not sound strange in their ears. Eddie was not known in Galloway, for he confined himself within the circle he had chosen on the north of Niths-dale. Eddie at length drew near ; and the men from the barn-yard, and Grizzy from the kitchen, all went out to meet him. " Ye are welcome to the Miny," cried Gilbert. "Thank ye, Gibby, thank ye, Gibby, and yer gude spouse ; I am glad to see ye a' weel, and in health." The creels were cautiously lifted from the donkey, and one especially, which contained the *article*, as Eddie archly termed it, was deposited in a secure place. The animal, now unladen, went instinctively to his stall, and Eddie took his place in the kitchen. It was now toward evening, and all further operations were suspended for the day. It was somewhat amusing to the strangers to notice the ceremony with which a poor cadger was treated by the inmates of the Miny. They could see nothing which demanded such attention, and which made him an object of so much consequence ; but they soon had reason to change their opinion. Eddie was something more than he seemed to be—cautious, shrewd, trustworthy, and a man of sterling principle, who possessed a vast fund of information, and that of a kind which more immediately concerned them all. Eddie had gained more experience since the time we last met with him. His character, as a Christian man, was more matured, and his plans for assisting the sufferers better laid, and more dexterously executed. He threw himself as a shield between the persecuted and their enemies ; and though a poor keelman, it was amazing how successful he was in this way. He succeeded where persons of greater influence, it might be, would have failed. If the persecutors had spies and informers on their side in a given locality, Eddie had his too, and faithful servants they were, and they furnished him with information from places far and near. All this Eddie treasured up and made his own use of it.

"Ye'll hae heard, nae doubt," said Eddie, "that the auld company o' troopers has left Muirkirk, and that Crichton, wi' his dragoons, has ta'en their place." "We have," replied Gilbert, "and we fear the change will not be for the better." "And ye hae gude reason to fear it," said Eddie. "Crichton is weel kent as a cruel, wicked man, and Cochrane, his assistant, is even worse. The whole party is a drunken, roisterous squad, who fear neither God nor devil, as they themselves declare. I was somewhat acquainted with the former commander, and could use a little freedom wi' him, but this man, I doubt, I doubt———" "I fear," said Grizzy, timidly, "I fear there will be muckle bluidy wark ere a' be done." "There *is* so, mistress. Bluid is already flowing in all quarters; and the dark cloud that has been gatherin' o'er puir Scotland for a quarter of a century is now bursting over our head in earnest." "But God can blow away that cloud," said Gilbert, "as he moved the thunder cloud from the conventicle that day at Friarminion." "Ay," replied Eddie, "but that, perchance, may not be till all its terrible contents are poured out." "The troopers at Muirkirk," said Gilbert, "are, as we hear, behaving very ill in their raids throughout the district." "They are; but Geordy Ga' is among them, and I hope to be able to do something through him." "Hae ye met wi' Crichton himsel' yet, Eddie?" "I have, and that very unexpectedly. I was one day in Glenmuir Water, and came the length o' the Shaw to stop a night, and when I was half way between it and Dalblair, the rain began to fa', and the thunder to growl on the tap o' the Tor Hill; but before I got to the house, I was drenched wi' the heaviest spate that ever fell on me in a' my wanderings in these wild moors. As I was sittin' afore a big fire in the kitchen drying my clothes, who should ride up to the door but Crichton and four o' his troopers.

They could go no farther ; the rain fell in torrents, and the thunder was terrible. The whole party was panic-struck. Crichton strode into the apartment with his streaming cloak, and his huge Bothwell Brig boots, like a pair o' yer stoups there filled to the brim wi' water, which, at every step, spurted on the floor as from a watering-pan. In a short time the kitchen was filled. Geordy Ga' was one of the party ; and when the commander observed that we kent each other, he turned a keen eye on me, and demanded who I was, and if I belonged to the house. 'I am Eddie, the keelman, yer honour,' said I. 'I traverse the uplands here all around, selling keel to the shepherds, and tobacco and pipes to the auld wives ; and here and there I gather a few eggs to give in exchange for my wares ; and as yer a' baith cauld and wet, I'll be glad if ye'll accept o' a pipe the piece and a thraw o' tobacco ; it will pit heat in ye, yer honour, for there's aiblins nae whisky in the house.' My gift was accepted, and Crichton smoked as freely as ony o' them. They were very quiet, for they were a' cowed wi' the thunner, which roared louder and louder, till we were like to be deevt a' thegether ; and then the lightnin', I sometimes thought I was stane blind. But the upshot came to be this, they were obliged to stop a' night. Crichton got the spense, and the men and me sat round the fire and crackit till a late hour. I got a chance o' Geordy, the very thing I wantit. Geordy tells me that he is pretty weel in Crichton's graces ; for Crichton, though a rude, swearing man, is for a' that fond o' a joke, and Geordy is first-rate at that, and can keep a whole company in roars of laughter for hours thegether, so that he is a general favourite baith wi' the men and their captain. Now it happens that Geordy does na drink like the rest, he never carries a flask, and he never errs in the moss, and as he always rides foremost, the others follow, trusting to his guidance, so that when they are half fu' he can lead them where he likes. E'en Cochrane, when he is

wi' them, lets Geordy lead, baith because he is aye sober,
and because he kens the country best.  Noo, my hope lies
here, that Geordy will ere long be put in Cochrane's place,
as I hear it is likely he will be sent to Kilmarnock ; and, if
this shall turn out to be the case, it will be a great help to
us in this district.  Geordy is a lad I can trust.  He is a sodger ;
but, as I told you once before, he is one merely for the sake
of the horsemanship part of it.   He aye takes an advice frae
me for his auld father's sake ; and I am sure I will get from
him very important information when it suits.   Noo, if
Cochrane were ance out o' the gate, I think Geordy will do
us gude service.   And I am glad that I met wi' Crichton
himsel', because he'll ken me noo, and not think it a queer,
a suspicious thing to see me ga'en about wi' my equipage,
and mair by token that his ain men converse familiarly wi'
me.   But the times are fearfu', and no one can tell what
may befa'; but it is a' in the hand o' Him that sits aboon,
and who makes even the wrath o' man to praise Him."

"But, Eddie," said Gilbert, "do ye really think that Cochrane is as bad a man as they say he is ?"   "There's nae
doubt o't ; nay, he is even worse.   It is but the other day
that he shot a man on this side o' the Birkencleuch.   There
were three o' them, but two escaped."   "And wha, think
ye," said Gilbert, "was the man that was shot, but the honest shoemaker that was here in the time o' the snaw storm ?
and these twa men there were his companions that have escaped to our house.'   "Indeed !" exclaimed Eddie, "but
that was a worthy man.   He was quiet ; but there was
something about him that drew my heart close to him.
Many a time since have I thought on his prayers in family
worship ; they aye meltit my heart.   And has he gained
the martyr's crown ?   O, but one's heart is crushed wi'
grief when we hear of so many of our dear acquaintances
falling by the shot of these men on muir and mountain !
And the tailor, the godly tailor, what of him ?"   "Shot

too," said Grizzy; "shot but the other day in the wilds o'
Galloway. I think my puir heart will e'en break a' thegither." "Ah me!" groaned Eddie, "these men were aboon
many, but they are gane, and are safely lodged in Christ.
And ye were their companions," said he to the men. "I
honour ye as sufferers in the same cause, and if at any time
I can help ye, I shall stand your friend." But little recked
they that these last words of Eddie were, in a sense, pro-
phetic.

"You say, Eddie, that Cochrane is a dangerous man."
"I do say so; and my advice to you is, that ye look about
ye, and see that the places hereabout may be put in such a
posture as that you shall be able to retreat in case of a visit
that may not be so pleasant. I told Geordy to do his utmost to wile the troopers from this place, and he tells me
that he was once here when the former captain came to bid
you farewell." "And what would you advise in this case?"
said Gilbert, "Why, I see you are inning your corn, and
a fine crop I think it is—the stooks are the tallest I have
seen in a' my travels, and if the grain be as gude as the
stalk is strong, you will not need to complain." "Indeed,"
said Gilbert, "our fields have been unusually productive;
we have been amply repaid for all the little hospitality
which we have shown to the Lord's poor people. But you
were going to propose a plan for our safety." "And it is
this," said Eddie, "in building your stacks, make one or
two rather larger, and make what is called a *boss* in the heart
of them, capable of containing two or three persons, and
keep a large sheaf of corn within, so that the hole can be
stopped with the stubble end of the sheaf outward, to prevent discovery. But then, as your stackyard cannot always
last, I would propose this other scheme. You have that
deep, wooded ravine a few yards behind the house; now I
would advise that an outgate should be made through the
wall there to the gully—it would not be convenient to break

a passage straight through the wall, but I have observed, in your little dairy there, a built-up doorway. This could easily be re-opened, and a door provided, having a strong bar in the inside ; from this you could issue on any occasion of alarm, and dive into the ravine, and there you are safe." " A good plan," exclaimed Gilbert, " but then the face of the ravine is so steep and dangerous that no one can reach the bottom." " That may be," said Eddie, " but you could easily tie a strong rope to the root of the tree in the linn, and then you could descend with all safety ; but there is more than this, you have the Auchty, and a better place can scarcely be found. I ken the Auchty weel, for many a night, as I told you before, hae I lodged in its vowts in the days when I followed the smuggling trade, but that's mony a year syne, and I heartily renounce a' that sort o' wark ; but I ken the Auchty weel, and wi' your leave, we will visit it before I take my journey, and I will show you mair about it than ony o' ye yet kens o'. The way from the linn into the Auchty is easy, if the weather be so that ye canna hide among the bushes wi' comfort." " We shall act on your advice, Eddie," said Gilbert ; " but I would like to examine the Auchty in company wi' ye, and we'll a' gang thegither, for the truth is, I never likit to look into that place, there was aye something sae eery and dismal about it." " Why, that's just one o' the things that renders it a place o' safety. Nobody will venture into it ; and the sodgers that were here before durstna go near it, and I'll tell Geordy Ga' to give the new sodgers an inklin' o' what sort o' place it is, should he and they ever happen to come this way."

They went to the old ruin, and when they stood in the vault, Gilbert said to the two strangers :—" This is the place in which the tailor and the shoemaker, who are now in their graves, lodged at first in the snow storm ; and they warmed themselves by kindling a fire of the dry birns and brush-wood that happened to be blown into it by the wind. Here

they remained two nights—till they were discovered." The
strangers regarded the place with deep interest, and looked
on it as a hallowed spot. "I hae lodged here mony a night,"
said Eddie, "wi' the kegs o' brandy standing around me ;
and mony a drucken scene I hae witnessed, and mony a
brawl and scuffle ; for we were a company o' rude, graceless
chaps, who carried on that smuggling trade ; but I bless
the grace that snatched me like a brand frae the burning.
But the secret I was going to show you is this : see you
that square hole in the roof there ?  Well, there is a chamber above, and a nice snug place it is, at least if it be as I
saw it thirty years ago.  We had a small ladder by which
we went up and down, and when we were all up and wished
concealment, we drew the ladder after us.  Now, if you
wish to see it, let one mount on the shoulders of another,
and you are up in an instant."  The experiment was tried,
and the place was found to be exactly as Eddie had described it.  No place could be more desirable for concealment ;
and they resolved to make their own use of it if necessity
should require.  Eddie's other suggestions were attended
to, and in a brief space the door was opened from the dairy.
The rope was tied to the root of the tree, and a stack or
two were constructed with a boss or "fause-house" in the
middle.  In this way, all things were ready for the use of
a surprisal, and that surprisal came in due time.

"In our part of the country," said one of the men from
the Glenkins ; "we also have to resort to various expedients.
Gordon of Earlston has a large bushy oak tree—the growth
of centuries.  The trunk is of enormous thickness—it is
clad with hundreds of leafy branches, and so dense, that no
eye can penetrate them.  In case of a surprisal, he has a
rope attached to one of the boughs, by which he can climb
with amazing speed unto the first cleft of the tree ; and
there, resting his foot, he springs up to the next branch,
and the next, till he is completely concealed by the mant-

ling of the leaves; and there in secrecy he can see and hear all that is going on below. I have proved the tree, and found it to answer the purpose admirably."

"In some houses with us, there is what is termed a double gable—that is, a gable built inside of the barn, leaving a space between it and the outer gable some yards wide, having an entrance at the inside corner, usually behind a heap of straw or bin of peats. These chambers are never suspected, and no soldier ever guesses at such a thing. We have frequently lodged in these hiding-places for several days together, and found them exceedingly comfortable. Sometimes a peat-stack is so constructed as to afford a very safe retreat. A square chamber is formed in the interior; the roof being supported by sticks, and the floor covered with hay. I once stayed with John Stevenson a night in his peat-stack at Craigdarroch, and never spent a happier time. The prayers of that saintly man always melted me, and his conversation never failed to quicken me."

As they were thus conversing in the kitchen of the Miny, a visitor appeared at the door. It was Sarah Gilry, the wife of honest Peter Corsan of Powmerlog—a mile or two distant on the south side of the moss. Sarah was a mother in Israel, and she and Grizzy were kindred spirits; nor were their husbands dissimilar. Sarah was a "gracious woman," by which was meant—in the language of those times —a woman richly endowed with Divine grace. Her memory was well stored with the Word of God; and her strong understanding, and sterling good sense, rendered her conversation remarkably edifying. She was among the women, what Priesthill was among the men. She loved Grizzy as a sister, and Grizzy loved her as more—as a mother as well as a sister. Their meetings were frequent; for the purpose of comparing notes, as they called it, both of their religious experience and of their ideas of the times. Sarah received a hearty welcome, and was introduced to all the friends;

but Eddie was no stranger to her, for he was her frequent
guest, and one whom she highly valued. "I have been
longing much to see you, sister Grizzy," said Sarah, "and so
I thought I would just come o'er the muir the day, to pay
you a visit, as the harvest would now be at a close." "Nane
mair welcome of womankind than you, dear Sarah," exclaimed the kindly-hearted mistress of the Miny. "Many a
time has the Lord sent you to me, as an angel from heaven,
with a message of comfort and strengthening in this the
day of our tribulation, and I am persuaded that good will
come of this visit." "And in like manner," said Sarah, "have
I often received refreshment to my spirit in the hour when
I was ready to despond, by what you were directed to say
to me. But, Gilbert, how are ye ?—and how fares it with
you in these times ?" "I am well in my health, dear Sarah,
but, like the rest of the Lord's people, I am distressed in
Zion's affliction ; but in darkness we look for light."

---

## CHAPTER VII.

AS the men were busy without, Sarah and Grizzy were
in close conversation within. "These are, indeed,
heavy times," said Sarah, "in which we live, and I
wot not what may be the end of these things. What a
bluidy sun gaed doon in the west the other night, and then,
after the sky darkened in, there appeared that fitfu' dead-
light that sprang up in the moss, and leapt from side to
side in the lonely muir, and danced up the hill, and stood
for mair than an hour by the side o' the dreary Birkencleuch,
and then came slowly doon the brae, and, starting here and
there along the moors, vanished at the very spot where it
first appeared—all this, I fear, bodes dismal things." "Yes,
dear Sarah, whatever it may bode, it was a light used on a
dismal occasion—it was the burial of a martyr on the hill:

the dear companion of these two men who are with us at this time. He was shot by Cochrane and his troopers when fleeing for their lives. He was the shoemaker who lodged with us during the snow storm, and of whom you have heard me speak. These shoes on my feet were made by him, and the coat that is on Gibby's back was made by the tailor, his companion, who was shot the other week by Lagg in the wilds of Galloway." "Alack-a-day!" exclaimed Sarah. "O that the Lord would lift up His feet unto these perpetual desolations, and that He would consider all that the enemy hath done wickedly in the sanctuary! Ours is a day of sore trouble. We are passing through the furnace; but we may rest assured of His sympathy in whose cause we suffer. 'In all their afflictions He was afflicted, and the angel of His presence saved them.'" In this way did these two Christian women encourage themselves in the Lord, and the Lord was with them, and their spirits were refreshed, and they felt as if they could undergo anything for Christ's sake, and though their hearts were not quiet from the fear of evil, yet they had peace.

As they were thus conversing, the boy Sandy, who had been out in the moor with the sheep, hastily approached the house, and cried that the troopers were on their way straight to the Miny. Considerable confusion ensued—the men assembled in the kitchen; it was considered the arrival of the troopers was from evil intent, and, therefore, the sooner they provided for their safety the better. It was agreed that the men should flee, and that the women should calmly abide in the house. Accordingly the four men issued from the back door, which was immediately bolted on their departure. None of the fugitives mentioned the spot to which they intended to betake themselves, so that the women could easily affirm that they knew not where they were. In this situation they waited, in trembling anxiety, till the cavalcade rode up to the door. In the meantime,

Gilbert took his place in the corn-stack, and having thrust
a sheaf into the entrance, continued quietly to await the
result; the men descended by the rope into the ravine,
where they were in perfect concealment. The prayers of
the fugitives were alike fervent and incessant for the
women, that the rude and wicked men might be restrained
from doing them injury, and that they might be blessed
with courage and enabled to answer rightly. The dragoons
were six in number, with Cochrane at their head; they
dismounted and entered the house without ceremony.
"Who is the mistress of this house!" demanded the officer.
"I am," replied Grizzy firmly, "I am, and what do you
want with me?" "Not so much with you as with your
husband; where is he?" " He is without, sir; but I cannot
say precisely where he may be." "Not *precisely*, of course,
but you know his whereabouts? Is he on a journey or
about the premises?" "I have told all I can tell you;
and if I knew exactly where he was, it is not likely that I
would say, if I thought you were going to do him harm."
"Come now, pretty mistress, this will not do; we cannot
be put off in this manner; tell us frankly, or we shall
extort it in another way. "You have my answer," replied
Grizzy. "Watson," cried the officer, "Watson, where is
Watson?" "Here, sir." "Then, fetch the matches; we
must apply the torture." "Why, to confess the truth,
Captain," said Watson, "I quite forgot to put them in my
pocket, though you reminded me a little before we started,
and I sincerely beg your pardon." "O, then perhaps a
piece of lighted candle will do as well; for you see,
mistress, we place the match or lighted candle exactly between the fingers in this way, and we burn the flesh to the
very bone, and so we soon extract a confession." "I hope,"
said Grizzy, "I shall be enabled to endure the pain rather
than betray my husband."
  At this moment Sarah, whose heart burned within her,

exclaimed, "The tender-mercies of the wicked are cruel;
have you no compassion in your breasts? Have you no
fear of God before your eyes? know ye not that God will
bring you unto judgment for all these doings?" "What, so
ho, have we got a preacher here, a female one too? where
do you hold your next conventicle, for we mean to do ourselves the honour to attend it, and——?" at this moment
a hubbub was heard without—"What's the matter there?"
cried the officer, "what is the matter, I say?" "Why,"
said Watson, "the horses in the stable are all broken loose,
and are kicking and tearing at one another violently." It
took a while to reduce the animals to order, and by this
time the affair of the matches was forgotten, and the whole
party commenced a strict search about the premises. The
out-houses were examined, the stack-yard was visited—and
Gilbert in his concealment could easily hear their threatening words as they stood beside the very stack in the heart
of which he lay; they investigated the dwelling-house,
they stabbed the beds with their swords, they thrust their
glittering points up between the boards of the garret floor
above their heads, they crept under the beds, peeped into
every recess, overturned the straw in the barn, tossed about
the heaps of corn; in short, there was not a conceivable
place or nook which they did not examine, but no person
was to be found.

They next looked at the cattle, but the cows did not suit
their purpose, and the horses were too small and too lean
to be of any avail. By this time it was past mid-day, and
the troopers, who were always ready for a meal, demanded
provisions. These were instantly set before them; and the
two women, with all promptitude, presented them with the
best the house could afford. The hearty manner in which
they were entertained had somewhat of a softening effect
upon the rude guests, and they showed a more becoming
demeanour than was usual in such cases; for, instead of

emptying the meal girnal on the floor, according to custom, and then trampling the contents of the beef barrels on the ground, they seemed disinclined to use this privilege. When they had appeased the keenness of their appetite with the wholesome food with which they were so amply provided, they resolved on searching the places at some distance around, hoping to come upon hiding-places that might furnish them with what they wanted. In their rambles, they reached the Auchty, and came to the mouth of the vault ; but one of the soldiers who belonged to the former party, and who knew the bad repute of the place, asserted that it was haunted, and frightful sights had been seen and suspicious sounds heard there ; that it was, in short, a place where deeds of darkness had been committed, and that the ghosts of the murdered had frequently appeared in its murky recesses. "I care for none of these things," vociferated Cochrane, "I fear neither ghost nor devil ;" and with this he dashed into the vault, while the rest timidly followed. When the party had got fairly within, a strange and unearthly sound was heard issuing from the little chamber at the far end of the vault, like the wailings of a person in great distress, and then a fluttering as of many wings over their heads, which made the arch resound as if with thunder ; and then, to crown the whole, a sight, the most appalling, presented itself—a coffin lying close by the wall ; a black coffin, with bright lace around the edges, and handles on the sides and ends. This completed the thing, and the whole party, terrorstruck, rushed to the entrance, and Cochrane himself the first. "The spirit of all that is evil," he exclaimed, "is certainly in this place !" and instantly retreated to the Miny. No time was lost ; the horses were immediately drawn from the stable, and without more ado they were all over the moor in a brief space. The women, relieved by their departure, recalled the fugitives from their hiding-places, who, when assembled in the Miny, thanked the Lord for their escape, and that the soldiers were prevented from misusing the women, and wasting the provisions in the wantonness of their mischief. It was now found that Eddie's plan was successful, and that the highest degree of safety was insured by this means.

It will be necessary here to say a few things respecting the occurrences in the Auchty. The unearthly sounds which the soldiers heard were the bleatings of a ewe that had strayed into the extreme part of the vault; the mysterious thundering above their head, was the flight of a number of bats that frequented the place, and that had been roused from their repose by the bustling of the soldiers; and the coffin, apparently the greatest mystery, was a veritable coffin that had been brought in a cart, under the cloud of night, from Douglas Water, and hidden in the vault till it should be conveyed to a place where a person had died, in the moors, of a disease caught by hard usage, and hiding in cold, damp caves from the pursuit of the troopers. The suffering people, in many cases, durst not carry their dead to the common churchyard, and had, therefore, to bury them in desert places. The preceding occurrences rendered the vault a place of much security, for it was well guarded by the superstitions which it created. The inmates of the Miny were at this time altogether ignorant of the incidents that befell the troopers in the vault, but Geordie Ga', to whom they were communicated by a fellow-soldier, related them to Eddie, by whom they became known at the Miny, and which was a subject of some amusement to them.

Glenmuir Water is a beautiful little strath that stretches up through the moorland, along the back of the hills that lie southward from Muirkirk. It has been celebrated in song: "Glenmuir's wild solitudes lengthened and deep." It is flanked on both sides with mountains and wild moorlands, and is, especially towards the upper part of the glen, a place of as complete seclusion as can well be desired. Far up in

the strath, in the very heart of the solitudes, stood an old
baronial hold—the ruins of which remain till the present
day.  A few large trees—the growth of centuries—guard
the venerable spot, and recall to our thoughts times that
are long gone by, when lordly barons, in a barbarous and
adventurous age, held sway over the wilds around them,
that were then thickly peopled, compared with what they
are now, or even in the times of our persecuted ancestors.
Glenmuir Shaw, as this place is called, is the farm-house in
the upper part of this moorland district, and is situated
close to the old castle ruins in the flat bottom, near the
stream that flows through the lonely glen.  Its distance
from the Miny was not great, and the worthy farmer of the
Shaw and Gilbert were dear friends.  It had been agreed
on at one of the prayer meetings held at Friarminion that a
conventicle should be kept at the Shaw, and that Mr Renwick should be invited to preach.  Accordingly the day
came round, and crowds of people flocked in from all parts
of the surrounding country.  It was a beautiful Sabbath
morning ; all nature seemed to be glad with joyousness,
and the people, with light foot and glad hearts, bounded
along the heath, and dived into the secluded glen, where
they were out of sight in a moment.  The throng gathered
around the tent in which the youthful preacher stood ready
to commence the services of the day ; but whether they
should be permitted to observe their solemnity without interruption, and gather the manna that rained around their
camp, without the sudden invasion of the troopers, was a
different question.  They had dared, however, to assemble
to worship God in the wilds ; and dared, even at the risk of
their lives, to engage in this service.  The work went on ;
the sound of so many voices singing in concert was wafted
adown the glen by the eastern breeze, and rose to the tops
of the hills, where the warders, stationed here and there on
the peaks of the heights, caught on their ears the sweet mel-

ody, though they could not distinguish the words of the song. The preacher, with his sweet and soft voice, in fervid eloquence, discoursed on the lofty subjects of the Christian faith, and on the affecting love of Him who shed His precious blood for the avail of sinners of the human race : and all this was done in a mood so tender and so pathetic, that all hearts seemed to be bowed and moved, as the trees of the forest by the wind. The amount of good done on that occasion can be known only on the great day of final reckoning ; but if signs be any evidence of effect, these certainly were not awanting. The preacher seemed to be preternaturally assisted—a tongue of fire rested on him, and the Lord was with his mouth. The people entered into his feelings, and were obviously carried away with him on the wings of a lofty spirituality. If it was not a day like that in Hyndbottom, it was, at least, a second to it, and a day that was long remembered. The firmament above smiled, and the glorious sun looked brightly down on the company in the solitary glen ; but the Sun of Righteousness shone brighter still from His place in the high heavens of God. They were a flock of His own sheep gathered in the wilderness, and His eye was on them, and "His rod and His staff they comforted them."

But the brightest morning is sometimes followed by a dark and scowling evening, and so it was on this day. Informers had given the watchword, though not in time to prevent the meeting, nor even to hinder the services till they were near a close. A warder that stood on the Tor Hill, immediately above the conventicle, observed in the distance something suspicious : and, looking narrowly and wistfully, plainly discerned, glancing in the sun, the armour of the troopers. The alarm was instantly given ; and the direction in which the enemy was advancing intimated that the conventiclers should flee in the opposite way. All was in confusion. The greater part took the steep brow of the height before them, up which, they knew, the troopers could not climb. Laing of Blagannoch, always the foremost in danger, took charge of Mr Renwick, and a small but nimble pony carried him down the glen in the direction of Dalblair, where he succeeded in making his escape. The great body of the people reached the top of the hill, and got beyond danger. All, however, were not equally successful. The troopers, seeing the people scattered on the heights and along the distant moor, were afraid of losing their prey and accordingly they pushed forward with great fury.

The people of the Miny, with Sarah and her husband, were fleeing in company, when they were encountered by a party of the dragoons who had separated to the right between the glen and the moor, with a view to prevent a flight in that direction. They were made prisoners. The women were dismissed, but the men were led away. The troopers having disposed themselves all over the district, fired at the fugitives, but without effect—as the companies were too far advanced in their flight for the heavy horses to follow in the sinking moss; so that the only persons seized were those mentioned. The four men were led back to the Shaw, and there confined till Crichton himself, who was not present, should pronounce sentence. In other circumstances, Cochrane, perhaps, would have shot them at once ; but the scene in the vault had produced a somewhat startling effect on him, and he was not prepared at once to perpetrate the deed. Sarah and Grizzy lingered about the place till they should see the upshot. Cochrane, however, ordered them off, and even sent some of his men to drive them over the moor. It was with heavy hearts that they were forced to turn their backs on all they loved best on earth. Their communings by the way were mournful, but they encouraged themselves in the Lord ; and Sarah quoted many a precious text of Holy Writ, from which they drew consolation in this their darkest hour.

In the meantime, the friends were closely confined in an old vault at the Shaw, and as Cochrane resolved to remain till next day, the soldiers were employed, in their turn, guarding the prisoners. In the early morning a messenger was despatched to Crichton with the news of what had occurred, who instantly set out with a small party to visit the Shaw and see what was proper to be done.

The good men in the vault, like Paul and Silas in the prison, prayed by turns, and sang praises to God at midnight; they rejoiced to be counted worthy to suffer for the sake of Him who died for them; they counted on a bloody death like their fellow-witnesses who were falling daily in all the wilderness around them; they were filled with peace and joyous anticipations, and felt as if they were even at the very gates of heaven itself. At length the morning dawned, and it was the dawn of the last day they expected to see on earth, but they were prepared for whatever might befall.

Crichton, with his cavalcade, at length arrived—the matter was inquired into—the men were examined, and confessed that they had been at the conventicle. "There needs no farther proof, then," said the commander; "you know the penalty?" "We do," replied they, "and we are prepared to abide it." "And you shall abide it, but in the meantime you must be conducted to Muirkirk, and there undergo your sentence."

The party now left the Shaw with Crichton at their head. The prisoners trudged on before, exhibiting no signs of dismay, although their feelings toward kindred and home wrought deeply within them. As they emerged from the glen, and had come the length of Ladyburn, Eddie Cringan —the constant friend of the sufferers, and who had learned the whole circumstances of the present case—crossed the path of the troopers with his equipage. He recognised the four men, and his heart was filled with concern. "Ho,

Eddie," cried Crichton, "is this you ? Why, man, you are everywhere." "And it is e'en gude for some folk that I am to be found here and there," said Eddie, "else it might be the worse for them; ye ken yoursel', yer honour." "I think I know what you mean; but there is no second danger of that sort here, I think." "Maybe no, maybe no; but whare are ye ga'en wi' thir puir men this morning, yer honour ?" "Why, they are rebels, to be sure; they have transgressed the Conventicle Act, and they must be shot." "Noo, hear me for ance, Captain; a word privately in yer lug. Ye mind the day I saved yer life in the moss. Noo, Captain, when you and yer horse, wi' yer reckless riding, were plunged baith o'er the head in that deep wellee, twenty feet to the bottom, but a' grown o'er on the surface wi' moss weeds, and when you came up wi' a bowt, and I held out the head end o' my staff to ye, and ye clutch it wi' a death's grasp, and I pulled, and ye struggled till ye got yer feet free o' the stirrups, and then wi' yer knees on the puir beast's back, and frae that took a step to the side, when ye plunged neck deep the second time; and then I got haud o' the cuff o' yer coat, and drew ye, like a dead salmon, to the hard turf, when ye fand yoursel' actually in life—a thing ye didna expect twa minutes afore; and when ye stood a' drookit and shiverin', mair frae fear than frae cald, cald as these wells are—I say, had it no been for me, ye would hae perished, for yer troopers were awa scourin' a mile a-gate afore ye, while ye stood haverin' wi' the drucken piper o' Sanquhar, as he was trudgin' through the muirs to play at the sodger's wedding in Douglas. Noo, Captain, what did ye say to me ? 'Eddie,' says ye, 'ye have saved my life. Had it not been for you, I must have perished in that *hell's-pit*.' These were yer verra words; and then ye added, in the overflowing o' yer heart, 'Eddie, can I do ye a favour ? Just ask, and I'll grant it.' 'I hae nae favour,' I said, 'to ask for mysel', for neither me nor the auld cuddie needs muckle ; but maybe I may hae occasion to ax a boon frae ye in anither direction,' and that occasion has come, and I earnestly request the lives o' these four men." "Eddie, you have asked a hard thing. You know the strictness of the laws ; and if I were to let these men go, my own life would be at stake." "But it has been at stake already ; and had it no been for me, ye wadna hae been standing here either to keep the laws or to break them." "You say the truth, Eddie. It is only three days since I was near the black bottom of that execrable well, and I feel a shuddering yet : but still, if I were to comply with your request, these fellows there, and Cochrane, would lodge information to my detriment ; for though they are under us as commanders, we are in some measure under them too." "I'll tell ye what to do, yer honour. Order them a' back to the Shaw again, and just say that if these men are to be shot, it is proper that they should be executed on the very spot where the conventicle was held, as a warning to a' others, and for a' time coming. Order Geordy Ga' and a company to guard them, and leave the rest to me." "Right, Eddie, right ; that is the very thing. I see the issue, but keep this secret, or, if you whisper it, a whizzing ball goes through your brains." "Chap me for that, yer honour ; it will fyke some folk to howk that out o' me."

Crichton then imparted his intentions to his men, and selected a company to conduct the prisoners to Glenmuir Shaw ; with the strict injunction, that on the morrow they were to be led out to the conventicle ground, and shot on the spot—as a more striking warning to others. "Ga'," said he, "I leave this business in your hand, as Cochrane must proceed to Kilmarnock this very afternoon." This ended the matter. Crichton marched to Muirkirk, and Ga' with his party, to the Shaw, and Eddie followed at a short distance.

"I dinna ken," said Eddie to the new commander of the

party, "I dinna ken how I could stand to see these poor
men shot on the green the morn." "Nor I," replied Ga';
"it's a black business, and I wish I had been a hundred
miles off." "But ye will be obliged to execute it, though ?"
"I am sure," answered Ga', "I most heartily wish they may
find some way of escape ere the morning." "I would like
to see," said Eddie, "how they are put up, and to take a
last fareweel o' them ; for I canna think of staying here till
the morning." By this Eddie wanted to see their prison-
house, that he might devise some way of escape. It was a
barn in which they were confined ; while two soldiers
guarded the door. Eddie saw his plan at once. "I think,"
said he to Ga', "if this business either pinch yer conscience
or pain yer feelings, that ye may possibly avoid it ; for it's
an unco thing to be accessory to the murder of gude folk ;
yer ain godly father wad sooner hae laid yer head in the
grave than—" "I understand you ; it is a wretched business this ; but, sooner than see these men shot, I will flee
the army." "There is no occasion for that either," said
Eddie, "for that would not save their lives ; these reckless
men would shoot them in your absence, and think it good
sport ; but if ye leave the thing to me—between us twa—
I'll manage it." "Do as you like." "Then," said Eddie,
"a' that I ask is, that after it is mirk dark, ye will ca' in
the guards to their supper, so that the ground without may
be clear."

When the darkness had fully set in, the soldiers were
convened, in the kitchen of the Shaw, to an inviting repast,
of which they stood in need ; and with keen appetites, and
not one of their number awanting, they fell, in their usual
graceless manner, on the food, and devoured it with great
voracity. Meanwhile, Eddie had gone to the door, and taking down the key of the barn from its nail in the passage,
crept out to the close, and quietly opening the door, stood
in the dark beside the prisoners. "Ye ken me," he said ;

"I have opened the way for your escape; the soldiers are in the kitchen at their supper, and they are not generally in a hurry with their meals; in five minutes after this—for I must return to the house to avoid suspicion—issue ye frae your prison-house, and when ye get to the close, lift every man a large stone and smash the barn door to pieces, and syne make the best o' yer way to the muir." Eddie instantly returned to the kitchen, and sat quietly down at a side bench, and partook of his supper. The troopers jeered and swore among themselves, and gulped down large mouthfuls of the viands with which they were so liberally supplied. In the midst of their hilarity, a crash, which Eddie impatiently waited for, was heard at one of the doors, as if the broad side of the house had been battered in. Instantly all were on their feet; a general rush was made to the door. The horses had probably broken loose, as they did at the Miny, but nothing could be seen in the darkness. A light was procured, and the door of the barn was broken to shivers and the prisoners were gone! Conjecture was useless, but the general opinion was that a rescue had taken place, and that assailants from without had done the deed. Eddie's end was gained, and Ga's mind was relieved. The friends now plodded their way through the moor in the direction of the Miny.

Meanwhile, Sarah and Grizzy, as disconsolate as may be, were brooding over the fate of their dear husbands, expecting, when the woeful tidings would reach them, that their blood had been shed on the heath. A thought struck Sarah. "Grizzy," said she, "does not our Lord say, 'If two of you shall agree on earth as touching anything that ye shall ask, it shall be done unto you?' Let us, then, kneel down, and joining hands, plead this promise, and why may we not expect an answer?" They knelt, and first Sarah prayed, and then Grizzy. Their prayers were cries of agony that rent the heavens, and the Lord heard, and first sent com-

posure to their hearts, and then their husbands to their
arms, for at this moment their well-known voices were
heard at the door, when Sarah exclaimed, "It shall come to
pass, that before they call I will answer, and while they are
yet speaking I will hear." In an instant the fugitives stood
in the kitchen of the Miny ; and it is easy to conceive the
mutual greetings that took place, and the sincere thanks
that would be rendered to the great Preserver of their lives.
This was a happy night in Gilbert Fleming's house, when
the Lord returned their captivity like streams in the south.

On the morrow, Eddie and his equipage appeared on the
moor, coming to ask how it fared with his friends after the
rescue. And never had a person greater satisfaction in per-
forming a deed than had honest Eddie in the feat which he
had accomplished. The Master whom he served, blessed
him with the fulness of peace in his own mind. When he
drew near, all went out to meet him ; and though they did
not know all, yet they knew this much, that he had been
the means of delivering them from death. Eddie was received with a shout, and such a welcome as a prince might
have been proud of. Every one strove to show him kindness, and to let him see how much they were indebted to
his interference. The honest man was much affected at this
display of cordial attachment, and he wept like a child, till
they all wept together, and fell down instinctively on their
knees, and prayed and gave thanks to the Lord. "My
dear friends," said he, "I have done my best to serve you ;
but had it not been for certain providential incidents that
otherwise befel, my poor interference would have been of
little avail ; it is the Lord that has done it, though He made
me the instrument." He then related the occurrence of
Crichton in the well, and the promise he had made when
delivered from his perilous situation; and how he pled for
the lives of his friends on that condition, and the secrecy
which Crichton imposed on him. "The same secrecy," said

Eddie, "I now impose on you; my life is at stake if this secret should ever become public."

The Miny was now found to be a place of almost perfect security, and the vault was a place which no soldier would dare to enter.

---

## CHAPTER VIII.

BOWIE of Lochgoin, in his "Alarm to a Secure Generation," mentions a number of wonderful appearances that were somewhat common in the days of our persecuted ancestors, and also in the age following; and which, owing to the superstitious views of the times, were considered as preternatural signs or tokens pointing to scenes and incidents that were to follow. This connection produced a deep impression on the popular mind, and led, it may be, to certain extravagances both in feeling and in conduct, which it was desirable to avoid. We shall here give a specimen or two of these appearances narrated by the venerable author of the "Scots Worthies," in the tract we have just mentioned. "In the year 1682, a little before John Findlay in Moorside was apprehended, and executed in Edinburgh, one night my great-grandfather, called David Thomson, having paid him a visit, as he was convoying him up a burn-side, they heard, a little above the house, a great noise, as if it had been horses, with the rattling of their harness, approaching; and taking it for the enemy, they both clapt in behind a little height upon the burn-side. In a little the noise ceased. One of them, I think the said David, creeping up to look if he saw anything, perceived plainly, upon the height just at hand, the appearance of a man standing without the head. The one communicated this to the other at parting, it was some thought to them both."

"In the year 1685, about eight days before that zealous
and faithful martyr, John Nisbet, was apprehended in the
Midland, by torch-light, with three others of his dear
friends and acquaintances, as he and some others were
travelling in a dark wet night, and no moon—a light
sprang from above their heads, which, for about two minutes' space, they thought exceeded the light of the sun,
with a noise as if a torch had been burning. And some
time before, upon the Midland crofthead, where his three
dear companions in tribulation were shot on their being
apprehended, some people saw, at a distance, the appearance of three linen shirts spread upon each ridge head
where they fell, lying all clean and white."

"In the year 1686, about two years before the raising of
the Angus regiment and the Revolution, and nearly three
years before the battles of Killiecrankie and Dunkeld, there
was seen in the months of June and July, about the Cross-
ford Boat, especially at the Mains, two miles below Lanark,
in the afternoon, the appearance of showers of swords, hats,
and bonnets, and companies of armed men marching in
battle array upon the water-side, which companies falling
down to the ground, their place was supplied by others,
which also falling down in the same manner, disappeared.
At the same time people could plainly perceive the
dimensions of the guns, the handles of the swords, and the
knots upon the bonnets, and whatever way they turned,
one of these would fall in their way and disappear."

The author then goes on to show that appearances of a
similar description, but even more wonderful, were witnessed in the moors of Fenwick, and other places, in the
middle of the last century, and even later. Howie obviously
regarded these things as preternatural, and even bordering
on the miraculous ; but the whole can easily be explained on
scientific principles. They were appearances which, through
a certain refracting or modifying powers in the atmosphere,

were thrown down like objects in a camera obscura, on particular localities. The Ettrick Shepherd mentions precisely similar appearances which he and his friends witnessed in Yarrow. In the days of our ancestors, however, when no explanations of such phenomena could be given, it is no wonder that such sights struck them with alarm, and that they were considered as something like miraculous foreshowings.

Grizzy of the Miny dreamed of blood falling like rain drops on the leaves of her Bible while she was reading it; and it is recorded in the history of those times "That one Janet Fraser, a pious young woman, the daughter of a weaver in Closeburn, in Nithsdale, went out one Sabbath morning in May, 1687, to the fields with a young female acquaintance, and sat down to read the Bible in a place not far from her father's house. Feeling thirsty, she went to the side of the river, the Nith, to get a drink, leaving her Bible open at the place where she had been reading, which presented the verses of the 34th chapter of Isaiah, beginning with the words, "My sword shall be bathed in heaven : behold it shall come down upon Idumea, and upon the people of my curse, to judgment,' etc. On returning, she found a patch of something like blood covering this very text. In great surprise, she carried the book home, where a young man tasted the substance with his tongue, and found it of a saltness or insipid flavour. On the two succeeding Sundays, while the same girl was reading her Bible in the open air, similar blotches of matter, like blood, fell upon the leaves. She did not perceive it in the act of falling till it was about an inch from the book. It is not blood, for it is as tough as glue, and will not be scraped off by a knife, as blood will ; but it is so like blood, as none can discern any difference by the colour." Such are some of the statements respecting the wonderful meteorologica appearances which were witnessed about this time, and all of which were held as having a special reference to the sufferings of the Lord's people in those days of trial.

It is no wonder, then that every fresh exhibition of this kind filled the minds of the people with uneasy forebodings. "I am convinced," said one of the friends who had resorted to the Miny to congratulate Gilbert and the others on their escape from the hands of the troopers, "I am convinced that we shall soon hear of bloodier doings than any that have hitherto been reported to us, bloody as these have been ; for as my friend here and I were coming over the heights to-day, and communing on the troubles of Zion, we were startled with the appearance of horsemen, in their armour, riding along the brow of the opposite hill, and in their march they proceeded along the face of the steep rocks and rugged precipices in perfect order and without a stumble. Now the face of that hill, as you know, even a goat cannot traverse. The officer who marched at their head, seemed, for all I have heard of him, to be Claverhouse himself. As we were gazing on the scene, there appeared all at once two men in full flight before the troopers. The horsemen spurred on with fury. We saw the smoke of the muskets, and one of the men fell, while the other continued to flee, when in a few seconds the entire apparation vanished. We were thunderstruck, and concluded that this fore-on shadowed some bloody work to follow. All this we can our honest word declare that we have witnessed." "Ay," said Grizzy, "it will not do to overlook these things ; the Lord above does wonders, and He shows His people things to come. Sarah was telling me that there fell some draps o' bluid on the linens which she was bleaching on the green beside the moss, she was startled at it; but she could neither scrape it off nor wash out the stains. Now surely there is something in this ; and I mysel' hae had troubled dreams and visions in the night."

As they were conversing, Willie from Lesmahagow

entered. "O Willie, dear Willie, is this you ?" "Yes,
dear aunt and my dear uncle, how fares it with you both ?"
"Oh !" exclaimed Gilbert, "it's mony a day since ye were
here—not since the snaw-storm—and muckle has come and
gaen since syne." "Yes," said Willie, "many a dear, dear
friend has found a gory winding-sheet and a martyr's grave
since I left your hospitable roof. I am sore oppressed at
the heart when I think of the havoc that has been wrought
among us, and when I think of the still greater havoc that
may yet be wrought." "But where have you been, dear
Willie, all this time ? We have never heard a word of you
since you left our abode." "I have been wandering up and
down the land, 'the bluidy land,' as Mr Peden calls it,
having no settled dwelling-place, but fleeing continually
from the face of the enemy, who seem to be everywhere
dogging our steps, and allowing us no rest by night nor by
day ; but blessed be He in whose cause we suffer, they cannot deprive us of our rest in Him ; and, indeed, I may say,
I never was happier than since I have been thus harassed
and deprived of anything like home ; and I sometimes think
that we are even obliged to the enemy for the hard usage
they make us to undergo, for it is then that the consolations
of the Lord most abound. I cannot utter the joyfulness I
have experienced in the cold damp caves, in the dark and
stormy nights, either when alone or with a friend—for
these were made times of high communion with Him who
sits as a refiner of the furnace, and who speaks more peace
to our hearts than all the terror our enemies can speak in
our ears."

"O Willie !" said Gilbert, "How much you cheer my
heart with these words ! That is exactly my own experience. But where have you been since you left us ; and
what has become of John, that kindly-hearted, godly youth,
who was so great a favourite with us all—what of him ?"
"Why, he is in the peel of Dunnotar, and there, as I hear,

the prisoners are very harshly treated. We travelled together in our wanderings ; thrice we were in the enemies
hands, and thrice we made our escape. John's father and
mother, the parents he so tenderly loved, and indeed they
were worthy of his love, are both in the grave ; and it was
when he had crept from his hiding-place to attend his
father's funeral, that he was caught while he was in the
churchyard lowering his honoured father's head into his
narrow resting-place. The troopers apprehended him on
the spot in the midst of the hisses and execrations of the
populace, whom they soon dispersed ; nor would they allow
the grave to be filled up, and so it lay open, and the coffin
exposed, till the dark night, when friendly persons shovelled
in the moulds, and covered all up with the green grass sod.
John was hurried off the ground, and banished with others
to Dunnotar. My heart bleeds for John ; alas ! my brother.

"The rehearsal of my own wanderings were a tale too
tedious for you to listen to. I have indeed experienced a
variety of hardships, but I complain not ; I grieve more for
the afflictions of Zion than for my own. I am a mere unit ;
but there are thousands enduring tribulation, and who have
no prospect of deliverance. What dreadful times are these !
they are justly termed the 'Killing Times,' for God's people
are drawn out like sheep for the slaughter. Everywhere we
hear of blood, nothing but blood ; blood shed in the moors and
on the hills around. Military license is used without restraint ;
and the troopers, like certain wild beasts, seem to be maddened
at the sight of blood, and their appetite for slaughter becomes
more keen. I have lately been in many places in the country around, and almost everywhere the wailings of distress
are to be heard. There have been shootings in the parish
of Kirkconnel, over in Nithsdale there. Hair and Corsan
were found singing psalms in a green hollow, and the
dragoons happening to pass along, were attracted to the
spot by the sound, and interrupting the solitary men in

their song of praise, put a few testing questions to them, and then shot them on the spot. In the parish of Sanquhar, the same work has been going on; two men, Brown and Morris, were shot on a hill that overlooks the water of Crawick. Another of the name of Crichton, was shot on a meadow a little below the farm-house of Conraik, and another still in the moors somewhere behind. Douglas of Drumlanrig has been chasing the poor people in all the hills and glens to the north of the burgh of Sanquhar, in the locality between the two parallel streams of Menock and Crawick. His party, however, were dispersed at a place called 'the Martyr's Knowe,' on the water of Cog, by a fearful thunder-storm, not far from the place where the mist covered Mr Peden and his friends when chased by the soldiers. They have been shooting in Dunisdeer; Daniel MacMichael has fallen at the mouth of the pass of Dalveen, by Dalziel of Kirkmichael. They have been capturing in Crawfordjohn and Douglas. Lesmahagow has come in for its share, and severely has it been handled. Cumnock has now its martyrs lying in the moss of Crossgellioch; and what an act of cruelty to shoot poor Marion Cameron, the sister of Richard! She, with a few female companions, were praying and singing praises in a green hollow place in the moss of Daljig, between the Cumnocks; and having been found incidentally by the troopers, they were shot, and now lie buried in the moor. I understand also that many murders have been committed in the higher parts of Galloway, and in the upland districts of Ayrshire, and the Upper Ward of Lanarkshire has suffered severely—in short, where, where is the place you can name in the south and west where the same deeds are not perpetrated? Truly the red car of persecution is dragged by furious steeds over a bleeding land; surely the cry of a suffering remnant has entered into the ears of the Lord God of Sabaoth, and He surely will arise and avenge the cause that is His own."

Gilbert informed Willie of the shooting of the tailor and the shoemaker, who were well known to him as his associates during the snow storm. On hearing the full account, he was deeply affected, and the tears streamed down his cheeks. "They were," he said, "men very dear to me, and often have I thought of them since, and the sweet and heavenly fellowship we had together; but know you anything of the other two worthy men that were found in the vault after the second snow fell?" "We know nothing of them," said Gilbert; "we have neither seen them nor heard of them since; it may be they are also in the martyr's grave."

"O Willie," said Grizzy, "what fearfu' sights are these we see, and unco sounds we hear in these dismal times! Bluid is seen to fa' frae the clouds; sodgers marching o'er the hills and through the muirs, and then vanishing in a moment. And then what strange sights at some times when the sun is setting! Truly our hearts are failing us for fear, and for looking on those things which are coming upon the earth." "Truly," replied Willie, "I know not what to make of these appearances; but certain it is that they are not uncommon—I myself have witnessed some of them, but it may be they can be explained, I cannot tell, only I know that all is in the Lord's hand, and He will make all things work together for good to His people."

"But," said Willie, "what means that track of blood that I crossed in my path coming through the moor?" "Ah!" said Grizzy, "everything I see I think is tinged wi' bluid—even the very leaves o' the Bible." "But saw ye bluid in the muir," inquired Gilbert, with some degree of anxiety, "saw ye bluid in the muir?" "I certainly did; and it seemed to dye the heath deeper as it proceeded into the moor." "Well, these poachers are always going about, and you know I am the gamekeeper, and it is my duty to look after them; and if you have no objections, we shall walk

out and see what's what." "I heard a shot gae aff in the
muir," said Sandy, "a gude while syne, but I did not go
to the tap o' the knowe to see wha fired it."

Gilbert and the friends, with Willie for their guide, proceeded to the moor, and after wandering about for some
time, came upon the track which Willie had mentioned.
They followed it, and came to a man lying on a soft, green
spot in the moss, and faint through loss of blood. They
had no restoratives with them, not expecting to find a man
in such a predicament. They attempted to raise him, but
he fell down again, being sore enfeebled. The question was,
What was to be done? The boy was despatched to the
house, with all speed, for a hand-barrow, which he found
readily at the side of the peat-stack, without informing
Grizzy of his errand. In a brief space he reached the spot,
and a quantity of soft heather having been spread as litter
on the barrow, he was gently laid on it; and while Gilbert
and Willie bore him along, the others assisted in holding up
his head. The poor man was in great pain, and could
scarcely utter a word. As they came near the house,
Grizzy saw the procession, and soon perceived that they
were bearing a wounded man, for the blood was dripping
on their path. A bed was instantly prepared, on which he
was softly laid till his wounds should be examined. This
was done with all gentleness; and it was found that a ball
had passed through a vital part, and that life must soon become extinct. The restoratives that were administered,
however, revived the weary man, and his spirit seemed to
come again. He looked about him with surprise, and soon
became aware of his situation; but what astonished them
was that he seemed to recognise them, and that he looked
on old familiar faces. He whispered in a low voice, "The
Miny! Gilbert! Grizzy!" and then said, "Do you not
know me? Do you not remember the two men whom, in
the time of the snow, you rescued when apparently dying

of sickness in the little chamber on the side of the vault?
I am one of them; you remember Henry and Andrew?"
He was now fully recognised; but his countenance was so
greatly changed that, without his own statement, they
would not have known him. "How," asked Gilbert, "met
you with this sore accident?" In broken accents he led
them to understand that, in coming through the moor with
the intention of visiting the Miny once more, he encountered
a party of troopers who were passing along, and that without a single question asked, but on the supposition that he
was a Covenanter, he was shot at, and fell on the heath
with his Bible in his hand, which, as he was walking slowly
along, he happened to be reading, and consequently did not
so readily observe their approach, and the more especially
as they had emerged on a sudden from behind a heathy knoll
before him. The sight of the book was enough ; a soldier
fired, and he fell. He felt he was fatally wounded ; but, rising to his feet, he attempted to proceed to the Miny, but became so bewildered that he mistook the direction, and at
last sank down in exhaustion. Gilbert inquired what had
become of his neighbour who had been formerly with him
at the Miny. The answer was that he had died of sickness
and other diseases, caught by means of the privations to
which he had been subjected. It turned out that this was
the person for whom the coffin which was discovered in the
vault was provided, and that he had died a few miles to the
west of Gilbert's residence, and that he was interred on a
green slope on the side of the hill, where a grey stone
marks his resting-place. Andrew lingered till the next
morning, when he died in great peace and comfort of the
Lord. A grave was dug in the deep moss at the end of
the dwelling-house. Grizzy wrapped his body in a pair of
her softest woollen blankets, and without any preparation,
except an armful of scented hay spread on the bottom of
the grave, the body was carried out by the small company

of sincere mourners, and solemnly lowered into its last bed, and all filled up and covered with the benty turf.

When all was over, and the company had gathered into the kitchen to talk over the recent incidents, Grizzy was deeply affected, and affirmed that the grave which she saw in her dream in the deep, dark moss at the end of the house, was precisely like the grave in which they had just laid the bleeding body of the martyr.

"Has it never struck you, dear friends," said Gilbert, "in what peace, and even assurance of their salvation, all our witnesses have died, whether shot on the fields or executed on the scaffold? I confess this is to me one of the strongest proofs of the rightness of our cause; for we see in this the Great Master bearing His testimony of approbation in behalf of His suffering people. We ourselves know, when but lately we were 'drawn to be slain,' with what composure we were enabled to look forward to our death, and with what fortitude, and even joy, the Lord inspired us. We loved life as well as others; we had no ambition to die merely to be honoured as martyrs, and an escape from being shot by those wild dragoons was as acceptable to us as it could have been to other men; still, I believe that every one of us felt as if the sting of death had been taken away. I do not know of one whose last words were heard, or whose last testimony has been given out, who did not die rejoicing in hope of the glory of God." "I trow," said Willie, "this was the case with all my acquaintances who were honoured to seal their testimony with their blood. I had two Lesmahagow friends, John Richmond and Archibald Stewart, who died eminently happy deaths in our Lord's cause. John Richmond said, 'Scare not at the cross of Christ; for O, if you knew what I have met with since I came to prison; what love, what matchless love from my sweet and lovely Lord—ye would long to be with Him, and would count it nought to go through a sea of blood for Him!'

And then what sweet expressions did Archibald Stewart,
that lovely youth of only nineteen years of age, utter in
the immediate prospect of his execution ! I have his very
words here on this paper. 'Now,' says he, 'this is the
sweetest and most joyful day that ever I had since I was
born. My soul blesseth the Lord that ever He made
choice of me to suffer for His noble cause and interest ; that
ever He set His love upon the like of me to give a faithful
testimony to His controverted truths, who was born an heir
of hell and wrath. But now He has redeemed my soul
through His precious blood and suffering, from the power
of sin and Satan, and hath made me to overcome by the
blood of the immaculate Lamb of God. I die not by con-
straint ; I am more willing to die for my lovely Lord and
His truths, than ever I was to live ; and my soul blesseth
the Lord that ever He did accept of a testimony from the
like of me. Scare not at the way of Christ because of
sufferings. He hath paved the cross all over with love, and
hath made all sweet and comfortable to me, and hath made
all my troubles fly away like the morning shadows. O I
cannot express His matchless love to me, neither can I make
mention of His goodness ! O it is but little I can speak to
the commendation of my lovely Lord and His cross !' Thus
speaks Archibald Stewart, my dear and constant friend,
and so then we are not to sorrow as those who have no
hope, for our friends are at rest with Jesus, in whose cause
they suffered, but through whose death, and not through
their own, they have entered into life. We may well
apply to all of them the inscription on the throughstone
that covers the graves of the worthies in Ayr's Moss—

    'Halt, curious passenger, come here and read,
    *Our souls triumph with Christ our glorious Head,*
    In self-defence we murdered here do lie,
    To witness 'gainst this nation's perjury.' "

"May the Lord prepare us all," said Gilbert, "for whatever may be before us ! We stand in jeopardy every hour.

Our churches are desolate, and their congregations are scattered on the mountains, and driven into desert places before ravening wolves. 'O God, how long shall the adversary reproach! Shall the enemy blaspheme Thy name for ever? Why withdrawest Thou Thy hand, even Thy right hand? Pluck it out of Thy bosom, for God is my King of old, working salvation in the midst of the earth.' Let our confidence be in God—we are safe in His hands."

"I expect," said Grizzy, "a visit this evening from the gudeman of Powmerlog, and my sister Sarah—a sister in affliction, and in the faith of Christ, and a sweet companion in tribulation. It was their wish to spend a night with us here, and to unite with us in giving thanks to the Lord for our late deliverance." Powmerlog, as we have already noticed, was on the other side of the moss, and was a small moorland farm, something like the Miny, and belonging to the same laird. Peter Corsan had possessed it for a number of years, and was a man much esteemed by his landlord. Indeed, his sterling character commanded the respect of all. He originally belonged to the parish of Sorn—the native place of Mr Peden; in consequence of this, and because they had been intimate in their younger days, Mr Peden made Powmerlog one of his places of resort, and always found a cordial welcome. On this account not a few conventicles were held by him in this secluded locality, though the troopers seldom visited the place, as it lay so much out of their way. On the day on which the man was shot on the moor, the soldiers paid this lonely place a visit. As they advanced but slowly through the moor, Peter, who saw them in the distance, absconded, driving his two horses before him up the hollow of the burn into a creek, where they were concealed from the view. When the horsemen were in sight of the place, Peter presented himself full in their view on the brow of the hill. His object was to decoy them from the dwelling-house; and to convince them that he was the man they were seeking, he threw off his coat, waved his bonnet in defiance, and betook himself to flight. As he fled he always allowed them to keep sight of him, till he had wiled them several miles out of their way; sometimes leading them into the morass, and sometimes up the face of the steep hill, and round the head of a ravine, and when they had doubled it, he mocked their pursuit by rushing down its precipitous bank, and appearing on the other side. In this way he twisted them backwards and forwards, and round the height, and across the morasses, till the day began to decline, and the evening mists to gather on the tops of the hills. His object was now to lead them into a path by which they might be able to find their way home, as they were now a number of miles from his house. Having thus gained his design, he soon disappeared from their view behind a rising ground, and then ensconsed himself in the deep channel of a dry water-course, from which he could trace their march in the right direction to their own quarters. Peter returned in safety, and was met at the door by Sarah, who, with a glad heart, saw him descending the height before the door, driving the horses before him. "You have been long away, my dear Peter, and I have been earnest in prayer for your safety, and the Lord has answered." Peter was never again troubled with a visit from the troopers, but this was much owing to Geordy Ga', now installed in room of Cochrane, and whose mother and Sarah had been intimate acquaintances.

We now return from our digression to notice the visit which Peter and Sarah paid on the projected evening to the Miny. It was about the dusk when they arrived, and the friends went out into the moor to meet them. The motherly Sarah clasped the affectionate Grizzy in her arms. "Our husbands have been spared to us, dear Grizzy ; it is the Lord's doing, and it is wondrous in our eyes, and to Him be our acknowledgements." The whole company now gath-

ered round the hearth of the Miny, consisting of the two
men from the Glenkens, Willie from Lesmahagow, Peter
and Sarah, with Gilbert, Grizzy, and the boy. The time
was spent in spiritual exercises till far on in the night.
Thanksgivings were rendered to the Lord for their preservation, and fervent prayer ascended to the throne on high
in behalf of their brethren, and particularly for those that
were appointed unto death, that the "Lord would spare
the green and take the ripe." Their meeting was a happy
one; for He in whose cause they suffered was in the midst
of them according to His promise. "O how happy!" exclaimed Sarah, "how happy are we here, and how safe
under our heavenly Father's protection! The enemies
think they make us miserable, but never were men so entirely outwitted. Our peace is with God, through the death
of His own Son, and who shall rob us of this peace? Nothing but sin can do this, and it must be our care to avoid it,
and then we need not fear the sufferings that may come
upon us." "It is indeed a bitter blast that blows in our
face," said Gilbert, "but we must breast the storm as best
we may, and better be beaten prostrate on the ground by
it, than seek a shelter which our conscience disavows. O
sirce, how difficult it is to keep our garments clean in these
defiling times! but surely the satisfaction of a good conscience is more to us than all the temporal security that we
can purchase by a foul compliance." In this way did they
strengthen one another, and encourage themselves in the
Lord their God, and the sweet refreshment of that meeting
remained on their spirits many days after.

---

## CHAPTER IX.

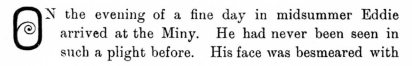

ON the evening of a fine day in midsummer Eddie
arrived at the Miny. He had never been seen in
such a plight before. His face was besmeared with

blood, his clothes hung in tatters, and the poor cuddie was
all beplastered with black moss. "Eddie, Eddie," exclaimed
honest Gilbert, "what is the matter? Why man, you seem
as if you had come from a battle-field. What in the world
has befallen you?" "Speak, dear Eddie," cried the tender-
hearted Grizzy. "Are you hurt or are you sick? Have
the troopers fa'en foul o' ye, or has the brute beast thrown
ye?—and sic a canny beast too." "Na, na, nane o' these
things," responded the worthy keelman, "but I hae faen
amang thieves—thieves, gude wife. I hae been set upon
wi' thieves, and that is what never befel me before, during a'
the tedious years I hae wandered among these wild muirs."
"Thieves!" exclaimed Gilbert, "whar came they frae?—
poachers you mean?" "Why, on that score," said Eddie,
"there is no very muckle difference, as I opine ; as the ane
is so is the other—for if a man poach he will steal, for what
is poachin' but stealin', and if a man will steal he will poach.

"But to make the matter plain, as the cuddie and me
were coming tentily through the moor yonder, and as the
moss was something dry, I thought I would take a near
cut and come straught through by the upper end o' the
flowe, thinking the moss might bear the craiter's weight and
mysel' alang wi' it, when a' at ance plump went donkey to
the belly. My twa feet restit on the surface, and I easily
steppit frae its back, but when I did so I sank to the knees,
and sae I could neither help the beast nor the beast me. I
struggled and warsled till I got out ane fit, and syne
anuther, for ye see I had but twa feet to release while the
cuddie had four. Weel, ye see, I fought away till I
warsled round to the other side, where the moss was firmer,
and then I took the helter, and poo'd and tuggit at the beast's
head, but he remained fixt. I then ventured to apply the
whip—a thing I seldom do, for indeed I would never carry
a whip at a' were it not for fashion's cause, and just to be
like other folk that ride and that hae a travellin' equipage

to guide—but a' wadna do, and then I fleetcht and straikit
the poor brute about the neck, and the kindly craiter lookit
wistfully in my face, as muckle as to say, 'I wad, but I
canna.' It made a struggle to get on to its knees, but sank
down again; then it tried to waggle frae side to side, but
still it lay. I saw that effort was useless, and resolved to
seek help, if aiblins I might meet wi' a shepherd, or some
stray wanderer on the moor. I wandered, I daur say, a
mile o' gate aff, lookin' up and doon for the needed help.
At length I spied two men at some distance, and I waved wi'
my bonnet, and they obeyed the signal. I mentioned the
circumstances to them, and asked their assistance. I led
them to the spot, and what was my surprise to find the
cuddie calmly grazing on the bent as if nathing had
happened. I was never mair astonished; and the men
plainly saw how the matter stood, for the animal was a'
smeared o'er wi' the moss, but hoo the thing happened
passes me."

"But what of the robbers, Eddie; how fared ye wi'
them?" exclaimed Gilbert. "Why," replied Eddie, "these
men were the robbers, as ye shall hear; so ye see, when
they perceived how the matter stood, they winkit at ane
another, and said—'But old man, what do you allow us
for our trouble? You have brought us far out of our
road, and we, having urgent business on hand, cannot
afford to be detained; so then, if you please, friend, we demand wages for our work.' I plainly saw that they were
set on mischief, and that they actually belonged to that
class of plunderers that are at present infesting the country
to such an extent. I found it was needless to resist, for
what could I do? I then said, 'What will please you?
and I shall willingly give what is reasonable.' 'Nothing
less than your entire equipage will please us,' said they.
'That is hard,' I replied; 'for you see I am but a poor
man, earning my daily bread by the sale o' the bits o' ar-

ticles I carry on the donkey's back, and indeed he is nearly
as frail as mysel'.  I hope you are not in earnest, and don't
intend to harry a poor body like me at my helpless time of
life.'  'None of your whining,' said they; 'Yield all up
instantly.  Robbery is our trade, and we follow it just as
you do yours;' and so they seized the creels and emptied
them on the turf, and when I remonstrated, one of them
struck me on the face with his staff, and so belaboured me
otherwise, that I was driven donart, and fell senseless on
the moss.  How long I lay in this condition, I cannot tell;
but I awoke as from a sleep, and found myself all sore and
bleeding.  The men were gone, and the cuddie was grazing
quietly on the bent.  On examining the state of matters, I
found that I was plundered of everything.  The creels were
emptied ; my pockets were rifled, and every farthing I had
was gone—nothing, I may say was left me but a morsel of
bread and cheese in my wallet, which, indeed, was a mercy ;
for, on eating a mouthful or two, I began to revive.  I now
found that no bones were broken, and that the wounds
though bleeding were not deep.  I washed off the blood in
the moss water, and felt much refreshed.  I then replaced
the creels—which were now light enough for the poor
animal to carry.  I mounted his back once more, and tentily
traced my way to your hospitable abode, and so I am here
again, although through fear and peril, thanks to the great
Preserver of our lives."

"O, Eddie, dear Eddie, you are most welcome to our
hame, and you must no more expose yourself in this way ;
we complain of the soldiers, and good reason have we, but
we have even more reason to complain of these heartless
plunderers, who, taking occasion of the troublous times,
steal and rob on all hands."

On the morrow, Peter Corsan entered the Miny almost
out of breath, for he had suspected that mischief had befallen his poor friend Eddie, in the moor.  He was, how-

ever agreeably surprised to see him sitting snugly in the
kitchen of the Miny. " Eddie," said he, " I was in deep
concern about you, for I imagined that you had met with
some severe disaster." " How did that strike you?" replied
Eddie. " Why in this way," said Peter ; " three men came
to our door in the dusk, and as the darkness and the mist
soon set down in the moor, we pressed them to abide with
us during the night. We found that they were brethren
in the suffering cause, who, along with others, had escaped
from the Canongate Tolbooth in Edinburgh, and had made
their way into the country, where they hid through the
day among the tall corn, and in the thickets by the wayside,
and travelled under the cloud of night. As they came
southward, and got into the mountainous districts, they
advanced with more freedom. Yesterday they crossed the
country from Douglas Water, and, getting into the uplands
of Kyle, they arrived incidentally at my house. As we
were conversing on many things, they mentioned an occur-
rance that gave me no small concern. They stated that in
passing through the moor, and on approaching the side of
the flowe, they encountered a donkey sunk to the belly in
the soft moss. No one was with the animal, and it seemed
to be much exhausted, and quite helpless. They then
applied all their strength and relieved the poor beast from
its lairy bed, where it must soon have expired. They left
it grazing on the heath, and then made their way over the
mosshags. It instantly occurred to me that it might be
your cuddie, and so I made further inquiries—if it carried
creels, if the half of its left ear was cropt, and if one of its
eyeballs was of a whitish colour—and having ascertained
all this to be the fact, I had not the shadow of a doubt that
the equipage was Eddie's. But the question was, What
had become of him? Was he buried in the flowe beside the
poor donkey? I got no rest during the night, and I resolved
that when the morning dawned I should set out for the

Miny, and now I find Eddie here, and I suppose the cuddie will not be far off." "I am here, dear Peter, and I thank you heartily for the interest you take in me, and I as cordially thank my dear friends in the Miny here for all their solicitude on my poor behalf. It was all true the men told you, and this explains to me a circumstance I could not well account for—namely, how the feckless cuddie found his footing on the hard turf. It appeared to me something like miraculous, but it seems to have been accomplished by ordinary means after all. God's providence gives us every thing, and blessed be His name." "Eddie, dear Eddie," replied honest Peter, "we can never repay you for your kind interference in getting our lives spared when we were led forth to execution." "Never mention that, Peter; it was not me, it was the Lord ; it was He who ordered the whole circumstances, and to Him be our acknowledgments."

"But, Peter," said Gilbert, "who were the men you entertained last night ? Are you sure they were not thieves and robbers ? Eddie fell among thieves when he met his mischance; they plundered his creels, and then wounded him, and left him for dead on the bent." "These ruffians," replied Peter, "are rife at present ; but the men whom I received are true men. They were on their way to the Vennel, at the mouth of Glen Aylmer, in Kirkconnel. They are well acquainted with the Hairs of Glenwharry. They were caught at a conventicle in Douglas Water, whence they were carried with others to Edinburgh, and there lodged in jail. Here they suffered many hardships, but they at length made their escape."

As they were conversing, a gentle rap was heard at the door, and Jonas Stewart, from the Mosscastle in Crawfordjohn, was introduced into the kitchen of the Miny. Gilbert and Jonas were old friends, but for a good while, owing to the troublous times and their distance from each other, they had had but little intercourse. Jonas was an intelligent, upright, godly man, and a friend who could be depended on at all times. He had sustained much injury from the persecuting party. He had been often spoiled of a considerable part of his property, but his life had hitherto been shielded, and he had never been captured by the enemy. His place of residence was in the heart of a wild locality, for Crawfordjohn was at that period characterised by its desert aspect and the rudeness of its population. It was long proverbial for its seclusion, so that the saying became common—"Out o' the warld and into Crawfordjohn." But the state of things in this parish is in our days entirely reversed. Crawfordjohn can now vie with any one of the contiguous parishes, both with regard to the culture of its soil and its inhabitants.

In the days of worthy Jonas, however, matters were at a very poor pass ; the very name of his domicile, the Mosscastle, or the castle in the moss, like the house of the Miny, or moss, indicates the condition of the parochial surface as being composed chiefly of moss and marshes. Some ancient feudal baron, of name now unknown, had reared in the moss his square tower, as best he might, for his defence. The whole country around was studded at certain distances with these towers, the ruins of which are everywhere apparent.

Jonas and Gilbert felt all the ardour of their former friendship revive, and their Christian fellowship was warm and edifying. Jonas spent some days at the Miny and got acquainted with Peter Corsan and others who occasionally resorted to Gilbert's house. As for Eddie, he knew him well, for Mosscastle was one of his stations in his trudging among the wilds. Eddie often imparted to him useful information regarding the designs of the enemy, which he had gathered in his journeyings ; and, indeed, it was much owing to Eddie that the visit of Jonas to the Miny was paid. From Eddie's account of the incidents that befel at the Miny, and especially the story of the capture and the rescue on the occasion of the conventicle at Glenmuirshaw, the heart of the honest patriarch at Mosscastle yearned over Gilbert and his worthy spouse, and he could not rest till he found himself before the hearth of the Miny.

It was when speaking of Eddie's adventure in the moss, and the loose state of the country through the disorganisation of society, caused by the persecution, that Jonas detailed the following disastrous incidents :—"We have," he said, "down in our parish of Crawfordjohn, there, experienced much distress, not only from the lawless interference of the military, which is bad enough, but also from these depredators who make it their business to live by plunder. My neighbour of Mountherick, was lately robbed of all his valuables, by a band of ruffians who invaded his house by night. They rifled every chest and drawer, and carried off all the money, and when he remonstrated, they bound him hand and foot, and left him in his helplessness on the floor. The dragoons never wrought more mischief than did these loose and wicked men. They run from place to place, and pretend that they have authority for all they do, and refer you to the conduct of the soldiers as their example."

"On another occasion," added Jonas, "my neighbour of the Glaspen met with the same treatment from these strolling robbers, but with even a worse result, for being violently opposed, they were so enraged that they set the barn on fire, and the stackyard, and consumed a great quantity of victual." "We heard of that," said Gilbert, "but did they not kill one of the household ?" "Not exactly," replied Jonas, "but a woman had her clothes set on fire, and she must have been burnt to death, had they not drenched her plentifully with water. The case you referred to happened in Glengonar, where a scuffle took place between the servants and the robbers. A worthy lad was killed on the spot while defending his master's property. But this is little thought of, for they scruple at no such deed in the way of gaining their object.

Stanehill has suffered, and so has Birkcleuch—nor has Whitecleuch been exempted. Mosscastle has come in for its share. I have been subjected once and again to these plunderings, but particularly one night before rent day, when I had collected the sum to pay it to the factor at Douglas on the following morning, these evil men beset my house, made a forcible entrance, and carried all off. Whether they understood anything about the rent, I cannot say, but they gained their end.

Two of my intimate acquaintances were one evening coming from a fair in Douglas, and when they reached the head of Earnsallach burn, they were confronted with a batch of these fellows, who instantly fell upon them and spoiled them of all they had. They were thankful to escape without further injury." "And so they might," said Eddie, "for what is siller to one's life, or to broken banes, either ?" "You mentioned Earnsallach burn," added Gilbert, "it was a sore affliction that befel honest James Gavin, the tailor from Douglas, when Claverhouse cropt off his ears that morning he passed the head of the linn." "Aye," replied Eddie ; "he was obliged to his tarrier dog that abode with him in the cave, for that gude turn ; the yelpin' craiter with its barking, made Clavers search the place." "Ah, but he was a worthy man, James Gavin ; I hae heard muckle gude o' him though I never saw him."

"I know him well," said Jonas, "we always employed him in our house, and no man ever entered my door that was more welcome than he. His conversation was aye heavenly, and he always bore himself so devoutly that he was an eniment example of goodness to all. He seemed to live in the constant expectation of being caught one day by the troopers, and to endure the martyrdom which fell to the lot of many of his brethren around. When he wrought

in my house he would sleep nowhere but in the barn or in
some out-place, lest he should be suddenly surprised by the
enemy.   It was this that led him to the cave the night before he was caught by Claverhouse."   "I understand," said
Eddie, "he is to be banished, with a number more, to the
West Indies."   "Aye," replied Grizzy, "they may banish
God's saints as they like; they may shoot them in the
moors; they may lock them in their jails; they may kill
them on the scaffolds; they may chase them in the wilderness, and hide them in dens and in caves of the earth—and
muckle waur than a' this, if they can; but the church of
Christ will survive, because the gates of hell shall not
prevail against her.   Mr Peden was just saying, that the
crack of our Lord's winding-sheet will scare the enemy like
the craws on the height, and awaken the slumbering church
to assert her right position."

"I now see," said Peter Corsan, "that we must tak' tent
o' these robbers.   The state of society is much disordered,
and we owe this to our persecutors.   They have driven men
from their holdings—servants, and masters, and merchants
have all been thrown loose, and sent forth as beggars and
thieves abroad on the community.   I live in a secluded
place beyond the moss, to which few can find their way,
and am therefore not much troubled; but I pity those who
are exposed to the plunderings of those lawless men."

All that Peter Corsan said was true.   The state of matters
at this time were, in reference to this same particular, most
distressing; and our remarks in this chapter are given
principally in elucidation of this.   It is the prominent
points observable in this great persecution that we wish to
take hold of, and to present to the notice of the reader.   Dr
Hetherington, in his history of the Church of Scotland, says
"that the twenty-eight years of tyranny and persecution
had wasted the land, reducing many of its fertile districts
to the condition of a wilderness, and throwing a vast pro-

portion of the middle and industrious classes into deep poverty. The inevitable consequence was that nearly all the lower classes of the population were both thrown completely out of employment by the ruin of the class immediately above them, and habituated to idleness, vagrance, and pillage, by the encouragement and example of the devastating soldiery, and the use made of them to assist in destroying the property of the respectable Presbyterians. Thus the existence of two hundred thousand vagrants, by whom the country was so greivously infested, was one of the direct results of the attempt to establish Prelacy in Scotland ; and it is no wonder that such people were ready, at the instigation of those around whose paths of carnage they had so long prowled and battened, to rush anew on their wonted task of perpetrating insult and violence against the persons of Presbyterian ministers, and of interrupting the most sacred ordinances of religion."

This witness is true—the people were thrown into confusion—men seemed not to know what to do, nor where to fix their abode. "The persecution called forth a host of bad characters, who practised on its stage during the time it lasted, and when it passed away, it left them as a residuum in the community. These evil men were not confined to one class of the community, they were to be found in all ranks, and they appeared boldly and in the face of day. The evil genius of the nation seemed to be evoked by the persecution, and wickedness was drawn forth and fostered as if it had been the only good—the only glory of a country." Hence the hosts of robbers, and thieves, and fire-raisers that were everywhere to be found in the south and west of Scotland."

"I well remember," said Gilbert, "the Highland host that came into the western parts in the *seventy-eight*, the year of Claverhouse, when he first appeared on the bloody theatre. The ravages of these kilted savages were excessive;

no classes were spared ; all were treated alike—Prelatists and Presbyterians—persecutors and persecuted—gentle and semple—no matter what might be their condition—high or low, rich or poor—wherever there was spoil to be had, all were plundered, friend and foe without distinction. To such an extremity were matters carried, that the persecutors themselves were most thankful to get free of them, and when they left the country it is well known what booty they carried with them."

"Ay," said Eddie, "and we hae the remnants of these Heelanders among us still, and they are as busy reivin' and stealing as they were eight years ago. I can assert from what I know that there are scores if not hundreds of these wild men still traversing the country, and that they are made use of by the troopers to do their dirty work. An ordinary trooper, bad as he is, is an honourable person compared with these northern savages. I hae forgethered wi' them frequently in company wi' the regular soldiers, so that I was the less afraid."

These remarks of Eddie were precisely in keeping with the facts of the case. The following are the statements of Patrick Walker, a man who lived in the persecuting period, and long after it, and a man of sincere godliness, who had suffered much, having been, as he says, twice in the enemy's hands. He left behind him a goodly number of reminiscences of some of the worthies of that time, especially of Peden, Cargill, Cameron, Wellwood, and James Renwick. He lived to correct some of the incidental mistakes of Wodrow, particularly as it regarded himself, and other matters of which he was personally cognisant. He states, "That there are many thousands yet alive, who can witness from their sad experience, that there were a thousand Highlanders, in the month of March, 1685, six years after Bothwell, who were sent to the south and west of Scotland, it being killing time, to assist the forces, they being more

swift of foot to run through bog and moss, hill and glen, to
apprehend the sufferers, than the standing forces, who were
turned fat and lazy with free quartering, and strong feed-
ing upon the ruins of the Lord's people.  As also these
Highlanders were brought to the west to rob and plunder,
and to frighten people, more especially women and children
by their strange, uncouth language, not knowing whether
they were to kill them or save them alive, which is a great
aggravation of a judgment ; and what great murder and
robbery they committed these three months that they were
in the south and west of Scotland !  There is one instance
among many that I could give which I cannot pass.  When
they came to the south, through the parish of Morrinside,
the curate there, Mr Andrew Ure, informed them of worthy
Peter Gilles, who lived in that parish, who apprehended
him, with John Brice, who lived in the parish of West Cal-
der, and when they went through the parish of Carluke,
they apprehended William Fenneson and Thomas Young,
who lived there, whom the Laird of Lee's footman apprehended, on whom they exercised great cruelty.  They carried these four prisoners to Machlon, and apprehended one
James Binning, waiting upon cattle, without either stocking
or shoe, and took their Bibles from them, and would suffer
none either to sell them, or to lend them Bibles—the first
four were my very dear acquaintances—and hanged them
all upon one gibbet, without suffering them to pray at their
death, and their corpses were buried upon the spot."

After this interview with his friends at the Miny, Jonas
set out for his home.  On his way he visited Friarminion
and Blagannoch, Gareland and Shielstanes, at all which
places he received a cordial welcome.  He then plodded his
way down the Spank, a streamlet that falls into the ancient
river Crawick.  In the dusk he reached Mosscastle, but
there heavy tidings awaited him.  The dragoons had been
there the day before, and Peter Inglis had seized the best

horse in the stable, an article always in request by the
troopers.  But this was not all ; a fat bullock was loosed
from the stall as a fair prize, and Inglis compelled Johas's
servant to drive the animal before them across the moor to
Douglas ; and so honest Jonas was left with one horse only,
and bereaved of the bullock, which was intended to be
slaughtered as food for his household.  But to all this the
good man submitted, and thanked the Lord that matters
were no worse—he might have been personally captured ;
his ears might have been cropped ; he might have been sent
to prison ; his premises might have been set on fire, or
himself unceremoniously shot on the bent.

   After the departure of the good Jonas, the household of
the Miny was somewhat thoughtful and silent.  At length
Grizzy said, "I think, sirce, we hae muckle need to spain
oursel's frae this warld and a' its concerns ; for, ye see, our
lives are not only uncertain, but a' that we possess is equally
uncertain.  The dragoons may shoot, and the robbers may
plunder—everything is at hazard.  Be it our wisdom, then,
to seek that life and those riches of which none can rob us."
"Ay," said Eddie, "I mysel' hae gotten a gude lesson with
regard to a' time's uncertainties ; my property is stown—
my life has been nearly at an end.  I might hae been lying
a corpse on the moor at this moment, and the puir cuddie
cauld dead beside me ; but I am alive, thanks to the great
Preserver of our lives ; and as to my future through-bear-
ing, I hope to maintain myself by my honest calling as
heretofore."  "Yes, Eddie," exclaimed Gilbert, "we will
ne'er see ye want.  Ye shall share the last morsel wi' us,
and ye hae a gude richt till't."  "Dinna speak o' richt,
Gibby, my man—dinna speak o' richt.  I claim naething ;
it is to Him who rules aboon, and guides a', that we owe
thanks for *what* we are and *where* we are at this moment."

## CHAPTER X.

IN our chapters relative to the sufferings of our Covenanting ancestry, it is necessary to notice the *curates*, and to give them some little prominence as actors in the persecution. It is well known that they were the main instigators of much of the mischief that befel the Nonconformists in those distressful days. At the commencement of the persecution, when upwards of four hundred of the Presbyterian ministers were ejected from their charges by what was termed "the Drunken Council," at Glasgow, it became necessary that their places should be supplied. Their successors, then, according to the Prelatic style, were termed curates, and the introduction of these officials forms a curious episode in the ecclesiastical history of Scotland. It is not easy to define their position ; but one thing is plain, that they formed an entire contrast to the worthy men who were their predecessors. Never was a class of individuals, in any official situation, more highly esteemed than were the Presbyterian ministers generally who occupied the Scottish pulpits immediately before the Restoration. They were all of them well-educated men—men of sincere piety—men well instructed in the gospel, and many of them connected with the best families in the land. They were universally beloved by their flocks, not only on account of their sanctity, but also on account of their kindliness and of the deep interest they took in the concerns of their people. The novel ministers, however, the Prelatic intruders, were persons of an entirely different stamp ; and both their official talents and their moral character were of such a nature as produced an uncontrollable revulsion in the popular mind. "They were," says the historian Wodrow, "they were mostly young men from the northern shires,

raw, and without any stock of reading or gifts. These were
brought west in a year or two after they had gone through
their philosophy in the college, and, having nothing to subsist upon, were greedily gaping after benefices. To such
the common people were ready to ascribe all the characters
of Jeroboam's priests ; and it must be owned great multitudes of them were as void of morality and gravity as they
were of learning and experience, and scarce had the very
appearance of religion and devotion. They came into the
parishes with much the same views as a herd hath when he
contracts to feed cattle ; and such plenty of them came from
the north at this time, that it is said a gentleman of that
country cursed the Presbyterian ministers heartily, 'for,'
said he, 'since they have been turned out we cannot have a
lad to keep our cows.'

"Their personal character was black ; and no wonder
their entertainment was coarse and cold. In some places
they were welcomed with tears in abundance, and entreaties
to be gone ; in others, with reasonings and arguments which
confounded them ; and some entertained them with threats,
affronts, and indignities, too many here to be repeated.
The bell's tongue in some places was stolen away, that the
parishioners might have an excuse for not coming to church.
The doors of the church in other places were barricaded,
and they made to enter by the window, literally. The
laxer of the gentry easily engaged them to join in drunken
cabals, which, with all iniquity, did now fearfully abound,
and sadly exposed them ; and in some places the people,
fretted with the dismal change, gathered together and
violently opposed their settlement, and received them with
showers of stones. This was not, indeed, the practice of
the religious and more judicious; such irregularities were
committed by the more ignorant vulgar. Such who were
really serious mourned in secret, as doves in the valley, and
from principle could never countenance them.

"Some of them—alas! too many—were heard swearing very rudely in the open streets. And this was but of a piece with the doctrine taught in their pulpits—that to swear by faith, conscience, and the like, were innocent ways of speaking. Instances were sadly common of their staggering in the streets and wallowing in the gutters, even in the canonical habits; and this needs be no surprise, when they were witnesses to Bishop Wishart's preaching publicly, that *he* was not to be reckoned a drunkard who was now and then overtaken with wine or strong liquor, but *he only* who made a trade of following after strong drink."

Such were the men whom the bishops employed in the parishes to promote the cause in which they had embarked. The doctrines of the Gospel—which it is the peculiar office of a preacher to announce to his audience—they understood not; and in this respect they were immeasurably inferior to the peasantry who had been soundly instructed by the holy and learned men who had been removed to make room for persons so unfit to occupy their place. Their sermons had no substance, no point, no doctrine—the glory was departed from the churches, and the sound of the Gospel was not heard within their walls. These curates were greedy hirelings; they had no sympathy with the people among whom they lived, for they were, for the most part, strangers and needy adventurers, who sought the fleece, but cared not for the flock. The Prelates and the Council had not a better organised agency in the land, one that was more widely spread, or more supple and subservient to their will. They had by this means a constituency in almost every parish on which they could firmly count, and which was on all occasions devoted to their interests. No class of persons, therefore, were more despised, and even hated, by the people than these curates. Their churches were for the most part deserted, and they were obliged to harangue to empty pews. The desertion of their places of worship was a matter of

severe mortification to these Prelatists.  No wonder that
the people retired to the conventicles, and that the great
Master of Assemblies retired with them.  How appropriate
are the following lines of Hislop the poet !—

"In cities the wells of salvation were seal'd,
More brightly to burst on the moor and the field,
And the spirit that fled from the dwellings of men,
Like a manna-cloud rained on the camp in the glen."

It is stated that one of these curates, either he of Muirkirk, or he of Strathaven, on entering the pulpit one Sabbath morning, and finding the church nearly empty, was so
exasperated that he vehemently exclaimed, "Black be my
fa' but they are a' aff to the hill folk thegether ; sorra gin I
dinna tell, and they'll be a' shot or hangit be Yule."

The curates kept a list of those who, in the parish, did
not attend the church, and when a company of soldiers
visited the place, they put the roll into the hand of the
commander, who, being guided by it, made special inquisition throughout the district, and captured or plundered all
the recusants they could find.  On the Sabbath the soldiers
were stationed at the church doors, and counted the people
as they retired, and took their names, so that the absentees
were easily ascertained.  In this way the curates wrought
the work of their masters, and became the cause of indescribable distress, particularly in the rural parts.  It is no
wonder, then, that the people wished to rid themselves of
these incumbents, or to flee from the places infested by them.

But even among these same curates there were cases
where compunctious visitings were strongly experienced,
and instances were not infrequent here and there of these
officials abandoning their position, and casting in their lot
with the persecuted Covenanters.  Mowat, the curate of
Kirkconnel, in Upper Nithsdale, is an example of this.
This Mowat lived at a place called Glen-muckcloch, or "the
glen of the boar's stone," as the name signifies, at a consider-

able distance from his Church, situated near the mouth of the romantic defile of Glen Aylmer, a magnificent gorge that cleaves the green mountains on the north, a grand feature in nature, to which few glens can be compared. It occured to Mowat to pay a visit to his neighbour, the curate of Muirkirk. He had many a weary step to trudge through the lonely moors that lay between him and his destination. He was a man of a somewhat generous disposition, and though he approved of Prelacy, and adhered to it as a system of ecclesiastical polity, yet he hesitated in giving his full concurrence to the measures which were employed for establishing it in the land. He wended his way by Penauchrie, a mountain streamlet that gurgles down a rugged gully on the slope of the hill, and reached the summit of the green height that overlooks the steep ravine of of Glenwharry. He then got into the footpath that leads through the moorland towards the house of Auchtytinch. As he pursued his way he encountered a person of a very patriarchal appearance, resting on a grey stone by the wayside. "Good day to ye," said the venerable man, "good day to ye ; I see you are sair forfochen wi' your journey." "I think," said Mowat, "that these rugged heights and rough moors are not for aged persons like you to traverse." "They are not," replied he, "but necessity compels. And I was just thinking before you came forward, in surveying that bleak and weary solitude that spreads itself before us, with its black moss hags, and deep mountain runners, how many worthy persons without a shelter and without a home may be concealed in these lonely wastes, in hunger, and in destitution of all things." "You allude to the Noncomformists, I opine," said Mowat, "but you know they are rebels and it is not for us to speak well of them." "Ah," replied the old man, "an avenging sword, an avenging sword, for thee, bluidy land ! Lord, when wilt Thou avenge the bluid of Cameron and Cargill, the bluid of Kid and King,

and all the bluid that has been shed in these dismal times ?
O Scotland, Scotland, a bluidy sword for thee !" And then
lifting his bonnet from his head, and fixing his eyes on the
blue heavens, while his silvery hairs were streaming in the
mountain breeze, he exclaimed with great energy, "Lord,
spare the green and take the ripe." And with this he
darted away, and left the astonished curate fixed to his
seat. " What a wild, warlock figure," said he to himself,
" can this be ? Surely the man is in a frenzy, or he is one
of those fanatical men who live in desert places, and are
driven about without an aim wherever their unhappy genius
impels them. Poor man ! I pity him ; how he speeds his
way as if pursued by a host every moment ready to seize
him. I am persuaded he has been chased before; perchance
he is one of those raving Covenanters whom the very
whistling of the bent in the wind puts to flight, as it does
the downy gossamer on the waste." Thus ruminated
Mowat, and then plodded his way along the mossy footpath
till he reached the base of the speckled height of Penbreck.

Here, as he crossed the rivulet that descends from the
hill, he encountered all at once a company of troopers in a
beautiful green hollow. The commander was well known
to Mowat, for he was the redoubted Crichton himself. "Ho,
Mowat, is this you ? Whereabouts in these parts ?" " I
am bound for Muirkirk, to visit my friend the curate there."
" What, ho, Winton !—our boon companion ; and a brave
fellow he is ; as void of grace as a pagan, but none the
worse of that, you know, for he just suits our purpose so
much the better. Why, I'll tell you, friend Mowat, if it
were not for you fellows—you worthy curates, I mean—I
humbly guess that our harvest-field of what these wild
mountain men call persecution, forsooth, would soon be
reaped, and the whole produce be gathered into the barn-
yard—I mean the kirkyard, or whatever place of deposit
may be assigned these same lusty sheaves that our well-

tempered sickles so deftly reap, whither on moor or mountain or grassy plain.   I say, were it not for you honest fellows, our harvest would soon be reaped ; for when we are
at a loss for work you find it for us, and conjure up Nonconformists on every side, and thus you furnish us with
abundance of congenial employment, for all which you deserve
our thanks, as leal-hearted cavaliers."   "But sir," said Mowat,
"what means your meeting here in this lonely spot?"   "Lonely
spot !  why, let me tell you there are no places better frequented   than   these   same   solitudes — for   what   with
conventiclers, and  troopers, and  persons  in  concealment,
these deserts are far from being solitary ; nay, the bees
among the heather blooms there, that go buzzing and booming past your ears, are scarcely as numerous as these
pestilent fellows that infest the wastes.   But as to your
question—why, we are about, as you may see, to shoot
these two dogs, surrounded by the troopers, for they have
transgressed the Conventicle Act.   A wild, grey-headed
rebel they call Peden—a fanatic who keeps the whole
uplands in a ferment, and on whom we have never yet been
able to lay our hands, for there seems to be some enchant-
ment about him ; but, however it be, the old wizard can
never be caught.   Well, I was saying this same madman,
and warlock, and rebel, has been holding a conventicle over
the hill there, and we caught these men in the act of flight,
but him we missed."   "The very man," said Mowat to
himself, "I met not an hour ago seated on the grey stone
by the footpath ;" but he revealed not the circumstance.

The two men stood ready to be sacrificed.   "Prepare,"
cried Crichton, "for immediate execution."   The men knelt
on the bent, and poured forth a prayer full of fervency and
tenderness, and of such implicit confidence in God, that it
produced a strange impression on all present.   "I think,"
said Mowat, who felt unusual emotions, "I think that the
lives of these men might be spared.   You may say that

they ought to suffer death as a warning to all others.  Now in my opinion, one living witness is worth two dead ones ; and therefore, instead of shooting them, I will crop off their ears and let them go, and this, perchance, may go further as a warning than if they were hidden in a mossy grave. This, you know, was the punishment inflicted on James Crosbie in Nithsdale, and on James Gavin in Douglas.  I think the experiment may at least be tried, and I am per- suaded it will have a good effect " This proposal was agreed to ; their ears were cropt, and the poor fellows, with the warm blood flowing down into their necks, and endur- ing intolerable pain, were dismissed with the plain warning that the next offence would be visited with the unsparing shot of the troopers.

The curate, along with Crichton and his dragoons, moved off in the direction of Muirkirk.  Mowat received a cordial welcome from the curate, with whom he had formerly spent many an evening in deep carousals.  On this occasion it happened that the curate was to give an entertainment to his intimate associates that same evening.  Crichton, and Strachon the trooper from Cumnock, Peter Inglis from Douglas, the curate of Sorn, and he of Strathaven, with a batch of riotous lairds and farmers, gathered from the neighbourhood, were invited to convene in the curate's domicile.  The night was spent in sheer debauchery, for what with eating, and drinking, and swearing, and bully- ing, it was next to unparalleled.  The whole company was in a perfect uproar, and blows were in some quarters very freely exchanged.  The noise was heard without, and the rabble convened before the door.  The uproar within was responded to by the crowd, and instantly a shower of stones and other missiles were sent smashing through the windows straight into the apartment.  All was confusion ; some were struck on the head, and others were wounded in various parts ; the bottles and glasses were shivered to pieces, and the precious liquor, as they deemed it, was swimming on the floor. The party was disconcerted. Crichton sprang to his feet; called for his dragoons; ordered the instant capture of the assailants, and swore ample vengeance. But he reckoned without his host, for neither the mob nor the troopers were forthcoming; the one had fled in the dark, and the other was drinking hard in the alehouse, and was utterly incapacitated for duty. Muirkirk was not then what it is now, a large and populous village; but it had its Kirkton with a considerable number of inhabitants, who were sorely oppressed by the soldiers who were quartered among them.

Mowat had witnessed many a debauch, but this baffled the whole. He felt sick at heart, and wished himself in his quiet retreat at Glenmuckcloch. At this meeting plans for circumventing the Covenanters were concocted, and every scheme against the party was entertained with great spirit.

Next day Mowat felt greatly distressed; his mind was in a maze, and his body was disordered, and he determined immediately to leave Muirkirk. The curate bantered and rallied him, but all would not do, and accordingly he retreated from the place with feelings of peculiar disgust. As he trudged southward, the breezes of the desert fanned his burning temples, and cooled his frame. His spirits began to recruit, and he felt calmed and refreshed, but the recollections of the preceding evening rushed upon him and made him miserable. The party with which he was identified began now to appear in a new light; the whole faction seemed to be a wicked, godless crew, fit only for the service of the devil, and actively engaged in it. The shooting of the harmless peasantry, plundering and robbing, committing the most atrocious deeds, violating all decency, and trampling everything like religion under foot, determined Mowat to adopt another course. He sat himself down on the stony seat by the footpath in the moor where the day before he encountered the mysterious stranger who, after certain fan-

atical exclamations, as he deemed them, darted away into
the heart of the moor, and disappeared in the moss hags.
"That man," he said, "must have been Peden, the wild
moorland preacher, everywhere spoken against but nowhere
to be caught; I wish I may encounter him again, for my
mind is ill at ease; I greatly desire information on certain
points." As he gazed around, a man was seen approaching
in the distance, he came near, but it was not Peden, it was
Hair of Burncrooks, he who eluded the dragoon on the
edge of the defile of Glen Aylmer, rolling himself adown
the steep slope till he reached the bottom. Hair recognised
Mowat, who kindly invited him to a seat beside him.
Mowat opened his mind to his companion, as a well-known
Covenanter, and in full confidence imparted to him his
determination, but added that he much needed instruction
on the question of Nonconformity. "I think," said Hair,
"I can trust you, and I may impart to you a secret which,
if you keep, and follow my advice, may be of use to you.
I am on my way, at present, to visit Mr Peden, who is now
at Cleckloe, to invite him to hold a conventicle to-morrow
evening in my brother's house, in Glenwharry, and if you
will come to that meeting, you shall hear the saintly man
preach, and a personal interview with him may help you
out of your difficulties." "But," replied Mowat, "you
must keep all this a dead secret, for you know the consequences that may attach both to you and me."

They parted, and the curate wending his way across the
slope of the hill, reached the grave of St Connel, the tra-
ditional patron of the parish, and from whom it derives its
name. He sat down on the rude stone which is said to
cover the remains of the saint, and ruminated on the state
of the times, and on his own situation. He was about to
take a step, the consequences of which he could not forecast,
but he committed himself to Him who judgeth righteously,
and lifting the bonnet from his head, he fervently prayed

that a double portion of that spirit which inspired the holy man whose dust reposed beneath, might come upon him whatever might betide. He rose refreshed, and pursued his way to his home, but a home that he was destined soon to leave.

The evening of the conventicle came, and Mr Peden preached to a goodly company that had convened under the cloud of night. The solemnity that pervaded the meeting was new to Mowat, and produced a very salutary effect. There was in the whole service something so contrary to the loose and perfunctory manner in which the curates performed their office in the church, and something withal so spiritual, and so holy, that at once convinced Mowat that the Divine presence was with them of a truth. Little was said in the sermon about the difference of parties, the main topic was salvation through the Great Redeemer. The poor curate often said in his heart, "surely God is in this place : I wonder what I have been doing these long years past; I am astonished at my blindness. And are these indeed the people they call rebels—the people who are everywhere pursued, and that like wild fowl on the heath, and the people whom I have been accustomed to regard as a nuisance in the land? If these are the people, I am from henceforth one with them."

When the services were ended he was introduced to Mr Peden, and received from him much instruction, and many faithful counsels. The conversation, in the presence of godly and intelligent men was kept up till far on in the night. The conversion of the curate was to them a matter of high gratulation, and before they parted, they prayed together, and gave thanks to the Lord for this display of His graciousness.

Glenmuckcloch was to be the abode of Mowat for only a few days more. He had now made up his mind, and was ready to depart, and to share with his brethren in the deserts the privations to which they were there subjected. There was now no halting between two opinions, and the fact was soon divulged, that the curate of Kirkconnel had abjured Prelacy, and adopted the cause of the Covenanters. All were now on the alert, curates, and dragoons, and Prelatists of every sort. Great was the indignation ; for a curate to revolt, was worse than for a dragoon to desert. The capture must now be made. The circumstance created a little seasonable excitement, acceptable enough to the troopers, who were always most hilarious when a raid was in question. The local troops, however, were spared the pleasure of the search, for a more illustrious cavalier himself rode into the field. The redoubted Clavers was at hand. His commission, at this time, was to scour Nithsdale, from New Cumnock to Sanquhar, in quest of all disaffected persons, and to search every nook, and ravine, and hut unsparingly on both sides of the river Nith. Not that this was undertaken to secure Mowat, for Claverhouse knew nothing of such a person ; it was a search that had been contemplated by the enemy, more especially on account of the rescue which had been accomplished by the Covenanters in the pass of Enterkin, which caused so much noise in the west. Claverhouse put his troopers in motion ; the one half sweeping along the north side of the river, and the other along the south. As it regarded the populace, no exemptions were to be made, the peasantry, men, women, and children, were to be driven like a flock of sheep before the soldiers to a given place, and there to be interrogated, and treated every one as the commander should dictate. The distress caused by this movement was very great, and the people were captured as if by the invasion of a foreign enemy.

In reference to this raid, Wodrow says—"That Claverhouse with a great body of militia and some soldiers, came down the Water of Nith, and in the parish of Kirkconnel, and on both sides of the water he apprehended multitudes, both men and women, and there caused many to swear that they would never lift arms against the king under pretence of religion." In another place he observes—"That where-ever Claverhouse came, he resolved upon a narrow and uni-versal work. He used to set the horse upon the hills and eminences, and that in different parties, that none might escape, and then his foot went through the lower marshes and mossy places where the horse could not do so well. The shire he parcelled out in so many divisions, six or eight miles square would be taken in at once. In every division the whole inhabitants, men, women, and children. young and old without distinction, were all driven into one convenient place. When thus got together, he called out as many of them as he saw proper at once, till he got through them, and interrogate them severally if they owned the Duke of York to be king. When any refused to swear he was most barbarous; the man was carried some few paces from the rest, and a napkin tied upon his face, and the soldiers were ordered to fire either blank powder, or to shoot over his head."

"Somewhat yet more cruel, if possible," adds the historian, "follows. All the children in the division were gathered together by themselves under ten years of age, and a party of soldiers were drawn out before them. Then they were bid pray for they were going to be shot. Some of them answered, Sir, we cannot pray. Then they were ordered to tell when they saw men with guns in their house. Sev-eral children of seven or eight years of age were carried about with the soldiers, who sometimes would offer them all fair things if they would tell of their parents, and what people used to come to them late at night. At other times they treated them most inhumanely; threatening them with death, and at some little distance would fire pistols without ball in their faces." In this way, according to

Wodrow, did the ruthless Clavers treat the people of Upper Nithsdale, and elsewhere.

The news was whispered that Claverhouse was on his way or about to commence his raid, but then the visitation was so sudden and secret, that few had time to escape. Some few made their way to other parts, among whom was Mowat. There were hiding places in the deep and impassable ravines, on the sunny braes of Glenmuckcloch, into which no dragoon durst venture to dive, and dark retreats under the procumbent rocks overshadowed by the umbrageous underwood, into which no soldier had courage to peer. But whether Mowat hid here or on the south side of the river, in the basky gorge of the Palmer's Burn, or whether he hid with Hepburn in his seclusion among the murky thickets of Connel Bush, we cannot say. How he fared after this we have no information. But as we have no doubt of Mowat's sincerity, so we have as little doubt that he would continue firm to the end. Some of the curates who at that time renounced Prelacy became preachers in the ranks of the Covenanters, and it would be gratifying to know that Mowat did the same.

As Claverhouse marched down the valley of the Nith, it is easy to see where his raid would terminate, though no mention was made of the circumstance, and that his resting-place must have been either at the peel of Sanquhar, or Eliock House in the wood. The likelihood is that he would enter the first port, and that was the residence of Queensberry, the ancient castle of Sanquhar. In either case the inhabitants of Sanquharburgh, as it was called, would get a view of Claverhouse, as he rode on his black war-steed at the head of his cavalcade, for the "bluidy Clavers," though an object of terror, was also an object of interest, and we may easily conceive some of the douce inhabitants of the "auld brugh" exclaiming, "Hech, sirs, sic a bonny face, and yet sic a cruel heart."

## CHAPTER XI.

THE haunted linn is a romantic gorge on the south side of the stately Carco Height, one of the most massive of the hills that flank the river Crawick, which flows through one of the most charming pastoral valleys that grace the south-western parts of Scotland. The linn is about two miles from the burgh of Sanquhar, and has long been famous for its eery traditions, and "auld warld stories." So firm a hold had the gloomy tales regarding it on the popular mind of the preceding generation that but few, as we have heard the old people say, durst venture into its murky recesses, even in the broad day. The defile, however, has been greatly cleared of its primeval wood, that erst densely covered its precipitous sides, and with this have been cleared away also the superstitious terrors connected with it. In the time of our persecuted ancestry, however, the linn was invested in all its gloomy grandeur, and was consequently a suitable retreat for those who were chased from the abodes of civilized men and driven into the wilderness. Near the foot of the wild gorge, there stood in a little grassy plot a small cottage ; it was so much buried in the thick and tangled wood that the passenger, in going along the road, could not possibly descry it. It was exactly such a spot as one would desire for a place of almost perfect concealment. The occupant was a Covenanter of the name of Andrew Hislop, a devout man, and one that feared God, with his wife, who was a mother in Israel. Andrew's door was ever open to the wanderers, and his table was always spread with a meal for the hungry outcast. Many a happy meeting was held in Andrew's hut. His cottage was a centrepoint to the Covenanting friends throughout the district, and if it was not so secure a retreat as the Miny, yet it afforded a high degree of safety.

There was in the upper part of the gorge in which Andrew
dwelt, an open space, cleared of underwood, at the mouth of
what is called the Shiel burn. Andrew sometimes contrived
to get up a conventicle in the lonely but lovely bosom of
the glen, and great gatherings were occasionally witnessed.
It occurred to our worthy that as the troopers were not
then in the hold, and that as Mr Peden was at the time in
the house of his neighbour, Andrew Clark of Auchengrouth,
he might invite him to preach. On the day appointed a
great company met in the linn, and Mr Peden preached, and
distributed the bread of life to the hungry flock that had
gathered around his tent.

In spreading the news of a projected conventicle, it was
impossible wholly to hide the thing from informers and
other interested persons, and so the matter was whispered
in the ears of the notorious Peter Inglis, who lay in Douglas
with his men, ready to sally out on any errand, and especially on that of dispersing a conventicle. Accordingly the dragoons, with their redoubted commander at their head, were
on the move by the break of day, as they had sixteen miles
to traverse through moor, and moss, and stream. They issued from Douglas by what is called "the Black Gait," and
then down the lea of Anershaw, and into Glaspen moor, and
on to Duneaton. The stream was somewhat swollen, but
the bold troopers dashed into it reckless of consequences,
and reached the opposite bank. It was still early, and not
wishing to arrive at their destination too soon, they halted
at Whitecleuch for the entertainment of men and horses.
By this time the clouds had gathered thick in the west, and
were pouring out their contents several miles to the north
of where the conventicle had assembled.

But it was now time for the cavalcade to move. An im-
pediment, however, lay in their way. The river Spank,
which flowed across their path, was in high flood, and what
was to be done ?—cross they must, be the consequences

what they might.  In they rushed, swearing, and swaggering, and spurring their war-steeds that swam the flood, and
sprang hilariously to the landing-place.  All reached the
dry ground but one, who was carried down by the torrent,
and, losing his seat, was drowned ; but the horse gained the
sandbank.  The hunting of the conventicle was likely to
cost them more than they cared to lose, but their object
must be attained.  The valley of the Crawick was, in those
days, difficult to traverse.  The river had to be crossed at
least six times, owing to its tortuous course, and there was
no formed road along its vale.  This was another retarda-
tion ; for the stream being full, they had to betake themselves to the heights, the tracks along the sides of which
were almost impassable, and then they had again to descend
to the level ground on the margin of the river.  And now
they were near their journey's end, but an unforeseen obstacle again presented itself.  The mountain torrent of Pow-
craigy, which rushes impetuously adown the steep face of
Carco hill, confined within a rocky channel, and falls into
the Crawick, had descended with such a precipitancy, and
such a full discharge of its waters, which ran straight across
the road, and had ploughed a trench of the depth of several
feet, and had diffused itself hundreds of yards on each side
of its course that rendered a passage impossible.  Here the
party was completely at a stand, while the linn was scarcely
a mile before them.  What, then, was to be done ?  To stand
still till the torrent discharged itself was to wait for hours.
"Let us scale the height," exclaimed Inglis, "and get round by
the top of the watercourse."   " Ay," said the guide, "that's
it, but then the men must go afoot, for no horse can get
through the thickets that cover the steep brow of that
mountain."
    Meanwhile the conventiclers were cowering in the glen,
and listening to the precious words that poured from the
mouth of the preacher.  We say they sat cowering ; for if

the troopers were overtaken with drenching rains, and had
to encounter dangerously flooded waters in their way, the
worshippers in the retreat of the linn came in for their
share of the same visitation. The teeming clouds that
hung on the brow of the height above at last dashed down
their contents with frightful energy, and drenched the timid
company, soaking their clothes with water as thoroughly as
if they had been dragged through the current that foamed
and chafed along the rugged gorge at their side. And yet
they sat with patience, regarding the watery baptism as a
light matter compared with the fiery attacks of the ruthless
troopers on the harmless companies that occasionally convened in the solitudes. This exposure to all sorts of
weather on the misty hills, and among the hazy marshes,
the people sitting on the turf, literally like a sponge filled
with water, and having their feet bathed in the smeary
moss, or on the cold snow wreath, by the sheltering side of
a lonely wood—listening for hours to the fervid words of
the preacher, nor thinking those hours long—all this, we
say, induced diseases that brought multitudes to sudden
graves. No constitution, however robust, could long resist the deleterious effects of such an exposure. The pining
sickness, the debilitated frame, the burning fevers, the
agues, the consumptions, the rheumatisms, and other name-
less diseases caught at winter conventicles, were far more
prevalent and severe than we have any precise conception
of; and all this was patiently, nay, even thankfully submitted to by the honest, and warm-hearted, and confiding people who fully followed the Lord in that dark and cloudy
day.

But the storm passed over, and the clear and warm sun
shone out in the blue firmament. And now all nature was
gladdened; the green leaves glistened in the bright sun-
beams; the mountain flowers looked coyly upwards; the
warblers in the bushes chanted their song and filled the

groves with melody; and the lambkins on the green slopes
sported around their dames. The valley of the Crawick
appeared most gorgeous; it was never seen in such array;
it was a perfect poem to look on, and the grand old hills of
Carco and Knockenhair were clad in living green, and tossed
their lofty heads proudly to the azure firmament. The
congregation assumed a joyous aspect, and were just engaged
in lifting, with a united voice, a song of high praise to the
God of their salvation, when the troopers, having gained the
steep ascent, stood breathless on the very edge of the declivity, at the bottom of which the congregation reposed. A
volley from their fire-arms was sent whizzing and booming
among the bushes. The conventicle was startled. The
warblers ceased their song. The raven, perched on the grey
cairn on the heath, rose on his jetty wing and soared away
afar into the moorland. The timid hare sprang from her
lair at the sharp report, and bounded off to the neighbouring height. The blue smoke issuing from the muskets,
which were discharged in a line across the margin of the
declivity, rose in lazy volumes above the trees, as if the
outskirts of the thickets had been caught by an incipient
conflagration, caused by the scathing thunderbolt from the
clouds.

The shot was speedily replied to from the bosom of the
thicket beneath. One ball went curving over the heads of
the troopers, and another came bounding after it, and struck
a tree, peeling the bark from its side, and flattening itself on
the face of a bare rock behind. Inglis started; for the bullet
passed close to him as he leaned his arm on the tree. The
party retreated a few paces, not caring to expose themselves
to what might perchance issue from the dark and impervious
underwood, and the question became, What was now to be
done ? "I think," said the informer who guided them, "I
think that as the men are jaded and exhausted, that
it would be madness to descend to that infernal gorge,

with its frightful recesses as dark as the black pit itself, and
infested by desperate men with murderous weapons, and
who in a trice might despatch our whole company, and none
left to tell where our carcases lie ; and so my advice is, that
for the present we retire to the Castle of Sanquhar, and
seek quarters in the Peel in the absence of Queensberry and
his party.  I am persuaded that he would feel offended if
we did not avail ourselves of the opportunity, and more
especially as we are on the king's service ; and besides, something is due to ourselves on the score of victuals, you know."
This proposal was adopted, and the party withdrew with
all convenient speed to the Peel.

The conventiclers kept themselves under the cover of the
thickets, in the deep bottom of the dark linn, till the troopers
withdrew, and then they betook themselves to their homes.
In the cottage a number of worthies convened around the
preacher, congratulating themselves on their deliverance.
These were Andrew Clark of Auchengrouth, Bryce Cairns
of Carco, Laing of Blagannoch, Peter Corsan, Hair of Burncrooks, William Tait of Whitecleuch, Patrick Adams, and
Edward Fraser, saintly men all, and all stern and unflinch-
ing Covenanters.   The cottage of Andrew Hislop contained
a batch of leal and stalwart men, all prepared for the defen-
sive, and each ready to expose his life in shielding the helpless.   The Apologetic Declaration inspired the military with
a salutary awe, and more especially when a leaden bullet
was commissioned from the murky covert of the basky ravine or the thicket by the wayside, and of which the doughty
Peter Inglis got something like a foretaste, though happily
no harm was done.   It was considered prudent to keep together for the night, and to disperse cautiously at the dawn
of day.   Many a hallowed hour had been spent in the cottage in the linn, but this night excelled them all.   Mr Peden
discoursed on the troubles of Zion, and his fervid words
stimulated the company to a still higher pitch of moral

heroism, and they were all prepared to die cheerfully in adherence to the great and good cause. A sleepless night was spent in Andrew's hut; and when the day broke, "each to his several home with speed repaired." Andrew Clark conducted Mr Peden to his house in Auchengrouth, where the venerable man always found himself at home, and more especially as he had a cave in the lonely thickets of the dark Glendyne.

Our chief object at present is to follow the steps of Patrick Adams and Edward Fraser who betook themselves to the heights on the north.

The troopers in the castle were highly exasperated; they considered in their secret minds that had it not been for their over cautiousness, or rather cowardice, they might have done something more decided in the affair of the conventicle, and they determined to wipe off any dishonour that they thought might attach to them. "What!" exclaimed the brave commander of his magnanimous troopers, —"What! shall a company of low, cowardly, fanatical conventiclers deter his Majesty's honourable cavaliers, well equipt, and full of martial ardour, in the execution of their high military enterprises? No; this shall not be. Peter Inglis was never known to be a poltroon—never known to be conquered; no, never but once, and *that*, I feel ashamed to say, was by a smirking maiden of Newmilns. But you know the circumstances, comrades, and I know you excuse me—we blithe blades are sometimes caught in silken snares, but even that, believe me, would not have happened had it not been for foi mer remembrances and——, but it is needless to descant, let us mount with the rising sun, and scour the face of that huge mountain, and dive suddenly into the glens beyond, and my name is not Peter Inglis, if we do not pounce on some game ere we make our retreat."

Patrick Adams and his companion wended their way over the heights, and entered the more remote solitudes, where

they had little expectation of being followed by the troopers.
But Adams was a well-known character; he was famous as
a Nonconformist, and a price was now set on his head as
a leading rebel in the district.  The liberal reward which
was offered for his apprehension increased his danger, and
obliged him to abide more closely in his hiding-places.  His
house, a shepherd's cot, stood in the centre of a lovely glen,
through which purled a sparkling rill, which descended with
a gentle murmur from a rocky cleft on the right; on its
margin grew the palmy willows, whose pliant branches,
bending over the stream, kissed the bosom of its limpid
waters, as they were bidding farewell to the upland solitudes, and hastening away to accompany their kindred rills
that were pursuing their course to the distant ocean.

When Adams with his friend entered the cottage, his
wife was sitting with a sickly child on her knee, bathed in
tears and apparently uttering a prayer—a tide of tenderness
overflowed his heart.  As to the mother, the half of her
sadness was lifted away from her heart when she saw standing in her presence the person, whom above all others, she
valued in this life, and she felt as if her sickly charge must
now recover.  The child, who could now scarcely lift her
heavy eyelids, recognised the voice and the face of her
father, and a momentary smile played on her features.  It
was obvious to the parents that death was about to make an
entrance into their dwelling, and the tone of their mutual
congratulations was greatly softened.  Adams now with a
full heart knelt beside the child and poured forth the fervour of his soul in earnest and importunate supplications.
The hearts of the worshippers were humbled in contrite
submission before God, and they rose from their knees with
a sweet refreshment on their spirits, and sat down to wait
with resignation the result.  Nor did they wait long, for in
a short time, the lovely child breathed her last.

At this juncture, a company of dragoons appeared wending their cautious way along the face of the opposite hill, with the obvious design of visiting the cottage. Adams and his companion betook themselves to the height behind the hut. They bedded themselves on the soft heather, among which the wild mountain bees were booming on airy wings from place to place as they sought the scented flowers that blushed unseen on the brown waste. The friends beheld the movements of the troopers with intense anxiety, and saw them reach the house. They entered, and, after a considerable delay, issued from the door, dragging by the arm Patrick's little son, a boy of about five years of age. "They are going to kill my boy, my dear boy!" exclaimed Adams, springing to his feet. "Stay," said Frazer, "perhaps they are only in sport; they will never shoot the child—the mere child." The object of the ruffians was to learn from the boy what they could not extort from the mother; and hence they threatened him with instant death unless he informed them of his father's hiding-place. By this time Adams and Fraser were in full race down the heathy slope to prevent the supposed murder. Their approach was instantly noticed by the soldiers, who, by this plan, gained their object in drawing the father from his concealment. They surrounded them and made them their prisoners. Adams was a noted character, and no favour was to be shown him, not even that of a mock trial, and he was condemned to be shot without further ceremony on the spot. A few moments were allowed for prayer. He knelt down on the heath, and with a countenance indicative of entire resignation, he prayed—that every covenanted blessing might descend on his wife and children—that God would return to His church in Scotland—that He would open the eyes of the enemies of His people—and that He would forgive all his sins, and receive his soul into the heavenly rest, for the sake of Him who loved sinners and shed His precious blood for their redemption. When he rose from his knees he said, "I deem this the happiest day of my life, and though my enemies count me wretched, I am full of joy by the light of God's countenance. What may be your fate, my dear cousin Fraser, I cannot tell, but if it ever be in your power, look to my poor widow and fatherless children, and the blessing of him that was ready to perish shall come upon you." When he had said this he embraced his beloved wife and children, and added, "the Lord will be with you when I am gone. Do not grieve for me, I see heaven as clearly before me as I see that sun, and in a few minutes I shall be there." When he had finished, the soldiers commanded him to kneel on the bent till they bound his arms and tied up his eyes with a napkin. "No," said he, "you need not bind me, nor tie up my eyes, I can afford to look death in the face without alarm, and can welcome the messenger that calls my soul to glory." Two of the dragoons then took their station before him and fired simultaneously. The one ball passed through his head, and the other entered his heart, and without a groan or a quiver he fell lifeless on the turf, and his happy soul, "from insult springing," was carried by angels to the Saviour's presence. The dragoons carried Fraser with them as their prisoner, and retired in silence from the scene, leaving the bleeding body of the martyr on the heath.

The poor widow's heart sank within her, and her enfeebled limbs could scarcely support her, but as she gazed on his countenance, now pale in death, she said, with a sweet and heavenly composure, "the archers have shot at thee, my husband, but they could not reach thy soul ; it has escaped like a dove far away, and is at rest."

She proceeded to adjust the body, that was yet warm, before it was stiffened in death—she closed down the eyelids with a gentle hand—she washed from his brow with the pure water of the streamlet the blood that still oozed from the wounds, and kissed the pale lips a thousand times.

She then covered the bleeding corpse with a plaid, and, having gathered her children around her, she lifted up her voice and wept, and the piercing cry of their distress entered into the ears of the Lord God of Sabaoth, and He sent the Comforter, and He spoke words of peace to their hearts.

As they were sitting by the mangled body of the martyr, two of the wanderers happened to pass that way. They had been well acquainted with the deceased, and they expressed their warmest sympathy with the afflicted widow and her children. They carried the body to the house, and having prepared it for interment, they made a deep grave in the very spot where he fell, and there they laid him and the babe by his side, and like the devout men who carried Stephen to his burial, "they made great lamentation over him."

Edward Fraser, who was captured at the time when his friend was shot, was banished to America. He returned at the Revolution, and the first place he visited in his native wilds was the scene of his cousin's martyrdom. He found his widow still living in the cottage, and her children growing up around her. He betook himself again to the occupation of a shepherd, on the same farm where Adams had been employed in a similar capacity. In process of time he married the widow of his friend, and reared her children with parental care. They lived together many a long and happy year, and at last descended in peace to an honoured grave. Thus ended the raid to the haunted linn.

## CHAPTER XII.

"I HEAR," said Peter Corsan to a few friends who had forgathered to the Miny, "I hear that a great ado is at present made down the valley yonder about the conventicle that was held last week in the haunted linn. It is considered by the authorities that the retreat of the troopers was a cowardly act, and that the ball shot from the thicket, which barked the side of the tree and had very nearly wounded the magnanimous commander, has converted Inglis into what they call a poltroon. They do not consider that his shooting of the noble-spirited and saintly Patrick Adams was enough to wipe out the stain; and now the valiant Peter and his roving troopers are all back again to their quarters in the Red Ha' in Douglas, where it is said they hold a riotous time of it, and are a perfect pest to the village and its neighbourhood, sowing wickedness and dishonour all around them." "No matter," said Gilbert, "they had no business to sally out on the errand they came. They richly deserved the dookin' they got, and now they as richly merit the reproaches they got from their ain party; it will teach them better manners for the time to come. Let them keep within their ain heftin, as the sheep on the hills do theirs." "But, Gibby," said Eddie, "ye dinna mean to blame the dragoons for no makin' havoc o' the conventiclers? Wad ye hae praised their bravery if they had shed the bluid o' the hale half o' them in the linn, and driven away the other half as prisoners? Noo, this is what the persecutors would call heroism. I think, therefore, that the like o' us should give them credit for their caution, or, if ye like, their cowardice. I dinna honour the men, for I hate their employment; nor do I admire their spirit, suppose they had been fechtin' in a gude cause, for then that cause wad hae been lost; but I say we should be thankfu' that their hearts failed them; for, depend upon it, it wad otherwise hae been bluidy wark." "Right, Eddie, right; I hae been misguarded in my language."

"I fear," added Peter Corsan, "that the same game will be played over again that was played last year after the rescue of the prisoners in Enterkin Pass, when the country for so many miles round was so fearfully harassed by the soldiers. Queensberry's men have arrived at the castle of Sanquhar, and terrible penalties will be exacted. I tremble for the consequences. I fear our honest friends in the Crawick and its neighbourhood will come in for their share of trouble." "Ay," said Grizzy, "Eddie often tells us that there is a race of rare folk in the Crawick; and where can the eagles gether but where the carcase is? But as the gude, godly Mr Semple used to say, 'He is aboon that guides the gully,' and sae our enemies can win na farther than their tether will let them; but still I fear the warst. I had an unco dream yesternight; and oh, hoo mony o' these have I had first and last! I am weary o' them, and I sometimes fear to close my een in sleep, lest I see eery visions and hear eery sounds. Weel, I dreamed that I was ga'en across the muir on a visit to my dear sister Sarah at Powmerlog. I saw in the black moss a deep, wide grave, and three men lying on their backs in bluidy winding-sheets. I thought I kenned the face o' ane o' them, and as I gazed in astonishment and fear, he seemed to open his pale lips, and softly say, 'We are not dead, but sleeping here;' and oh, how calm they slept, and what a heavenly look they had! It appeared as if they were in some deep, and holy, and happy dream, or carried away in the visions of God to some beauteous and blessed land. As I gazed on their peaceful faces, and felt in a manner entranced, I heard a sound in the air above me, as of a multitude of sweet and heavenly voices chanting the words, 'These are they who have come out of great tribulation, and have washed their robes, and made them white in the blood of the Lamb, therefore are they before the throne of God, and serve Him day and night in His temple.' I turned to look around me, but both the vision and the sound vanished, and I awoke." "That was indeed a wonderful dream," said Peter Corsan; "It both cheers and admonishes us. But, Grizzy, who was the man whose face ye kenned ?" "But that I cannot tell you, Peter. I have considered again and again, and I canna make it out ava ; but I am sure that at the time his face was kent to me." "It's aiblins as weel," said Gilbert, "that ye hae tynt the recollection o't, for if the person be alive it might hae rendered us uneasy about his fate. But a' dreams are not realities, and sae we will leave a' in the hands o' Him wha can best preserve us." "But, Gibby, my man, ye'll alloo that dreams are sometimes realities. Ye ken yersel' what we hae already experienced, and sae we manna fling a' to the winds." "Na, na," exclaimed Eddie, "I ken mysel' that dreams are no a' vanities. It was a dream that once saved my life in the moss, but I'se no trouble ye wi' it• The puir cuddie and me are standin' witnesses to the truth of that admonition. Dreams or no dreams, let us be on our guard, my friends, for more mischief is brewing than we wot o'."

"I hear," said Peter, " that the Laird of Gairland is likely to be brought to trouble in consequence of the conventicle. The meeting was held on his lands, for all the linn from the top of the cleuch to where it falls into the Crawick belongs to him, and has belonged to the name of Crichton for generations past. He is not a Covenanter ; he is one of their own party, though a moderate man, and does not seem to be troublesome. He is connected with the old family of the Peel, for the Crichtons have been the lords of that stronghold for ages past, and though the lands are now in the family of Queensberry, yet the name of Crichton is still common in the district around Old Sanquhar. The fact that he belongs to the Prelatic faction will not exempt him. Now Gairland is a laird, and therefore there is something on which they can pounce, for wherever property is in question a sonsy fine is sure to be exacted. The wealthy people are the fit subjects for a' persecutors to batten on. There is no friendship even among themselves, and how can we expect their favour ? The conventicle was held on his lands, and therefore he is responsible."

The state of matters on which Peter Corsan grounded his suspicions was the following :—An act of a most stringent kind had been passed by the Council, to the effect that every man was to be responsible for his neighbour. It was most comprehensive, and so distinct that none could evade its import. Lairds were made answerable for their tenants, in case they frequented conventicles, farmers again were answerable for their cottars and servants, heads of families were answerable for the members of their households, children were expected to inform on their parents, and neighbours, and acquaintances, and all were bound to delate one another, so that the entire community were comprehended, and every man made responsible for another. A more tyrannical law could scarcely have been concocted, or one more ensnaring. The consequence was that a strong spirit of jealousy was excited in the community, and every man dreaded his neighbour. Many were ruined in this way, entirely ruined, for every one was at the mercy of some ill-set individual, whose information, however false, was always assumed to be correct by the party who simply wished it to be so. In the case of a laird, a conventicle kept on any part of his estate was enough to confiscate the entire property, and in cases where this was not actually done, the most ruinous fines were extorted. It signified nothing whether the laird knew of the conventicle being kept or not ; his ignorance, or his disapproval of the thing, did not at all exculpate him ; the deed was done on his lands, and that was enough—he was liable to the penalty. It was the same with a tenant ; he forfeited all he had, and he might be captured and lodged in jail. The fines exacted in those cases were generally absorbed by those who uplifted them, and the estates confiscated were frequently bestowed on favourites, so that very little of all this came into the public

treasury.  These exactions were made use of by the persecutors to enrich themselves ; they demanded just what they
pleased, and it was fruitless to remonstrate.  The local
Courts had ample powers conferred on them, and without
responsibility they could make the most exorbitant demands.
And then the military commanders had powers no less ample, and if they had not they assumed them, and who was
to gainsay them ?  When they besieged a farmer's house,
or that of a small proprietor, they usually carried off all the
money they could find, and drove before them what of the
cattle suited them, and when they were at a certain distance
from the premises they offered to restore them, provided a
goodly sum was paid by the owners.  All this was done
under the sanction of law, so that there was no appeal.  The
Laird of Gairland, then, on whose lands the conventicle was
held, though unknown to him, was not to be exempted from
the usual plundering exactions.  His was precisely such a
case as they desiderated, but then there was this difference,
that his small estate being in the immediate vicinity of
Queensberry's large domains, the exactions made were more
likely to come into the public purse, and consequently it
was more likely that a smaller share would fall to the public
harpies.  Douglas of Drumlanrig, it is said was infamous
for his exactions, and the laying of field to field, so that
when Alison, his factor, whose horrific death-scene is so gra-
phically depicted by the historian Wodrow, was laid in his
grave, Douglas is reported to have exclaimed, "There lies
he who, had he lived other ten years, would have secured
for me all the lands between this and the green-clad Corsancone."  Gairland had a house in the town of Sanquhar,
which stands to this day, and to which it is likely that his
crippled resources would then confine him.

  " Hard eneuch, hard eneuch," said Eddie, "but no harder
than the lot of others.  I ken the laird ; he is an honest
man—a quiet body, and no sae ill to the like o' us after a'.

I hae quartered mony a night in his house up in the cleuch yonder. It was in his cleuch that the queer chapman, that was sae lang amissin', was found dead, lying at the side o' the great muckle round stane in the bottom o' the deep ravine. I hae mony a time wondered where yon stane cam frae; for I'm sure it's no a native—it's as round as an egg. It couldna hae been brought yonder by human strength, and I am certain the puir silly fairies could hae had nae hand in't; but be it as it may, mony an eerie story has been tauld about yon stane. Draps o' bluid have been seen on't, and ghostly shapes hae been seen pacing slowly round and round it, and a pale licht flickerin' on the tap o't, and deep moans, and heavy sounds hae been heard at the mirk hour o' midnicht, and strange and unearthly lookin' craiters hae been seen in braid day licht. I dinna wonder that they ca' it the hauntit linn." "But ye see," said Gilbert, "that's just a security to our persecuted friends. It is to them yonder what the Auchty is to us here; and no doubt the eery things about that linn have been the means of keeping the friends in hiding there from no small molestation."

"I fear," added Peter Corsan, "that our friends down in that quarter will soon be made to feel the vengeance of the enemy on account of this conventicle business."

"And that they are just doing," said Eddie, "the dragoons have come to the castle, and they are scouring the country round and round. This I can weel testify, for I hae come in for some o' the misuse mysel'. I was at Auchengrouth, in the house of our leal friend Andrew Clark. Mr Peden was in hiding; for the conventicle affair made it perilous for him to be seen abroad. He has a cave in the thickets of Glendyne, to which he can betake himself in case of a hasty visit from the enemy. Weel, we were a' sittin' in the kitchen, as we are here just now in the Miny, when a' at ance there appeared on the edge o' the muir a company o' troopers making straucht for the house. Cap-

tain John Mathieson frae Closeburn was wi' us, who had
also been at the conventicle.  He fled wi' Mr Peden and a
few towards the heights of Auchengrouth, and in full view
of the sodgers, who, seeing the movement, rode wi' desperate haste.  The friends kept to hill, but Mr Peden's strength
began to fail.  He stood still and said—' Lads, let us pray ;
for if the Lord do not help us, we are undone ;' and then,
taking off his bonnet, he lifted up his voice and cried—
' Lord, we are ever needing at Thy hand, and if we had not
Thy command to call upon Thee in the day of our trouble,
and Thy promise of answering us in the day of our distress
we wot not what would become of us.  If Thou have any
more work for us in Thy world, allow us the lap of Thy
cloak the day again, and if this be the day of our going off
the stage, let us walk honestly off, and comfortably through,
and our souls will sing forth Thy praises to eternity for
what Thou hast done to us and for us."  When ended, he
ran alone a little, and came quickly back, saying, 'Lads, the
bitterest of this blast is over, we will be no more troubled
with them to-day.'  I was in great anxiety about the upshot, but was much relieved when I saw the horsemen returning, chased down the hill by the creeping mist, which
came on and on and drove them before it.  I wondered at
the thing ; there was the soft, white mist which, like a band
of armed men, compelled them to retreat, while it enfolded
within its ample curtain the poor fugitives whose prayer
had brought down instant help from the clouds.  The party
came to Auchengrouth in a great rage, and uttering the most
horrid oaths, both on the fugitives and the mist.  They had
dogs with them, and as I was sittin' on the cuddie afore the
door ready to depart, one of the men hounded one of the
fiercest on the poor donkey, which making its attack on the
heels of the harmless beast, it began to kick violently, and
struck the vicious dog on the head so firmly that it daiver'd
him and sent him whumlin' on his back, where he lay for

dead. The dragoon instantly drew his sword to hew the cuddie on the hind legs, but as the blow was descending, the craiter, which was still kickin', met the sword wi' his airn heel, and shivered it in twa. The sodgers leuch like to split, whereupon he, in a red-wud rage, drew his pistol frae his belt to shoot, it may be, baith the puir beast and my puirer sel', but the commander interfered, and ordered him to stay his hand. I was obleeged to the Captain, for he kenn'd me, and so did the rest o' them, for I had dealt wi' them a' in the tobacco line. And so, when the hubbub had ceased, and all was restored to quietness, the party entered the house, and got refreshments, and the very man who had done me the injury, came out and shook hands wi' me, and axed my pardon, which was readily granted, and a twist of tobacco into the bargain, and so I came trudging through the moor thankfu' to get rid o' sic customers. And so you see the affair of the conventicle is not ended ; we shall hear mair of it yet."

"I hear," said Peter, "that a price is set on Mr Renwick's head. His conventicle meetings are giving unbearable offence, but he always contrives to avoid the enemy." "Ay, and will do," said Gilbert, "so long as the Lord has work for him. His services are much needed. Our conventicle preachers are now reduced to the smallest number, and if he and Mr Peden were out of the way, I wot not what would become of the poor hungry flock in the wilderness. I think none will be so base as to become his betrayers." "Ye forget, Gibby," said Eddie, "that these spies, and informers, and troopers, will consider themselves as blessed as ever Bonshaw did when he captured the good Cargill, and delivered him up for the reward which was promised. Ye may depend upon it, they'll consider that fifty pounds sterling is no to be girned at, and that any one o' them will speedily rax out the greedy loof to keep the cauld siller whenever it is drappit in till't. Na, na, they'll no grudge to steek their neeve on a guerdon like that."

As the friends were thus quietly conversing in the Miny, two persons entered—Willie of Lesmahagow, who had been in the West, and William Tait of Whitecleuch, near the source of the Crawick.  Both were bearers of tidings.  "Ye are welcome, my friends," said Gilbert, in his usually hospitable manner, "ye are welcome to our biggin' here.  In these precarious times it is dangerous to be abroad.  There are troopers, and robbers, and reivers, and plunderers of all sorts, that infest the country, especially in our landward districts.  Society seems to be let loose, and all is in a state of disorder together.  And so, then, friends, I say again I am glad to see you here safe and sound."  "It is now many a day since I was at the Miny," said William Tait, "and I felt an urgent desire to see you and honest Grizzy once more, and particularly as the times are so uncertain, and as our lives hang in doubt before our eyes.  How many of the excellent ones of the land have gained the martyr's crown since we met last! and even you yourselves have been in the enemy's hand, and were led forth to a cruel execution, but the Lord delivered you, and that by a wonderful providence, as Eddie informed us, and therefore we should cling the closer to each other in this the day of our common trial.  My worthy neighbour, the gudeman of Mosscastle, was telling me of his visit to you, and this stirred up within me a strong desire to see you."  "You are welcome a thousand times, my dear old friend, and I hope our intercourse shall be blessed.  But how fares it with honest Mosscastle ?  He is a man that fears the Lord above many, and has had his own tribulations in these heavy times."  "Mosscastle is well, and though he is but low in worldly circumstances— yet he is prosperous in spiritual riches.  The poorer he is made the more heavenly does he become, and, like the rest of our sufferers, he is taught to sit the more loosely to the things of time, and to take a firmer hold of the heavenly inheritance.  The house of Mosscastle is a place of refuge

to many a sufferer for Christ's sake." "Is there," asked
Peter Corsan, "any farther news about the conventicle
affair? Have any of the friends been caught?" "Only
one, so far as I have heard," replied William, "and that is
young Andrew Clark of Auchengrouth. James Douglas of
Drumlanrig apprehended him, and was preparing to shoot
him on the green before his father's door, but the youth
was spared on the intercession of an aged matron, whose
husband had once done Douglas's father or uncle a good
turn. Douglas is cruel; he is, like Peter Inglis, more a
savage than a hero; and it was a wonder to every one that
he was induced to let go his prey. The soldiers are roam-
ing all around, and are scouring the hills and glens between
the Menock and the Crawick, and catching all they meet
with. One day they had made a goodly capture, and were
boasting of their success, but a heavy thunder-cloud that
had been gathering on the tops of the hills burst with a
fearful crash over the narrow glen of the Cog, where they
had met, and the gleaming of the lightning, with the peal-
ing of the thunder, so scared the horses, that they became
unmanageable, and broke away from their riders, who themselves were still more alarmed, and felt as if the voice of
God was speaking in angry tones from the firmament
against their misdeeds. By this means the captives got
free, and fled away apace. 'The Martyr's Knowe,' in the
glen, is the place where this occurred. The troopers who
came from Douglas to disperse the conventicle in the linn,
visited Whitecleuch on their return, adown the moors of
Duneaton, where they had been pursuing some of the fugitives, and I could easily perceive that Inglis was somewhat
crestfallen. The men behaved civilly on the whole, although
they took what suited them in the way of provisions and in
driving off my best horses; but we were thankful that matters were no worse, and so we put up with what befel."

"I have," said Willie of Lesmahagow, "this very day

witnessed a scene I will not soon forget. Several of our
brethren were returning from a conventicle held in the parish of Carsphairn, and on their way encountered Claverhouse
and his troop. They were instantly apprehended, and
without more ado were shot on the spot. The report of
the firing was heard at a distance, and attracted the notice
of some persons on the moor. On the withdrawment of the
dragoons they visited the place, and found three men
weltering in their blood. They were instantly recognised.
Their names were Joseph Wilson, John Jamieson, and
John Humphrey. When I reached the spot, which I did
by mere accident in crossing the moor, I found the friends
preparing a grave in the black moss at Crossgellioch. It
was wide and somewhat deep, and when all was ready the
bodies of the blessed martyrs were adjusted one by one,
and laid side by side in their soft resting-place. Their
clothes were their winding-sheets, and their bonnets were
on their heads. They were laid on their back, and we gazed
on their pale faces on which the sun shone in his brightness.
How placid were their features? They seemed to be in
a deep and quiet sleep. There was nothing unsightly,
for the blood stains had been washed from their faces, and
the blooming heather, torn from the moss, was strewed upon
their bodies before the clods were thrown into the grave.
We were in no hurry in covering them up, for they were
so pleasant to look on. It was proposed that one of the
party should pray, and so we fell on our knees around their
lowly resting-place, and Hugh Hutchison poured forth a
prayer with such melting fervour that we were all bathed
in tears, and our hearts were bowed down before the Lord
in entire submission to the dispensation. He then read
from the blessed book of grace that passage in the seventh
chapter of Revelation : ' What are these that are arrayed in
white robes, and whence came they ? These are they which
came out of great tribulation, and have washed their robes,

and made them white in the blood of the Lamb. Therefore are they before the throne of God, and serve Him day and night in His temple.' 'Yes,' said Hugh, as he closed the book, 'they have washed their robes, not in their own red blood which has streamed forth on the heath here, but in the blood of the Lamb—that precious, precious blood that taketh away the sin of the world, so that we may heartily exclaim, Unto Him that loved us, and that washed us from our sins in *His own blood*, unto Him be glory and dominion for ever and ever, Amen.'

"We then stood and sang part of the twenty-seventh Psalm. With tearful eyes we took our last look of the slaughtered bodies of these witnesses for Christ, and having pulled handfuls of soft grass from the bent, we spread it lightly on their faces, and let the moss gently down, as if afraid to disturb the repose of death ; and, having filled up the grave, and covered it with the blooming heath sod, we sat down and wept again, and then withdrew from the spot, and left the bodies there to sleep till the blessed resurrection."

"And now," said Grizzy softly, "I hae my dream read, and I now ken the face of him that I thought was going to speak to me—that face was John Jamieson's, a kinsman of our own, and a man whom we have not seen for a long season, yet he lived in our memory as one of the excellent of the land. And has he, too, gained the martyr's crown? Wae's me, what havoc the wolf is now making in the fold of Christ! Oh, but this is a sair dispensation! but what need we say? they are falling all around us on hill and moss. Oh, Willie, Willie! I am happy to see you safely here ; and may ye lang be preserved from the destroyers on the right hand and on the left!"

"There are," said William Tait, "deaths caused by the persecution of another kind besides those by shooting in the moors, and hangings on the scaffold. There are deaths caused by exposure in cold, damp caves in the darkly

wooded ravines. And I may now mention that our godly
friend and fellow-sufferer, Bryce Cairns of Carco, in the
Crawick, died last week of sickness caught in this way.
You know he often accompanied Mr Renwick in his hidings,
and slept with him whole nights in caves here and there in
lonely places, and in the furthest solitudes. The dripping
of the water through the rocks drenched them to the skin,
and produced cold shiverings which, in Bryce's case, terminated in a fever which ended his days. He died in a vault
in the old castle of Spoath. The old castle is something
like your own Auchty here. The lower story is strongly
vaulted, and the upper one contains a variety of chambers
with small windows and loopholes. It is curious that, like
the Auchty, it has the repute of being haunted, so that
people are afraid to come near it, and this renders it a convenient hiding-place. A bed was made in the vault, and
the good man was carefully tended by his friends, who
watched him night and day till he expired. On his death-
bed he manifested the strongest confidence in the Saviour,
and experienced a sweet and heavenly peace. ' I know,' he
said, ' that I have caught my death by exposure to inclement
weather in my wanderings, and in my lodging in the dreary
caves, and cold damp thickets but I do not regret. I have,
perhaps, endured twenty times more pain in this, my last
sickness, than any of our martyrs have sustained, even
when the fatal shot glided through their bodies ; but in all
this I have been upheld by a mighty ·arm, and consoled by
a sweet peace, and nearness to the blessed Redeemer, so
that at times I feel a joy that I cannot express. Jesus has
long been precious to me, but never more so than at this
present moment. Death has no terrors to me, all fears are
gone. O eternal life ; eternal life ! This is the promise
that He has promised us even eternal life ! Dear friends,'
he added, ' cleave firmly to the persecuted cause. Never
fear a suffering lot for Christ; His grace can make up for

all.  Oh, if our adversaries but knew in what peace I die,
they would envy me!'  He ceased for a while, and lay
calmly, as if in a soft slumber, and then roused himself, he
said, 'What's that I see?  Blessed Saviour, art thou come?
Lord, into thy hands I commit my spirit!'—and then
expired.  His death was edifying to all, and all blessed the
Lord for His grace shown to His servant.  He was buried
in the dead of night, carried by friends along the face of the
hill to the old kirkyard of Kirkconnel, near the mouth of
Glen Aylmer.  The night was dark and the way precarious,
so that lanterns had to be used to show the footing in the
morasses and through the ravines.  The lights were seen
from the town of Sanquhar, and by the people on the south
side of the Nith, and many wondered and feared, and all
considered it an evil omen.  As the procession was moving
slowly past the mouth of a basky gorge, they were arrested
by sounds that seemed strange and unearthly, that issued
from the midst of the thicket close at hand, and as the
night was calm, though dark, they listened, and the following lines were sung in a low and plaintive voice :

> O call to thy remembrance
>   Thy congregation,
> Which thou hast purchased of old ;
>   The same still think upon.

> To these long desolations
>   Thy feet lift ; do not tarry
> For all the ills thy foes have done
>   Within thy sanctuary.

These must be hidden worshippers, we said, who have fled
to this lonely retreat, and here, under the cloud of night,
to call on the name of the Lord.  Let us seek them out, for
they are fellow-sufferers.  In a moment the sound ceased,
and all was still as the grave.  The mourners then moved
on, and reached the burying-ground, while the inhabitants
of the little Kirkton were sunk in deep sleep.  We soon
dug the grave, and laid the precious dust in its last resting

place, and the company retired as they came.  This is the
end of the good Bryce Cairns, who shone as a light in a
dark place."

"It is e'en thus," said Gilbert, "that our worthies are
wasted away by pining sickness as well as wede from
among us by the shot of the troopers ; but the Lord will
raise up witnesses to supply their place, and to hold up the
standard, however torn or blood-stained it may be, for the
rod of the wicked shall not always lie on the lot of the
righteous."  "Ay ; but it may be sometime ere that," said
honest Peter Corsan, "and there may be a great falling
away in the midst of the land.  Days of trial are still awaiting us, and so we must yet abide awhile in the furnace, for
it would seem that a farther purification is needed."

## CHAPTER XIII.

"I HAVE been thinking," said Gilbert, to a few friends at
the Miny, "I have been thinking on some of the remarkable deliverances which in the course of these
troublous years have been experienced by many of the Lord's
people in their wanderings in desert places.  I think if
these were carefully recorded, they would furnish instances
bordering on something like the miraculous.  It is true
that miracles are not to be looked for now-a-days.  Still,
the Lord's arm is not shortened that it cannot save, and He
has doubtless reserved things in His own hand out of the
ordinary way of His providence, in answer to special prayer
in the day of distress.  I would not like to shut God out of
His own world, as some folk seem to do who think it enthusi-
asm to suppose that the Lord should interfere in a necessi-
tous case when we cry to Him, as godly Mr Peden did at
the foot of Auchengrouth hill, when the mist hastened
down the brae to cover him and his company frae the

sight of his pursuers." This remark made by honest Gilbert
opened up a wide field to the friends around the hearth in the
Miny. Almost every one of them had either met with such
deliverances, or had known of them in the case of their friends.
To many now-a-days the startling things that frequently
occurred in the experience of our persecuted ancestors must
appear as bordering on the superstitious. But whatever
such persons may opine, the facts are nevertheless unassailable. No one can scan the veritable pages of the historians
of that period without being struck, and even overawed, at
the apparently supernatural interferences which God's
suffering people experienced from the hand of the great and
good Shepherd. No man can survey even his own little
history without noticing that Providence has often interfered and wrought deliverances at a juncture when
absolutely required.

In speaking of these matters, however, there is no doubt
that much caution and discrimination are necessary; while at
the same time we ought to be on our guard lest we be
ready to explain away what was real in the experience of
those godly but sore-tried men. MacGavin in one of his
notes to the "Scots' Worthies," makes the following
judicious remarks :—"I am," he says, "not so wedded to
my opinion on this subject as not to admit that men who
lived in such intimate daily communion with God as Mr
Peden did, may have had *presentiments* of things with regard
to themselves and the church, of which Christians of lesser
growth can form no conception."

Wodrow, in recording the sufferings of the persecuted in
the year 1684, says :—"Wonderful were the preservations
of the persecuted about this time. The soldiers frequently
got their clothes and cloaks, and yet missed themselves.
They would have gone by the mouths of the caves and dens
in which they were lurking, and the dogs would snook and
smell about the stones under which they were hid, and yet

remain undiscovered." This is a general statement, on the truth of which many a particular might be made to bear.

"I think," said Willie of Lesmahagow, "we need not travel far to gather instances of very particular deliverances vouchsafed to our suffering friends. The house of the Miny itself is not barren of such incidents, and I myself, in company with my dear friend John, have been favoured with very strange deliverances. If our enemies are everywhere among us, the Divine presence is everywhere too. It is true that we are not always to expect deliverances; for in that case none of our witnesses would ever fall by the murderous hands of our persecutors ; but, then, when we do experience protection, and especially if it be in answer to prayer, we should not hide the Lord's kindness, but should tell it for the encouragement of others who need their confidence in the Lord strengthened. I think that if we were carefully to gather up the instances known among us of the special interferences of the Lord in our behalf, we might easily fill a volume. We should record them to the praise of Him who is the preserver of our lives. When I was out this time at the Ken in Galloway, I forgathered with two brethren from the Carsphairn neighbourhood, and they made the following statements :—'They were,' they said, 'on the banks of the Dee, where they happened to meet in their wanderings, and not having seen one another for a long season, they agreed that before they parted they should retire into the heart of a thicket by the wayside and pray together.' As they were engaged in this exercise, a company of troopers marched along the side of the river and passed on their way. Now, the certainty is, that had they stood a few minutes longer, or had each of them pursued his own way along the road, they would have been captured, and most likely shot on the spot.

"On another occasion, one of these men met with a deliverance equally remarkable. He was one day, in high summer, wending his weary way from the head of the Water of Yochan towards the lonely Monthraw, of which I have also a story to tell you of no little interest, and as he entered the defile of the gloomy Afton with its bold and precipitous mountains, what should he see, on looking back, but a company of horsemen rounding the hench of the hill a short distance behind him! He ran, and they pursued; but, as the ground was firm, the horses easily scoured along, and every minute gained ground. His strength had nearly failed him, when, turning round a projecting rock, he was for a minute concealed from their view, and losing his footing, he was projected straight into the heart of a dense hazel bush, where he was hid all but the feet. The troopers came up, and by this time they had dismounted, and were leading their horses leisurely down the declivity. They passed the bush, lashing it with their heavy whips, and swearing at the disappearance of the fugitive. Two of them even stood for a while pulling the green nuts from the hazel twigs, but happily on the side opposite to where the feet were exposed. He listened to their conversation, and heard them state, distinctly state, that the whole party were, on that same night at twelve o'clook, to attack a place called Dehana, where dwelt a man of the name of Campbell, whose house was a noted receptacle for rebels. He learned from them that a small conventicle was to be kept there that night. After a short time they left the bush, and the poor man was relieved from his anxieties. This deliverance was somewhat striking, and more especially as the worthy man who, on a former part of the day, felt a strong presentment that a certain undefined danger was before him, had been wrestling more than ordinary in fervent prayer for the Lord's special protection."

"I ken Dehana weel," said Eddie, "he is a worthy man Campbell. He is ane o' my customers. His house is a

stage o' mine. I may say he ance saved my life, for as I
was comin' alang the muirland parts where there are deep,
narrow trenches worn by the water-courses from the hills,
and a' covered over wi' lang tufts o' heather, which hides
the black ditch from the view, so that you are not aware of
the danger. Weel, ye see, as I was coming cannily and
tentily alang, sittin' on the cuddy to keep my feet dry, and
Dehana crackin' by my side, all at once the poor donkey
stumbled into ane o' these trenches, and I flew richt forward and lichtit on my broo amang the heather on the ither
side. The cuddie was doon to the neck ; the creels were
o'er his head, and a' that was in them was toomed into the
ditch. I lay in my helplessness, quite daivert, and the
cuddie mair sae. I scrambled up ; nae banes were broken
—a matter o' thankfulness ; but the case o' the donkey
seemed hopeless. He was immovably fixed in the mossy
trench, and he could not make even a struggle to help himsel'. Dehana went to the tap o' the knowe, and cried and
waved his bonnet for help. At last two strong lads made
their appearance, and we got the puir beast dragged on to
the bent, and the creels gathered frae the smeary moss. I
am weel acquainted wi' the Afton ; for as I informed ye
ance afore, it was our smugglin' route frae the Galloway
side, wi' the kegs o' brandy swinging on baith sides o' our
ponies. I hae seen thirty o' us a' in a raw comin' doon the
glen o' the Afton—the bonny Afton, wi' its crystal stream,
and a' its woods filled wi' sweet singin' birds. I love the
Afton as I love the Glenmuir, and the Crawick, and a' the
pleasant hills and the wild moors covered wi' the heather
bloom. I like the deserts, and I like them the mair that
they are the sleepin' places o' our martyrs whose bluid has
dyed the wilderness. I could not live out o' these muirs,
and I hope my dust will find its last resting-place in their
solitudes. But, as I was saying, I hae seen thirty o' us a' in
a raw comin' doon that Afton, and every ane had a weapon

o' defence, so that it was no easy matter for gaugers or excisemen to offer an onslaught, and if ance offered, my certes, they wadna green to ettel't again. We marched chiefly in moonlicht, and the Auchty was our next stage. But these were bad practices, and I hae renounced them lang syne, for I hate them."

"But, Willie," said Gilbert, "what of the conventicle at Dehana —how fared it ?"

"The man," replied Willie, "said that he went straight to the place for the purpose of forewarning the household. At first the family was shy, not being sure how to regard him. He might be a spy, he might be a friend, who could tell ? At length he convinced them that he was a true man. Arrangements had been made for a pretty full meeting that night. The services were to be conducted, not by a preacher, but by some of the members of the praying societies. It was now too late to warn the friends not to come that night ; but just as the people came, one by one, in the most stealthy manner, they were directed to resort to another spot that had been agreed on farther up the defile, where the meeting was held under the cloud of night at the bottom of a majestic rock, called 'The Stey Amory,' where they were completely out of the range of the soldiers.

At the time agreed on among themselves, the troopers advanced cautiously towards the house, in the full expecttation of pouncing at once on the little conventicle. But to their utter surprise, no sound was heard, no light was seen, no movement of any kind. They besieged the doors, the windows, the out-houses, but nothing was to be found. They were determined, however, not to leave without invading the premises ; but, just as they were going to dismount, a person came in haste with information that the conventicle was holding at the foot of the craig at some distance. On this they hastened away in hopes of surprising the company in the very act of worship ; but then there was an obstacle, the way was difficult to traverse, and the night was pitchy dark.  To remedy this inconvenience, as far as possible, a lantern was employed, and which, being carried a short way before the party, was found to be a wonderful help.  But here again a precaution was necessary.  The night was calm, though murky, and any peep of light could be discerned at a considerable distance.  It was therefore agreed on that, to prevent suspicion of their approach, a soldier's cloak should be held up at full stretch between two men before the lantern, which would shine behind without being perceived by any right in the front of it.  This scheme appeared to be quite successful and so the party moved on with confidence.  They were now approaching the place, and were within no great distance of the little conventicle, when one of the men who held the cloak stumbled into a mossy trench, and letting go his hold of the screen, the lantern shot its light across the moor, and, in the deep darkness, it shone like a bright star.  This was instantly observed by the person who was on the watch.  He at first thought it might be wild-fire in the bogs—a sight not uncommon—but as it did not seem to leap from place to place, but to advance in a straight line, he began to suspect that mischief might be approaching, and accordingly he gave due warning.  It was soon ascertained that a company was drawing near, and it was thought likely that it was a party of troopers led on by a spy.  Under this impression the little conventicle withdrew, and sought concealment in a thicket not far off.  In order to prevent the further intrusion of the enemy, a lantern which had guided some of the conventiclers themselves through the rough places of the moors, was put in instant requisition, and two or three strong men, acting as a decoy, moved away from the place, and speaking pretty loudly among themselves, so as to be heard by the troopers, for the purpose of directing the pursuit after them.  Nor were they disappointed, for the soldiers, supposing that this was the entire body of the conventiclers moving homewards, followed them in the full persuasion that they were now wholly in their power. The men from the conventicle had now all their suspicions confirmed, and they moved on, guiding the troopers after them by always keeping at a proper distance, till they led them near the high road which leads ˙ between the two Cumnocks. When they had reached this point, the friends extinguished their light, and withdrew into the heart of a dense thicket, and left the dragoons to plod their way to their garrison."

"But, Willie," said Gilbert, "ye mentioned Monthraw, what about it ?"   "I ken Monthraw weel," interrupted Eddie, "I ken Monthraw ; it was ane o' our stations in the smuggling times, and a safe and cosy place it was ; for it was far frae mortal habitation, and we never felt alarm when we spent the time there, either by night or day."

The story concerning this place, alluded to by Willie, was as follows, and we shall here quote it, word for word, from the "Voice from the Desert." It is a veritable story of thrilling interest, and shows us that facts are sometimes stranger than fiction.

"It was in the dark and stormy month of December, in the persecuting days, that the family of Monthraw were thrown into no little consternation by the incident we are now about to notice. Monthraw was one of the loneliest places among the hills. It is situated in the heart of the bleak moorlands beyond the source of the Afton toward the wilds of Upper Galloway ; and its solitudes seem to justify the old adage respecting it—

> ' The lone Monthraw,
> Where man never heard
> His neighbour's cock craw.' "

And verily it is a solitude, but yet a solitude that has its features of intererst.

But to our story.   "It was a dark night in December ;

the wind blew a hurricane ; the rain covered the sides of
the heathy hills with foam, and all the rills and the burns
were in high flood.   The family of Monthraw had barred
the door of their cottage against the storm, and piled on the
hearth the brick-like peats—the flame of which sent a
cheerful glow through the apartment.   They were more
than ordinarily happy.   The gudeman had on a previous
part of the day received a considerable sum of money which
was due to him, and which he had carefully locked in his
chest.   The storm without enhanced the idea of comfort
within, and the inmates felt assured that on such a night
there was no likelihood of any intrusion from an unwelcome
visitant.   As they were enjoying the quietude of their little
dusky chamber, and lifting up their hearts in gratitude to
the Giver of all good, they were startled by a rude and
hasty knocking at the door.   ' What can this mean ?' exclaimed they in astonishment, ' who can be abroad on the
lonely moor in this wild tempest ?'   But there was no time
for questioning.   The knocking was repeated with fury, and
a stern voice demanded instant admittance.   ' Who, and
what are you ?' vociferated the master of the hut, whose
words were scarcely audible in the raving of the tempest.
' Open the door, I demand, or I'll burst it in with a crash.'
On this the gudeman undid the bar, and in bursted a stalwart, burly dragoon, and stood in his military accoutrements
in the middle of the dusky apartment.   The consternation
of the household may easily be conceived.   The wild troopers had invaded the dwelling, and ' the thing that they had
greatly feared had come upon them.'

" ' I have lost my way in this execrable moor,' said the
soldier ;   ' and had it not been for the light that gleamed
from the window of your hut, I must have perished on the
wild.   The storm is terrific, and has rendered my horse
almost unmanageable.   I was never so thankful to meet
with a human habitation, and I mean to make my residence

here for the night.' The man spoke discreetly, and the
fears of the inmates were gradually allayed. ' I wish to
sit by your fire during the night,' said he, ' and I will put
you to as little trouble as may be. I am so thankful that I
have found a shelter from the tearing wind and the splash-
ing rain.' 'We will give you the best accommodation in our
power,' replied the gudewife; · and we will hang up your
dripping clothes before the fire, and have them all dry for
you in the morning.' A suitable meal was provided, and
everything that the hospitality of the moorlands could
afford was forthcoming to render the stranger comfortable.
His weary horse found a corner in the cow-house.

" In due time the inmates retired to rest, and the soldier,
before stretching himself among the warm bed-clothes, had
his pistols loaded and carefully placed on his pillow, and the
sword, in its ponderous scabbard, was laid on the table before the bed. The family, fully convinced that the trooper
meant no harm, but the contrary, resigned themselves to
sleep. The soldier slept well and soundly in the forepart
of the night, but afterwards became restless ; and though
he could not sleep, felt comfortable among the downy
blankets. As he lay ruminating, and the storm had abated,
his ear caught a slight noise at the little window, on the
back part of the room, near the bed. The aperture called
the window had no glass in it—it was closed with a square
board which turned on leathern hinges, either to admit the
air or to let out the smoke. As he listened, the noise increased, and he at length plainly saw by the flickering light
on the hearth that the board was moving on its hinges, and
was gradually pushed inward. ' Who is there ?' exclaimed
the soldier. No voice responded, and all was quiet again.
The trooper was now on the alert. He was convinced that
it was not the wind, for that had ceased, but it might be
some domestic animal that sought admittance by its accustomed path of entrance into the house. But whatever it

might be, the soldier, as he was not inclined to sleep, was resolved to watch the issue. In a short time the window-board again began to move, and to move with a persistency which appeared to him to be somewhat suspicious. He again demanded who was there, but no answer. 'Be you who you may,' said he, 'I fairly warn you that I will fire if you do not desist.' No attention was paid to the warning, and the soldier, hastily seizing one of his pistols, fired. A rustling was heard, and then a heavy fall under the window. The household was alarmed at the rousing report of the pistol, and in a moment all were out of bed. They were at a loss what to think, knowing that they had a soldier sleeping in the house ; and the dragoons were always objects of suspicion, and for the most part, of terrible dread. Did the man intend to murder the helpless family? the man to whom they had shown kindness in receiving him under their roof from the storm, the man who had professed so much thankfulness for the hospitality shown him? They knew they were wholly in his power, and they knew not how many of his fellows might be at hand, and ready to pounce on them like beasts of prey. They were terror-struck. The matter, however, was soon explained. The soldier, who saw how naturally they were alarmed, soon composed their fears, by relating the occurrence simply as it stood, and they retired to rest as if nothing had happened.

"At length the morning dawned. The storm had passed away, leaving the streamlets flowing brim full, and all the mossy ground soaked in water. The soldier, anxious to know what had really befallen in consequence of his firing through the aperture, donned his clothes and hastened to the back of the house, and to his amazement, perceived that he had shot a man, who lay dead in a pool of his own blood. The gudeman of Monthraw at once recognised the person : but could not divine the cause that had brought him to his house at the dead of night, and in a night so tempestuous,

when there was no apparent inducement for him to leave
his own home and travel so far into the heart of the dreary
wilderness.   And then, what did he want at the window ?
Why did he not seek admittance by the door ?   What
could all this mean ?   The mystery, however, was soon un-
folded ; for, on examining the body, there were found implements of murder, plainly intimating that a deadly onslaught on the family of Monthraw was meditated, and that
the assailant, like a thief, sought an entrance by the narrow
aperture unsuspected.   But why all this ?   Why come to
murder an unoffending family ?   Why should a neighbour,
with whom they had lived on terms of friendship, venture,
without seeming provocation, on so nefarious a deed ?   The
thing appeared inexplicable.   A thought, however, occurred
to the gudeman of Monthraw, and a suspicion flashed like
lightning through his mind.   This was the person from
whom he had received the sum of money, which he had so
carefully deposited in his chest the day preceding.   He was
the only individual acquainted with the circumstance, and
he had actually come with the wicked intent of again recovering the sum, and to kill the inmates rather than be defeated in his vile project.   In this way the whole mystery
was at once cleared up ; there could be no doubt respecting
the man's design.   He had travelled miles in the dark
storm, and he had exposed his life in the perils of the
night, so powerful was the stimulance of his avarice.

" How wonderfully was the shield of the Divine protection thrown over the family of Monthraw !   What visitor
could be more unacceptable than the bluff dragoon? and
yet in the person of this man did the Lord send them a
guardian—an armed soldier of the enemy to save their lives.
He who knows every occurrence that is to befall, foresaw
the plot that was laid for the ruin of that family ; and He
ordered all the circumstances that were to result in the
counteraction of the contemplated mischief.   The household

of Monthraw might think that no incident was more to be
depreciated than a visit from a fierce dragoon, one of a class
whose vocation was to shed the blood of God's saints by
special license in the moors and wilds of the country.
There is no doubt that, but for the soldier's presence in the
household of Monthraw, the evil man who plotted their
ruin would easily have effected his purpose. It often
happens that things which appear to us to wear a calamitous
aspect are actually blessings in disguise. The storm in the
wilds belated the trooper, and drove him from his path, and
the light from the window of the hut, flickering over the
wastes, was the star that led the man to a shelter, to the
saving both of his own life and the lives of the people in
the cottage—so wonderfully does the Lord work. We know
that the house of Monthraw was the occasional resort of
the persecuted people, who sought its obscure retreat as a
pretty safe hiding-place. Hence, if a cup of cold water,
given to a disciple of Christ for His sake, shall not lose its
reward, this worthy family received their reward on the
night of the storm." Such is the story of Monthraw.

"Andrew Clark," said Eddie, "was telling me, the last
time I was at Auchengrouth, that Mr Peden had a very
remarkable escape in the muirs beyond Sanquhar. He was
one day surprised by a party of troopers who were crossing
the bent at a considerable distance behind him. He ran to
seek a hiding place, and coming to a mountain streamlet
where for a few minutes he was concealed frae the view o'
the sodgers, he got his eye on a hollow place beneath the
brae o' the burn, which had been scooped out by the floods;
he crept down under the green projecting sod, where he
stretched himself at full length, hoping to remain undiscovered. At length the troopers came on straight to the
place, with a view to cross the burn. He heard the
thundering o' the horses' feet as they came prancing along
the turf behind, close by his hiding-place. They bounced

over the streamlet one after another; but the last one, in crossing precisely above where the good man lay praying for protection, crushed one of his hind legs right down through the sod, and so near his head, that the animal's foot squeezed his bonnet into the soft clay beneath. The horse sprang to the other side, and left the lowly man unscathed.

"Geordy Ga' tells me that he has been mair than ance, or twice either, useful to persons in concealment. One day, in traversing the muirs in the van o' his party, he observed the feet of a man, who, on seeing the troopers coming up, had crept into a heathery trench, in the moor, sic as the ane into whilk the cuddie and me fell near Dehana. 'Creep farer ben,' whispered Geordy; 'your feet are seen,' and then turned away frae the spot.

"He tells me he ance saved a man on another occasion. The sodgers had come to a house in pursuit of a person whom they saw running in the muir, and who, they observed entered the door of a hut. They searched the house but found nothing. When the sodgers left the place, Geordy, on pretence he wanted something, rode hastily back, and entering the house, pointed to the clothes-press that stood in a corner of the apartment, and said, 'Mistress, next time you hide any one, hide better. Part of your husband's coat is locked without the press,' and then left the house. The poor woman was astonished on finding matters as Geordy had stated, and who had observed the thing without saying a word about it to his fellow-troopers."

"Ay, ay," replied Gilbert, "it's e'en sae. The Lord hides His people in the hollow of His hand in the day of peril, and screens till their work and their working-day be ended."

"I forgot to mention to ye," said Eddie, "the remarkable deliverence that Mr Peden had at Garrick Fell. He was preachin' in a lonely shepherd's hut in the wilds, and during

the exercise there came a ewe bleetin' to the door, and
bleetin' sae loudly as to disturb the worship, whereupon the
shepherd rose to drive it away.   As he was chasing it along
the bent, he observed, to his surprise, a company of soldiers
advancing in the distance.   He ran back and informed the
friends within.   In an instant they fled, and hid themselves
as best they might.   Mr Peden betook himself to the Fell,
and a friend with him.   He had a cave at the bottom o'
the hill, the mouth of which was curiously concealed.
There was a tuft of heather that hung from the top of the
opening straight down for more than half way, and then
there was a fanlike braken bush that grew from the bottom
and met the bloomin' heather above.   This formed a screen,
behind which the fugitives hid themselves, so that when the
sodgers came up the glen, and close past the mouth o' the
cave, Mr Peden could distinctly see their faces, and as distinctly hear what they said ; and I am informed they were
sayin' nae braw things about him.   But he was secure, and
the only danger feared was frae a doug that was saunterin'
ahint the horses, and cam' snookin' amang the stanes about
the caves mouth, and even keekit ben for a moment and
glowert about, and coor'd back, and syne ran aff wi' his tail
clappit atween his twa hint shanks.   I never was at this
cave, because I dinna deal wi' the herds in that quarter, but
I hae kent them that were often there, and hid wi' Mr
Peden, too.   Auld Robert Braidfit, a worthy man, weel
acquaintit in these parts, used to tell me a' about it.   But
he has been mony a year in his grave, and a douce man he
was.   Hech, sirce, hoo these sauntly folk are weedin' away
frae 'mang us !"

## CHAPTER XIV.

THE furnace of the Persecution was now heated in right earnest, and its scorching fires scathed all around. It was now the obvious design of the ruling party to extirpate the Nonconformists from the land, and every pretext was adopted to accomplish this end. It was not enough that a man had been at Bothwell or any of the risings only, to secure his destruction; but if a person did not attend the curate of his parish, or if he had been known to frequent a conventicle, however peaceably attended, in the remote solitudes, or if a Bible were found in his house, or if he were ever seen with a book in his hand, any one of these was sufficient to subject him to military outrage. The patience of the Council that sat at Edinburgh, and conducted the machinery of the Persecution, was beginning to be exhausted; not that they were tired of the work, but fretted and exasperated at the tardiness of the full execution of their designs. Hence the armies that were let loose over the south and west—the great field of persecuting violence—so that, as Wodrow remarks, the country had the appearance of a conquered land lying prostrate under the feet of the foe. In the upland districts, which were incessantly traversed by the troopers, especially in the *eighty-four* and *eighty-five*, "the Killing Time," the reports of murders committed by the military were every day reaching the ears of the peasantry. The most exaggerated accounts of outrage and slaughter were never deemed too incredible, considering the character of the persons employed in the work.

On the evening of the first day of summer, 1685, Eddie Cringan and his equipage were seen coming slowly over the moor in the direction of the Miny. He was always a welcome guest, but now more than usual; the services he had

rendered were never to be forgotten. "I hae come," said
he, "straight frae Glenbuck, and I am the bearer of heavy
tidings.   Priesthill is no more ; the godly carrier is at this
moment lying in his bloody winding-sheet; he fell this
morning at the end of his own house by the cruel Claverhouse and his troopers." It was as if the knell of destiny
had fallen on the ears of every one in the house, and a flood
of tears gushed from every eye.   Priesthill shot ! A character so blameless !  Who now can expect to escape ! What
had he done? he had been at none of the risings ; all his
offending lay in this, he did not attend the curate of Muirkirk.   This was all—this was the head and front of his
offence.   What next?   But it was needless to enquire, what
next? for there were scores of men as blameless as John
Brown who were falling in the desert places all around.
The light of John Brown, like that of many others around
him, shone too conspicuously not to attract the notice of the
persecutors ; and therefore it was to be expected, as Mr
Peden opined, that he would one day fall by their hand.
The household of the Miny was stupified at this report ;
they sat in amazement ; the heart was too full for utterance.
Gilbert threw himself on the langsettle behind the fire, and
there gave vent to his grief ; and poor Grizzy, covering her
face with her apron, sat rocking her head from side to side
in the deepest affliction.   Eddie felt sick at the heart, and
could not express his emotions, and the boy Sandy stood
bathed in tears, casting a glance at one, and then at another,
in the group of sincere mourners that were before him.
Willie was in the moor when Eddie arrived, and it was
some time ere he returned.   When he entered, he was
astonished on seeing the deep affliction of the family.
"What has happened now, dear friends?" asked he.
"Priesthill," replied Gilbert, "has been shot this morning
by Clavers and his band ; that dear man has won the
martyr's crown ; that great light that shone so clearly in a

dark place has been extinguished." "I never knew him," said Willie, "but, from report, I am as familiar with his character and doings as if I had lived with him. Our David Steel of Lesmahagow was his bosom friend; and many a hallowed hour did they spend in the solitudes together. But he has shared the fate of his brethren, and a fate that may soon be ours."

"But, Eddie," said Gilbert, "what were the circumstances of his death?" "I had the account," he replied, "from one who was present, and who hurried down to Glenbuck with the news. It appears that Claverhouse, having heard of the nonconformity of the Christian carrier, hastened, in the early morning, over the moors to reach the house of Priesthill before the inmates were up, to secure his victim. John Brown, according to his custom, had risen with the dawn, and having spent some time in devotion, next assembled the family for worship, which being performed, he went out with a spade to prepare some peat ground for fuel, when all at once there appeared, on the ridge of the brown height behind the house, a company of horsemen. In a brief space they descended to the moorland, and with eager haste seized on their prey. They led him, or rather he went before, leading them, more like a conqueror than a captive. Isabel Weir, his wife, was informed by one of the children that a company of soldiers were coming over the bent behind the house, and that their father was walking before them. She instantly suspected the true state of the matter, and snatching up the infant in her arms, exclaimed, 'The thing that I feared has come upon me; Oh! give me grace for this hour.' She then went forth to meet them, and, for the first time in her life, she saw the face of the dreaded Claverhouse, whose name had spread terror over all the western parts. There are seasons when the mind rises above all the terror of circumstances that wear the most gloomy and threatening aspect, and when we feel a fortitude and buoyancy of spirit which bear us up and carry us triumphantly over every fear. This was fully experienced by the wife of Priesthill when she was called to her trial. The work was short; Claverhouse commanded him instantly to prepare for death. But this preparation was not to make. The good man was willing to die, and to die on the spot as a witness for Christ. When he was praying his last prayer aloud on his knees, Claverhouse commanded him to rise, for that was not praying, but preaching. He replied, 'Ye ken little what either praying or preaching is, if you call this preaching.' He then took an affectionate farewell of his dear wife and children, and commended them to Him who is a husband to the widow, and a father to the fatherless, and having committed his spirit into the hands of his Redeemer, he stood ready to receive the fatal shot. That shot was fired, and the martyr fell dead on the heath. When the deed was done, Claverhouse, with insulting language, said, 'What thinkest thou of thy husband now, woman?' 'I ever thought muckle gude of him,' said she, 'and now mair than ever.' He then cruelly said, 'It would be but justice to lay thee beside him.' 'I doubt not,' replied she, 'but your cruelty would lead you that length; but how will you answer for this morning's work?' 'To *man*,' he impiously replied, 'to man I can be answerable; and as for *God*, I will take Him in my own hand.' He then hastily retreated, for he had been twice vanquished—vanquished by the resignation of the martyr, and vanquished by the fortitude of the widow. Poor Isabel then tied up his shattered head with a napkin, and covered the dead body with a plaid, and when she had nothing further to do or contend with, she drew her children to her, and wept over the mangled body of her husband. Such is the account," said Eddie, "I received before I left Glenbuck."

This was indeed mournful tidings, but tidings, nevertheless, which were to be expected; for who could look for exemption when the slaughter of God's people was the order of the day? Every one felt deeply for the widow at Priest-hill, and Grizzy and Sarah resolved to pay her a visit on an early day.

The raids of the troopers were now more frequent and destructive than ever—even children did not escape their cruel usage. One of the men from the Glenkens related the following story :—"A worthy man of our acquaintance had often been sought for by the troopers, but had as uniformly avoided them. This stimulated the furious men more and more, who felt chagrined that their dexterity in capturing the rebels, as they were called, should be so successfully eluded. On their next visit to the place, the officer resolved to try another plan. There was a fine little boy, about ten years of age, whom he had observed in the house, and on him he pounced, with a view to expiscate information respecting his father. The poor boy was terrified at the sight of the gruff dragoons, and he stood shivering with fear in their presence. The commander, with a stern voice, asked where his father was, and if he came home at night, or if any persons lodged in the house with him. The poor boy, shaking like a leaf in the wind, would answer nothing. 'I'll make you speak,' cried he, 'if there is a tongue in your mouth.' He then tied a cord round his thumbs, and suspended him from a joist in the kitchen, in the presence of his mother. He hung, screaming with agony, but still would answer nothing. He was then taken down, and his face was next held close to a large fire, till his eyes were ready to start from their sockets, and his face like to burst with the heat, still he would answer nothing. 'Cast the brat into the flames,' cried a dragoon, 'and burn him to a cinder for his obstinacy.' 'You cruel-hearted man,' said the mother, whose bowels yearned over her poor and faith-ful boy, 'you cruel-hearted man, thus to abuse a child; have you forgotten that there is a lake of fire into which wicked men and murderers shall be cast, there to be tormented for ever ?'

" 'Take him out to the green,' vociferated the officer, 'and let him be shot there, unless he answer our questions ; we are not to be baffled by an ape like that in this way.' He was then placed on his knees before two of the troopers, who stood with their fire-arms ready to shoot. 'Now,' said they, ' answer all we ask, else we will blow out your brains.' But no answer could be elicited. His eyes were then tied up with a napkin, and the dragoons fired a volley over his head. The boy was stupified and almost out of his reason. In this way were these redoubted men vanquished by a mere child, whose firmness was indeed remarkable."

"I remember," said Willie, "another case of cruel treatment in regard to a boy a few years older than the one you mention. The soldiers tied a sharp cord round his brow, and twisted it with the butt end of a pistol till it cut the flesh through into the very bone. His cries were dreadful. He lingered a few days and then died." Such were the cruelties practised by the soldiers on timid children and weakly women ; and had they not been recorded by the veritable historians of the period, we would not have ventured to imagine them.

But time passed on. Renwick's Declaration had been published at the Cross of Sanquhar, on the demise of Charles II. —which circumstance made a great noise in the western parts, and on account of which many suffered cruel deaths. The prisons were ready to burst with the crowds that were immured within them. Not a few escaped from confinement, and returned to the rural parts from which they had been taken. John of Lesmahagow, and a few more, escaped from Dunnotar, and made their way southward. He reached his native place ; and having visited his friends by stealth, he next proceeded to discover, if possible, the hiding-place of Willie. He was not to be found in all the district round.

John was greatly cast down ; and, dreading the worst, he
determined to proceed to the westward, to see how it fared
with the people of the Miny.  Accordingly, he arrived here
one evening, and found them all in life, and Willie as their
guest.  It is easy to imagine the mutual greetings that took
place.  Next day, after a recital of what had befallen Gilbert's household, and their narrow escapes, John was requested to give a recital of his adventures from the time of
his capture, and especially the treatment he met with in
Dunnotar.

It may be necessary to remark here that Dunnotar, like
the Bass, was, in the time of the Persecution, used as a state
prison, in the dungeons of which were immured crowds of
Nonconformists, who endured cruelties such as have rarely
been equalled.  It is a fortress of great antiquity.  It was
built in the reign of Edward I. by Sir William Keith, the
Great Marshall of Scotland.  It is situated on the top of an
immense rock that projects into the sea, and has more the
appearance of a desolate city than a ruined castle.  It was
in the times of the patriot Wallace that no fewer than four
thousand Englishmen were here burnt alive.

It was in the month of May, 1685, that the Council in
Edinburgh, having received alarming accounts of the invasion of Argyle, and dreading the consequences if the Nonconformists should join his standard, resolved to send all
the prisoners who had been captured in the south and west
to the dungeons of Dunnotar.  It is to the dreadful privations endured in that frightful hold that we intend to direct the attention of the reader.  Could "the Whig's Vault,"
in the peel of Dunnotar speak, it would tell a story enough
to rend a heart of stone.

The Nonconformists in the various prisons in the south
were hastily and without due warning marched northward
to Kincardineshire, to become the inmates of the dark and
frowning hold of Dunnotar.  The hardships they endured

on their journey are almost incredible.   In one part of their
march they were kept all night on a bridge, and the soldiers
were stationed on guard at each end.   It was a very inclement night, and many of them were worn out with fatigue.
They were condemned to stand on the cold bridge till three
or four in the morning.   From this they were conveyed to
Dunnotar, and were entered as state prisoners in its
gloomy keep.   The condition of the prisoners in this
wretched receptacle was described by John in the following
words :—

"At Dunnotar," he said, " we were received by George
Keith, Sheriff-Depute of the Mearns.   Our large company,
consisting of a hundred and seventy persons, was thrust into a dark vault under ground—one of the most uncomfort-
able places poor people could be in.   It was full of mire,
ankle deep, and had but one window—toward the sea.   So
throng were we in it, that we could not sit without leaning
on one another.   We had not the least accommodation for
sitting, leaning, or lying ; and we were perfectly stifled for
want of air.   In this miserable vault we were pent up, and
it was a miracle of mercy we were not all killed.   The barbarities of our keepers and of the soldiers are beyond expression.   The prisoners had nothing allowed them but what
was paid for, and even money was paid for cold water.   And
when the soldiers brought in barrels of water and had sold
it out in parcels to them till they began to weary of it, they
would pour it into the vault to incommode us the more.
Considerable numbers of us died, and no wonder, through
such hardships.

"When our whole number had continued for some days in
the great vault, the governor was pleased to remove about
forty of us to another small vault, which being narrow and
low, they were not much less straitened than in the great
vault, and they were in hazard of being stifled, their being
no air nor light there but what came in by a very small slit

or chink.  The walls were a little decayed, and some little
air came in at the bottom of the vault ; and they used to lie
down one by one on their belly, on the ground, that they
might have some of the fresh air.  By this means some of
them, particularly the Rev. Mr Fraser, contracted a violent
cold and dysentery.  After some time spent in this melancholy posture, the governor's lady came in to see the prisoners in the two vaults, and prevailed with her husband to
make them a little more easy.  Twelve of the men were
removed, from the forty, to a better place, where they had
room and air enough, and put into two several rooms.

"As to meat and drink, nothing was allowed them but
what they bought, and the governor made even a monopoly
of this.  When the country people were bringing in provisions to the prisoners for their money, they were stopped,
and the soldiers were ordered to allow them no access ; and
one of them was roughly treated for insisting to get into
the prisoners with what he had to sell.  The reason of this
was, the governor's brother, who lived at Stonehouse, not
far from Dunnotar, resolved to have any money the
prisoners had, and none were suffered to provide for them
but he."

"Such who were in the great vault were in the greatest
misery, and not a few of them died.  It was no great wonder that, under such grievious hardships, they essayed all
innocent methods for their own safety.  In order to this,
they endeavoured, and got at length out by the window in
the vault, which was just over the sea, one night, and crept
along a most dangerous rock to the utmost hazard of their
lives.  About twenty-five escaped before the alarm was
given to the guard, by some women who were washing
near the rock, and the rest were stopped.  Upon the alarm,
the outer gates were shut, and the hue and cry raised.
Fifteen of them were apprehended ; and it was a wonder all
were not catched, being so weak that they were not able to

flee far, and *the country around being disaffected to them and
their way.* Such as were seized were most barbarously used.
Not only were they most inhumanely beaten and bruised
when apprehended, but when brought back to their prison,
they were put in the guard-house, bound and laid on their
backs on the floor, and most dreadfully tortured. In three
different parts of the room they were tormented. William
Niven, and Peter Russell, and Alexander Dalgleish, in
Kilbride, were laid upon their backs upon a form, and their
hands bound down to the foot of the form, and a fiery
match put bewixt every finger of both hands, and six
soldiers waiting, by turns, one after another, to blow the
match, and keep it equal with the fingers. This was continued for three hours without intermission, by the
governor's order. By this treatment William Niven lost
one of the fingers of his left hand. Alexander Dalgleish
died of the pain and the wounds he got, and an inflamm-
ation rising thereupon. Several others had their fingers
burnt, and the very bone turned to ashes; and some, besides
the last-mentioned, died of this torture. Some account of
these barbarities was sent to Edinburgh, and methods
taken to lay them before the Council. By the influence of
some there, not altogether so merciless as others, orders
were sent to the governor to treat the prisoners with a little
more humanity, and to accommodate them with some better
rooms."

These words of the historian Wodrow, which we have
put in John's mouth, sufficiently attest the barbarities
practised in that heartless age. In addition to this, we
may here notice the complaints made in a petition to the
Council, by two women in behalf of their husbands confined
in this execrable den, as confirmatory of the preceding
averments. They state :—" That the petitioners' husbands,
who are under no sentence—with many others—having
been sent prisoners to the castle (Dunnotar), they are in a most

lamentable condition, there being a hundred and ten of them in one vault, where there is little or no daylight at all, and, contrary to all modesty, men and women promiscuously together, and forty-two more in another room in the same condition, and no person allowed to come near them with meat or drink, but such meat and drink as scarce any rational creature can live upon, and yet at extraordinary rates—being twenty pennies each pint of ale, which is not worth a plack the pint, and the peck of sandy, dusty meal is offered to them at eighteen shillings per peck, and not so much as a drink of water allowed to be carried to them, whereby they are not only in a starving condition, but must inevitably incur a plague or other fearful diseases, without the Council provide a speedy remedy, and therefore, humbly supplicating that warrant may be granted to the effect underwritten."

On the presentation of this petition, the Council recommended more lenient measures; but the governor was greatly exasperated at the interference of the Council, and immediately drew up an exculpatory paper, which he forced several of the prisoners to sign, and those who refused to do so were treated with more than ordinary harshness. On this occasion Keith acted the part of a monster rather than that of a common jailer. It does not appear that this unfeeling and brutal person would ever have sought to mitigate the injuries inflicted on the poor prisoners, had not the dread of a visitation of a somewhat startling description overawed him. He began to entertain the suspicion that, from the state of matters in the vault, the plague might, perchance break out, and this induced him to moderate his severities, and to treat the prisoners a little more humanely.

Dunnotar, then, is a notable place in persecuting history; and the eye of the traveller, as he passes along the highway, is instinctively turned toward it. There is, in the churchyard of Dunnotar, a tomb-stone erected to the memory of those who died when imprisoned in its holds, bearing the following inscription :—"Here lies John Scott, James Aitchison, James Russell, and William Brown, and one whose name we have not gotten ; and two women also whose names we know not ; and two who perished coming doune the rock ; and one whose name was James Watson, the other not known, who all died prisoners in Dunnotar Castle, anno 1685, for their adherence to the Word of God and Scotland's Covenanted work of reformation."

———※———

## CHAPTER XV.

ONE day in autumn, as it drew near the dusk, Eddie and his donkey appeared before the door of the Miny. "Whaur hae ye come frae the day ?" exclaimed Gilbert Fleming, when he saw his honest old friend stand once more before him, "I hae come frae the burgh— the auld burgh o' Sanquhar ; and I hae had an unco speel up the face o' that weary Bale Hill. It is a sair, toilsome ascent, and there is always something eery in passing that wild-looking spot they call Laganaweel ; where, the shepherds say, unsonsy things hae been seen. They say the name means 'The Bluidy Hollow,' where a kind o' folk called Druids offered sacrifices—and they say even human sacrifices—but be that as it may, what a glorious view presents itself from the top o' that lofty hill ! I hae often, in the way of my calling, climbed to the height of that eminence, but I may say I never saw its beauties till this afternoon. The pure Nith winded its way through the bottom of the valley like a silver thread till it lost itself among the woods of Eliock. The town of Sanquhar, with its old frowning castle, lay, as it were, at your feet. In the east corner, the majestic Lowther Hills were seen towering

above all the lesser mountains and overlooking the terrible
gorge of Enterkin, where the rescue took place last year,
and which has caused so much distress to all the parishes
around. And there were the heights of Afton—the green
Corsancone—the charming defile of Glen Aylmer—the hills
of Kily and Yochan, and the dark mountains of the 'wild
Disdeer.' My spirits were raised; but my heart sank within
me when I thought that, throughout all the district around,
and as far as the eye can reach, there lie the mangled bodies
of many of our martyred brethren. I trembled when I
looked around, and trudged on with a heavy heart, not
knowing but in an instant I, too, might be stretched lifeless
on the bent." "And indeed, Eddie," said Gilbert, "we ourselves have made a narrow escape since ye were here; but tell
us how it has fared with you since you left us." "I hae been
at the ancient burgh of Sanquhar, as I was saying just now.
I deal wi' the Provost, who occasionally takes some of my
wares, and especially keel. It is lang since we were acquainted, and he wishes me weel, and does his best to extend my
trade, and as I deal in various articles, he got me introduced
to the castle. Hech, sirce! but it is an unco place yon castle
they ca' Crichton Peel. It's a gowsty auld pile o' a biggin,
and of great dimensions, capable o' haudin' hundreds o' folk,
great and sma'; and, then, there is Wallace's Tower in the
south corner, and there was the great big iron yett, wi' its
heavy portkillus, as they ca' it, for I am sure it is eneuch
to kill us a' if it were to plump doun on our heads, and so I
think its weel named. It hangs frightfully aboon, wi' its
great iron teeth girnin' as it were for a bite. Weel, then,
as I was creepin toward the peel wi' considerable caution,
wha should I forgether wi' but Queensberry himsel'—no so
frightfu' a looking man after a'. He glowered at me a blink,
but I appeared naething daunted. 'What do you here with
that miserable-looking creature you are leading behind you?'
'An't please yer honour,' said I, 'I am een auld Eddie

Cringan, the keelman ; and I deal in sundry articles, such
as tobacco and pipes, and the sodgers are often gude customers.'  When he heard me name the sodgers, he said, 'Ye
are an honest fellow, I opine ; here, Sergeant Turner, take
the old fool into the kitchen, and give him something to eat
and drink.'   'Thank yer honour,' stammered I, and he
passed on.

"And now I am going to tell you what happened.  A
company of Airly's troops is lying at the castle.  I had
no acquaintance with any of them, but my ears were open
to listen to what might be said ; and I resolved to gather
what information I could with regard to their movements.
All was bustle about the peel, and what wi' sodgers, and
what wi' servants, I was amaist dung donnart a' thegither.
The troopers dined in the same place, and I was seated a-
mong them, but I didna at a' find mysel' at hame as I do
here at the Miny.   The entertainment was plentiful ; and
whisky, and ale, and a' sorts of liquors, were in abundance.
The men seemed as if they had not broken their fast for
half a week, and the drinking was prodigious.   Scarcely a
single person was sober.  Angus Macbane, one of Airly's
men, was a first-rate hand at the bagpipes ; and it was
agreed that the whole party should sally out and hae a dance
on the green under the castle wa'—and such a mingling,
and a shouting, and a capering, I never saw.  Some drew
their swords and waved them above their heads, and others
threatened to run their fellows right through the body.
Bonnets were tossed high in the air ; and the kilted lads
footed it most nimbly on the swaird.  Some were tripping
their neighbours prostrate on the ground, others were boxing
like rams, and pushing like wild bulls.   I could see, through
a hole, the braw folks keekin' frae the high windows, obviously enjoying the scene, and one fair lady displayed her
handkerchief from the balcony, when a loud shout arose
from the crowd that was perfectly deafening.   The town's

people assembled at the head of the avenue of stately trees
that leads from the foot of the street to the high gate of the
peel, but they stood quietly, not willing to attract the notice
of the sodgers, lest an onset might be made by the reckless men. The auld story o' the king's visit to the castle
was naething to yon.

"The hubbub rose higher and higher, the shouts waxed
louder and louder; and I could easily discern that danger
was apprehended even by the officers themselves. The inferior commanders were utterly disregarded. All was in
confusion. Upwards of thirty stalwart dragoons, together
with a strong band of male servants, and other officials belonging to the castle, were all jumbled together, and fighting, and bawling, became quite unmanageable. I wished
myself once more in the moors of Kyle, bad as things are
about us here and round Muirkirk. I at first thought myself pretty secure in my little out-house, with the door
closed on me and the puir cuddie; but ere long I began to
dread the upshot. A roisterous party, in the frenzy of their
excitement, approached my hiding-place, and fighting furiously, and roaring terribly, came with a crash against the
frail door, behind which I stood. It flew to shivers, and in
tumbled half-a-dozen of boisterous troopers, heels over head,
on the floor. When they had recovered themselves, they
instantly recognised the keelman and his cuddie. 'Come
now,' yelled they, 'come now, old fellow, unpack, and let us
see what sort of wares you have got in those miserable creels
and wallets of yours. You are a fair prize captured, forsooth on the battle-field, and now for the spoil. It was needless to remonstrate. The poor cuddie was speedily eased of
his burden. The creels were opened, and tobacco and pipes,
and snuff and eggs, were all tumbled together on the floor.
The tobacco was picked up, and so was the snuff—the pipes
were useless. The eggs they seized and flung at one
another. Nor did the cuddie and me escape. We came in

for our peppering, as they called it, so that the yellow
yowks were running down my breast and back like water.
I was utterly despoiled. They untied the cuddie and led
him out into the midst of the hubblement, and they insisted
that I should mount him and ride round the green, all besmeared with the eggs as I was. They next insisted that
I should perform certain feats of horsemanship for the general amusement, otherwise I should forthwith be ducked in
the pond, which certainly would have been the case, had
not an event occurred which changed the scene.

" A spy from the moors was seen coming in haste toward
the castle, bearing tidings of a large conventicle being held
northward among the hills. He stated that a goodly proportion of the conventiclers were armed. The bugle sounded,
and every man girt on his armour, and drew the war-steed
from the stall. In an instant the castle court was empty,
and with their captain at their head, were scouring along
the moor, under the conduct of the spy, whom they placed
on horseback to hasten their march. All this occurred on
Saturday afternoon last. Queensberry and Airly abode in
the castle, swilling themselves with wine, and Kirkwood,
the witty curate of Sanquhar, was their companion. I like
Kirkwood, for he is kind to the suffering people. I never
like ony one to speak to his discredit ; he is always discreet
to me since the time I helped him to extricate his mare
from the moss at the Shielbog yonder, at the end of the
bonny green hill of Knockenhair. He has aye had a warm
side to me sin syne, and he treats me kindly when I ca' at
the manse. Weel, as I was saying, Kirkwood was there,
and Airly was greatly taken wi' him, and kept him to a late
hour wi' jokes, and stories, and daffin'. His conscience now
and then pinched him a wee, for he kenned he was to preach
on the morrow, and he attempted several times to rise and
retire to his home ; but Airly always held him to his seat,
and said, 'One glass more, and then,' but the night wore

away and the dawn began to appear. He was then allowed to depart, and stealing quietly along by the edge of the river, he reached the manse unseen.

"Next day he appeared in the church, and Airly and Queensberry, with all their retinue, placed themselves in the loft—exactly opposite the pulpit. I was in the kirk, and a great crowd there was that day to see the grand equipage o' the folk frae the castle. I was in a corner where I could weel see baith the minister and the gentry; and I observed how the grand folk sometimes baith frowned and smiled, as the curate went on in his dashing way, when preaching from the text, 'The Lord will destroy the wicked, and that early.' He pronounced the word *early* with a strong voice, and looked straight to the loft where Airly sat, and thumpt on the book-board, and stampt wi' his feet till the bottom o' the pu'pit rang like a drum; and the folk glowered and stared, and winkit and noddit, and leuch some o' them at the courage and spirit o' their minister, and wondered sair what it a' meant. When he had drawn to the ordinary length o' a sermon, he bawl'd oot to his precentor, 'Jasper, turn the sand-glass, for I mean to have another glass, and then.' When he had uttered these words, I observed that Airly and Queensberry laid their heads on the book-board, and hotched and leuch, to the amazement of all around them. When the sand had run its course a second time, the same command was repeated—'Jasper, another glass, and then—.' In this way he detained the party in the Queensberry loft, as they had detained him in the hall of the castle the night before. Kirkwood is a merry blade, and he pleases the peel folk vastly; and liberties seem to be granted him, which in another would not have been allowed. I was in the seat ahint the Provost, and as the kirk was skailin', he says to me, 'Eddie,' says he, 'what think ye o' this day's wark?' 'It will, at least,' says I, 'have this good reward: that the curate will get an invitation to dine at the castle this afternoon, and to spend another night wi' the family in their carousals.' 'Right—right, Eddie ; he is, in fact, a man they canna want. He has a certain influence wi' Queensberry, and he again has influence with the Council in Edinburgh, and so ye see how one thing hangs on another. I am certain, if the family have not been instructed to-day, they have at least been amused. Did ye observe how the people enjoyed the thing ? They hate the persecuting party, and they are much gratified when they think that anything like a blow has been dealt. There are many staunch friends of the good cause in this place, and not a few of them have had friends whose blood has been shed in the moorlands around.' Thus spoke the Provost ; and when we parted at the kirk stile he asked me to visit him in the evening."

"But, Eddie," said Gilbert, "ye havena tauld how ye came on after the affair of the plunder, and yer waggery in riding round the circle." "Waggery ! I trow it was nae waggery in me, but a very sair trial, the upshot of which I couldna weel guess. Weel, then, ye see, I was in a sad plight—a' besmeared wi' the broken eggs, as if I had been standing for a misdeamour in the jugs at the kirk door, or at the cross o' the burgh, when mischievous callans and ill-behauden women are privileged to fling a' sorts o' nuisance in yer face. The tobacco was stown ; the pipes smashed a' tae staples ; the creels crushed flat as a scone; and the cuddie shaking as if he had the ague. I went to the edge o' the pond and stript my coat and vest and proceeded to get mysel a' nicely syndit in the dub, in the whilk I at one time expeckit a dookin' in case o' the failure of my horse-manship. I then lifted the auld creels and placed them tentily on the cuddie's back, and walked quietly up to the auld burgh, where I met wi' muckle sympathy, for ilka ane said, 'Eddie, ye are an ill-used man ;' and some straikit and clappit the donkey, and others held out a wisp o' new hay

to the craiter's mouth. At last I came on, wi' a heap o'
bairns following, till I reached Deacon Weir's door, when
the honest man much bemoaned me. The Deacon is of the
Weirs of Lesmahagow, I was his lodger, and the cuddie had
its stance in the byre. When he had closed his shop, and
we had drawn round the ingle in the dusk, said he, 'Eddie,
ye hae met wi' a sair misfortune, and muckle ill-usage, and
I hae a mind to gi'e ye a lift out o' yer difficulties. I'll gi'e
ye a pair o' new creels, and fill them wi' a' that ye hae lost,
and set ye fairly on yer feet again ; and if ever ye can repay me, gude and weel, but if not, there'll be nae mair about
it, and sae ye hae my gude will.' 'Hoot, awa', Deacon,'
says I, 'it's come to muckle, but it's no come to that. I am
greatly obliged to ye for yer truly friendly offer ; I feel it
to be a kindness which I cannot soon repay ; but I have a
posy here which the thieves have not lighted on. My siller
is a' safe. It is not much, to be sure : still, it serves my
turn ; and, besides, I hae something in the hands o' a worthy
man in Douglas Water, on which I can fa' back if need be.'
'Indeed, Eddie,' said he, 'I am glad to hear o't, and I shall
be ready to supply ye wi' the articles ye may require.' And
so ye see, I bought new creels, and got them weel packit
wi' gudes, and paid ready siller for the whole, and so I
owe no man a plack. I placed the poother and the shot
among the packages in the bottom, and set out on my travels—glad to escape without mair scathe.

"The Deacon is a worthy man, and weel informed on
many subjects, and we spent some hours in the forenight in
close conversation. 'Eddie,' said he, 'these are heavy
times in which we live, and were it not for our kindly curate, who never informs on any of his parishoners, I durst
not stay in this place. Kirkwood knows my leanings, and
we sometimes converse on these matters, and we do it freely,
for we can trust each other. He has great weight with
Queensberry, who, I believe, is himself not ill-inclined, some-

times, towards the Nonconformists. I have known Kirkwood, after he came from a feast in the castle, where he
learned the designs of the enemy, come to my house and
tell me quietly how matters stood. He did not say, 'tell
any of the friends in hiding,' but I knew what he meant,
and I took my measures accordingly, and in this way we
saved the lives or the capture of not a few. We were all
thrown into deep distress the other week by the shooting of
the godly William Crichton, on the brae of Conrick. He
had been visiting Mr Peden in his hiding-place in the
thickets of Glendyne, and wending his way through the
moors behind the town common, he encountered a company
of troopers who, without more ado, shot him where he
stood. We stand more in fear of James Douglas of Drumlanrig than we do of Queensberry. Douglas is a cruel
man, and unsparing in his acts. I know this, that I always
feel more secure when the Marquis is at his seat here, than
when the peel is empty. I believe my bit shop would often
be plundered by these locusts, were it not that when the
soldiers are lying here, they see the family from the castle
frequently entering it and buying what articles they
occasionally require. But for all this, we are never safe ;
for the riotous troopers, filled with liquor from the castle,
come roaring and swaggering up the street, and, entering
the inn, sit till midnight, and then in the darkness they
work all manner of mischief. I find, however, that the
most of these soldiers are mere bullies, and that a bad conscience, joined to a superstitious dread, makes them cowardly
in the dark. Not one of them will pass the Churchyard at
the head of the town in the mirk night ; they are always
seeing spectres or hearing eery sounds. And then there are
the reputed witches of Crawick Mill, that are a perpetual
terror to them alike by day and night, so that auld Winnie
Crichton o' the Brig End will keep them mair in awe than a
whole meeting of armed conventiclers.

"You had a specimen this afternoon of the state of things at the castle. It is one of the worst specimens, I admit— still it is a specimen. The peel, when the dragoons are there, is a nest of wickedness; and if the garrison at Lesmahagow be justly termed 'Hell's Byke,' Crichton Peel may be termed the 'Deil's Den.' Since the publication of the 'Sanquhar Declaration,' (you were here that day), this has always been considered a more than ordinarily suspected place, and the soldiers think themselves more at liberty to act outrageously. You about Muirkirk are much better situated in this respect than we doun in the valley here.' 'No,' said I, 'we may in some things be even worse. We have Crichton yonder, a cruel man, though I have some little influence with him since the affair of the well; and then there is Cochrane, a man who riots in mischief, and scarcely a week passes without a murder. But, Deacon, I was going to ask if you know anything at present respecting the movements of the troopers, because, you see, while I carry about my articles for sale, I make it my endeavour to gather what information I can respecting the designs of the enemy in a particular district, that I may give due warning to the wanderers.' 'I know nothing just now, dear Eddie,' said he; 'for I have no confidential friend in the castle at present since Meck Grant, the woodman, who brought fuel from the moor to the peel, left us. The only person at all likely to give information is the Provost, and you know his leanings. He and I understand each other, and our mutual confidence has not been misplaced—try the Provost.'

"I stayed with the worthy Deacon all night, and next day went with him to the church, as I have mentioned. And now I come to tell you o' my interview with the Provost on the Sabbath evening, as he invited me to his house. 'Come away, Eddie,' said he, 'I am glad to see you in my abode. Come away and tell me what you think of this day's work. Was not our curate on his high horse to-day?

I trow both Queensberry and Airly got a hearing ; but he
is a queer man the curate, and the lord of the peel here
finds him useful.   Kirkwood is soon forgiven for any supposed offence of that kind ; and I understand he is at the
castle this afternoon again, and I warrant you they will
have a brave night of it.  But how are you after the abuse
which these reckless men heaped on you?  These troopers
are a class of the worst fellows that ever bestrode a war-
steed ; and how can it be otherwise, when their officers set
them such an example?'  'It's a' true ye say, Provost, a'
true ; and mair than that is true.  We hae the same sort o'
work in Muirkirk, and Douglas, and Cumnock, and, indeed,
in a' the places around.  My blood boils when I think o'
their villanies in town, and village, and moorland cottage.
Among us—o'er the hill there—the bluid o' God's witnesses
has been running like water in the mossy streams.  But
our wailings are needless ; and the thing that I wad be at
wi' ye the night, Provost, is this—Can ye gi' me ony inklin'
o' what the enemy is likely to do in this quarter at present?
for, ye understand me, I am in the habit not only of retailing the articles in my bits o' creels, but in furnishing
information, when it is in my power, respecting the movements o' the sodgers, to the friends who may be in hiding.
Ye ken I·am not a suspeckit person, and I can gang freely
baith amang sodgers and cottagers without being called in
question.  Noo, Provost, gin ye ken onything, ye may
safely entrust it wi' me—I will not betray a secret.'  'I
well know that, Eddie : you are the last man that I would
suspect of acting a dishonest part.  I have a confidential
friend in the castle who communicates with me on matters
of moment ; and you know, as I have a number of farms
that I rent from the Marquis, and as some of the shepherds
are staunch Covenanters, and, besides, are often guilty of
what the enemy calls reset, and as heavy penalties are
exacted in all such cases, it requires me constantly to be on

the outlook, that I may give them notice when anything is
astir.   This is necessary for my own safety, you know, as
well as for the safety of the poor lads, whom the troopers
would despatch in a trice, and with less ceremony than I
take this pinch of snuff : and, indeed, I may say, were it
not for the kindly curate, I would have been fined, and imprisoned, and utterly ruined long ago.  Nay, Kirkwood
himself has often given me a hint as he returned from the
castle, where he became acquainted with the designs of the
officers.

   " ' Well, then, this is Sabbath evening, and to-morrow
there is to be a fetê at the castle, on the occasion of the
birth-day or birth-night of one of the family, and that is
the reason why we have a more than ordinary company at
the peel at present ; on Tuesday they are to rest after their
debauch ; but on Wednesday morning, by the dawn of day,
the soldiers are to be on the tramp, and if possible, seize
the unsuspecting people in their houses.   The troopers are
to go in three divisions—one is to take the valley of the
Yochan, where my farms chiefly lie, and the people there
are already warned ; another takes the Crawick, and the
third scours the Menock and the braes on either side.
Dalziel of Carnwath, who is at present at Eliock in the
woods there, intends a move towards Muirkirk to meet
with Claverhouse, who is somewhere in those parts.   Now,
this more immediately concerns you, for it is likely he will
take the track over the Bale Hill, under the conduct of a
sure guide, and it is reported that Sandilands, the spy from
Crawfordjohn, is in our neighbourhood, so that it is probable
that Blagannoch, Gareland, and Friarminion, Penbreck,
the Miny, and the Shaw will all receive a visit, and it may
be a very unsparing one.   Now, Eddie,' said he, ' you have
enough for the present ; off with your donkey in the morning, and give warning to all along the route, and much
mischief will be prevented.'   ' I thank you, I do thank you,

sir,' said I, 'for your kindness ; it is well that I happened to
come to Sanquhar on this occasion ; I am richly rewarded for
all the abuse and misuse I met wi' yesterday.  But, Provost,
what of Menock and Crawick: have the folk there got
warning?' 'They have, Eddie, for you know I have
an interest in both of these localities.  Andrew Clark of
Auchengrouth and his manly sons, in Glenim, are in posession of the secret, and a trusty friend in the Crawick has
been told this evening, and so, all things considered, I now
feel comparatively at my ease on the matter ; and now,
good Eddie, I advise you to keep out of harm's way as
much as possible.' 'I thank ye, Provost,' said I, 'I again
thank ye for a' yer friendly hints, and I pray that the
blessing of them that are ready to perish may come upon
ye, and I know it will ; and now I will to the Deacon's and
confer with him a little further, and I shall depart early in
the morning, and plod my way over that wild hill till I get
among the moors of Kyle.'

"'Well,' said the Deacon, when I entered, 'I can now
see the result of the raid of the troopers, who were so unceremoniously called away last evening when they were
insulting you and working mischief among themselves.  A
conventicle met in Glenshilloch, on the north side of the
Cog—that lonely streamlet that falls into the Crawick.  Mr
Peden was the preacher, and a goodly number has assembled.  A spy was lying in wait, ready to carry information
to the troopers down here, and no sooner were the services
begun, than he sped his way to Sanquhar.  You saw the
soldiers depart, and merrily they paced along.  Not a few
of them found a bed on the Sanquhar moor, as the heavy
horses plunged and leapt over its rugged and broken surface,
where they lay insensible, while there fellows scampered
off, they knew not where.  A sentinel was stationed at
the head of Glenairn, who, when he observed the movements
of the dragoons, advancing over the moorland below, gave

warning, by a certain signal of the approach of the enemy. The valley of the Cog, you know, is deep, and the horsemen could make but little progress, and so the conventiclers made their entire escape ere ever the soldiers once came in sight. Mr Peden escaped by Castle Robert, and found a refuge with Laing in Blagannoch.' 'I am much indebted to the good friends in Sanquhar,' said I; 'I see you have here some who, like myself, are endeavouring to act as a breakwater between the persecutors and the persecuted, and God grant that we may be even more successful than we have hitherto been.' 'But we have much need of caution, dear Eddie; you may have heard how they shot the old piper the other day beside the cairn beyond the Black Loch on the Sanquhar moor. He was a drunken creature, and many a day he skirled his pipes between the Gallows Knowe and the Piper's Thorn, the whole length of the street. He was a harmless body, and was a favourite with all the town's-people. He met with his death in this way : —He was coming along the "Black Moor," and, being under the influence of liquor, he stumbled and fell at the side of the cairn. Some of the soldiers were traversing the moor, and, seeing him fall, imagined it was a Covenanter trying to conceal himself from their view. Accordingly they ran forward, and firing, killed him on the spot. They soon discovered their mistake, and seemed to lament the fate of their old drunken crony. On the day of his burial, there was a large gathering to follow him to the grave, for he had piped in the streets of Sanquhar for upwards of fifty years ; and Angus MacBane, piper to Airly's company, headed the procession, and played till the welkin rang again. The soldiers all marched in order, and Queensberry and Airly followed up behind. The gathering at the Sanquhar Declaration was nothing to the numbers met at the funeral of the piper.' 'I weel mind the piper,' said I; 'a' the country round has heard o' the drucken piper o'

Sanquhar, and it was when he was on his way through the
moors to play at the marriage of the sodger in Douglas,
that Captain Crighton met him, and, standin' and haverin'
wi' him, missed his way, and fell into the deep wellee, from
which I rescued him, and for once saved the life o' an
enemy.'"

"And now," said Eddie to the folk in the Miny, "ye hae
my story, and I feel relieved. I breathe a freer air at the
fireside of the Miny than anywhere else, and I will make
my journeys shorter for the time to come ; but how hae ye
fared since I left you ?" "Weel, on the whole," said Gilbert,
"with the exception of one unsought visit from the wasteful
locusts that are flying about. It was a misty forenoon, and
we were dreading little harm, when Sandy, who had been
out on the moor, observed, when the wind lifted a wave of
the white mist, a company of horsemen advancing. We
had just time to escape by the back door there when the
cavalcade entered the close. Grizzy was alone in the kitchen, and she avoided their enquiries surprisingly. They
did not behave so very ill, but the worst was, they stayed
all night, for the mist terrified them. We took up our residence in the Auchty, and made ourselves as comfortable as
possible, for we were in perfect safety in the bogle-hole.
They left us in the morning, and seemed not ungrateful for
the treatment they had received ; and so things have passed
off pretty well since you left us."

---

## CHAPTER XVI.

"I THINK," said Gilbert, to a company of friends who
he had met one day in his house, and among whom
was Eddie Cringan, who was now a more frequent
visitor at the Miny than ever—"I think that as the summer
is drawing to a close, we should have a conventicle some-

where among these hills.  The flock of Christ is now longing to taste again of the rich pastures on which it fed in
the blessed days when conventicles were rife.  Our standard-
bearers are now few indeed ; for unless it be Mr Peden and
James Renwick, we can scarcely count on any, at least in
this part.  And my opinion is, that, as Mr Renwick is now
in Galloway, we should send for Mr Peden, who, I hear, is
now in Sorn."  It seemed good to the friends that a conventicle should be held, and that Mr Peden should be brought,
and that notice of the meeting should be given to all the
friends throughout the wide locality, as secretly and speedily
as possible.

But the meeting place—that was the next question—
where was it to be ?  Dangers were on every side, and the
least whisper would bring the enemy on them from different
quarters.  Some spot hitherto unoccupied was deemed most
suitable.  "Weel, then," said Eddie, "if I may give my
opinion, I think the Gareland Cleuch should be that place.
I passed that way the other week on my road from Douglas,
and I wondered that no meeting had ever been held in that
spot.  In all my journeyings among these hills and glens, I
never saw a retreat equal to it for the purpose."  Eddie
was right, and all agreed that this should be the place.  The
Gareland Cleuch is a wonderful feature in the topography
of the moorlands.  It is an immense trench scooped out by
some watercourse in the almost level face of the desert.  It
is like a wide street in some of our large cities, with lofty
houses on either side, and nearly as perpendicular.  The
present brooklet that purls through it, is utterly inadequate
to account for the erosion of the trench ; and yet it has
been eroded, and that too by the action of water, but when
we cannot tell.  Probably its existence may be attributed
to some prior condition of the earth, for plainly it cannot be
attributed to anything in its present condition.  We have
many a time thought it strange that our geologists, who

visit the more distant parts of the globe, seldom think it
worth their while to look nearer home, especially in our
Scottish deserts, where things somewhat striking, and, shall
we say, staggering too, might perchance meet their view.

But the Gareland Cleuch was the very place for a conventicle.  The worshippers could sit in the deep bottom of the
cleuch, afar in the bosom of the wilderness, and no eye
could possibly descry them ; for the sides of the trench,
even within a short distance, appear to meet, so that a person would never dream that there was such an opening in
the surface of the moorland.

"I hae mair reasons than ane," said Eddie, "for fixing on
the Gareland Cleuch.  It is a central place, and equally convenient for the parishes of Douglas, Crawfordjohn, Sanquhar,
Muirkirk, Auchinleck, and Cumnock, so that if the day is
favourable, a goodly meeting may be expected.  And there
is another thing, the troopers are called elsewhere : there
are no dragoons in the castle of Sanquhar just now, for
Airly has marched to the lower parts of Nithsdale, and
Geordy Ga' tells me that their bit garrison is to be quartered for a few days, partly in Mauchline, and partly in Dal-
mellington ; and so I think there could scarcely be a more
favourable opportunity for holding a meeting."

In little more than a week after this, the projected meeting was held.  It turned out to be one of the largest conventicles that had assembled for a long time ; and the venerable Peden, though his constitution was greatly reduced
through the hardships to which he had been subjected for
more than a quarter of a century, presented himself in the
tent which had been reared in the deep dell, to screen him
from the burning sun.  The day was remarkably fine ; the
sun shone brightly on the multitude ; and the lambkins
sported among the bleating sheep on the brown bent above.
The warders lay flat on the side of the precipice, in full
view of the congregation, and could hear every word that
was spoken.

The preacher went on in his peculiar way, borrowing, with great facility, illustrations of his subject from the scenery around and from the incidents of the day. He had a dash of the poetic in his temperament, and far excelled in the imaginative faculty all his contemporaries who preached in the wilderness. He was an original; and had his mind been trained, he would have cut a figure in his time. But whatever were his qualifications, he was a man of God, and deeply imbued with the spirit of his Master. To preach the gospel was his meat and his drink, and he gladly embraced any opportunity of announcing the good news of salvation to sinners. His oratory was peculiar; it wanted fluency, but it was full of fervency. His manner was abrupt; he frequently diverged from the continuous line of his subject; but then his episodes were always striking and full of sentiment, so that they became little sermons in themselves, and were well suited to the diversified circumstances of his hearers. It was no ordinary treat to listen to the saintly Peden, whose ministrations were so greatly countenanced by his Master. The wilderness was his home; he had traversed it in its breadth and length—he knew all its retreats —all its hiding-places in the solitary dells. He knew every friendly household in the upland wastes—the amount of their means—the shelter they could afford—and all the ways of escape about the premises. The people of the desert counted him their man—he was one of themselves, and all of them had heard his voice again and again. At the conventicle, his preaching was regarded as something like a Divine communication immediately from heaven; for he used now and then to pause, as if he listened to a voice speaking in his ear, and then he burst out in all the fervour of his utterance with some weighty sentiment, or with some fresh and impressive view of Divine truth. It is needless to remark that Christ and Him crucified was the great theme of his preaching, for this was common to all the

conventicle preachers; this was the one leading topic, though
it did not exclude other topics of subordinate interest.

The conventicle held in Gareland Cleuch, as has been
remarked, was large, being convened from all the surrounding parishes. The worshippers sat in the bottom of the
deep dell, whence proceeded the song of praise and the voice
of fervent prayer. The discourse was powerful, and a hallowed influence from the Lord descended on many hearts,
and the children of the moorlands were fed with heavenly
manna. The day passed on without interruption, and
when the time of dismissal came, the company seemed un-
willing to separate. The spot was hallowed to them where
they had met with God, and they felt themselves endeared
to one another. Aged men and elders crowded around the
venerable preacher as he emerged from the tent, and women
and children pressed to be near him and receive his blessing,
but chiefly a company of strong young men, and men in the
prime of life, came near his person, determined to form his
body-guard should mischief befal. Conspicuous among
these were John Laing of Blagannoch and his brother Patrick—he, with the perplexing squint, who defeated the
Italian bully on a public stage in London—for Patrick had
served for many a year in the foreign wars, but returned to
his home among the mountains in the very heat of the persecution; and there was Andrew Clark of Auchengrouth, in
the moors of Sanquhar, with his nine brave and stalwart
sons at his back—one of whom suffered martyrdom in the
Grassmarket of Edinburgh, and another, who was doomed
to be shot on the bent before his father's door by Douglas
of Drumlanrig, but was saved by the intervention of an
aged woman who lived in the neighbourhood. There were
the Hairs from Glenwharry and Burncrooks, in the parish
of Kirkconnel; the Wilsons from Penauchrie; the Smiths
from the mouth of Glen Aylmer; and the Weirs from Tod-
holes, with many others of equal note, who were all pre-

pared to defend the man of God, who had that day conducted the services with so much profit to the Covenanters.

Hitherto all things had gone on well, but an event befel
which was not anticipated. There was a garrison that had
been recently established in the parish of Crawford, on the
Clyde, at a goodly distance from the place of meeting, and
it did not occur to any of the friends that any danger was
to be apprehended from it ; but Sandilands, the informer,
who wonned in Crawfordjohn, and whom Laing had caught
in the braken on the day of the conventicle at Friarminion,
as has already been detailed, was on the alert, and the news
had reached him of the projected conventicle, and though it
was at a late hour that he had received information, he hastened to Crawford on the Sabbath morning to rouse the
garrison. The commander hastily drew out his troops ;
but the way was long and rugged, and without almost a single footpath. At length they reached the wilds of Duneaton, but by this time the conventicle was leisurely dispersing. The troopers found they were too late to
attack the people in a body, but they resolved to pursue
them in detached parties. The greatest body of the people,
when they saw the soldiers, turned down what is called the
river Spank, with a view to reach the woods of Crawick. On
seeing this, the dragoons collected, and pursued the fugitives along the stream, but the way was rough, and greatly
retarded the horsemen. Some of the people took to the
heights on both sides, and thus eluded their pursuers. The
rest, however, continued their course down the valley, and
still kept before the troopers, till, nearing the river Crawick,
the soldiers came close up to them and fired, when one man
fell, and the rest escaped into the thickets. The name of
the worthy who was shot is not now known, but his grave
was to be seen within the last generation on the beautiful
green a little above the present bridge of Spank.

Mr Peden and his friends got safely to the Miny, among

whom were Laing, and Peter Corsan, and Sarah. The Miny
was now considered the place that afforded the greatest security of any in all the wide locality, so that the friends
who had convened here on this Sabbath evening considered
themselves out of danger. This evening was spent in holding something like a house conventicle. As they were conversing on many things, and as all looked up to Mr Peden
with the greatest veneration, and regarded him as an oracle,
Gilbert said, "What think ye, sir, will be the result of these
dismal times ?"  "A sword," he replied, "a sword hangs
over the bluidy land, and a woful time awaits this covenant-
breaking, perjured nation, and the Lord will avenge all our
right hand and our left hand defections; but our heads may
be under the sod ere all the judgments which I foresee coming shall descend on these apostate lands."  "But, sir,
what shall become of the poor, suffering remnant ?  I fear
we shall be worn out a' thegither, and the land become
spiritually desolate ; for unless it be yersel', and the kindly
lad Renwick, that is haudin' up his fainting mother's head
so tenderly, we would be utterly destitute. The hungry
flock of Christ in the desert is greatly famished, and is now
becoming weary and faint. I trow our meals are but few
and scanty, and there is a great bleating and wailing among
the flock."  "If," replied the venerable man, "if ye think
Christ's house be bare and ill-provided, harder than ye
looked for, assure yourselves Christ minds only to diet you,
not to hunger you. Our steward kens when to spend and
when to spare. Christ knows well whether heaping or
straiking agrees with our narrow-mouthed vessels, for both
are alike to Him; sparing will not enrich Him, and spending
will not impoverish Him.  He thinks it is ill won that is
holden off His people—grace and glory come out of Christ's
lucky hand. It is easy for Christ to be holden busy in di-
viding the fulness of His Father's house to His poor friends.
He delights not to keep mercy over night ; every new day

brings new mercies to the people of God." "But, sir," said the worthy Peter Corsan, "there is a waefu' scatterin' among us, and they are leaving us on the right hand and on the left, so that we may indeed be called a remnant; and I fear if this bluidy time continue much longer, that we shall scarcely have even a name left us." "It is true," replied the apostle of the desert, "it is true that this is indeed a winnowing time. A strong and mighty wind has arisen, but it is certain Christ's corn cannot be driven away, He will not want a hair of His people's head; He knows them all by head mark. I defy the world to steal a lamb out of Christ's flock unmissed. The storm will not lie long when the people of God have the worst of it, and when the wind is both in their back and in their face. A great fire in God's furnace will soon divide the gold from the dross. God is giving the saints a little trial, somewhat sharper than ordinary, that they may come out of the furnace as a refined lump." These are the identical words of Mr Peden, and in this way was the Sabbath evening spent, and even till far on in the night, in fervent prayer, in reading the Scriptures, and in singing the high praises of the Lord. Next day Peter Corsan and Sarah took leave of the company, and of the minister whom they so fervently loved.

Mr Peden lingered for a few days at the Miny, every one of which was spent more like a Sabbath than an ordinary day, for the words of grace and goodness were always distilling from his lips, and every household in which he sojourned, for even the shortest period, was always refreshed by means of his visit. At length, however, he left the hospitable abode of Gilbert Fleming, and in company with another person, he traversed the moors in the direction of the Wellwood, the residence of Captain John Campbell, a warm friend to the persecuted cause, and himself a sufferer. At the time of Mr Peden's visit he had left home to go to America, to avoid the persecutions in his native land.

When Mr Peden arrived at the Wellwood he asked the Captain's mother where he was. "He is," replied the worthy matron, "gone to America, for he can find no rest in his own country, and he is obliged to flee to the land of strangers, and we know not how it may be with him, nor how we shall fend in his absence." "No, no," said Mr Peden, "he is not gone : send for him, for he will never see America "—and it was even so, for a storm had arisen which endangered all on board, and the captain, not liking to encounter such tempests on the high seas, put back to the port again, and Campbell returned to his mother's house. He lived many years after the persecution ceased.

From Wellwood Mr Peden proceeded to Cameron's grave in Ayr's Moss. This was a spot he was fond of visiting. He used to sit on the gravestone and muse on past events ; and with a yearning he lifted his bonnet from his head, and looking up to heaven, exclaimed, "O, to be wi' Ritchie !" From this he went across the lonely moors to Sorn, to his brother's house, where, lingering for a few months in concealment, he died. He had a cave near the house, in which he resided for some time, and in which he fell into a sickness of which he died. "One morning early," says one who writes of him, "he left his cave and came to his brother's door ; his brother's wife said—'Sir, where are you going? —the enemy will be here.' He said, 'I know that.' 'Alas, sir,' said she, 'what will become of you?—you must go back to your cave again.' He said, 'I have done with that, for it has been discovered ; but there is no matter, for within forty-eight hours I will be beyond the reach of all the devil's temptations, and his instruments in hell and in earth shall trouble me no more.' About three hours after he entered the house, the enemy came, and having found him not in the cave, searched the barn narrowly, casting about the unthrashed corn, went through the house, stabbed the beds, but entered not into the place where he lay ; and within forty-eight hours after this he closed his pilgrimage, and became an inhabitant of that land where the weary are at rest, being beyond sixty years of age.

Eddie Cringan had been at the conventicle in Gareland Cleuch, and he received his own share of the impression which the services of that day had made on the audience. He had been acquainted with Mr Peden, and had done him service as he had done to others, but he had never been located with him in the same house for any length of time, and consequently had not the opportunity of hearing his conversation, which was so much distinguished for its spirituality and heavenliness. All this was new to him, and produced an ineffaceable impression on him; and he resolved to occupy the place of a middle-man no longer, but to take a decided step. He had now become a regular inmate of the Miny. It was to be his future home; for honest Gilbert Fleming thought he could never sufficiently requite him for the service of saving his life and the lives of his companions; and poor Grizzy, with her womanly heart, looked on him as her greatest benefactor. It was with no grudging hospitality, therefore, that Eddie was entertained at the Miny ; while, at the same time, he was at liberty to go occasionally about the country with his equipage as he thought fit.

One winter evening, towards the end of the *eighty-five*, as the household had gathered round the hearth, and as Eddie had just returned from one of his excursions, he appeared to be in a more than usually solemn mood, and something seemed to weigh heavily on his mind. At length, as if summoning all his courage, he said :—"My dear friends, I hae noo formed a resolution—I noo clearly see what the godly Priesthill said, that I did not rightly apprehend the cause for which ye are a' suffering sae muckle, and seem willing to suffer still mair ; but noo, laying a' things thegether, and especially considering what Mr

Peden said yon Sabbath night in this house, I hae resolved,
for better and for worse, to cast in my lot, decidedly, wi'
the suffering party ; and, as Grizzy said to me lang syne,
though I should bear witness in the Grassmarket, or be
shot in the muirs for my adherence to the cause, I am noo,
by the grace of God, resolved to abide by that truth.  I
mean to make no display regarding the step I hae ta'en.  I
do not intend to invite persecution, but neither do I intend
to avoid it by cowardly compliance.  I throw myself on
God's protection.  I am His, and let Him do with me as
seemeth good to Him."  Here the worthy man burst into
tears, and the whole household wept with him ; but none
seemed more affected than young Sandy, who was now a
decided Christian, and a firm adherent to the cause for
which his master suffered.  All congratulated Eddie on his
virtuous confession, and prayed that the grace which supported them might now support him.

"But," said Eddie, "I hae mair news than this to tell ye.
We hear many heavy tidings, and it is but right, when we
can do it, to make known something that may cheer us.  I
hear no news of the abatement of the persecution.  They
are burning the farm-steadings and the corn-stacks ; they
are driving away the cattle frae the stalls, and the sheep
frae the folds ; they are chasing parents from their dwellings,
and leaving children to beg their bread.  There is no abatement in these respects ; and how long this state of things
may continue, He only knows who knows all things.  But
still there are things occurring now and then that may cheer
us.  I hear that Mowat, the curate of Kirkconnel, over the
hills there, has renounced Prelacy, and cast in his lot wi'
the suffering people in this dark and cloudy day.  But what
I was ga'en to tell you is this : Geordy Ga' has left the
troopers ; he has become so disgusted wi' the profession,
and wi' the cruelties and wickedness practised by the sodgers,
that he could stand it nae langer ; and sae, on the Sabbath

night, when a' was dowf and mirk, and when the troopers, after a day of rioting and drunkenness, were sound asleep in the garrison, he quietly took his leave ; but before his departure, he stepped softly into the stable to take a last farewell of his charger, for the kindly brute likit him, and Geordy straikit him on the neck, and clappit him on the face, and the puir beast made an unco ado. Noo, the puir lad weel kens that instant death will be his lot if he should happen to be caught. A wonderfu' change has come o'er Geordy ; he tells me that his mother's prayers are to this day sounding in his ears, and that the advices of his godly father, auld Saun- Ga', grip his conscience sairly. He struggled lang against the voice within him, and tried to drown reflections in joining in the senseless mirth of his godless companions; but a' wadna do. Poor Geordy is in difficulties ; he kens na where to hide his head, baith for shame o' his conduct, and for fear o' the enemy. I left him in a friendly house in Douglas Water, but hoo lang he may succeed in avoiding the foe, I canna say."

"I trust," exclaimed Gilbert, "he'll never rue the step ; and, Eddie, I request it as a particular favour, that ye'll jist gang awa' and bring him here. The puir lad must be looked after ; and we will do our endeavour to screen him ; and not only so, but to instruct him in the way of salvation."

Accordingly, Eddie set out in quest of the penitent trooper early next morning, and by mid-day reached his residence. Geordy agreed to accompany him to the Miny, and when the night set in, the two friends proceeded over the moorlands to the friendly abode of Gilbert Fleming. It was past midnight ere they reached their destination, but what was their surprise to find the Miny occupied by the troopers, who were roaring, and swearing, and blustering about the premises. They had come in quest of both Geordy and Eddie. The poor inmates were in great distress, not knowing what might be the issue, in regard even to themselves.

Geordy's heart boiled with indignation, and old Eddie's manhood rose within him. Geordy proposed an instant attack upon the soldiers, but against this Eddie remonstrated, "for," said he, "what are we to so many ? and either our lives would go for it on the spot, or our capture would be certain ; let us stand aside for a little, for I think the thing is at its height, and they will soon depart." "I know one thing," said Geordy, "that will at least divert their attention ;" with this he ran straight to the stable, and, in the dark, turned out the horses into the close. In an instant all was in confusion ; the animals leaped, and pranced, and neighed, and ran one here and another there in the obscurity, so that the men were in the utmost consternation lest any of their chargers should be lost or injured, for in that case they knew the penalty. It was long before the animals were collected and reduced to order ; and before all things were assorted day began to dawn, and as the mist threatened to descend on the moors, the horsemen mounted and rode off. Eddie and Geordy watched their movements, and did not enter the house till they ascertained their complete departure, and the likelihood that they would not return.

When the troopers were fairly gone, Eddie and Geordy presented themselves in the kitchen of the Miny. Gilbert and his good spouse were delighted at seeing them, and expressed their wonder how they had reached the place without interruption. The whole circumstances were detailed on both sides, and much gratitude was expressed to the Giver of all good for the deliverance granted. Geordy was received with the warmest expression of friendship, as a strayed sheep that had returned to the fold of Christ. It was the particular request of Gilbert that Eddie and Geordy should now consider themselves as a part of the household: and that, as the Miny and the places adjacent were regarded as affording no small security to persons under hiding, everything should be so arranged as to admit of immediate concealment in case of a hasty visit from the enemy. The way of escape by the dairy was all prepared anew, but the vault at the Auchty was considered as the chief place of retreat. The troopers had not yet forgotten the affright from the ewe, and the bats, and the coffin, and Geordy asserted that they would never venture to enter a place of such bad repute. The apartment above the little chamber, on the right side of the farthest extremity of the vault, was put in order for a dormitory; and it was agreed that when summer came, Eddie and Geordy should sleep there, and that in the meantime they should sleep in the house.

Gilbert now took into earnest consideration the instruction of Geordy. He had now seen the evil of his conduct generally, and the sinfulness of the step particularly in joining the persecuting party; but then the question with Gilbert was, did he know the way of being saved? did he understand the ground of a sinner's hope before God? did he plainly perceive that the death of Christ, as the great sacrifice for man's sin, was that alone on which a sinner can rest for acceptance with God now, and for eternal life hereafter? These were the points in which Gilbert wished to instruct him, with a view to bring him fully to the faith of Jesus, and to a genuine repentance. Nor were Gilbert's efforts in vain, for he soon found in his pupil an apt scholar, who received the truth with all readiness of mind, and was sanctified by its influence, through the power of the Holy Spirit upon his heart. Geordy became, in short, a new man, and arrived at no ordinary stability in the faith. The family at the Miny were a truly happy household, living in the fear of God, and in sweet Christian intercourse; and though there were fears on every side, yet they encouraged themselves in the Lord their God, and left all their concerns in His hand, and were at rest.

## CHAPTER XVII.

IT was about the commencement of winter, a dreary period in the moorlands, and a season generally looked
forward to with considerable anxiety by the children
of the desert, for no one could tell how it might fare with
them as it respected weather, and other hardships ; we say
it was about the commencement of winter, when at a close
of a cold November day, a few friends convened around the
hearth of the Miny. Among others who had foregathered
on this occasion was Peter Corsan with two strangers.
These were Andrew Mar and John Weir, the one from Leadhills, and the other from the moors of Crawford. Gilbert
had often heard of the two men, and he felt particularly
gratified at meeting with them. They were eminently
Christian persons, and were well known to Peter, who had
often described their sufferings and their worth to Gilbert.
A wonderful sympathy pervaded the society of the persecuted in those trying days ; they all knew one another, if
not personally, at least by name, and when one suffered, all
suffered in common. Andrew was a miner, and John was a
shepherd. They were men of like mind, equally attached
to the common cause, and both possessed of ardent piety.
They travelled in company to conventicles in the loneliest
places, and were always found prepared to defend the helpless in the case of an onslaught by the enemy.

"I hail you as brethren," said the worthy host of the
Miny, "and I deem myself honoured in entertaining you
under my roof for the Master's sake." "We feel particularly grateful to you," replied they, "for your kind reception
of us, and the more especially as, since the time of the rescue in the Pass of Enterkin, we have sought refuge among
strangers."

"And," said Gilbert, whose curiosity was awakened to
know something of the incident which had made such a
noise throughout the country, and which had so dreadfully
exasperated the persecutors, "what may be the particulars
of that rescue ? or had you any concern in it?"   "We had;
we were both present; the one, a rescuer, and the other,
rescued.   We happened to be at a conventicle down in
Nithsdale, which was scattered by the military, when he was
caught, and I escaped."   "And how were ye treated?"
asked Gilbert, " it is a wonder you were not shot on the
spot."   "We were not, however," said John, "but we were
carried to Dumfries, and imprisoned there.   We were kept
for a short time and the command was given that we should
be conveyed to Edinburgh, and there treated as it should be
seen fit.   There were nine of us in all, including the
preacher.   The troopers who guarded us were twenty-eight
in number, a set of rough and cruel fellows.   At first they
made us trudge along as fast as their horses trotted.   We
proceeded in this way for a number of miles, till we became
so exhausted that they were obliged to seek some means of
conveyance.   Their horses were all occupied, but, to remedy
this, they seized the horses at the farm-steadings as they
passed along, and demanded provisions otherwise.   As for
the prisoners, we got nothing, but were placed on the horses,
two and two of us bound together on the bare-backed animals
with a halter for a bridle.   In this manner, after much
jolting and hard riding, we reached the mouth of the pass,
where our road became more and more perilous; and
then what was a matter of concern to us all, the mist
began to settle on the top of the mountain, and to creep
gradually down its sides, when we expected every instant
to be enfolded in its haze and lose our way.   But the
moment of our deliverance was just at hand.   The minister
was placed behind a powerful dragoon, to whom he was attached by a belt, so that we could have no intercourse with

him ; but the man with whom I was seated, a very devout
person, and who seemed to be incessantly engaged in prayer,
expressed his strong confidence that the Lord would appear
in some way or other for our help, in this the day of our
perplexity.   I said that the Lord was the Hearer of Prayer,
and that He could rescue us in the most unlooked-for way,
but that it was necessary that we should be prepared for
the worst, and be contented to die like our brethren, whose
blood was flowing on field and scaffold.   I said that, on
reaching Edinburgh, there was no doubt that we would
either be publicly executed, or banished beyond the seas ;
but that it was a happy thing to rest without carefulness on
Him who did all things well, and in whose cause we were
suffering.   As we were thus conversing, a sort of hubbub
was perceived in the front of the long line of the procession
as it moved forward on the narrow path, and a strong and
stern voice was heard to issue from the skirts of the mist,
which had now moved down almost to the edge of the footpath, 'Deliver our minister,' was the demand.    'Who are
ye ?' exclaimed the commander of the party, 'and what
want ye ?'   'We want our minister ; will ye deliver him
up, and the prisoners who are with him ?   If you do so, we
will not harm you, but if not, we will rescue them by force.'
'No,' replied the captain ; 'I will not deliver them up ;
stand on your guard.   Soldiers, fire !'   A volley was forthwith poured into the bosom of the mist, but without effect.
The men on the hill, to the number of twelve, now emerged
from behind the hazy screen, and fired in return.   A ball
reached the commander, and, gliding through his brain, he
immediately fell from his horse and tumbled into the abyss
beneath, and the animal with him, and was dashed to pieces.
The next in command, fearing lest the mountain-men should
fire again, and, perchance, send the whole party over the
precipice together, demanded a parley, and this the more
especially as two of their scouts had just returned with the

intelligence that a large company was stationed in warlike attitude at the top of the pass ready, as they conceived, to obstruct their progress in case of a refusal to deliver their charge.  This put the party entirely at a stand, who saw themselves between two fires, and the commander declared himself ready to come to terms.  The minister and the prisoners were now surrendered.  'And now,' said the officer, 'I request you to order the assailants at the head of the pass to retire, and not to hinder our march.'  'These persons belong not to us,' said the leader of the hillmen; 'they are unarmed people; travellers waiting till you pass by, that they may pursue their journey.'  'Indeed!' exclaimed the trooper, 'had I known that, you should not so easily have obtained the prisoners.'  'May be,' answered the Covenanter; 'but we have another company in reserve behind this mist.  Here are twenty-five men in addition to the twelve you see.  We are in all thirty-seven, and able to cope with you at this moment if you be so disposed.  We have the advantage of the height above, and if you think you can match us, you can try your skill.'  'No,' replied the officer, 'I think ye be brave fellows—e'en gang yer gate.  But,' said he to the minister, 'ye owe yer life to this execrable mountain.'  'Nay, rather,' replied he, 'to the God that made the mountain.'

"One of the prisoners, however, was retained by the soldiers; but how this happened, it is not easy to say.  His name was John M'Kechnie, a native of Galloway, a singularly pious man.  He was shot through the arm, and carried to Edinburgh, where he died of his wounds.  Lochear, another of the prisoners, was the laird of a small estate in the parish of Glencairn.  He was one of the rescued; but, after he was released, he became stupified, and fell in among the soldiers, who used him barbarously, and fired small shot in his face, which deprived him of his sight.  He was afterward severely wounded, and left on the hill by the troopers

for dead.  He was, in this condition, found by friends, and
carried to a cottage, where he was taken care of.  Such is
the rescue at Enterkin Pass, which has made such a noise
in the district, and of which our persecutors have made such
a handle."

" A wonderful deliverance !" exclaimed Gilbert ; "a most
wonderful deliverance !   Behold, what hath God wrought !
But how came all the circumstances connected with this
rescue to be so well and properly managed ?"    " I was one
of the party," said Andrew Mar, " who accomplished the
rescue, and I can tell you something of that.  A friend of
mine, who happened to be in the town of Dumfries on the
day before the prisoners were to be conveyed to Edinburgh,
was informed of the circumstance, and it immediately
occurred to him that something might be done for their
rescue.  Accordingly, he hastened forward to Durisdeer,
and informed the friends in that locality, and the news was
secretly conveyed to the friends in Leadhills and Wanlock-
head.  A party was instantly formed, and we agreed to post
ourselves at a particular part in the pass, where our object
was likely to be best accomplished, and where, as you have
heard, we did accomplish it.  The steep side of Auchenlone
height was almost unassailable from below.  It was like
scaling a high wall—a wall of hundreds and hundreds of
feet in sloping altitude, and the footing was so slippery that
few could maintain an upright position, so that the assailants stationed on the slope had the full advantage of those
beneath, and this is the reason why the rescue was made
with so much ease."

The famed Pass of Enterkin is a deep and terrific defile
on the south side of the Lowther Hills, a few miles to the
east of Sanquhar—the centre of the persecuting field in
Upper Nithsdale.  The majestic Lowthers, clad in green
from top to bottom, were long regarded as the loftiest
mountains in the south-west of Scotland ; but recent obser-

vations have shown that they are somewhat inferior in elevation to Hartfell, near Moffat, and also to another mountain in the upper wilds of Galloway. But none of these mountains can be compared in beauty to the verdant Lowthers, from the summit of which the most extensive view, perhaps, is to be obtained of any in the south of Scotland. In a clear day, and with a good prospect, the Firth of Clyde can be seen in the one direction, and the Firth, of Solway in the other. From this height the mountains eastward present an extraordinary appearance. The great proportion of the spacious field of the persecution in the south and west is plainly discernible ; and there is scarcely a moorland, or height, or glen, that appears in sight, that has not its own associations, pleasant or painful, connected with the suffering times. A whole volume might be written on the various matters which come up before the view in the different localities that spread themselves all around. Is there a place within the precincts of this vast space that was not traversed by our persecuted ancestors? No ; and it is true what the saintly Renwick said—"The moors and the mosses of the west of Scotland are flowered with martyrs."

But the Pass, what of it? Enterkin Path, as it is also called, was for many generations the defile through which travellers from the lower parts of Nithsdale journeyed in their way to the metropolis. It is an extremely narrow gorge ; for the two enormous mountains — the Lowthers on the north side, and the stupendous height of Auchenlone on the south—touch at their bases, and leave room only for the streamlet that gurgles through the strait. It is on the Auchenlone side of the defile that the narrow foot-path wends upward to the top of the glen. The precipitous sides of both hills are in some places like a wall in steepness, and rise for thousands of feet in the slope upwards. The path on the slope of Auchenlone is sometimes

covered over with the rubbish that rushes from the side of
the hill in time of heavy rain or melting snow, and this
renders the footing particularly perilous, and not infre-
quently leads to fatal accidents, so that, in the dark
especially, the hazard to be apprehended is imminent. No
place along the whole route from Dumfries to Edinburgh
could have been more favourable for the rescue than this.

"I ken the Enterkin," said Eddie, "and I hae gude
reason to mind it weel. I never was so near my latter, end
till I be really at it, as I was ance in that fearfu' pass. I
had occasion to visit Durisdeer in the way of my calling.
I had come up that lonely stream they ca' Glengonar, where
lang syne, they say, a man frae Germany, of the name o'
Bulmer, gathered goud, and hid it in the auld castle o'
Crawford, or in some other secret place, for a heap o' goud
is a fine posy, and no tac be shyled at. Weel, as I was
saying, I cam' up Glengonar, sellin' the keel on baith sides o'
the water, and reaching Leadhills, I stayed a' nicht in the
house o' a douce man o' the name o' Saunders Watson. I
hae been lang acquainted wi' Saunders. In our younger
days we followed the smuggling trade thegether, but
Saunders, like me, cam' to see the evil o' the profession, and
he became a miner, and I became a keelman. Saunders
has few equals in yon quarter, and I aften wonder how he
has escaped the grasp o' the enemy sae lang, but he has
escaped as yet, and is the means o' nae sma' gude in Leadhills, and the parts around. Weel, as I was saying, I had
occasion to visit Durisdeer, and I left my quarters in the
forenoon o' a bonny sunny day, and reached the head o' the
pass in my descent to the lower parts. As me and the cuddie were steppin' tentilie along, I saw in the distance afore
me a row of men on horseback entering the mouth o' the
pass below. I couldna discern by their dress wha they
micht be, but I thought they micht be carriers wha were
joggin' slowly up the ascent, wi' their packs thrown across

the horses. I soon discerned, however, that they were a
very different squad—they were in short a company o'
dragoons wending their way wi' muckle caution along the
precarious footpath. We met exactly at the spot where
the rescue took place. Douglas of Drumlanrig was the
commander, a cruel, reckless blade, who thinks as little o'
sheddin' human blood as of swallowing a glass o' red wine.

"Weel, then I encountered the party, but Douglas
wasna first, he was last; a wise precaution, for the horses
going before him made for him a beaten path, so he could
move with greater security. I was for creepin' cannily to
the upper side o' the path to let them pass, horse after
horse, but when the foremost dragoon saw this he shouted,
'Ho, fellow, with your miserable donkey there, enough to
frighten a whole gang of demons themselves, not to speak
of horses made of flesh and blood, keep to the side next to
the precipice, I say, else we will tumble you and your equipage heels over head right down into the gulf there, and no
ceremony.' I then moved to the lower side as I was commanded, and the poor cuddie stood shaking, as horse after
horse passed haughtily along, in scorn, it would appear, of
their more humble fellow-quadruped that stood cowering by
their side. They moved on jeerin' me and passing their
jokes at the expense o' baith the cuddie and me.

"But the thing was this—Douglas at length came forward, and seeing the plight I was in, and hearin' the gibes o'
the sodgers, he lookit sternly in my face, and then gave the
bit cuddie a push, and syne a kytch on the braid side, when
the puir beast stagger'd—for I was still sittin' on him, and
missing his footing, he slid down, side foremost, away and
away, while I keepit my seat, to the infinite amusement of
the troopers, who made the hills ring with their peals of
laughter, and the whole cavalcade was arrested on the spot,
eager to witness the upshot. I heard one of them cry, 'So
then, old fellow, your race is nearly run; and so it was, for

it happened that the puir beast was caught by the stump of
an old tree that was firmly rooted among the sklithery
stanes that covered the steep side o' the hill ; and lucky it
was—for steep as our descent had been, the portion that
lay below was steeper still, and, indeed, had we slid over
the brow, no earthly power could have saved us. The
sodgers moved on and left us to our fate. I still sat on
the animal, not daring to stir. In a short space the
troopers were out of sight, and no friendly hand near to
help. I said to mysel' now, if the Lord do not send help
we are over. I lifted up my heart to Him who is the preserver of our life, and besought His aid who has said, 'Call
on me in the day of trouble, and I will deliver thee, and
thou shalt glorify me.' Surely, thought I, this is a time of
extremity, and I will lift up my eyes to Him from whom
cometh mine aid. As I was ruminating on my sad case, I
observed two shepherd lads descending the steep side of
the green hill before me. They had observed my situation,
but durst not move till the sodgers were out of view, and
then they hasted to my rescue.

"They went round by the head of the cleuch, and at length
reached me sitting on the trembling beast. They scrambled
down among the shingly stones, for the distance from the
road was not more than twenty steps, but, then, the fearfu'
gulf below. The first thing was to get me aff the cuddie's
back without much movement. I then got my feet somewhat securely fixt among the shifting rubbish, and stood at
the poor brute's head and straikit, and clappit him, and
spoke kindly to him. The twa active young men then removed the creels tentilie frae his back, and creepin' up the
best way they could to the road, placed them in safety
there. But the main difficulty yet remained—how was the
cuddie to be got up ? I began to think that the attempt
would be needless, and that the harmless beast must just be
left to his fate, and sairly did the thought of this pain me.

It was not for the price of the animal—*that* I caredna a
snuff for—I could easily supply that, but him and me had
been lang friends, and mony a weary mile hae we journeyed
thegether, baith in storm and in sunshine, by nicht and by
day, and the puir craiter had a wark wi' me, for I never
used him ill, but rather fondled him, and aye was ready wi'
something for his mouth    And so, as I was saying, I couldna
think to see the auld cuddie's mischance ; it went near my
heart, and I wad rather hae seen the creels and a' that was
in them harried ten times o'er, than seen the beast's ill.    At
last one of the shepherds said, ' I think I see a way of man-
aging the thing, and if we had a shovel it could be easily
done, but, then, that we have not, only let us do our best.'
They then set to work wi' hands and feet, and formed a sort
of path along the side of the declivity among the loose rubbish, and then came out in a slenting way to the edge of the
regular road.    This work took a long time, and cost no little
labour, but it answered the end.    I then pulled the donkey
gently by the bridle, and he, seeing me before him, began
to move, and the two men behind pushing firmly along, he
ventured forward step by step till we got him to the road.
And, oh, what a matter o' thankfulness to us a'! and I could
not fail to see the good hand of Providence in the thing.    I
offered the lads a reward for their trouble, but they would
take nothing ; they said they had their reward in the satisfaction of helping a fellow-creature in distress.    And so we
met with no adventure farther till we came to the farm-
house of Dalveen, to which I was bound wi' keel to the
shepherds."

"Oh, Eddie, Eddie," exclaimed Gilbert, "but ye are an
unco man !   Ye hae met wi' muckle scathe in yer time, and
ye are here yet in life, and as yauld for the moors as ever.'
"We are all indebted to Eddie," said Peter Corsan, "for he
was the eminent means of preserving our lives on the occasion of the conventicle at the Shaw, and in how many more

instances he has been the means of preventing the shedding of innocent blood, owing to the seasonable information he has communicated, cannot well be known, but the day will declare it."

"I think," said Andrew Mar, "that all the attempts that our persecuted friends have made, first and last, for deliverance, have only aggravated the severity of our condition. Drumclog and Bothwell, the Archbishop's death, and the Sanquhar Declaration, have only tended to heat the furnace seven times, and now this last affair of the rescue has brought great distress on all the district around. The seven parishes in the immediate neighbourhood—Kirkbride, Durisdeer, Morton, Sanquhar, Kirkconnel, Crawford, and Crawfordjohn—are all prostrated under the power of the military, who are searching everywhere, and capturing all suspected persons."

This statement, made by honest Andrew, is not in the least degree exaggerated. The rescue in Enterkin Pass cost the country much. The following are the words of the historian Wodrow on this same subject:—"Orders," he says, "came from Edinburgh to all above fifteen years of age in Nithsdale to arm, and meet the gentlemen and soldiers in their appointed places, that they might search the whole shire for the rescuers of the prisoners ; and warning was given next Sabbath in the churches. Accordingly, every parish met, having some soldiers with them, searching mosses, muirs, and mountains, woods, and every corner of the shire ; but I do not find they catched any prisoners that day of the general search. When this failed them, the next Lord's-day intimation is made from pulpits in ten or twelve parish churches, nearest Enterkin, that all persons above fifteen years should meet at New Dalgerno next, and declare upon oath what should be inquired at them. Multitudes came, and were interrogate as to reset or converse—if they knew any guilty of it—if they knew who rescued the pris-

oners, or which way they went, or where they are now.   It
was but a few they could examine that day, and so the
soldiers divided into the several parishes, and appointed several districts up and down the country, and with
them Mr James Alexander, Sheriff-Depute.   The Laird
of Stonehouse, and other heritors of the different parishes,
accomplished yet a more diligent search.   The sheriff-
officers went from house to house, and they were appointed
to return written executions of their summons, that there
might be none omitted by paction, bribes, or the like ; and
the Episcopal ministers in each parish were obliged to give
in their rolls upon oath.   At those courts the forementioned
queries were proposed, and the strictest inquiry possible
was made—who kept not the church, who heard, married,
or baptised with outed ministers, and the like, as to which
many had been interrogate—I know not how often—formerly.   The absents had soldiers sent upon them, and multitudes were imprisoned or found caution to answer.   This
work continued about six weeks, and then the Circuit met,
of which already.   The reader will easily guess what a vast
trouble this inquisition brought upon that country.

"Ken ye," asked Gilbert at Andrew Mar, "ken ye what
befel the rescuers ?   Did any of them fall into the enemy's
hand ?"   "Why," replied Andrew, "out of thirty-seven
men engaged in that affair, it is not to be expected that
every one would escape.   James Harkness of Locherben
was seized with others and carried to Edinburgh, where
he was tried and condemned to die, but, with a number
more, escaped from the Canongate Jail, and thus saved his
life.   His brother Thomas, however, was not so fortunate.
He, with other two friends, Andrew Clark, smith in Leadhills, and Samuel McEwen, were apprehended by Claverhouse, who came upon them lying fast asleep in the woods
of Closeburn.   The three were conveyed to Edinburgh,
where, arriving at one o'clock, they were publicly executed

at five on the same day.  Clark was one of the nine brave
sons of Andrew Clark of Auchengrouth, in the moors of
Sanquhar.  The black Macmichael—the brother of the
saintly Daniel of Lurgfoot, in the parish of Morton, who
was lately shot at the mouth of the Pass of Dalveen by
Dalyell of Kirkmichael—took an active part in the rescue,
he who shot in self-defence Peter Pearson, the violent curate of Carsphairn, is still alive, but under hiding like ourselves."

"Let us pray," said Gilbert, "for the preservation of our
friends in the day of their peril."  The little company then
kneeled down, and Gilbert poured forth a most fervent
prayer, during which all were melted into tears.

---※---

## CHAPTER  XVIII.

OF the persecutors that traversed the spacious field of
Martyrland, in its breadth and length, a few of the
most renowned names are well-known ; but the fry
that overspread the country, and whose fame was more of a
local kind, is, now-a-days, comparatively little known.
Every one knows Claverhouse, and Lagg, and Dalzell, and
so on, but there were behind these a host of others no less
keen and cruel, and whose names are now considerably in
the shade.  The general reader, therefore, is in danger of
supposing that Claverhouse, and Lagg, with a few others,
were all that were employed in this work of mischief, and
that all the atrocities of the persecution, especially in the
upland districts, are to be attributed to them.  That they
were fell and valorous in the work of their masters cannot
be denied, but the main mischief in the moorland localities
was perpetrated by the subalterns, and petty officers clothed
with a little brief authority.  These were the persons who
were emphatically a curse to the poor peasantry, and who,

possessing no honourable principle, could condescend to acts of the lowest villainy without degrading a reputation which could not well stand lower. The number of such infamous persons that were let loose over the south and west cannot now be accurately ascertained, but there must have been scores of such individuals. We may here give a few of the names of these subordinates. These were Strachan, and Crichton, and Inglis, and Bruce, and Bannatyne, and Douglas, and Cornet Grɩham, and Bonshaw, and Westerhall, and Nisbet, and Dalzell of Carmichael, and bluidy Dumbarton, and the Laird of Lee, Watson, Alison, White, Lawrie, and the scapegrace Peter Inglis, son of the Captain Inglis above mentioned. These, with a host of others, needless to name, were all spread abroad, causing vexation and distress in every quarter. Their depredations were so extensive and severe that they were familiarly denominated locusts, and Sir Walter Scott relates the following anecdote :—That some years after the persecution had terminated, when a company of soldiers had occasion to march through a moorland district, a farmer's wife, on observing them from the door of her house, exclaimed, " Hech, sirs, but there are our ain auld locusts come back again."

It is, however, chiefly to Claverhouse and Lagg, the two most redoubted leaders in the fierce crusade against the Covenanters in the days of persecution, that in this chapter we would direct the notice of the reader. As the Miny was the great resort in the moors for the persecuted wanderers, so Gilbert Fleming was seldom without visitors, either strangers, or former friends. Their conversation, as was natural, turned on the posture of affairs in the country, and on the situation of matters as it regarded themselves individually. A small company of such persons happened to convene around the hearth of the Miny one lonely winter night, when the frost lay hard on the wide moorlands. The conversation turned on the raids of Claverhouse, of whom the peasantry stood in terrible affright. There were present David Dun, from the wilds of Ayrshire, good John Fraser, from lone Dalwhairn, near the source of Ken, Peter Clark, from the Water of Dee in Galloway, and Andrew Wilson from Carsphairn. These four had forgathered at a conventicle in the deserts beyond Monthraw. The meeting was surprised by the troopers, who chased the scattered people in every direction, and the friends just now mentioned found their way in the dusk to the Miny, led by David Dun, who knew the place.

"I think," said Gilbert, "that the wickedness of these men must now be near its height ; it's awful and unbearable to think of their oppressions ; the Lord will not much longer tolerate this work. Shall all the prayers put up in moors, and glens, and cottages, by living witnesses and slain martyrs, not be answered ? The Great Intercessor will prevail, and the day of retribution will come round."

" True, Gilbert, true," replied David Dun, "the Lord is certainly on our side, for the cause in which we suffer is His. Claverhouse has been raging sadly about the head of the Water of Ken, and in the places about the Water of Scar, where he has wrought terrible mischief, especially in the Scar."

"Ah," said Grizzy, "I weel mind the Scar; I stayed when I was a bit lassie wi' the auld gudewife o' Hallscar. She was my grand-aunt, and a Christian weel worthy o' her name. Many a gude advice I gat frae her, and many a fervent prayer did she put up for me, while I knelt at her knee, and hid my face in her lap. Many a time in her reeky room, sittin' afore an ingle o' bleezin' peats, wi' the tobacco pipe in her cheek, and puffin' the smoke up the lum, and wi' a sweet smile on her withered features, for she was an auld woman, and full of days, I say many a time hae I seen her wi' her eyes lookin' upwards, and her hands spread in the attitude o' prayer, and mutterin' words that I didna

understand, except that once I heard her say, O Lord, bless
this puir bit lassie, and may she be spared to be a mother
in Israel. I kent she meant me, and my bit heart filled,
and the tears stood in my een. She then took me on her
knee, and pressed me to her bosom, and rockit me frae side
to side, and said, 'My puir feckless bairny, it's hard to wit
what God may mak' o' thee yet ; the Lord be your guide
through life, and your portion through eternity, and when
my auld head is hidden in the cauld, cauld grave, may ye
live as a witness for Jesus Christ.' Muckle mair she said
that I didna weel understand, but mony a time hae I thought
on these things since. Her last days, as I hae heard tell,
were peaceful, and relying on the blessed Saviour and His
merits, she fell asleep. She was a gracious woman, and I
turned unco brodent on her, and it was like to break my
wee heart a'thegither to part frae her."

"I ken the Scar," said Eddie, "I ken the Scar, for our
route in the smuggling days was past the head of it, and
we often hid in the deep moss hags that lie between it and
the Ken. But it is wi' the middle o' the Scar that I hae
maist to do, for I used to deal wi' the shepherds o' Glen-
manna, and Dalyen, and Auld Glenwhargen, and Hallscar,
and the Shiel, and even as far up as Polgowan, and Dal-
gonar, and Powskeoch, and a' these quarters. There's a
cluster o' Christians in yon glen, the like o' whilk is
scarcely to be met wi'. The enemy kens this, and hence
the troopers pay them frequent visits. There's a fearfu'
rock yonder they ca' Glenwhargen Craig, towering some
hundreds o' feet high. They say that Claverhouse, on a
black war-steed, rode richt doon the face o't, and that the
animal on which he was mounted was not his own bold
charger, made o' flesh and bluid, but the Evil One himsel'.
I hae seen o'er muckle o' the oots and ins o' the warld to
hae ony faith in that. It's lang since I was in yon bonnie
glen, but my thoughts often revert to it. I never weary o'

lookin' at these great swelling mountains, liftin' their proud
heads high up to the bright blue sky, and their green sides a'
dotted o'er wi' bleatin' sheep, and their bits o' lambies
trottin' at their heels.

"I remember of being ance favoured wi' ane o' the finest
scenes my auld een ever beheld, frae the tap o' the hill that
lies between the Nith and the Scar. I left Sanquhar in the
morning, when the valley was filled wi' mist, and syne I
made my way wi' the cuddie up the slope o' the green hill
they ca' the Whang, and when I reached the summit, the
brown tops o' a' the hills round and round were quite clear
o' the haze, and, oh, what a sight! I will never forget it.
The valleys beneath were fu' o' pure white mist, and the
heads of the hills were seen like a hundred islands in the
midst of the great ocean. The whole country, as far as the
eye could reach, appeared as if sunk in deep water, and leaving only the higher parts bare, and showing them gilded in
the morning sun.

"We hae often heard of the Scar Water Christians,"
said Gilbert, "they are something like the Christians of
Carsphairn, of whom Mr Peden often speaks ; and it seems
that Claverhouse has found them out, as he does all others,
however remote their dwelling-places. The evil genius of
his party spurs him on, and he seems to have a keen scent
in sniffing out the hiding places of the wanderers ; and, besides, one would think that he was everywhere. There is
no dallying with him ; he grasps his victim, and ends his
life at once." "It is not easy," added David Dun, "to re-
count the raids of Claverhouse, or to retail his exploits of
cruelty, or, with all this, his mean and shabby deeds of
pilfering and robbery. From our own certain knowledge,
we can produce facts respecting this man that would dis-
grace any ordinary character. For instance, when, some
time ago, he came into the parish of Bar, in Ayrshire, there
was a worthy man of the name of M'Leweyend who had

beenat Bothwell, and was a prisoner in the Greyfriars' Churchyard in Edinburgh, and whom his wife, through certain
influential gentlemen, had succeeded in liberating. When
they were on their way home, Claverhouse came to his
house and plundered it of everything valuable. He carried
away all the clothes, and took with him two horses worth
six pounds sterling; and shortly after he lost nine cows, an
ox, a horse, and twenty fine sheep, with all the crop of that
year, and everything of household furniture that could be
removed."

"I remember," added Andrew Wilson, "when Claverhouse came to Carsphairn, when he seized all the horses
that were available for his purpose. From one man in
Craigengillen he took three that were worth eleven nobles
a-piece. In the same parish he robbed a poor widow of the
sum of fifty pounds, because, as he pretended, a servant of
her's had been at Bothwell. In the neighbouring parish of
Ballmaclellan, he acted in a similar manner. In the parish
of Glencairn he wrought fearful havoc. He apprehended a
harmless youth at his work, and pressed him strongly to
tell who of his neighbours had been at Bothwell. The poor
lad either could not or would not inform him; whereupon
they began to torture him, and twisted a cord so firmly
about his head, that it cut through the flesh into the bone.
The pain was inexpressible, and his cries were heart-rending,
but no confession could be extorted, and he died. Another
boy was caught in the same parish, and of him they demanded information respecting his master, who, they said,
had been at Bothwell. He refused to utter a word; and in
order to chastise his obstinacy, as they called it, they suspended him from the balk in the house, by means of cords
attached to his thumbs. The torture he endured was
excessive, but nothing could be got from him."

The preceding statements, made by Andrew Wilson and
David Dun are true, and are recorded in the veritable page

of the historian in nearly the very words we have given. In support of the fact of the injuries so gratuitously inflicted on mere boys and young lads by these ruthless men, we may here give a quotation from the diary of Sergeant James Nisbet respecting his own young brother. "The cruel enemy," he says, "got my dear brother into their hands. They examined him respecting the persecuted people, where they haunted, or if he knew where any of them was, but he would not open his mouth to speak one word to them. They held the point of a drawn sword to his naked breast ; they fired a pistol over his head ; they set him on horseback behind one of themselves, to be taken away and hanged ; they tied a cloth on his face, and set him on his knees to be shot to death. They beat him with their swords and with their fists ; they kicked him several times with their feet to the ground ; yet after they had used all the cruelty they could, he would not open his mouth to speak one word to them ; and although he was a very comely, proper child, going in ten years of age, yet they called him a vile, ugly, dumb devil, and beat him very sore, and went their way, leaving him lying on the ground, sore bleeding in the open fields." Such is the sergeant's account of the matter, and such was the victory gained by a mere child over a whole host of the enemy.

But we have not yet done with the "bluidy Clavers," as he was familiarly called. Andrew stated farther, "that in the parish of New Glenluce, Claverhouse seized John Archibald, Anthony M'Bryde, John MacLeanochan, and John Wallace. They were brought to Stranraer, and lay in prison twelve weeks, and because they refused to bind themselves to attend the curates, they were not only kept in prison, but the troopers were sent to their houses to live and riot at will, till all the provisions for men and horses were utterly consumed. After these poor men had been three months in prison, and had sustained the spoiling of their goods, Claverhouse ordered them to be tied two and two together, and set upon bare-backed horses, and to be carried to Edinburgh, there to be tried. When they had gone one day's journey, he made the proposal that if they would pay him a thousand merks a-piece, he would set them at liberty. To this they agreed, and were sent home ; but this did not prevent them from being subjected to future hardships." This, also, the historian Wodrow asserts.

Peter Clark who lived on the Water of Dee in Galloway, related the following story :— " Claverhouse," he said, "when ranging up and down in Galloway, came with his troopers to the Water of Dee, and surprised six persons in concealment there. He shot four of them on the spot. Their friends came and buried their bodies, but Claverhouse learning this, ordered their graves to be opened, which was done accordingly, and the coffins were exposed for three or four days, till the soldiers departed. The body of James Macmichan was taken from the grave and suspended on a tree. They were buried in the churchyard of Dalry in Galloway." This also is verified by the historian, and with more circumstantial statement.

"Ay," said Grizzy, "after his shootin' o' the godly John Brown we may easily believe a' that o' him. Oh ! but it was a waesome morning that at Priesthill. I saw Isabel the other day nae farther gane, when I paid her a visit o'er the muir, and she was tellin' me how kind the Lord had been to her, and how she was enabled to forgive the murderer frae her very heart, and to pray for him, and she said she had muckle peace in doing this. She says she sometimes feels lonely in yon muir, but then she just gangs to her closet and comes away cheered, and as happy as if she had a' her kind friends about her. She tells me she has great comfort in wee Janet, who sympathises wi' her in a' things, though she binna her mother. The puir bairn amaist tynt her reason a' thegether on the mornin' that her father was

shot, she gat sic a fricht that she wasna hersel' for lang.  I
am sure, dear friends, that we winna see Isabel want, and
we maun gang aye noo and then to see her and the bairns;
I am aye wae when I think o' them."

"Na, na," replied Gilbert, "they shall never see want as
lang as I hae a bawbee in my pouch, or a sheep on the muir,
or a peck o' meal in the barrel.  But we were speakin' o'
Claverhouse, the man that did the bluidy deed.  O that
we could a' do frae the heart as Isabel does, e'en pray for
him."

"The last time I was down at Crawfordjohn," said Eddie,
"I heard that Claverhouse had treated a worthy man of the
name of Brown very barbarously.  He lived in the parish
of Coulter.  One day when fishing quietly in the river,
Claverhouse came suddenly upon him and made him his
prisoner.  A powder-horn was found on him, and for this,
Claverhouse said he must die.  He was placed before six
dragoons, who were prepared to fire ; but happily the Laird
of Coulterallers, who was present, succeeded in getting his
execution delayed till next day.  He was carried by the
soldiers to the English border, tightly bound with cords.
When they came to Selkirk, he was lodged in jail, from
which he made his lucky escape."

"But," said Gilbert, leaving Claverhouse for the present,
"what of Lagg ?  We hae heard muckle o' him, though he
has never been in our parts, as Claverhouse has been in
Douglas Water, and in the Upper Ward of Nithsdale, o'er
the hills there frae Cumnock to Sanquhar, driving the folk
before like a flock o' sheep to the slaughter."  "And may
ye never ken mair o' Lagg," added the saintly John Fraser
of the lone Dalwhairn, near the bonny green hills that feed
the Founts of Ken, and "where rivers, there but brooks,
disport to different seas," "may ye never see his face, for it
has been a gruesome sicht to many, and to mysel' among
the rest.  He is a tiger in human shape, and nothing can

satisfy his craving but bluid, which he sheds without scruple on muir and hill. Lagg's character is of a deeper dye than even that of Claverhouse, for there is something so coarse and fiendish about him. I may instance some of his deeds of savageness—his cruel treatment of that excellent gentleman, Mr Bell of Whitside, in Galloway. Mr Bell was well known to Lagg, but for all this he apprehended him as a Nonconformist, and prepared to put him instantly to death. The good man requested a short time to pray, but this Lagg peremptorily refused ; and in his usual way of cursing and swearing, exclaimed, "What, the devil ! Have you not had time enough to prepare since Bothwell ?", and immediately shot him, and a few others along with him, and would not suffer their bodies to be buried. Sometime after this barbarous deed, the Viscount Kenmuir, Claverhouse, and Lagg happened to meet at Kirkcudbright, where Kenmuir challenged Lagg for his cruelty to one whom he knew to be a gentleman, and so nearly related to himself, and in an especial manner that he would not permit his body to be buried. Lagg replied with an oath, ' Take him if you will, and salt him in your beef-barrel.' Upon this the Viscount drew his sword, and if Claverhouse had not interfered would have run him through the body."

"Oh, but these be sad deeds !" exclaimed Gilbert, " but what can we say ? they are just the common doings of all the commanders and petty officers throughout the land. We here have our own Crichton in Muirkirk, and Peter Inglis in Douglas, both of whom have been raging with more than ordinary fury since Claverhouse was in Douglas Water. The evil spirit that is in that man appears to be injected into Crichton, and he now pursues the wanderers with the most unbridled keenness. Even his dragoons affirm that he is becoming quite unbearable, and that he gets into a towering passion on the least occasion, and threatens to shoot even his own men, and he would have killed Jasper Middleton,

the trooper, for almost no fault, had not Clavers, who was
present, prevented.  Some attribute all this to inordinate
drinking, and some again to other reasons.  But this I know,
at least, from the best information—and perhaps Geordy
Ga', here, can bear me out in what I am going to state—
that Crichton has never been altogether himself since the
mischance at the well, when our good friend Eddie dragged
him from its black depths.  His intellect then received a
shock, which makes him totter yet.  And the other thing
is his shooting of that godly man, David Steel of Lesmahagow, and the faithless way in which he accomplished his object, first promising the man quarters, and then to blow out
his brains in the presence of his poor wife and children."

"I think," said Geordy Ga', "that Peter is right regarding the affair of the well, but as to the shooting of David
Steel, that took place after I left the troop, and, therefore,
I can say nothing regarding his feelings in consequence of
that deed, but I know when I was with them that he often
alluded to the well.  I remember he said to me one day
when he and I were riding together, 'Ga', I wish all my
troop were as temperate in the way of their liquor as you
are—not that I care a fig for temperance in itself, but it
might tend to keep these riotous fellows quiet, and then——'
At this moment we were approaching the well in which he
had been plunged, and when we reached it he shuddered,
and said, 'there is that bottomless pit out of which I never
expected to come alive.'  At this instant a loud scream was
heard ; we were startled, and perceiving a hubbub among
the troopers in advance, we hastened to the spot, and found
that one of the men, in a state of high intoxication, had
been spurring his high-spirited charger with a view to force
him to cross the mouth of what is called the moss well.
This feat the animal refused to perform, and plunged and
capered till he tossed his rider from his seat, and pitched
him with violence head foremost into the dark pool twenty

feet deep, and covered with a mossy vault round and round like an inner arch. The trooper was never more seen, but lay like a stone, dead at the bottom. Crichton turned pale, and shuddered all over, as he saw in the fate of the poor soldier what once might have been his own."

"Think for a moment," said Gilbert, "on the difference between these men and our sufferers, as it respects the state of their mind in perilous circumstances ; our poor friends in their wanderings, in destitution of all things, and with a hasty and cruel death before them, are all peace, and even joy ; while their persecutors, though free from any fear of man, and in the full posession of all the enjoyments they desire, are yet miserable." "Yes," added Geordy, "we all knew in our quiet moments that we were fearfully wrong, and we had often the unwelcome suspicion that we were drifting downward to perdition. The boldest among us could not face an eery object in the dark. We were one day skirting the sides of Cairntable when we encountered a heavy thunderstorm. One of our band, a reckless, drunken blade, the contents of whose flask had highly excited him, and in his swaggering, impious manner drew his long sword, and pointing it at the lightning, dared it to the combat, when a vivid flash caught his glittering weapon, ran along it, and killed him on the spot. The party was horror-struck, and were ready to sink into the ground for very fear. It seemed as if the arm of the Almighty had been made bare to smite, and smite it did with a precision that could not be mistaken. Cochrane was with us that day, and he grew as pale as the mist that was creeping down the sides of the mountain. Not a word was uttered, and we could easily see at a little distance from our track a small company of the hiding wanderers at worship in a little green hollow, from which the sound of praise was heard in gentle tones through the roaring of the thunder. Their uncovered heads were turned heaven-wards, not fearing the scathing lightning that was playing around, and striking the projecting rocks on the brow of the height, and ploughing the turf close by their side.  They were at home on the lonely waste—at home, as I now understand it, with God, and in peace a-midst the raging of the tempest.  Not one of our troop dared to notice them, though all of us knew right well who they were, and what they were about.

"Next day we were somewhat sobered, and all felt that we had indeed been in peril.  'Swinge me,' said Bob Piper, 'but there must be a difference between us riotous fellows and these same hill folks whom we noticed yesterday sitting so composedly in the storm ; yes, I say, a difference that seems to have something of the mysterious in it.  The poor fellows sat under the gushing thunder-spate with as much composure as if they had been basking in the gentle sun-shine, while we trembled and shook as if we had been on our way to the gallows.  Now, I say, all this is what I do not rightly comprehend, and probably we chaps who opine we are doing right good service to king and country, may after all be in the wrong.'"

"In this way spoke Bob—an honest fellow on the whole, but one who, like myself, did not scruple to act the part of a trooper, thinking no evil of the profession.  How Bob stands affected now I cannot say, but I am persuaded that in these matters he did not think and feel alone."

---

## CHAPTER XIX.

TIME passed on, and many incidents occurred, both of a painful and of a pleasant nature.  The enemy, like wild beasts, roamed at pleasure throughout the land, and many a cottage was filled with wailing for the dead, and with wailing for the banished.  Through the im-policy and recklessness of the persecutors, everything was at a stand. Agriculture, and commerce, and industry were almost at an end. Farmers, and tradesmen, and shopkeepers, and labourers, were in vast numbers thrown loose on society, and so great was the general derangement, that Fletcher of Saltoun affirms that no fewer than *two hundred thousand* mendicants were found strolling over the land in want of all things. What a disorganisation in the general condition of society does this indicate, and all arising from the insane and unprincipled management of a wicked and irresponsible faction

One evening, as the household of the Miny were convened around the hearth, Peter Corsan, from Powermerlog, entered in company with a stranger. He was a man in the prime of life—tall and buirdly in his make, with an open and generous countenance, and eyes beaming with intelligence—with his plaid about his shoulders, and a sturdy staff in his hand, he stood eyeing the party with a smile playing on his features. " Ken ye this man ?" said Peter to Gilbert, who had risen from the langsettle to welcome the visitors. " No," he replied, " I think I do not recognise him." Grizzy gazed for a moment, and exclaimed, "Arthur Allan !" " Arthur Allan !" cried Gilbert, "where were my eyes that I didna ken *you !* O Arthur ! Arthur ! many a weary thought hae I had about ye, but I tynt the track o' ye a'thegither. O, my dear friend, where hae ye been ? and hoo are yer worthy parents ? Arthur, it was your father that brought me to the knowledge of the Saviour, and it was your mother that was the means of Grizzy's conversion, so that your father is my father, and your mother is Grizzy's. You are to us a brother beloved for their sake, and for your own. You are a thousand times welcome under my roof— the very sight of you cheers my heart. Sit ye down, my friends ; how happy you have made me this evening !" Such was the reception of Arthur Allan at the Miny.

" Arthur," said Gilbert, " I am anxious to know some-

thing of your personal history ; but, first, what of your parents ?"  " When we left Auchtercairn," said Arthur, " we
removed into the higher parts of Galloway, and lived in the
parish of Carsphairn.  My parents were greatly edified
under the preaching of the good Mr Semple, the indulged
minister of the parish ; but, when he died, the curate who
succeeded him being a very fiery man, and a garrison having
been established in the neighbourhood, we removed to near
Minygaff, where my dear parents died, and died in the Lord.
We were never exactly in want, for I was strong and able
for work ; and my father, through his industry when in the
farm in Ayrshire, saved a little money.  After their decease,
I was left alone, and having no interest in that part of the
country, I resolved to return to Ayrshire to revisit the
scenes of my childhood.  I came to our former residence,
but there no one knew me.  I next sought out your farm-
steading, and trod up with hopeful step to the door ; but
you also were gone, and none could tell the place of your
abode.  My heart died within me, and I seemed alone in
the world ; and in my loneliness I said with the Psalmist,
' Lover and friend hast Thou put far from me, and mine acquaintance into darkness.'  The Highland host was at this
time ravaging the west, and I had enough ado to keep myself out of their way.  Weeks and months passed on in this
way, till the rising at Bothwell began, when I joined the
covenanting forces, and fought in the battle.  I was taken
prisoner, with many hundreds besides ; and you have, no
doubt, heard of the usage which the poor prisoners received,
but having been one myself, and subjected to the treatment
which all alike received, I shall state, with as much accuracy
as I can, all the circumstances in which we were placed.
After the battle, about thirteen hundred of us, as prisoners,
were forthwith marched straight to Edinburgh.  We were
subjected to much ill-usage by the way.  In many cases the
clothes were stripped from our persons ; some of us half-

naked, and all of us in great destitution, reached the metropolis, where we were confined as state prisoners in the Greyfriars churchyard. Here we were subjected to the greatest hardships, and treated with the utmost rigour. If we had been the greatest miscreants on the face of the earth, we could not have been worse used. During the night we were forced to lie flat on the ground, and if any of us happened to raise our heads above the common level, we were instantly fired at by the sentinels. We were exposed to all sorts of weather without shelter, at least for a long time. Our food was scantily supplied, and our clothes scarcely served us for a covering. The friends who came to visit us, and to show their Christian sympathy, were rudely repulsed by the soldiers; and the necessary supplies of food and clothing which were brought, were sternly forbidden. It was chiefly in cases where bribes were given to the guards that access could be had to the sufferers. The Council deemed these rigorous measures all justifiable, because the men were caught in an act of rebellion, as they called it, against the Government. It may easily be conceived how much the rulers were gratified on finding what they reckoned a fair pretext for resorting to the harshest measures. The Highland host was sent into the west for the purpose of exciting the populace to insubordination, but the project utterly failed, and failed, no doubt, to the deep mortification of those who planned the scheme. In our case, however, they found the very thing they had so ardently wished, and now they judged that their procedure would be justified in the sight of the entire nation."

"After a long season of confinement and cruel treatment in our little corner of the churchyard, about two hundred and fifty-seven of us were drafted from the crowd, and sentenced to be transported to Barbadoes. On the fifteenth day of November we were taken out of the churchyard, early in the morning, before any of our friends knew of it,

and neither had we ourselves any previous intimation of
what was to take place. We embarked at Leith ; but the
barbarities exercised on us when in the ship cannot be expressed.  We were stowed under deck in so narrow a space,
that the most part of us were obliged to stand to give room
to those who were sickly and apparently dying.  We were so
closely crowded that we could scarcely move, and were almost
stifled for want of air.  Two hundred and fifty-seven of us
were pent up within a space that could scarcely have contained a hundred.  Many fainted from mere suffocation.
The rudeness and inhumanity of the seamen were singular.
When lying in the road, not only did they hinder our
friends from visiting us and to minister to our necessities,
but they even reduced the quantity of bread we ought to
have had, and allowed us no drink, though the master of
the ship had contracted to give us both.  All the troubles
we had met with since Bothwell, though put together, are
not to be compared with the troubles of even one day in
that ship.  Our distress was beyond conception, but yet,
as one of our friends remarked, in the midst of all our
tribulations, the consolations of God abounded.

"After we sailed from Leith we met with very severe
storms.  In the month of December we were off the Orkneys
and, in a very dangerous sea, we came pretty near the
shore, and cast anchor.  In the tempest that lay upon us,
the prisoners, fearing that all would go to the bottom,
begged to be set on shore, and to be sent to any prison the
master pleased, but this was positively refused.  The captain, who, I am told, was a papist, was indignant at the
proposal, and commanded the seamen to nail down the
hatches, that no prisoner might escape.  About ten o'clock
at night the ship was torn from her anchor by a violent
gust, and being forcibly driven on a rock, broke in the
middle.  The seamen quickly got down the mast, and laying it between the broken ship and the rock, got ashore ;

but so barbarous were they, that, though the poor prisoners cried vehemently to be released from the suffocating hold, they would not even open the hatches to give them an opportunity to save their lives, and those of them who did release themselves were driven back by the master and his sailors, who, getting upon the rock above them, struck them violently and forced them back into the boiling sea; notwithstanding this opposition, however, about fifty of us escaped, while about two hundred were drowned." Such was Arthur Allan's account of this atrocious affair, and such, too, were the real and veritable facts of the case, as the accredited historians of the period fully show.

"Ah! Arthur, my son," exclaimed Gilbert, "what matter of thankfulness is it that the Lord has brought you through all these disasters, and that you are now sitting under my roof in safety! But how came you, my dear lad, to find my house?" "In traversing the country," said Arthur, "I always inquired at those with whom I lodged if they knew one of the name of Gilbert Fleming anywhere in the district, and yesterday, in coming across the mountains there, I accidentally came upon the house of my friend here, who has conducted me to your long-sought-for dwelling; I put the same question to him that I had put to others, and found that you were just in the neighbourhood." "You will remain with us," said Grizzy, "and we will hide you from the enemy, for we have the means of concealment—only remain contented for a season." "I heartily accept of your invitation," replied Arthur, "for indeed I need repose, as I have been tossed of late from one district to another, and without any certain dwelling-place, but in this I am just like the rest of my brethren; yet all this is weary work, and often makes me wish that I were in the rest above." "Indeed," said Gilbert, "in these days of peril none of us can tell how soon we may be summoned from this world. How many of our friends have fallen all around us ! The cruelty of the enemy seems to be inexhaustable, for the more they shed blood, the keener is their relish for it." "Yes," said Arthur, "the cruelty of the soldiery is great ; but the cruelty of the Council that sits in Edinburgh and stimulates the persecution is still greater. An intimate acquaintance of mine, who was brought before that tribunal, told me that he was subjected to the most infamous tortures. He was subjected to what is called thumbkins first, and then to the bootkins. His thumbs were placed in a sort of iron vice, which was screwed so hard that the bones crashed within the instrument, and the blood and marrow spouted out, and so intense was the suffering that he fainted away in their hands. He was sent back to prison, where he lay a number of weeks, and then, when his tormentors could get nothing criminative out of him, they applied the boots, and if the thumbkins were dreadful, the boots were tenfold more so. These boots were of iron, adjusted to the leg, and wedges were inserted between the limb and the boot, which a man drove in with a large mall, till the bone within this instrument of torture was compressed and crushed in the most frightful manner, and the shrieks of the person writhing in agony were unendurable ; and yet, he said, the monsters who sat in Council laughed, and winked, and jeered; and none enjoyed the scene more than the Duke of York, to whom it seemed to afford the greatest delight. Such are the ways of these men, and to such torture was my dear acquaintance subjected."

To show that this account given by Arthur is not overcharged, but given according to the strictest verity, we shall here adduce the case of Hugh Mackail, to whom this instrument of torture was applied :—" When he was," says the historian, " brought before the Council, he was interrogated respecting the leaders of the insurrection, and what correspondence they had, either at home or abroad. He declared himself utterly unacquainted with any such correspondence, and frankly stated how far he had taken part in the proceedings. The instrument of torture was then laid before him, and he was informed that, if he did not confess, it should be applied next day. On the following day he was again brought before the Council, and again ordered to confess ; on immediate pain of torture. He declared solemnly that he had no more to confess. The executioner then placed his leg in the horrid instrument, applied the wedge, and proceeded to his hideous task. When one heavy blow had driven in the wedge, and crushed the limb severely, he was again urged to confess, but in vain. Blow after blow succeeded, at considerable intervals, protracting the terrible agony, but still, with true Christian fortitude, the heroic martyr possessed his soul with patience. Seven or eight successive blows had crushed the flesh and sinews to the very bone, when he protested solemnly, in the sight of God, that he could say no more, though all the joints of his body were in as great torture as that poor leg. Yet thrice more the wedge was driven in, till the bone itself was shattered by its iron compression, and a heavy swoon relieved him from further consciousness of the mortal agony ; he was carried back to prison, and soon afterwards condemned to death." " The tender-mercies of the wicked are cruel."

Arthur Allan found his abode at the Miny exceedingly agreeable, and he formed a very intimate acquaintanceship with Eddie and Geordy Ga' from whom he received a great deal of information regarding the tactics of the troopers in their raids through the country. Geordy stated that they had spies and informers in their pay, stationed in every quarter, all of whom gathered information, and then deposited it in the proper quarter. The curates, he said, and the lairds, and the officers, often concerted together over their cups, and formed plans of mischief, which were executed on the earliest opportunity, so that the poor people were often

pounced upon at a moment when they least expected it.
He said that they frequently set out on their excursions
more with a view to their own advantage, than even to promote the designs of their masters; and that not only were
eating and drinking their object, but plunder also, for they
uniformly seized on what money they could find in the
houses they visited.    In this way they enriched themselves,
while the officers uniformly got the lion's share.    This
money was consumed in deep carousals in the various public-
houses to which they had access, and then scenes of riot
and outrage occurred which beggared description.    So great,
sometimes, were the tumults on these occasions, that even
the officers themselves could not suppress them.    In short,
he affirmed that a garrison, for the most part, was a sort of
hell upon earth, where wickedness that cannot be named
was unblushingly practised.    Geordy said that he was
surprised that the Covenanters, from their long experience,
had not learned the two following things, that a fine day
always afforded them more safety in their own homes than
a stormy one, unless it were snow and drift ; and that an
exposed situation was better for a conventicle than a concealed place ; because, said he, we imagined that on a fine
day the persons in concealment would be hiding in some
place at a distance from their dwelling-houses, and that
when a conventicle met on a hill-side, or on some conspicuous
place, the troopers seldom thought of attacking ; for the
worshippers, having the view of miles before them, were up
and away long before the soldiers could approach them.
He said that he had often stated these things to Eddie, that
he might give a hint to those concerned.

But Arthur found the Miny not only an agreeable residence—he found it also a place of much security, and more
especially when Geordy informed him of the horror which
the troopers felt at the mention of the dark vault in the
Auchty.  Gilbert and Grizzy were father and mother to him ;

they cared for him in every way in which parents could care for a child, and Gilbert was never happy when he was out of his sight. He felt as if Arthur's coming to his house was a sacred trust committed to him by the God of his parents, who had been instruments of such essential benefit to himself and Grizzy. His manly form and noble countenance filled honest Gilbert's eye, and he was often noticed scanning him from head to foot, as if his whole soul centred in him, and then the smile of an unutterable complacency would play on his features. O Gilbert! Gilbert! beware of making an idol of that darling lad, lest that idol be smitten, and smitten, who knows, for your sake. And truly Gilbert needed the kindly caution, for a stroke was pending, which was to descend with vengeful effect. Arthur, in all the bloom of manhood, was to fill an early grave, and to lie down in his resting-place, in the martyr's shroud. He had gone to a conventicle that was held in the upper wilds of the Afton, and which was dispersed by a company of troopers from Carsphairn, who incidentally came upon it in marching through the wastes. Arthur fled in the direction of New Cumnock, whence he took the rising ground on the west of Corsancone, and the troopers in full pursuit. He struck into the moors of Kyle, with a view to reach the Miny, but strength failed him, and he fell down through exhaustion on the moss. The horsemen galloped up to him, and made him their prisoner. He had been at the conventicle—that needed no proof? and the questions put to him not being satisfactorily answered, it was resolved to shoot him on the spot. He was ordered to prepare for the result; and bending on his knees, he poured out his heart in prayer to his Father in heaven. He then rose to his feet, and stood undaunted and erect, and opened his breast to receive the deadly shot. They bade him pull his bonnet over his face; but he replied, "I am not ashamed of what I have done, and am not afraid to meet death as a witness for Jesus

Christ and His precious truths." He then uncovered his
head, and waving his bonnet in his left hand, stretched out
his right, holding in it his open Bible, and with his plaid
wrapped about his buirdly shoulders, he stood with his eyes
gazing up to heaven, and his lip moving in silent prayer.
In this attitude the command was given ; the flash and report instantly followed, and the martyr fell on the heath,
and immediately expired. The sound of the firing was
heard at a distance, and attracted the attention of two shepherds on the moor, and who, seeing the dragoons marching
westward, ran to the spot, and found Arthur Allan lying in
a pool of his own blood. The nearest house was the Miny,
and to this they ran, and stated that a man was shot on the
moor. Gilbert and his lodgers hastened to the spot, and
what was their astonishment on finding their dear friend
dead on the bent. Gilbert gave way to the most uncontrollable grief, and rolled himself on the heath. On the
manly countenance, now pale in death, there sat a placidity
indescribable. His plaid and his garments were literally
soaked in the crimson tide of life that gushed from his mangled body. It was proposed to carry his corpse to the Miny,
but, on second thoughts, it was deemed best to bury him
where he fell. Sandy ran back to the house for a spade to
dig the grave ; and Grizzy came trudging after, with one of
her best blankets for a winding-sheet. Her poor heart was
like to break in pieces when she beheld the dear lad lying
slaughtered on the moor, and his blood all curdled around
him. She washed his face with water from the moss—adjusted the body—kissed his clay-cold lips—covered his face
with a napkin—and when the grave was prepared, wrapped
the blanket around him, and then the body was lowered
into the mossy trench, which was immediately filled up ;
and when nothing more was to be done, the mourners sat
down in a circle, and gave vent to a flood of tears. They
retired sorrowfully homewards, and the Miny for that night
was a house of affliction.

After this, Eddie and Geordy found it necessary to exercise a more than ordinary circumspection, and to frequent as much as possible their little upper chamber in the vault. The ladder by which they ascended to it they took care to draw up after them, so that they felt secure in the night season, in a degree which allowed them to sleep soundly.

———✳———

## CHAPTER XX.

ONE day as Geordy was traversing the moor in the direction of Hyndbottom, to visit the scene of Cameron's Conventicle, he perceived a party of Crichton's troopers wending their way along the side of Mount Stewart, and, as he was on the rugged moss, he instantly cowered down in one of its deep trenches, and escaped detection. When the party had gone round the height, and were fairly out of view, he emerged from his smeary hiding-place, thinking that all danger was over.   He left the moor, and was beginning to ascend the hill, when, all at once, a trooper, who for some reason had lagged behind his company, confronted him.   "Ha, ha!" vociferated the dragoon, "what now, Geordy Ga'!   Upon the word of an honourable cavalier, the same worthy who saw fit to desert our honest service ; a goodly price is set on your head, my lad, and in the name of our liege lord, the good King James, you are my prisoner."   "Not so fast, Ringan, my good fellow," exclaimed the deserter, "not so fast; I shall first measure weapons with you before you shall claim me as your captive."   "Weapons, man," said the soldier, drawing his pistol from his belt, but forgot that it was unloaded ; he drew the trigger, but nothing followed; he then brandished his ponderous glaive, but here Geordy, though he had no blade nor lance, could cope with him, for he had a massive club in his hand, with which he could do brave execution when wielded by his brawny arm.  The soldier drew a powerful stroke with his keen-edged sword, but it met the club in Geordy's hand, and was shivered in two.  "Come down," cried Geordy, "and let us try an equal combat on the bent."  The trooper dismounted in a rage, but found himself without his armour. He was now in Geordy's power, and voluntarily yielded on the spot.  "And now," said our hero, "I will let you go ; we were old acquaintances, and have been companions in iniquity.  You may go and tell Crichton that you have met with Geordy Ga', and that he has beaten you in single combat."  "Well, Geordy," said Ringan, "you are a brave fellow."  "Ay, and the braver that I have conquered you, the bravest of the brave."  "None of your taunting, Geordy, this is not the first time that we have met in conflict in our riotous days, nor is it the first time that you have conquered me, and another with me too, and, upon my sooth, I would not have ventured on you now, had it not been the tempting reward offered for your capture, and that I saw you had no warlike implements with you, but I own myself beat, as I have done aforetime.  And now, honest Geordy, I advise you to keep out of the way, for Crichton is dreadfully exasperated ; he is determined to search every nook and corner for you—nay, he is resolved to call in more assistance, and there are inklings that Claverhouse and his troopers are to be sent for, so that all the district round and round is to be laid under contribution to find you, and we have been out on a raid this very day for the purpose, and I marvel how you escaped the party that preceded me."  "I did so," said Geordy, "by hiding in the moss, and when I thought all danger was over, I came out, and thus met you."  "And well it was so," replied the trooper, "else you would have been stretched a bloody corpse on the heath by this time ; but what are you doing wandering here in the broad daylight ; don't you know that there are spies out in every direction, and the more eager are they for the prize they expect ?"

All this astonished Geordy, for he had not the slightest idea that his capture was deemed of such importance, nor that such an array of soldiers and of spies was put in motion for apprehending him—a poor fugitive soldier.

"Now," said the trooper, "I will not divulge this accidental encounter, both for my own credit as a soldier, and also for my safety, for in these angry times none of us can tell what may befal. You know old Eddie the keelman? If you meet him, put him on his guard, for though Crichton has hitherto treated him as a privileged person, he is determined to do so no more. He suspects him of treachery; and he understands that he conveys information to the rebels of the designs of the military, and in this way has often defeated our purposes. He is an arch old fellow, I know him, and has more cunning about him that he lets wit; but I do not wish any evil to befal the creature, for he often supplied me with a twist of tobacco and a pipe gratis, which, you know, is no small boon to us fellows, who have nothing to spare past our liquor. I have mentioned him to you, so that if you chance to encounter him, and his equipage, as he calls it, tell him to keep his douce cuddie and his pawky self out of sight for a season.

"But I would mention further, since we are on this same subject, that if you have any acquaintance with that silly, whining creature, the farmer of the Miny, and the laird's gamekeeper withal, you may inform him that he is suspected of reset, and that he must endeavour to keep his premises clear of poachers—you understand me—lest he be favoured with a visit which, perchance, may not be very acceptable. By the by, there's a frightful vault in the neighbourhood of that moss-house, the Miny. I shudder when I think of it; a coffin lying on the floor, and the devil and his witches holding their revelries within! I never saw Crichton in such a plight; but you were there with the party that day."

"I was, and I would advise no person, soldier, or peasant,

to enter that place." "No more, no more, my blood runs
cold ; if I wished to listen at the mouth of pandemonium,
it would be to that vault I would go." "But I question,"
said Geordy, "if Claverhouse would be so squeamish."
"You are wrong there, Geordy ; I know Claverhouse—I
was more than a year in his troop ; and though brave in
battle, he is as timid as a child when eery things are concerned. You know how he dreads the soft and silent mist.
I have known him start and shudder in the dark ; and when
in our raids we had occasion to pass a lonely and deserted
churchyard in a glen, when night was beginning to set in,
he always turned away his head, that he might see no
sights, and hear no sounds ; at least we, uncharitable
rogues, thought so. Depend upon it, Crichton will not
venture there with the cavaliers.

"But as to Fleming, I say again, give him the watchword ;
for though he be a weak, superstitious saintling, I pity him,
and would not like to see any mischief befal him—he once
did me a good turn. I may mention, also, that Crichton
has two particular spies in his pay who are remarkably
dexterous and insinuating. The one has a squint in his
left eye, and red hair, and he attempts to pass himself off
as the redoubted Patrick Laing of Blagonnoch : and in this
way he has wormed himself into the confidence of not a
few unsuspecting families. He professes to be a devout
Covenanter, and he can practise his saint-craft admirably.
The other is a pedlar ; he has a deep scar in his chin,
inflicted by the sword of a soldier in a drunken squabble.
He comes creeping in with his pack on his back, and in a
timid sort of way he tries to bespeak the favour of the mistress, before whom he modestly displays his wares, and
promises a good bargain. He generally comes at the close
of the day, when he expects quarters for the night. He
takes his seat behind the hallen, where he pretends to be
dozing in consequence of the day's fatigue ; and this is done

that he may catch, without being suspected, all that is said in reference to the persons in hiding, or otherwise, whom it is his object to betray. These are the spies that are mainly employed at present. I know I am speaking to an old friend who will not entrap me." "I am certainly much in your debt, Ringan, for your information, and shall not fail to profit by it ; but how stands it with your garrison just now?" "Why, since you left us, Cochran has been recalled, and it is he who is at the head of the party before us there ; but we don't like him. And there is Jasper, our roisterous friend ; he lies at present with a broken leg, from a blow which he received from his horse in the stables, one day when misusing him in a fit of drunkenness. And there is Jackson on his death-bed, swearing, and bidding defiance to all the fiends in the pit. Crichton is more moody than usual ; I think there is something distressing his mind. On the whole, we are a set of sad chaps—every one is doing what is right in his own eyes. And now I must be off lest I be called in question for delay, though I can easily furnish the old excuse, you know—a pain in the head." "Yes," said Geordy, "a pain more frequently there than in the conscience." "You are wrong, Ga'; I feel many a qualm which I do not express—it is a cursed occupation this of ours. I could sometimes almost wish that I were dead and in my grave ; for how dreadful is it to see these poor fellows shot dead in the moors, without trial and often without warning! and, then, to hear their prayers, and to witness the confidence with which they meet death! I cannot look when the shot goes off, and I sometimes fall staggering backwards like a boy who fires a gun for the first time." "Why, then," said Geordy earnestly, "do you not quit the service?" "Why, there are considerations, Ga' —I say there are considerations, and I cannot quit at present ; but I contemplate a time. And so, move on, my good charger ; good-bye, Ga', and mind what I say." He urged the steed forward but he would not move ; he spurred and whipped, but the horse capered and pranced, and threatened to throw his rider.    What could be the matter? Geordy looked, and behold here stood his own old war-steed, who kept his eye on his former master, and would not leave the ground.    Geordy caressed him, and the poor animal fondled on him, and laid his head on his shoulder, and when Geordy moved he followed him like a shepherd's dog.    Geordy felt a strong emotion, though it was only to an animal.    The result was, that the dragoon was obliged to lead him away, for to ride was impossible.

This information from his old fellow-soldier caused thoughts of heart to Geordy, and he returned instantly to the Miny to communicate there what he had learned.    It was now certain that matters were about to assume a still more serious aspect.    It was clear that these spies were enemies much more insidious and dangerous than even the troopers themselves.    The approach of the soldiers might be seen, but the spies would silently steal in on them before they were aware, and see who were in the house before any one had time to elude their observation.    Accordingly, when Geordy arrived at the Miny, he imparted the news he had gathered from Ringan, and a consultation was held respecting what was best to be done.    The information regarding the appearance of the spies was a great point gained, so that Gilbert or Grizzy could easily detect from the marks given, the precise individuals.    Geordy thought of making his escape to a different part of the country, but Eddie remonstrated, and warmly dissuaded him from this step.    "The Miny," he said, "had always been found the safest place of concealment in the whole district.    It had the natural advantage of the ravine, and it had the vault which was well guarded by superstitious terrors.    It is my advice, then," he added, "that you, Geordy Ga', should remain here for your own safety, and, it may be also, for the safety of this household."

Next day a man was seen slowly plodding his way across the moor, with a staff in his hand, searching the moss here and there for a safe footing, and obviously advancing in the direction of the house. Eddie and Geordy made their way by the back door to the ravine—Gilbert and Grizzy remained quietly within. At length a timid sort of knock was heard at the door. Gilbert rose to open, and there stood before him a man with a squinting eye and red hair, attired like a Covenanter going to a conventicle. "May a stranger venture in," he said, "who, in these suffering times, is glad to repose for an hour under a friendly roof? Our lot is hard, and we are driven from place to place, seeking a shelter from the face of the foe, when our brethren are falling around us, and their blood running like water on the waste. 'When wilt Thou lift up Thy feet, O Lord, to these long desolations?'" "If you belong to that party," said Gilbert, "my advice is, that you make your escape as quickly as possible. We want none of *your* kind here, and I have a mind to call in assistance, and deliver you up to the proper party to be dealt with accordingly. You are the troublers of the land; and I have authority to deal with any intruder that encroaches on these grounds; and so, without any further parley, friend, I request you to ease us of your presence. We wish to harbour no such customers. Grizzy," he added, "rax me that pistol frae the shelf." The man began to remonstrate. "No, no," cried Gilbert, "away, away, not another word: you may keep your conventicle where you please, but it shall not be here." This altercation was heard by Eddie and Geordy, who crept near the back door, lest any violence should be offered, and they could scarcely refrain from bursting into loud laughter.

The information communicated by Ringan, the trooper, respecting the spies, was of vast consequence to the friends at the Miny. But, in order to render it generally useful through the district around, it was necessary that it should be made known to every household within reach.  Accordingly, Sandy was despatched, without delay, first to Powmerlog, to put Peter and Sarah on their guard, next to Friarminion, then to Blagannoch, and Shielstanes, and Gareland, and Shawhead, and Penbreck.  On the following day he was sent westward to Cleckloe, and down into Glenmuir Water.  The people in these localities spread the information to those next them, into Nithsdale, the head of Douglas Water, and the valley of the Crawick, and other parts adjacent.  It turned out that this prompt information completely defeated the efforts of the spies, for in every place they met with the same reception as at the Miny.  Nothing could be expiscated ; for no arts that they employed could induce the people to receive them as friends, while no suspicions of their real character were in the remotest degree expressed ; but had no warning been given, the artless people would most certainly have fallen into the snare.  It was a fortunate circumstance, also, that the two spies were entire strangers in the locality, and hence the religious leanings of the various families were unknown to them.

It was now necessary that Eddie and Geordy should be more than ordinarily cautious.  They were the individuals more especially whose capture was determined on.  Eddie had his donkey still grazing about the Miny, and it was plain that a sight of the animal, so well known, would lead to the discovery of its master.  Geordy proposed that, as it was aged and worn-out, it should be shot and buried in the moss ; but Eddie remonstrated.  He had a strong affection for the poor brute ; it had been his companion for many a long year, and he could not think of its life being taken.  It was then agreed that it should be imprisoned in the vault, in the little dark chamber, immediately under the sleeping apartment of the two fugitives.  The thought was good, for it served a useful purpose, as we shall presently see.  Eddie was much pleased that his old companion in travel should

be so near him, although its loud and unearthly braying was
a frequent annoyance.   For whole days Eddie and Geordy
never left their hiding-place in the Auchty; and it was only
on a clear day, when all the moorlands could be distinctly
seen, that they durst venture to the dwelling-house.   In
their prison, however, they were not alone.   Gilbert and
Peter Corsan were often with them, and their religious
intercourse was greatly edifying.   Through good instruction,
Geordy became a decided convert, not a convert to nonconformity merely, but a convert to the Saviour.   The evil of
his past conduct came vividly before him, and all the
prayers and instructions of his godly parents were im-
pressively presented to him.   He felt himself a new man,
and experienced a happiness he never knew before.   The
reading of the Bible was his constant employment, and he
grew in knowledge and in grace.   The seeds of instruction
that had been sown in his youthful mind at length germin-
ated, grew and bore fruit.

As a visit from the troopers was daily expected since
Claverhouse had come into the neighbourhood, whose movements were rapid and fitful, it was found necessary to station
a watch.   It was agreed that Sandy should be the warder,
especially as his occupation was to tend the *hirsel* on the
moor.   For a visit by night, however, no precautions of this
kind could be taken.   Accordingly, the dreaded visitation
befel.   Claverhouse, with his troopers at his back, entered
the head of Douglas Water, with a view to scour the valley
on both sides, till he reached the castle.   This line he chose
as being the more populous locality, while Crichton and
Cochrane took the wilds on the south and west.   Every
cottage and farm-steading were to be visited, and every glen
and bosky ravine were to be searched.   No imaginable place
of concealment was to be omitted.   Accordingly, one day
at high noon, Crichton and his dragoons appeared on the
edge of the moss, plainly advancing in the direction of the

Miny.   What was to be done ?   Gilbert, at the solicitation
of honest Grizzy, betook himself to the retreat in the
Auchty ; while she should remain busy in the house, and as
apparently heedless as if nothing unusual had taken place.
The troopers alighted at the door, and rushed into the
house—nobody was to be found but the mistress, who did
not seem in the least degree disconcerted.   It was not the
first time that she had been so visited, nor the first time
that she had succeeded in avoiding their interrogations.
Crichton, after due search, was satisfied that there was nobody about the dwelling-house.   He next proceeded to the
out-houses, but there he was as unsuccessful; only an occurrence befel which afforded some amusement.   It was their
custom to search for cheese, and poultry, and eggs, or whatever suited them in the way of edibles.   In this search one
of the soldiers clambered up into what was called the "hen-
balks," in quest of eggs, and while rumbling and stamping
about, the frail flooring gave way, and trooper, and balks,
and all came down in dust and divots on the head of Crichton, and some of the men who were standing below.   They
were extricated without much damage, but, to the infinite
merriment of the rest, Grizzy, on hearing the disturbance,
hastened to the spot, and when she saw the catastrophe,
exclaimed—"Hech, sirce ! it's a gude thing the kye wasna
i' the byre, else they might hae been smoored."   The incident seemed to put the party in pretty good humour, and
even Crichton himself, though he was partially *smoored* by
the inglorious descent of the hen-balks, appeared to enjoy it
not a little.

    After the hilarious incident of the balks, one of the sol-
diers, who happened to be strolling about, reported that he
had discovered the mouth of a vault in an old ruin just at
hand, and said it might be proper to search it.   Cochran
and Ringan the trooper exchanged looks, and ominously
shook their heads.   "What mean ye, friends ?" said Crich-

ton. "Nothing," replied Cochran, "but that vault is haunted. Horrible deeds are reported to have been committed within its dark walls in the olden times, and the very last time we were here, what sounds we heard and what sights we saw were dreadful. Yes, sounds unearthly, and coffins lying on the floor, and thunder rolling above our heads; it appeared as if we were standing at the very mouth of the black pit itself—visit that place who may, I shall not." All this was confirmed by Ringan and others who were there at the time. Crichton appeared to hesitate, "but," said he, "it can at least do no harm to go round and look at it. Who goes with me—who?" "We go," answered half-a-dozen of voices at once, "we go, and will dare all the devils it can hold; for, as we opine, they can scarcely be more of the devil-kind than we ourselves are." With this they hastened most courageously to the mouth of the murky pend. Here Eddie's donkey, which generally began to bray whenever a foot was heard in the vault, roared at such a rate that the vault resounded like thunder, or like the screaming of twenty gongs all playing at once, and the bats fluttering above their heads, seemed as if all the fiends had been roused from their slumbers to resent the invasion of their gloomy domains. The retreat of Crichton and his party was speedy, and no further search was dared.

After the disastrous affair of the hen-balks, and the rout of the troopers from the mouth of the vault by the braying of the donkey, like the scattering of withered leaves from the outlet of a narrow glen by the descent of a sudden gust of wind, the Miny was never more troubled, neither by troopers nor by spies. Notwithstanding this, however, Eddie and Geordy were obliged to keep themselves in close confinement, and so close that their residence at the Miny was not known in the locality save to a few of the Covenanting friends. These friends often resorted to Gilbert's house where much profitable intercourse was held, in which Eddie

and Geordy took a deep interest.  Their abode at the Miny
was upwards of two years, for Gilbert would on no account
consent to their removing to another quarter.   In their seclusion, however, they were not idle ; they wrought regu-
larly on the farm, and assisted the worthy gudeman in anything that came before them; and though it could not be
said that they earned wages, they, at least, earned their
food, so that here Gilbert was in reality no loser by them,
nay, he was a gainer, for the Lord blessed him for his hospitality.   Geordy sometimes stole, in the moonlight, to Blagannoch, and sojourned a while with Laing, in his retreat in
the deep and lonely glen by the purling stream that issued
from the high lands above.   Here, along with the men of
Shielstanes, and Gareland, and Shawhead, and Finglanfoot
—intelligent and godly men all, and all of them sufferers in
those times, and often plundered by the dragoons, but
staunch friends to the good cause—Geordy enjoyed a happy
pastime ; his head-quarters, however, was the Miny, where
he always experienced a much greater feeling of security
than elsewhere ; and, indeed, Gilbert was never easy when
he was out of his sight.

Some time after this the persecution in some degree
abated.   This arose from two causes : the one was that
the fire wanted fuel—the witnesses were now greatly reduced in numbers, not through defection, but owing to the
incessant shootings in the fields, the imprisonments, the
wholesale banishments, and the diseases caught through
the hardships to which they were subjected, and the volun-
tary withdrawments to other countries — an accurate
account has never yet been given of the number that were
drained off in these various ways, and at this distance of
time cannot now be given ; the other was the introduction
of measures somewhat more lenient on the part of the King,
for the purpose of preparing the way to the full introduction
of Popery.   Still the shootings went on wherever the sol-

diers could find what they called a rebel, or meet with a conventicle. We have, however, traversed the darkest and bloodiest period of the persecution in Scotland, for the purpose of bringing out, in a somewhat condensed shape, the cruelties exercised by the soldiery, and the magnanimous endurance of sufferings on the part of the persecuted ; not that the subject is exhausted—far from it ;—a whole vintage might yet be gathered, and what is here given may be considered merely in the light of a specimen ; the subject is still pregnant with many woes and many deliverances, with many outrages and many providential interferences, and with many lessons to us to hold fast our privileges.

The review of the dismal period of the persecution, from the Restoration in 1660 onward till the Revolution in 1688, is suggestive of many things. It is perfectly clear to us now-a-days, that the great moving spring of the whole was Popery, which, like the restless sea, is ever casting forth its mire and filth. The popish claimants wrought in secret, wrought perseveringly, and wrought with great effect ; the principle was indeed hidden, it was enveloped in a variety of coverings, but there it was, and there it operated. Popery has been at the bottom of all the mischief that has been plotted against the Church since the Reformation.

The history of the past is intended to serve as a lesson for the future. Popery is precisely the same at this day that it has ever been. It is unchanged, and wears the same hostile aspect to Protestantism that ever it did, even in its most rampant times. The same spirit of all evil, that instigated its movements in times past, is its animating soul still. It breathes out the same threatenings and slaughter against the people of the Lord as ever. Itself is not a church, though it is conventionally so-called. It is a great system of idolatry and image worship. It has in it everything that is superstitious, and vile, and degrading. " It is," as the Scriptures say, "the habitation of devils, the hold of every

foul spirit, and the cage of every unclean and hateful bird."
What an association for a church !  A confederacy doomed
to destruction, and only biding its time to be involved in a
much more terrific overthrow than that which befel Sodom
and the cities of the plain.  "She shall be utterly burned
with fire, for strong is the Lord God that judgeth her."  She
shall receive the due reward of her deeds when God shall
arise to judgment.

No institution has been a more emphatic curse to the
world than Popery, if you except its twin sister Mohamm-
edanism.  It has been well termed the very masterpiece of
the devil's invention for evil, to which there is nothing like ;
and when it fails and comes to nought, then may the devil
despair, for he has nothing left among his resources that he
can evoke as an adequate substitute.  Jonathan Edwards
calls the devil "the greatest fool in the world ;" and an
arrant fool he is ; still this device of his shows that his in-
tellects are not yet so utterly at fault that he cannot plan
schemes admirably calculated to serve his ends : but all his
devices shall perish with him.

Popery is still at work among us, and is mining its way
like the mole underground, for it cannot endure the clear
light of day ; and we can trace its hidden track by the up-
tossings here and there of little heaps of putrid matter that
has been festering beneath.  It becomes us, then, to be on
our guard, for we may rest assured that its determination
is to work us the same mischief that it did our fore-fathers,
whose blood is to this day found in her skirts.  Let Popery
work its ends, and in a brief space the whole land will be
enveloped in more than Egyptian darkness ; the crimson
car of persecution will be driven ruthlessly over the nation ;
all our privileges, civil and religious, will be annihilated ;
we will become a nation of serfs ; soul and body will be alike
enslaved ; we will be made the devotees of an abject and
disgusting superstition ; our popular intellect will be dwarf-

ed, and all the lights of literature and science will be gradually extinguished by the dingy smoke that issues from the
bottomless pit.  Popery spares nothing ; it eats, as doth a
canker, into the very vitals, and ends in the utter destruction of everything on which it fastens its loathsome grasp.
Let us, then, resist to the last, and by every constitutional
and scriptural means, the encroachments of this vile and
hateful thing.  Let the spirit of our ancestors kindle within
us, and let its fire burn with an honest vehemence in every
patriotic and Christian breast, till the monster evil be swept
from the face of the earth.  The great system of Romanism,
which is just a conspiracy against the rights and liberties
of human nature, is now putting forth convulsive efforts to
regain its ascendancy, and hence we must fight, and fight
valiantly.  No Scotsman can look back on the sufferings of
a Nonconformist ancestry without a manly indignation, and
an undaunted determination to withstand the advances of
"the Man of sin," even though it should be to the spilling
of his own blood in an honourable martyrdom.

In winding up our sketches here, we may remark that all
the friends at that time resident at the Miny survived the
persecution.  Gilbert and Grizzy lived to a good old age,
and were greatly prosperous in the world.  For it was remarkable that the households which the troopers plundered,
and often made them, as Eddie expressed it, "as bare as a
birk at yule," were greatly blessed in temporal things, so
that the bared birk budded afresh with green and fragrant
foliage.  But the prosperity of the house of the Miny did
not rob them of their spirituality, nor shrivel their hearts in
selfishness ; for the Miny continued to be the same hospitable receptacle that ever it had been, and, if possible, more
so.  Honest Eddie resided with them all his days, for they
never forgot the obligations under which they lay to him.
Poor as Eddie and his equipage were, yet the Lord made
use of him for allaying the storm of a local persecution, or

of diverting its force.   He died in great peace in the faith of Jesus, and was laid in an honoured grave.   His wish was to be buried in the moorland with the martyrs, but no stone marks his resting-place.   The poor donkey that strolled about the moor was found dead on the day of his master's funeral, and was hidden in a deep moss hag.

Geordy became a most respectable man and occupied a farm in Douglas Water.   He lived far on in the century that succeeded the persecution, but whether he was an ancestor of the persons of the same name who at this day reside in the fair strath of Douglas, we cannot say.

Peter Corsan and Sarah, who lived long after the trying times, cultivated the closest friendship with the family at the Miny, and many a time did they sit together at the hearth, recounting the woes of the suffering times; and when they thought on the blessed martyrs—many of whom were their dearest friends—their cheeks were often bathed in tears, and they resolved to follow their footsteps, up and up, to that high heaven of rest, where now—

"Their souls triumph
With Christ their glorious Head."

Willie and John of Lesmahagow were equally blessed in their surviving years.   Laing of Blagannoch, the staunch Covenanter, has his lineal descendants among us to this day, and so has Andrew Clark of Auchengrouth, in the moors of Sanquhar.   The upland people who live in the localities we have specified, are, in a great proportion, descended from the sufferers in the persecuting days, and they cherish their memory with the warmest interest ; and in instances not a few, they imitate their Christian character.

The places we have mentioned are almost all familiar to us, and the characters and incidents are equally so ; and the people who won in the moorlands will easily recognise all that we have depicted of the scenes and detailed of the circumstances.

# Other Solid Ground Titles

Printed in the United States
87541LV00002B/112/A